Introduction

Who is the Steam Highwayman?

You are the Steam Highwayman. Whatever brought you here, you now stand on the verge of an exciting adventure. Within this book you can explore a world of different choices, consequences, puzzles, mysteries and quests, discovering your own story as you turn from passage to passage. You will need a **pencil** and **eraser** to mark your **Adventure Sheet** (found at the back of this book) to track your progress and **two dice** (**d6** or normal six-sided dice) to help calculate the effects of chance in your tale. Your decisions will be matters of life and death, not just for yourself, but for many others too.

Options

From the very first passage in this book you are presented with choices: where to travel; how to answer a challenge; to kill or to spare a villain. Choices presented beneath a passage's main text are optional; instructions within a passage must be followed to maintain the narrative: this allows you the freedom to make choices but also means you are subject to their consequences. To make a choice, simply turn to the passage indicated and continue to read from there. You will encounter choices marked with the title of another volume of Steam Highwayman: to choose these, you should turn to the passage in the relevant volume. If you don't have it yet, you'll always have another option to choose within this book.

Tickboxes

Some passages include tickboxes which track your progress. You will be instructed to tick them with a pencil when you encounter them and either read on or proceed to a different passage. When the time comes to restart your adventure, you will need to erase any ticks before beginning afresh.

Codewords

As you travel throughout the realm you will learn many secrets, hear many rumours and experience strange and wonderful adventures: codewords allow the book to track this. When you gain a codeword, tick that codeword in the back of this book. When you are asked if you have a particular codeword, check to see if it is ticked in your codeword list. Some options are only available if you have ticked a certain codeword. When travelling to another book in the series, retain your codewords, but if you restart your adventure you will need to erase all the codewords you have collected.

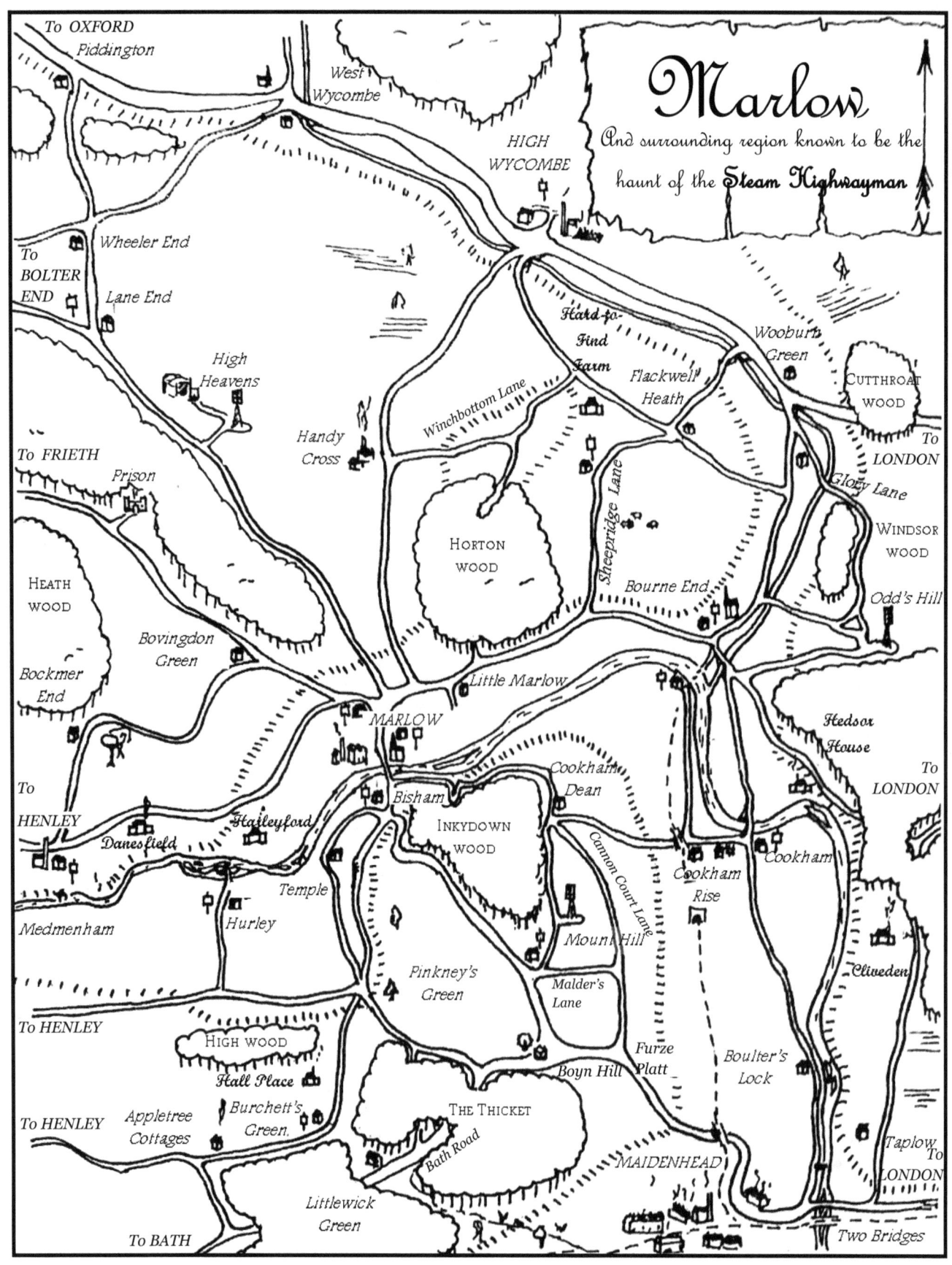

Steam Highwayman

Volume I

Smog and Ambuscade

by

Martin Barnabus Noutch

Illustrated by

Ben May

Your Adventure Sheet

Abilities
Your adventure will require you to use a diverse set of skills, which the following list represents:

RUTHLESSNESS	How threatening you seem, both in appearance and reputation
ENGINEERING	Your skill with pneumo-mechanics and steam machinery
MOTORING	The knowledge of road lore and the art of handling an engine
INGENUITY	Your mental ability to solve problems
NIMBLENESS	Your physical quickness and agility
GALLANTRY	The appeal of your manners, words and deeds

To make an ability roll you must **roll two dice and add the total to the appropriate ability score**, plus any modifiers. If the total score is **greater than** the **difficulty**, you have succeeded. Your natural ability score may rise or fall as you adventure: it cannot increase beyond 12. However, unique items can improve your score beyond 12.

Possessions
You will collect, find and buy many items as you travel the land. You may carry up to 12 possessions in your inventory (representing your saddlebags) at any time. Many items modify your ability scores. These modifiers are cumulative as long as the items are unique. For example, your ENGINEERING score of 4 could be improved by possession of a **pneumatic manual (ENG+3)** and an **adjustable wrench (ENG+1)** to total 8, but could not be improved by two **adjustable wrenches (ENG+1)**. Some options are only available to you if you possess a certain item. If these do not indicate that you should discard or use up the item, you may retain that item for later. Limited use objects are followed by tickboxes: these bonuses to ability scores are temporary and will revert after a single fight or skill check. Tick after each use and after the final tick, erase the object from your **Adventure Sheet**.

Money
The realm uses the Imperial monetary system - pounds (£), shillings (s) and pence (d). You will normally deal only in shillings, but when making deposits at the bank or expensive purchases you will need to do a little maths: there are 20 shillings to the pound or sovereign, and 21 shillings to the guinea. Paper money is normally only used by the wealthiest and is not always easy to exchange. A bundle of notes such as **thirty guineas in notes** may not be spent as normal - you will need to find someone to accept it as a deposit or exchange it for hard money (sometimes at a discount). Paper money does not take up a possession slot in your inventory.

Weapons

Shooting Guns
Each gun has an ACCURACY rating (eg **blunderpistol (ACC 6)**). To shoot, roll two dice and add the score to your gun's ACCURACY together with any other modifiers. A score **greater than** the **difficulty** is a success.

Fighting enemies
Combat proceeds in rounds and in each round you have an opportunity to wound your opponent before they have a chance to hurt you. When the number of **Wounds** you have inflicted is equal to your opponent's TOUGHNESS, or when you have **five Wounds**, the fight is over. To calculate whether you wound your enemy, roll two dice and add the score to your NIMBLENESS, together with any modifiers. If the total is **greater than** your opponent's PARRY, you will succeed in wounding them.

Your opponent then has the same chance: the sum of two dice is added to their NIMBLENESS and if the total is **greater than** your PARRY then you gain a **Wound**. Your PARRY score is the total of your NIMBLENESS plus the PAR value of your weapon. Note: if your opponent has a weapon with modifiers, these have already been added to the NIMBLENESS, PARRY and TOUGHNESS scores printed. You may take this weapon as a trophy if you win.

Wounds

A highwayman's life is a dangerous one: you may be wounded in single combat, shot at by angry constables or hurt in a road accident. Keep track of each **Wound** on your Adventure Sheet, as your fifth **Wound** will incapacitate you and will hasten the end of your adventure. You are able to treat your **Wounds** in a safe location either through rest or paying for medical treatment, which will normally result in your **Wounds** converting to **Scars**.

Scars

The normal process when a wound is healed is to erase the **Wound** from your Adventure Sheet and add a **Scar** to your scar tally. Roll two dice and a score of 11 or 12 will result in an **intimidating scar (RUTH+1)**, which should be noted in your **Other Modifiers**.

Velosteam

Your velosteam is your most prized possession: a finely-tuned and carefully engineered two-wheeled road engine of unsurpassed mechanical beauty, it runs on readily available coal-gas and can achieve considerable speed. However, it can be damaged by accidents or risk-taking. Keep track of any **Damage Points** on your Adventure Sheet, along with any customisations like a **strengthened boiler** that you manage to fit. You must take care! Your velosteam can sustain three **Damage Points**, but should you suffer the fourth your machine will be **Beyond Repair**. At this point you will be forced to abandon your adventure on the road - so ensure you know a trustworthy mechanic who can help you repair your velosteam before you reach that stage.

Reputation

As you proceed on your lawless way you are bound to make enemies as well as friends. Record your notoriety (for example, **Wanted by the Coal Board**) and your friendships (for example, **Friend of Lord Dashwood**) on your **Adventure Sheet**. These will decide your fate at many a turn.

Great Deeds

Some adventures may result in you becoming known for your **Great Deeds**. Note these on your Adventure Sheet: they will influence your eventual fate when you come to retire from this life.

Solidarity Points

The common people of Britain are oppressed and disenfranchised: it is their poverty that enables the wealth of the landed, the gentry, the industrialists and the political classes. Some of your choices may result in you gaining **Solidarity Points**, which indicate whether the poor of the land know you as a saviour or as an oppressor. Should you gain 50 or more **Solidarity Points** you will be known as the **People's Champion**. However, you may lose **Solidarity Points** for participating in the oppression of the common people. It is not possible to have a negative number of **Solidarity Points**.

Retirement and the End of your Adventure

Once you have fully explored the world of Smog and Ambuscade, you may adventure on into the other books in this series, riding airships, infiltrating government, fighting for Cornish independence or riding the Great North Road. However, your good fortune cannot last forever and when you decide to settle down and retire from the road you will be invited to turn to the **Epilogue**. Several important factors will decide the happiness and security of your later years: the number of **Friendships** that you have made, the amount of money you have banked with Coulter's Bank, the number of **Solidarity Points** and **Great Deeds** that you have collected, and your health, represented by the number of **Scars** you bear. All of these will also help you calculate a score to share with other riders of the midnight road, or to better in another adventure.

1

The tarmacadam of the midnight road glitters with dew and reflected moonlight. Over the hills you can see distant furnaces glowing, telegraph towers winking and airships lumbering slowly across the sky but here the woods are dark with secrets. The only light is the hard white beam thrown by the lime lantern of your velosteam.

Somewhere in the night is your next target: a steam-carriage, carrying rich passengers in warmth and privilege, insulated from the struggles of their countrymen by ignorance and indulgence. Little do they expect the sudden and terrible attack of the Steam Highwayman.

How did you come here?

"My master was imprisoned for his inventions..."	**585**
"I fled servitude on a guild roadtrain..."	**420**
"An early death in the factories of London was to be my fate..."	**778**
"I am a disgraced and penniless heir..."	**125**

2

High Wood sits atop a steep hill directly overlooking the Hurley road. It is dense and quiet - the perfect place to create a hideout. If you wish to do so, you will need a **tarpaulin**, an **axe** and an INGENUITY score of at least 5. Discard the **tarpaulin** and tick the option below.

If you choose to pass through the wood, you will travel over farmland towards Burchett's Green and eventually reach the Bath Road, running far to the west. The noise and bustle of the turnpike seem like another world from this haunt of kites and crows.

☐Head to your hideout...	**78**
Ride down the slope to Hurley Bottom...	**513**
Ride south over the fields...	**353**

3

Boulter's Lock Hotel is a glamorous place, full of the gentry. Their servants scurry around below stairs, readying hampers for the next river excursion, pressing suits for waterborne dinners, finding watermen and musicians and boats and parasols.

A crowd of finely-dressed customers are mingling on the terrace by the restaurant and through the French windows you can see a fine grand pianola awaiting a skilled player. If you have the codeword *Charged*, turn to **217**.

Offer your services as a musician...	**748**
Leave the hotel...	**94**

4

Marlow is a prosperous and self-satisfied little town, fat from the tolls on the Thames barges passing through the lock and the steamers that cross over the suspension bridge. The high street is lined with shops and wholesalers, and the chimneys of the Wethered Brewery send out a thick smoke tinted with gold.

Visit Hunt's Hardware...	**33**
Visit the Ship Inn...	**86**
Visit the Two Brewers...	**265**
Visit All Saints Church...	**681**
Visit the Freight Yard...	**669**
Visit the Wethered Brewery...	**899**
Visit Marlow Lock...	**109**
Leave town...	**169**

5

Several days later you are prepared for the race. The Wagtail has proven itself in practice laps of the track and you, Harris and the mechanics have worked to refine and tweak the steering, the fuel delivery system and the brakes. At last the day of the race has come.

First there is a parade of entrants. Fifteen vehicles, their owners, drivers, sponsors, in some cases all the same person, make their way around the track to the thunderous applause of crowds, thousands-strong. Newspapermen, reporters with portable telegraph towers and photographers form knots around any new development or scandal. Lords and ladies of Imperial industry are sat in the stands and the King's mistress herself, with entourage, has arrived to watch the race. Bets are taken, odds fluctuating wildly. The Wagtail does not excite the favour of many of the gamblers. It is too small, too low and of an unconventional shape.

"How can that little tin pipe carry sufficient steam away from the boiler?" queries one bearded lord skeptically. "A locomotive should have a good stack, that's for sure."

Certainly the Wagtail is different in its principles to many of the entrants. There are massive, heavy-wheeled engines like the American Eagle and Ramoni's Spirito del Vento. There are coal-fueled and gas-fueled creations, high-pressure and low-pressure engines, boilers mounted centrally, slung beneath the chassis, front-mounted or rear-mounted.

Many of the bets are on Lord Akroyd's True Patriot to win. He is going to drive his own machine: a red-painted engine with a small cockpit mounted over a long, barrel-shaped boiler. As the teams make their final preparations, his mechanics come out to fit axle-blades to his wheels. Ostensibly for cutting through wreck debris, you know they are more likely to be used to prevent Akroyd's rivals passing him. This will be the drive of your life.

Strap in...   **796**

6

The narrow lane winds sharply up the hill, up several hairpin bends before you reach the high ground north of Wheeler End. Beside the road you pass a rotting wooden cart: yesterday's technology, discarded by some farmer or trader in an iron-bound, steam-powered race to the future. Roll a dice:

Score 1-2	A travelling saleswoman...	**75**
Score 3-4	You reach Wheeler End...	**137**
Score 5-6	A Coal Board official...	**699**

7

As you hand back the purse, the freighter recognises you. "I remember your face!" he grins. "We met you here before, and blow me down if you didn't make jest such a donation. Well, God bless you."

Leave them...   **202**

8

The steam wagon chugging down the slope is pulling a trailer laden with goods: barrels of apples, bundles of staves, hoops for the cooper, bales of raw wool, baskets of hops. A boy handles the steering while the master leans out from an iron stanchion and peers towards you with narrow eyes.

Threaten them...   **623**
Attack them...   **828**
Hail them...   **746**

9

With no-one to help you and no-where to turn, you really are in a dire situation. Perhaps it is time to end this desperate way of life. Although you manage to make it to the night-shrouded outskirts of High Wycombe somehow, you are unable to go any further and fall from your velosteam. Count your **Scars**:

12 or more...   **357**
11 or fewer...   **242**

10

The road over the hill leads you steadily towards Wooburn Green. You find yourself riding above a steep, west-facing wood above the smoking town. Just to the north of here is the London road, passing beneath the dark branches of Cutthroat Wood. You are within striking distance, yet here it is quiet and secluded.

Head down the steep hill into Wooburn Green...**199**
Look around the woods here...   **709**

11

Winchbottom Lane runs down the bottom of one of the steep, enclosed Chiltern valleys that are so common around here. An isolated barn stands here at a junction, and up on the hillside to the West stands Hard-to-Find Farm.

Visit the farm...   **714**
Take the road south-west...   **465**
Take the road east...   **50**

12

Cookham Lock is a short distance from the village, on one of the thin islands that have provided the opportunity for entrepreneurial engineers to control and manage the river's flow. Many barges are loading grain here for London and the bargees and their families, dressed in their bright clothes, make a picturesque sight.

Go aboard your boat, if it is docked here...   **328**
Try to cross the weir...   **467**
Return to Cookham...   **246**

13

It takes you several days of hard work camped out on the riverbank, dredging the mud and water out of the hull, unbolting the machinery and cleaning it out, refitting pipes and valves and re-waterproofing the hull. Thankfully you have the help of a keen youth from the nearby village of Hurley, who will do anything for a chance to get on the water: he is steam-boat mad!

After all your efforts you are rewarded with a small, but working, steam skiff, large enough for you to embark your velosteam and single unit of cargo. You are ready to take to the water! The young man, who impressed you with his honesty and determination, agrees to come aboard as your mate, to look after the boat when you moor it and to help load cargo and handle the skiff through locks and congested stretches of the water.

"Won't your parents wonder where you have gone?" you ask.

He snorts. "Not at all. They'll figure I've just found work along the riverboats - I've been looking long enough."

Give your **small skiff** a name, mark it on your adventure sheet and gain the codeword *Appropriate*.

Raise steam and head onto the river...   **877**

14

The World's End Music Hall stands behind a row of steam-cabriolets disgorging wealthy socialites and fur-trimmed ladies. Gaslight suffuses the evening mists and smog and the glowing, slowly-spinning globe atop the building's green copper dome seems to reel with decadent drunkenness. Folk come from miles around to see the legendary floorshows here - the projectionists' magic and the dancing girls' glittered legs. You can find heirs to business empires, painters, musicians, clerks and coders from the telegraph works, urchins selling paper flowers and great obese Lords selling court favours. Nothing is for free here. The house and its entertainers all have their own bills to pay: you must front up a florin to enter.

At the stage door stands Lenny the doorman, who takes care of the dancing girls. He prefers to keep his employment and his charges secure and makes sure no-one but friends of the house can enter.

Go inside the music hall...   (**2s**)   **395**
Head to the stage door...(**Friend of Mrs Juste**) **91**
Leave the World's End...   **594**

15

The cutting sides provide you with the barest of chances to escape. With shots ringing out from the railway guards posted on the tunnel mouth, you manage to gun your velosteam over a ditch and onto a narrow path. A hairpin bend, a desperate charge across a disintegrating plank bridge over a muddy torrent and a dash beneath the low branches of a fallen tree and you are away!

Ride on!   **186**

16

It is a long race to Cookham weir, and the shouts of the Constables behind you prove they are convinced they have you trapped! However, you steer nimbly over the lock gates just as they swing closed, take a sharp left and approach the weir. Make a MOTORING roll of difficulty 10 to cross and leave your pursuers behind. You can add

1 to your roll if you have **off-road tyres** fitted to your velosteam.

Successful MOTORING roll!   **48**
Failed MOTORING roll!   **207**

17

Mr Hibbert greets you with a wave as you ride into the yard, then turns to his dogs. "Jasper, Moggett, down. Good fellows. Hello my friend! Come and warm yourself by the fire. Tell me how you fare." Before long you are sat in a comfortable chair with a glass of sherry in your hand and a good meal inside you. Mr Hibbert will have his servants tend your **Wounds** if you are hurt: remove any **Wounds** and convert them each to **Scars**, rolling two dice for each and gaining an **intimidating scar (RUTH+1)** for each roll of 11 or 12.

Enjoy Mr Hibbert's library...   **736**
Leave the farm...   **11**

18

The road slopes gently down to Marlow. You pass some large iron tanks being refilled from a massive water bowser, almost blocking the road. Then a gang of navvies are digging a trench along the street, laying a new sewer pipe. If you are **Wanted by the Constables**, turn to **132** immediately.

Continue down into Marlow...   **4**

19

Gain the codeword *Ammonium* and cross off your **explosives**. The explosion tears apart the tracks and scatters the gravel like shotgun pellets. Thankfully you took the precaution to retreat to a proper distance and are not hurt. The Imperial Western Railway will not be happy at all: you are now **Wanted by the Railway Guards**.

Make your getaway!   **351**

20

Lose the codeword *Aurum*. It was around here that the rainbow you found came to ground. If you want to calculate the exact location of the rainbow's root, you will need to do some mathematics. Make an INGENUITY roll of difficulty 10, adding 1 if you have a pair of **binoculars** or a **telescope**.

Successful roll!   **417**
Failed roll!   **264**

21

The tall wall is punctuated by a series of small windows and a pair of green gates. Behind here stands the kitchen garden and the greenhouses and Cliveden House itself stands some way beyond that, behind a smart drive and a fountain. But there is no way through here without a **gardener's key** or a **skeleton key**.

Back to the roadside...   **366**
Enter the gate...
    (**gardener's key** or **skeleton key**)   **462**

22

You miss your footing, tumble to the ground and narrowly dodge being run over by the steamer's heavy wheels. Nonetheless, when you pick yourself up it feels as though you may have cracked a rib. Gain a **Wound**.

If you have **five Wounds**...   **90**
Remount your velosteam...   **528**

23

The lights of a nearby roadhouse draw you in and soon you are seated in a warm nook, facing the fire, with a tankard of ale and a hearty meal in front of you. The wind and rain are forgotten - the risk and danger have passed and your heart is beginning to beat at its proper pace.

There is a sudden commotion at the door and a too-familiar figure limps in dramatically and falls in a chair.

"House! House, I say. I've been robbed on the road. A posse of highwayman - must have been at least four. Had to fight for my life! House! I thought this was a reputable place?"

Sit back into the shadows...   **259**

24

The stream trickles slowly eastwards and the bankside path is just broad enough for the wheels of your velosteam. Travelling slowly and brushing past the nodding white flowers of wild garlic, ducking beneath the zig-zagging beech twigs, you eventually reach the gravel and iron of the Occidental Railway line. You cross where an enterprising local has placed some boards between the rails and find yourself on an unpaved lane by a short row of cottages. You have reached the outskirts of Maidenhead, just as you were told you would, entirely bypassing the constables' checkpoints on the main roads.

Ride down to Maidenhead...   **594**

25

The pistons churn smoothly as you accelerate up the hill. Before long you are atop the high-ground, with all the countryside laid out before you. A chill evening is coming on and the earth's shadow looms in the east. Here, at Handy Cross, a huddle of buildings stands at the crest of the hill: a forge and a large shed beside a farmhouse. On each side the road streams down the hill and in the distance you can see road trains labouring heavily up the slope, their front lamps lit and fire-boxes glowing.

Investigate the forge...   **60**
Ride north towards Wycombe...   **313**
Take the road south towards Marlow...   **279**
Head east to Winchbottom Lane...   **465**
Turn west through the honeysuckle-covered gate...
                                      1003

26

The tax collectors came ready for resistance. Two large men with clubs step towards you: you will have to defeat them both to scare off the posse. Fight them as if they were one opponent - but note you will have to wound them twice as much as normal to win!

Tax Collectors   Weapon: **cudgel (PAR 4)**
Parry: 8
Nimbleness: 4
Toughness: 6

Victory!   **59**
Defeat!   **798**

27

You twist and bank over the soft woodland floor, crushing the undergrowth before you and leading the Constables deeper and deeper into the wood. Over a fallen tree-trunk, through a plashy mire thick with leaves like spear-points raised towards the sun, on over chalk and flint and broken ground.

Then the path you are following abruptly ends in an old landslip opening up like a waiting mouth. You manage to glimpse the threat in just enough time and pull your velosteam up onto the bank and between the beech trunks. The Constables, however, are still accelerating as they launch off into space. They crash to the valley floor in a scalding explosion of metal and steam. You had better put some distance between yourself and the carnage!

Steam away...   **67**

28

With your final blow you knock the bandit chief to the ground and his gang melt away into the bushes. You find some of his loot hidden nearby - a purse containing **£4 3s**, a **gold necklace** and a **dark cloak** (RUTH+1).

Return to the convoy...   556

29

Your shot misses and the deer leaps away into the depths of the wood. You will not have another chance today, as the animals will all be more than usually wary after gun-fire in their wood. You make your way back to the velosteam and ride off.

Leave the wood...   289

30

You put the dirt of Wooburn Green behind you. You steam up out of the Wye valley and into farmland. Sunshine breaks through the heavy clouds and for a moment you can enjoy the sight of golden wheat and red kites flying overhead.

Ride up Glory Lane...   530
Head on to Loudwater...   574
Take the road to Flackwell Heath...   50
Steam south towards Wooburn...   310

31

"Good to see you!" Lord Dashwood approaches, a glass of champagne in his hand and a young woman on either arm. "You made it - excellent. Now, we can't race without a **lady's colours**. How you charm one of these delightful guests is up to you!"

Plenty of the guests are racing enthusiasts and Dashwood tows you round, introducing you here and there. There are rude stares and titters as the people size you up, but there are also genuine well-wishers. The food is good - although the portions are small - and there is free-flowing champagne to keep the mood merry.

You have to do something to net this sponsor!

Tell some tales of the road...   72
Join the dancing...   479
Remain aloof...   522

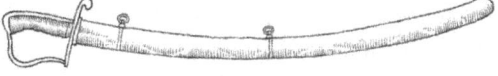

32

Shortly after entering the gloom of the bank, a heavy hand lands on your shoulder: you have been recognised from your attempted robbery!

Bank Guard   Weapon: **cudgel (PAR 4)**
Parry: 9
Nimbleness: 5
Toughness: 4

Victory!   377
Defeated!   779

33

Hunt's Hardware shop is tucked away down a side-street between a row of cottages and a barbers, but when you enter it is plain why this is a destination emporium for any self-respecting engineer. The staff are all one extended family and are keen to send every customer away satisfied.

Clothing	To buy	To sell
dungarees (GAL-2)	**£1 10s**	**15s**
goggles (MOT+1)	**£2 15s**	**£2 2s**
engineer's gloves (ENG +1)	**£3**	**£2 5s**
engineer's gauntlets (ENG+2)	**£5**	**£4**

Tools	To buy	To sell
rope	**4s**	**2s**
waterproof paint	**6s**	**-**
rope ladder	**9s**	**7s**
lantern	**6s**	**4s**
shovel	**8s**	**5s**
wirecutters	**12s**	**9s**
heavy wrench	**18s**	**12s**
welding tools	**£2 2s**	**£1 10s**
grappling iron	**12s**	**8s**
tarpaulin	**4s**	**4s**
brass flange joint	**8s**	**5s**
copper pipe	**6s**	**4s**
high pressure valve	**18s**	**9s**

Other items	To buy	To sell
pneumatic manual (ENG+3) -		**£6 10s**
skeleton key	**£4**	**£2 10s**

If you have a **strongbox** and you want Old Hunt to open it for you, pay **£1** and note this passage number before turning to **821**.

Leave the shop...   4
Leave Marlow...   169

34

Within the cool chalk and brick halls of the Abbey, the monks of the Order of St Aloysius pad to and fro in their rope-soled sandals, pondering God's ways and their part in bringing His kingdom on earth.

In the Refectory the monks keep an open table for any traveller in need of refreshment. You sit alongside traders, travellers and beggars, vagrants of the most ragged kind, loafers and wandering cripples. The meal is simple and hearty and a serious quiet pervades the room. After eating, you talk with some of the travellers and hear their stories: escape from the anarchy of Cornwall, hard labour in Wales, destitution and cholera in London. Here, at least, there is fresh air and freedom, even if work is hard to come by. If you are **Wanted by the Constables**, turn to **352**.

Leave by road...	**737**
Sail away... (if your boat is moored here)	**745**

35

There is something thoughtless about the authorities' decision to lock all the law-breakers together: in the company of thieves, pickpockets, fraudsters and all manner of creatively felonious individuals, you learn many tricks of the trade. Increase your INGENUITY score by 1.

Turn to...	**227**

36

"Stop your engine," barks a voice from inside the armoured wagon. "You have been identified. Halt immediately for searching."

Of course you have no intention of stopping! You put out your foot, pivot around exactly the way you came and accelerate off. The Enforcer doesn't give any more warnings but immediately begins to fire. Bullets whizz over your head as you duck and weave across the road, tucking in tight behind freight wagons coming down from Lane End. The guild are close behind: their multi-wheeled vehicle is designed to be a pursuit vehicle.

There is only one option: an off-road dash, testing the limits of your MOTORING skill. A gap in the hedge presents itself and you have a split-second to make your decision.

Steer through the hedge and inbetween the trees... **712**
Leave the road to the right through the farmland... **824**

37

The people of Temple village work hard for the owners of the Estate - the monks at Bisham Abbey. The rich soil is pressed hard, and everything squeezed for the maximum profit. You can see the lock beyond a fence and a line of trees, but the monks strictly control any access from the road and there is no mooring for riverboats.

Ride south...	**662**
Take the path to Hurley...	**569**
Travel to Bisham...	**737**

38

The girl rewards you with a kiss and her thanks. "That's my uncle you just beat down, dirty beggar. I'm off to Honduras, myself." She hitches up her skirts.

Return to Maidenhead...	**594**

39

A few minutes later Judge Hector, Master of Hedsor house, appears on the steps in his frock coat and wig. "Well?" he demands. "What do you have for me?"

"Your doom," you reply, preparing to fight. He draws his sword and takes a fencer's position.

Judge Hector		Weapon: **rapier (PAR 7)**
Parry:	13	
Nimbleness:	6	
Toughness:	2	

Victory!	**87**
Defeat!	**255**

40

When your blindfold is taken off, you are standing in front of a young woman in engineer's dungarees and a headscarf sitting behind a full desk. She holds a mechanically printed image of your portrait, together with a long report on your background.

"So you want to join the revolution? I must ask you several questions, to find whether you really believe in the people or whether you simply want to escape their wrath!" Comrade Feaver leans towards you. "Firstly - why do the people suffer?"

"Life is a struggle and many are too weak to help themselves."	**994**
"Human selfishness is the root cause."	**963**
"The owners of capital believe they are owners of individuals."	**973**

41

"Stop that engine!" you cry. To intimidate the crew of the Haulage Guild Steamer you must make a RUTHLESSNESS roll of difficulty 13. You can add 2 if you have a **double headlamp**, as the bright beam will dazzle the crew.

Successful RUTHLESSNESS roll!	**179**
Failed RUTHLESSNESS roll!	**281**

42

Recognising your face from the many wanted posters, the guildsmen steam directly towards you. The two guards begin firing their carbines and as the wagon swings to a halt, blocking the road ahead, you are amazed to see a carbine-toting posse clamber down from the wagon and race towards you!

Race back the way you came...	**247**
Take off across the fields...	**96**

43

The chattering girls take their photograph, in which you pull your most heartless grimace. They stand around for a moment, then one of the ringleaders steps up to you. "I say, you wouldn't kidnap our teacher for us, would you? Miss Evans is trying to take us to the Winchester Chamber of Commerce for a field trip, but we'd much rather take the charabanc to the sea. All we need is for you to keep her out of the way for a day. What do you say?"

"I'm not the one to interrupt your studies, girls."	**587**
"Alright. I'll happily kidnap your teacher."	**88**

44

Deep in the wood you come across a little old man in a shapeless hat, a mossy green suit and a bright pink scarf. His white beard gives him a rather mischievous, gnome-like appearance. You ask what he is doing in the wood.

"I'm measuring these hazel coppices," he replies. "Very difficult to age, hazel coppices. Now if it were hornbeam, like over there, or even ash I'd have a clue." He is a professor of trees, studying woodland and its history. "Important fuel source, I'd say, all these woods round here. Charcoal, of course. And more."

He fixes you with a beady eye. "I love really old trees. Do you know of any I can study?" If you have the codeword *Anthill*, turn to **818**. Otherwise you must leave the old man to his measuring and pottering and ride further into the wood.

Turn to...	**190**

45

A posse of long-coated men are making their way through the streets as you ride along. Something about their demeanour catches your attention: they are tax collectors. You overhear one conversation with a mother at her door.

"That's twice what we was told to pay, and we paid it last week!"

The tax collector replies smoothly, "Then you'll have the receipt for that, I guess. No? Then I'm afraid to say that the visitor was probably an imposter. We've had reports."

"How do I know you're not an imposter?"

"Madam, I am Officer Smiteby of the City Financial Affairs Office. No-one can doubt me."

"But we already paid our city tax, I tells you."

"Not, alas, according to our records."

"Well the devil take you and your records!"

Offer to pay the woman's tax...	(£2)	**117**
Turn the tax collectors away...		**26**
Ride on by...		**650**

46

It would be foolhardy to try and ride straight into the Haulage Guild's compound even as they are searching for you! You had better find a way to get them off your trail - maybe by disguising yourself or changing your Citizen Identification Number.

Return to the Two Bridges...	**282**

47

Your mate finds you a secure mooring amongst the islands and stows the travelling gear. You leave him warming his feet by the cabin stove as you wheel your velosteam ashore. Note that you are moored at **Hurley Lock (Downstream)**.

Turn to...	**569**

48

Once you are over the weir, you have plenty of time to empty the water from your footwear. You park and check your velosteam under the cover of some nearby willow trees. For just a few moments, you can rest here in the river's calm before heading on. Where will you ride next?

Towards Bourne End...	**703**
Towards Hedsor wharf...	**214**

49

After taking some time looking through the undergrowth for signs of animal tracks, you choose a likely-looking spot and lay your trap. Discard the **snare** and roll a dice:

Score 1-2 You catch nothing
Score 3-4 A **pheasant** strolls into the noose
Score 5-6 You find a **rabbit** in your trap

Leave the wood...   **289**

50

You steam through Flackwell Heath, its cottages strung out along the hilltop road. This place is known for its cattle-breeding and its strong ale.

Stop at the Three Horseshoes...   **228**
Head east towards Wooburn Green...   **199**
Head north-east to Loudwater...   **574**
Head north-west towards Winchbottom lane... **11**
Ride down Sheepridge Lane...   **291**

51

You moor up against the old dock. The other wharves are busy, as machinery brought up from London is transferred onto freight wagons before being hauled up to High Wycombe. The route is slower, but also cheaper than making the whole journey by road. This wharf is quiet, however, and For Sale signs hang on the machinery and cranes. If you wish to fit a **cargo crane** to your boat, the wharf foreman will gladly see his men working rather than waiting around, and will charge you a mere **£10**.

	To buy	To sell
Charcoal	£12	-
Furniture	-	-
Machinery	£24	£24
Pottery	-	-
Cotton	-	-
Woollen cloth	-	-
Coal	£12	£11
Beer	-	£16
Wheat	-	-
Malt	-	£8
Frozen Meat	-	-
Ice	-	-

There are no moorings for a private barge here, so once you have bought or sold any cargo, you must return to the Thames. If you have a cargo of "Mineral Samples", turn to **789**. If you are a **Member of the Compact for Worker's Equality**, you may address the workers.

Address the wharvesmen...
   (**Member of the CWE**)   **866**
Unmoor...   **693**

52

The Henley road is full of traffic, so you ride over the verges and take a shortcut through a wheatfield. The Constables are still close behind you as you approach Hurley village and just as you approach the lock, the gates open to let a barge through. You must jump the gap to reach the Harleyford estate footbridge and the safety of the north bank! Make a MOTORING roll of difficulty 12, adding 1 if you have a **gas pressuriser**.

Successful MOTORING roll!   **65**
Failed MOTORING roll!   **207**

53

The little room you keep here at the Crooked Billet is at the top of a winding stair that passes up behind a warm chimney breast and deposits you high in the roof, with a window commanding a prudent view of the road in both directions. It will be hard for the authorities to surprise you here.

You may leave possessions here in safety, returning to collect them at your leisure.

Looking out over the garden and the hedgerows of the little valley, you also have the opportunity to weigh up your past. Can it be time to retire from this life on the road while you are still well? There may be other adventures open to you in other parts of this lawless land - particularly if the authorities in this region have become watchful. Perhaps there is even a way, somewhere in this region, of wiping your name clean and erasing your notorious reputation, leaving you to retire in peace.

Rest and tend your **Wounds**...	**382**
Return to the parlour...	**180**
Consider retirement...	**1017**

54

The straight road down towards Marlow is well-drained and firm beneath your velosteam's wheels. Roll a dice to see if you meet anyone coming down the hill towards you:

Score 1-2	A local haulier...	**8**
Score 3-4	Nothing obstructs you...	**202**
Score 5-6	The Haulage Guild...	**673**

55

The stalk takes you deep into the wood, over ice-cold streams and between ancient coppice stools, under fallen trees and along tracks so forgotten that they begin in the middle of nowhere and end in the middle of nowhere. Your eyes are sharp, though, from all your road-watching, and ignoring the squirrels and birds, you are sure that something is not far ahead of you, moving deeper into the wood.

Suddenly you come to a cliff: the lip of an old quarry. Cold water pooled below and a carpet of bronze beech leaves provides the backdrop to a magnificent stag bowing his head to drink. He looks up for a moment - you have one opportunity to shoot! Make an ACCURACY roll of difficulty 14.

Successful ACCURACY roll!	**810**
Failed ACCURACY roll!	**29**

56

You are knocked down by the guard who laughs and stands over you gleefully. "You should have known better than to try it," he chuckles, despite his wounds.

Suddenly, a shadow moves across the room. Someone strikes the guard from behind and he falls onto the carpet beside you with a thump. You just manage to see a figure swooping down on the jewel case before you too black out from your wounds.

Turn to...   **621**

57

You steam down the hill towards Wooburn and the River Wye. Roll a dice to see what you encounter:

Score 1-2	An entrepreneur...	**111**
Score 3-4	Wooburn...	**310**
Score 5-6	Strange tracks...	**174**

58

He immediately steps away. "What are you doing on the road at this time of night... mother?" He has seen through your disguise and suspects a trap. You can quickly change your plan: will you draw your sabre and attack him or attempt to scare him into giving up his purse?

Threaten him...	**838**
Attack him...	**555**

59

At the sight of their downed colleagues, the tax collectors disappear into the streets around. They will certainly be back, however, and you have done little more than earn the poor people of the slum a brief reprieve.

"It's just typical," says a crippled, wizened man. "Taxes, taxes, taxes, while we're paid less and less for working longer hours. The time is coming when there'll be revolution in this land, oh yes. A youngster like you may live to see it. I know it's being planned."

"Where can I find such people?" you ask.

"They meet up in Wooburn and Loudwater," says one woman. "Print flyers and suchlike, decrying the oppressive upper classes. But will they ever do anything? I don't know, and that's the truth."

You have gained **1 Solidarity Point** for your actions.

Ride on out of the slums...   **650**

60

Steam rises from a boiler powering a donkey-headed power-hammer, repeatedly slamming down on the cherry-red bars the smith is forge-welding here. A wide bed of charcoal glows with blue and white heat, venti-

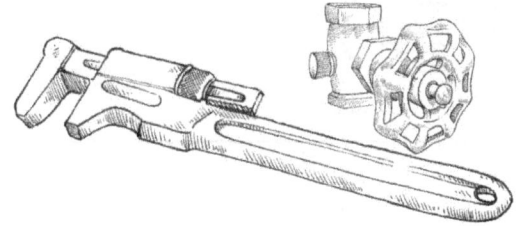

lated by more machinery and fed, automatically, by a mechanized hopper and rake. The forge at the crest of the hill is kept busy here: a constant flow of traffic between Marlow and Henley needs repairs and upgrades and the smith is well-known as a wizard with machinery.

Clothing	To buy	To sell
cloak	£1	15s
dungarees (GAL-2)	£1 10s	15s
engineer's gloves (ENG +1)	£3	£2 5s

Tools	To buy	To sell
shovel	8s	5s
axe	8s	6s
wirecutters	12s	9s
heavy wrench	18s	1
brass flange joint	8s	5s
copper pipe	6s	4s
roll of oiled silk	-	£5

Velosteam Customisations	To buy
muffled exhaust	£3 15s
enlarged fuel tank	£6 18s
reinforced boiler	£12

Repairs	To buy
Per **Damage Point**	£1 10s

Chat to the blacksmith...   459
Ask about **titanium alloy**...   635
Leave the forge...   25

61

Gregory the natural has been replaced by a mechanical box-organ. The pieces it plays are complicated and impressive, but you can't help but feel it lacks expression, and wonder what happened to the boy it replaced.

Leave the church...   4

62

After handing your precious **letter of introduction** to the gateman (cross it off), an imperious butler arrives to bring you to Lord Dashwood himself. He greets you on the drive in front of his home and is immediately interested by your Ferguson velosteam.

"Beautiful machine," he says. "Such crafting. Tell me - how does she ride?"

Lord Dashwood is a keen engineer and racer. He is currently working on a new steam road carriage, built exclusively to compete in the Spenser Cup. He shows you the vehicle in a garage behind the house. "A birchwood frame and aluminium streamlining," he points out. "And the engine is a thing of beauty. But it still needs work. I'm topping ninety, but I want a hundred miles an hour! Will you help me? I've been trying to enlist the help of the engineer Lalage Harris down in Littlewick Green. I've offered her money, I've offered her a position, but I can't convince her yet. Perhaps another enthusiast like yourself can convince her that this beauty has a chance of winning the cup - that it isn't just an aristocrat's vanity project. Return here with Lalage Harris and I will be very grateful."

Gain the codeword *Agile*.

Leave West Wycombe House...   492

63

The window slides open. The guard is facing the door. You creep behind him and quickly whip a pad soaked in chloroform over his mouth. He struggles, of course, and it takes all your strength to press the sleeping draught into his face as he fights. Then you lower him to the floor.

The jewels are in a fine brass and walnut box on the dresser: you find the key in the guard's pocket. Opening the lid, you are presented with the sight of a glittering river of diamonds set in silver, a pear-shaped black sapphire hanging in a pendant beneath them like the tear of an Indian god.

Then, as you stretch out to take it, you are struck from behind. Everything goes black.

Turn to...   621

64

"An interesting reply," says Feaver. "You seem to have thought about this for yourself. Still, I do not yet know whether I can admit you into our ranks. Answer me this: you find yourself rescuing the passengers from a sinking ship and three swimmers plead for your help. A mill-owner, cruel to his workers but influential and likely to repay your help, waves to you. A poor woman from steerage class, unable ever to repay you, begs to be saved. And a comrade-in-arms, a fellow member of the Compact, holds up his hand in desperate help. Whom will you save?"

"The mill-owner."   996
"The poor woman."   982
"The comrade."   275

65

You leap the gap directly over the bargee's head. The Constables are left on the far side, staring and trying to aim their weapons. However, a quick dash between the lock buildings and through the private gate and you are onto the Squire's private bridge. Arching elegantly over the northern stream of the river, it takes you across the Thames to safety.

Ride towards the main road...   **786**

66

Your trusty velosteam smashes through the blockade and you tear away before the Constables have an opportunity to mount their steam wagons. Dr Smollett hangs on grimly behind you, without a word, and you carry on towards Bullocks Farm.

Ride on through the rain...   **726**

67

You have left the outskirts of smoky Maidenhead behind you. Here is Widbrook Common, its buttercups and tall grasses unbesmirched by progress.

Ride north to Cookham...   **246**
Ride onto the Common...   **264**
Ride south to Boulter's Lock...   **280**

68

There is no sign over the low door and no bar inside the front room. A few slovenly workers are sat on benches by the light of a single window, drinking from tumblers of gin, laughing, arguing, rolling dice. This is not a refined place or a particularly safe one. The looks of desperation in the faces of the men and women drinking here indicate that you are as likely to be a target as a guest.

Order some gin...   (2s)   **688**
Buy a round of drinks and listen for rumours...**256**
Ask about the Compact for Workers' Equality... **989**
Leave the gin shop...   **199**

69

"Go on and kill 'im," shrieks the woman. "He's only another nob - there are more where he came from."

You turn your velosteam around and head up towards Hedsor House. The gates are open, so it is a simple matter to ride in up the drive. A shout from a man tending the garden rings out from behind you, but you con-

tinue up the front steps and into the courtyard.

A footman cleaning boots looks up as you stop the velosteam. "What do you want?" he asks. "Never seen you before."

"An urgent message for the master of Hedsor," you reply. "News from the city."

The footman gets up, confused. "I'll tell the butler," he says. "Wait here."

Wait where you are...   **39**
Follow the footman in...   **766**

70

A small fair has been set up on the green alongside the road. Most of the stalls are selling produce from the hills and pasturelands around, but several mechanics are showing their ingenious inventions.

Food and Drink	To buy	To sell
bird's eggs	4s	3s
rabbit	2s	1s
pheasant	4s	3s
tin of fruit	3s	2s
wheel of cheese	£1 2s	14s

Clothing	To buy	To sell
cloak	£1	15s
eyepatch (RUTH+1)	15s	5s
wide-brimmed hat	£1 10s	18s

Tools	To buy	To sell
rope	4s	2s
lantern	6s	4s
fishing line	1s	-

Medical items	To buy	To sell
cough medicine	8s	-
false teeth	-	8s

Other items	To buy	To sell
constable's whistle	-	2s
deck of marked cards	15s	4s
parasol	-	£2
chess set	£2 2s	£2

As you skirt the fair, a pair of constables on Imperial velosteams peer at you, then consult their wallet of notorious brigands and dangerous criminals. If you are **Wanted by the Constables**, turn to **694**.

Leave the common...   **5**

71

If you are **Wanted by the Haulage Guild**, turn to **46**.

A burly guard looks you over and punches your Citizen's Identity Number into a machine before opening the barrier. You can enter the compound of the Haulage Guild - after all, members of the public use their services all the time. Inside the yard several road trains are being prepared for freight journeys across the land. If you have a **Guildsman's medallion**, turn to **178**.

Try to see the regional director...	**306**
Leave the compound...	**282**

72

You amuse several of the guests with one of your tales of the road - and the laughter attracts the interest of Mrs Roberts. She brings her hangers-on over and somebody finds her a chair while you tell more of your near misses, close escapes and most death-defying moments on your velosteam. Whistles of appreciation accompany your telling and Maria Roberts' eyes flash with interest as you tell her.

"Wonderful!" she enthuses. "There really is no fear in you, eh? And now the Spenser Cup. With that sort of attitude, I think you could do very well. How would you like to drive under my colours?" She unwinds a white silk scarf and hands it over. You now have a **lady's colours** and gain the codeword *Able* as well. "Now Dashwood's engine had better be as good as his driver," says Mrs Roberts. "I shall bet heavily on you."

The ball continues long into the night. Dashwood is elated that you have managed to pique the interest of the King's mistress. "Just think what that connection could do for us!" It is many hours later that you steam out of Cliveden gates, a little wobbly, into the morning mist.

Leave the ball... **612**

73

If you are **Wanted by the Constables**, turn to **356** immediately.

A wide column of steam rising between the trees indicates a wide-funnelled wagon coming your way - maybe a Levison engine, used by the Constables. Sure enough, Constabulary blue and brass soon gleams in-between the trees and you stay hidden behind a holly bush as they steam by. You mount up and ride in the opposite direction.

Head to Bisham... **737**

74

You are overcome by the loss of blood and left for dead at the side of the road. When you come to, your velosteam is in the ditch beside you, but all your **money** has been taken and many of your possessions as well. For each **possession** or item of **clothing**, roll a dice. A score of 4 or lower means that you must cross it off.

You must now see if you can survive long enough to get to safety.

If you are the **Friend of Mr Hibbert**...	**639**
If you are the **Friend of Lord Dashwood**...	**797**
If you have the codeword *Adoption*, turn to...	**755**
If you have the codeword *Ashen*, turn to...	**518**
Bandage your most serious wound... (**bandages** or a **cloak**)	**219**
Otherwise, turn to...	**9**

75

A woman pushing a cart flags you down. No sooner have you stopped than she unfolds a banner, a jangling display and a tiny automated steam-organ that plays a jaunty tune. "Mistress DeFancy's Fancy Goods, all at your disposal," she says with a bow. "Unique equipments for the technically minded, guaranteed workmanship from Sheffield, Boston and Paris."

Jewellery	To buy	To sell
locket	6s	4s
pocket watch	-	£1 15s
silver ring	10s	7s
silver bracelet	£2	£1 5s
silver necklace	£1	10s
gold ring	-	£1 1s
gold bracelet	-	£2 2s
gold necklace	-	£5

Medical items	To buy	To sell
cough medicine	5s	-
pink pills (NIM+2) ☐ ☐ ☐	£2 5s	-

Other items	To buy	To sell
constable's whistle	3s	2s
ivory fan	£2	£1 8s
clockwork bird	£2 2s	£2
punchcards (Aramanth A)	£10	£7 4s

Continue on your way... **137**

76

You are surprised to see a herd of cattle come tearing along the lane, mooing and lowing fit to burst. They must have got away from their drovers and they are headed right towards you.

If you have a level of **Animal Friendship** or a **whistle** of any kind, you will be able to calm them down. Otherwise they will knock you off your velosteam and trample you!

Calm the cows...	**144**
Otherwise...	**372**

77

After a long wait with no likely-looking targets approaching, you have no choice other than to find shelter for what remains of the night. Your velosteam is low on pressure and your bones feel the cold. Where will you find warmth?

The Cross Keys at Burchett's Green...	**628**
The Bull at Bisham...	**801**
The Golden Ball Inn...	**394**

78

The path to your secret hideout is well hidden. Roll two dice and add 1 for every **Wanted** status you possess.

Score 2-11	Secrecy preserved	**220**
Score 12+	Discovered!	**336**

79

The Freighter's Haven is right alongside the yard where the long-distance hauliers refuel and repair their road wagons. The parlour is part workshop and part bar, serving hearty meals for the men and women who ply this route. Everyone wears hard-wearing road clothes, unashamed of their mud splashes, coal dust, oil smears and filthy hands. Up on the chalkboard are today's options: steak n' kidney pie, potato pie, lamb pie and meat pie.

If you wish to take a room, pay a deposit of **£2** and tick the box next to the option below.

☐ Head to your room...	(ticked box)	**645**
Buy a drink...	(1s)	**829**
Buy drinks for the freighters...	(6s)	**241**
Talk to the mechanic...		**759**
Leave the Freighter's Haven...		**684**

80

The road here is full of smoking traffic. Steam bursts out from badly-adjusted pistons on every side. Farmers try to drive their herds through the confusion, pedestrians brawl and shove their way into town. Roll two dice:

Score 2-4	Freighters...	**8**
Score 5-8	You make your way through...	**313**
Score 9-12	The Co-Operative...	**343**

81

A nasty scene is playing out on the coke-scattered yard as you arrive. A large woman armed with a leather strap is cursing her apprentice, who seems to have made one mistake too many, and means to give him the beating of his life.

Let her discipline the boy...	**396**
Invite the boy to hop on your velosteam...	**491**
Knock a sense of fairness into the woman...	**659**

82

Your mate helps you unload your velosteam down a plank onto dry land. "We'll wait for you just here, boss," he says. "Don't be away too long."

Mark **Two Bridges** as your mooring on your barge **Adventure Sheet**.

Turn to...	**282**

83

Unfortunately the soaking seems to have affected you more than you realised. You have the symptoms of a bad fever coming on. Note the **Fever** on the **Other Modifiers** section of your Adventure Sheet. Until you recover from the Fever, you must suffer -1 to your GALLANTRY, INGENUITY, NIMBLENESS and ENGINEERING scores.

Ride on regardless...	**650**

84

The strongbox contains a fine set of **emerald jewellery** in a velvet bag. The rich colour of the stones and the fine setting would make even a scullery maid look like a princess. This loot must be worth a great deal - if you can find someone to take it off your hands. Emeralds can come with a curse, after all.

Continue...	Return to your noted passage

85

You manage to subdue the engineer and rifle his fallen body. You can take his **club (PAR 4)**, a **box of cigars**, a **pneumatic manual (ENG+3)** and **£1 19s.**

Ride away to the shelter of the Inn...   737

86

You have to duck to enter the Ship Inn, then choose between two parlours in which to drink and recuperate. On one side is a jolly, raucous crowd of navvies, songsters, brewer's mates and hauliers, while on the quieter side sit fat merchants supping port and soup.

Order a bumper of port and sit quietly... **(4s)** 373
Buy a round of drinks for the crowd... **(8s)** 99
Return to the High Street...   4

87

The Judge falls to the ground, dead, and the grieving mother is avenged. The story of your wild championing of those too poor to protect themselves will travel far and wide - and maybe give other nobles cause to think how they treat the lower classes. Gain **2 Solidarity Points**. As the Judge's servants flee, you have the opportunity to take the purse of **£5 4s** from his coat, if you want to mix robbery with revenge. Then you must flee: you are now **Wanted by the Constables** if you are not already and gain the codeword *Astrakhan*.

Ride away into the woods...   709

88

The girls cheer as you strongarm Miss Evans off the bus and blindfold her. Before you know it, the bus has turned around and sped off. For the rest of the day you babysit her, listening to her woes and cares as she talks to you about a schoolmistress' life. She is more than happy for the girls to enjoy a day's adventure but would feel guilty if she were to take them to the sea without a good educational reason.

  The bus of schoolgirls is late to their rendezvous, but you reunite them with their teacher and regain your own freedom. Miss Evans is grateful and the girls even more so. One of them presents you with a stick of **seaside rock**. Miss Evans points out the school on your map just outside Henley. "If you are ever steaming past, do drop in for a cup of tea," she says with a smile. Gain the codeword *Awful*.

Ride on to Bourne End...   703

89

Your decision to renege on your agreement will certainly hurt your reputation, as well as the freighter's chance of a new life for herself and her family. Lose **three Solidarity Points**. Add the **£50** to your wallet before you ride away and leave her to face the consequences. You will also be **Wanted by the Constables** and **Wanted by the Wallingford Town Guard**.

Ride away...   546

90

Lying beside the road, you have the slimmest of chances to make it back on your feet and back to health. If you have a **cloak** or **bandages**, you can try to staunch the flow of your wounds yourself. If you have friends nearby, you may be able to reach them for help.

Bandage your wounds... (**cloak** or **bandages**) 481
If you have the codeword *Alba*...   451
If you are the **Friend of Madam Juste**...   508
If you are the **Friend of Wellesley Garman**... 753
Otherwise...   9

91

Madame Juste welcomes you to the back room above the stage. The dancing girls are changing just along the corridor. "Welcome back, darling," she says. "Anything you need?"

Rest and bandage your wounds...   341
Leave the World's End...   594
Head downstairs to the show...   641
Visit the bar...   678

92

The landlady snorts. "I knew I shouldn't have trusted you," she says. "Get out before I sets the boys on you." Lose the codeword *Aspirin*.

Leave in a hurry...   774

93

Languishing in prison is no place for a person to build up their strength and you are unfortunate enough to catch a touch of typhoid from the other inmates. Somehow you manage to survive, but at a dreadful cost. You must lower your MOTORING and NIMBLENESS scores by 2 points each due to your physical weakness.

Turn to...   227

94

The river and the riverbanks bustle with fashionable life. For those rich enough to afford a leisurable day on the water, Boulter's Lock is the place to be seen. A tall hotel has been built here and on the veranda and balconies stand couples peering at the quaint boatmen and their families toiling with the heavy machinery. Skiffs nip backwards and forwards like insects on the water surface, carrying tokens of affection, challenges, bets and bottles of champagne. A city hatter has set up a fashionable shop here at the waterside and next to that stands Wilby's Guns, known up and down the land for their fine pieces. There is also a photography studio doing excellent business.

Park by the hotel...	**3**
Enter Wilby's guns...	**116**
Visit the hatter...	**656**
Board your boat (if it is moored here)	**844**
Leave and ride north...	**67**
Leave and head south...	**239**

95

When Ma Curtis discovers that you mean to treat your own wounds, she insists on coming over to bathe and clean them herself. "You ain't got no more idea how to do that than my stupid boys have," she says firmly. "Now get those clothes off and let me have a proper look. I got knitbone for your fractures and borage for the heart and poppy for the pain."

Under Ma Curtis's care your **wounds** heal quickly. For each **wound** you have, roll two dice. A roll of 12 indicates it has become an **intimidating scar (RUTH+1)** which should be noted on your adventure sheet, and any other roll means that it will become a normal **scar**. In either case remove the **wound** from your adventure sheet. If you have the codeword *Arthropod*, *Astrakhan* or *Apogee*, turn to **704** immediately. If you now have more than 10 scars, turn to **990**. Otherwise you enjoy a restful sleep and should turn to **743**.

96

A track through a field of wheat is your best chance of getting away, but the shots from the guildsmen's carbines are getting closer. Poppies in the wheat flash red as blood as you charge past. Make a MOTORING roll of difficulty 12 to get away!

Successful MOTORING roll!	**279**
Failed MOTORING roll!	**629**

97

The Wagtail is built for maneuverability and speed, not outright track warfare, so you hold back your steam until approaching a wide bend near the top of the track. As Da Silva and then Anderson head into the bend their vehicles begin to veer outwards under the force of their own weight, and both are forced to brake, kicking up clouds of dust, and re-align. You however enter at a moderate speed and then release more steam and a little more oil into the pistons, accelerating through the bend and leaving them both behind. Gain a Race Point!

Focus on the steamers ahead!	**103**

98

The vicar is unimpressed. He doesn't seem to want to get into a conversation about your personal deeds, ill or otherwise. "We must each find our path to God," he says, "And make peace with ourselves one way or another. It is not up to me to judge you or tell you how to live, oh no. Bad dreams are usually the result of an over-large dinner, I find. But perhaps you would like to make a penitential offering to the church in recognition of your... mistakes?"

Make a gift...	**(1s or more)**	**135**
Leave the church...		**4**

99

☐ ☐ ☐

If the boxes above are empty, tick the first and turn to **290**. If one is ticked, tick the second and turn to **414**. If two are ticked, tick the third and turn to **361**. If all three are ticked, turn to **257**.

100

A stream-lined green steamer slows as you approach. It has a fearsome looking turret mounted atop the boiler, armed with a mechanical repeat-loading gun: this is one of the Telegraph Guild's Enforcer engines, licensed to protect their wagons and convoys. Normally only found in the wild lands of the west or abroad where the guild are still claiming territory for their telegraph stations, the machinery is quite out of scale for the leafy roads of Buckinghamshire.

If you are **Wanted by the Telegraph Guild**, turn to **36**.

Ride past...	**247**

101

"Yes?" asks the small, bespectacled man in front of you. "Have we reached our destination?"

"Consider this something like a toll," you advise him, "Not a robbery. Perhaps you can get it on university expenses."

He gloomily hands you his wallet, containing **£4**, a **pocket watch** and a **pink scarf**.

Head to a nearby inn...   **394**

102

Your struggle in the water is painful but brief. Your wounded body will be fished out at the next lock downstream and your adventure is over. Never again will you ride the midnight roads in search of gold and glory. Perhaps the reputation you leave behind you will live on as a legend? Turn to the **Epilogue** to find out.

103

The race is well underway now. Several steamers have retired or crashed out and you tear around the track, only just within the top six. The Wagtail is capable of more in terms of straight-line speed, but the condition of the track and the other, equally determined and increasingly desperate drivers are slowing you down.

Ahead of you, the long red and yellow shape of Edward Hall's Zephyr pulls in to the service lane to top up his water and to refuel with a fresh tank of coal-gas. You see the flags calling you in to stop, but for every minute you burn ground coal and boil water the Wagtail lightens.

Another lap round, however, and you too are forced to stop. Harris, overseeing the refueling, leans in to the cockpit. "Pressure Jackson and you'll pass him. His engine is more than he can handle. Watch out for Akroyd - he's already sent two other drivers in for repairs. Try to pass him at full speed on the straight."

As soon as the Wagtail's tank is refilled you are back on the track. Initially the machine is a little slower to respond - the weight and the temperature change affect all parts of the engine - but you push up back towards the leaders. You can see them bunched behind Lord Akroyd's True Patriot, which he is driving defensively on the bends to prevents overtaking, then accelerating to an unmatchable speed on the straights.

Head straight into the mix and out-steam Akroyd... **458**
Pick off the vehicles one by one on the bends... **723**
Drive offensively, forcing the other drivers to slow... **520**
Wait for another driver to make a mistake... **856**

104

Cross off your **explosives**. Your inexperience with demolition takes a dreadful toll. A premature explosion as you are laying a charge spoils your attempt, casting gravel and earth up into the sky. You are tossed aside, dazed and bloody, but must get up and get away if you are to escape the Railway Guards. already running towards you. Gain 2 **Wounds** and you are now **Wanted by the Railway Guards**.

If you have 3 or more **Wounds**...   90
If you survive...   299

105

You open the firebox to stop the pressure rising too quickly, grab hold of the steering lever and regulator and allow the mounted brigands to ride alongside. Then a sharp tug to the left and you slam massive road-wheels into one rider with a crunch and send two others into the ditch. Their leader checks her horse, puts on a burst of speed and jumps onto the footplate beside you. You must fight her off!

Brigand Leader   Weapon: **sabre (PAR 6)**

Parry: 10
Nimbleness: 4
Toughness: 3

Victory!   **173**
Defeated!   **74**

106

The dusty lane falls quiet as you ride into Horton Wood. No birdsong, no steam engines other than the finely-tuned whirr of your own brass and iron wonder. Roll a dice to see what you encounter:

Score 1-2   A historical ecologist...   **44**
Score 3-4   Ride further into the wood...   **190**
Score 5-6   A mound of leaves...   **562**

107

The road south of Cookham is full of traffic. A steam wagon carrying sacks of grain is jammed at a bend in the road trying to pass a traction engine towing an oversize burden of hay. Roll two dice:

Score 2-4   An accident!   **154**
Score 5-8   You squeeze past...   **280**
Score 9-12   Wild cattle...   **76**

108

The velosteam throbs with concentrated power. Turning off the front lamp and trusting to your road sense, you accelerate around the bend and straight towards the roadblock. The Constables, unsure of who exactly is approaching, first call out warnings, then begin to fire their carbines. There is one way through: a single trestle blocks the space between two steam wagons. If you can hit it at sufficient speed to smash the wood with your heavy front wheel, then weave through, you can deliver the Doctor to his destination. Make a MOTORING roll of difficulty 12, adding 2 if you have a **reinforced boiler**.

Successful MOTORING roll!	66
Failed MOTORING roll!	767

109

Marlow Lock is always busy. Steam barges queue both sides of the gates and the powerhouse chimney smokes all day and all night. There are wharves here belonging to the papermill, the sawmill and the brewery. If you have a boat docked here you will be able to purchase or offload cargo, as well as going aboard and making your way along the Thames.

Inquire about passage along the river...	571
Go aboard your boat, if it is docked here...	120
Return to the High Street...	4

110

The driver falls back, a hole through his head. Lose a **Solidarity Point**. The steam carriage careers onwards and crashes into the ditch.

Turn to...	149

111

"Make an investment, kind traveller," cries a woman at the roadside. "I have just returned from the Indies, where there are riches to be gained for small capital investments. Buy a share in one of the many fine hotels now being built to house travellers - and receive your own stay there too... Or become a salesperson for this new herbal product, proven by Dr Smithson P. Smithson to alleviate symptoms of machine work. Or perhaps you would care to donate to the Cause for the Workers' Emancipation and become one of only eighty silver-grade sponsors? Rewards are limited and exclusive, kind traveller..."

Her voice trails away. It seems she has an endless stream of reasons for you to give her money.

Leave her at the roadside...	310

112

With all your hard work, the Wagtail soon tops a hundred miles an hour in trials and Lord Dashwood is confident about his entry in the Spenser Cup. "I owe it all to you," he says. "My home is your home. Come and stay whenever you wish." You are now the **Friend of Lord Dashwood**.

Continue...	172

113

The wide road is quiet beneath the shadows of the trees. Ahead, it begins to climb steadily up the slope towards Pinkney's Green and another road leading off to the north-west. There is an encampment of caravans here, circled around a large fireplace. Deep in Maidenhead thicket many a steam carriage has met its demise. Consequently most who travel this way pay for guards to accompany them.

Prepare an ambush here...	140
Enter the encampment...	911
Ride up to Pinkney's Green...	535
Take the smaller road north-west...	370
Head south-west along the Bath Road...	707
Take the path by the stream... (*Abstruse*)	24

114

You find Comrade Robin with the help of Comrade Feaver's description and hand over the **heavy parcel**. He looks at you queryingly. "Did you open it?"

"No," you reply.

He shakes his head. "Very strange attitude." He gives you **passdisc 21**.

Return to the Freight Yard...	888

115

A steam carriage comes chugging up the hill, towing a trailer load of luggage behind it. The driver is plainly conserving water. This is your moment: how will you try to rob the passengers?

Ride alongside...	284
Shoot at the driver...	191
Show yourself...	276

116

The gunsmith is a woman called Miss Wilby. The steely eye she fixes you with convinces you that there will be no opportunities for funny business here. That and the loaded pistol slung around her neck.

Weapons	To buy	To sell
blunderpistol (ACC 6)	**£4**	**£1 10s**
dueling pistols (ACC 7)	**£10**	**£7**
gamekeeper's shotgun (ACC 7)	**£10**	**£6**
Leboutier hunting rifle (ACC 10)	**£35**	**£20**

The gunsmith can upgrade your guns, improving each one by up to 3 ACCURACY points each. However, each gun can only be improved once (and should be marked as an **improved** weapon on your adventure sheet).

Upgrade gun by +1 ACC	**£7**
Upgrade gun by +2 ACC	**£15**
Upgrade gun by +3 ACC	**£42**

Return to Boulter's Lock...   **94**

117

The officer takes your money without a word, stamps a piece of paper, hands the woman at the door a docket and walks on to another house. All down the street his men are doing the same: what you have done could never be more than a gesture. Nonetheless, it is appreciated by the woman in front of you, who thanks you tearfully, then takes her children back inside. Gain **a Solidarity Point**.

Leave the slums behind...   **650**

118

Heath Wood extends some way to the west and several holloways and tracks lead through it. There are the signs of deer here too.

Lay a **snare** here...	**(snare)**	**49**
Try stalking a deer...		**633**
Head further into the wood...		
	Highways and Holloways 130	
Leave the wood...		**289**

119

A man lies on the verge cooking something over a fire, turning the spit with his toe. He bursts into song as you slow to watch.

"A traveller on a steed of brass

Took a moment to sit on the grass.
For the road is hard and the road is long
And there's always time for a bite and a song."

He is a minstrel. You may join him at the roadside if you have anything to contribute: a **rabbit**, **pheasant**, or **deer carcass**, a **bottle of wine** or **beer** or any other food or drink will do.

Eat with the minstrel...	**475**
Nothing to share...	**288**

120

If your boat is moored at **Marlow (Upstream)**, turn to **498**. If it is moored at **Marlow (Downstream)**, turn to **776**.

121

You manage to convince the jury that you have been framed for these awful crimes. They are unwilling to find you guilty and in the end the exasperated judge is forced to release you onto the streets of Maidenhead. You are no longer **Wanted by the Constables** and may go completely free. But beware - you may not be so lucky next time!

Turn to...   **594**

122

You pass several grand houses and a long, picturesque green. Roll two dice.

Score 2-5	An airship enthusiast...	**316**
Score 6-8	An empty road...	**575**
Score 9-12	Fair on the Common...	**70**

123

Erase the codeword *About*. When you enter the doctor's office he is slumped face-down on his desk. He groggily raises himself up as you enter.

"Ah, it's the wanderer," he says. "The resolute, ruthless, reckless roadster. Excuse me. I was working all night."

"How's that hippocratic oath treating you, doctor? And how is the farmer's baby?"

He gets up. "The baby's fine. The mother's struggling, frankly. Depression. But that's half of medicine. The mind. I didn't thank you at the time and I don't easily find words for such things but I appreciated your help that night. Now what do you want?"

The doctor is ready to treat your **Wounds**, and this time his manner is a little gentler. For each **Wound** the doctor will charge you **15s**. However, his treatment does not result in your **Wounds** becoming **Scars** - you can simply erase them from your sheet. As a result of his gratitude for your late-night velosteam rescue, you are now the **Friend of Dr Smollett** if you were not already.

Leave the Doctor's Surgery...   **684**

124

The Bounty stands on a low green on the Cookham bank of the river, between a row of small warehouses and several small riverside villas built by London clerks. It is well known as a place to relax, drawing custom from up and down the river. Several boats are moored up against the jetty and an outdoor bar serves thirsty bargees.

Moor here...   **570**
Cross the River to Bourne End...   **713**
Sail towards Marlow...   **525**

125

Every individual is truly alone in this world - that is clear. Your past mistakes may have cost you your inheritance and your place in society, but they cannot decide your future. Perhaps the gambling addiction that ate up your family fortune and lands is not yet sated. Well, now you will gamble with your own life. As the disgraced and penniless heir to a noble line, it was less shameful to flee than to return to your father's house empty-handed. There is little for you but the desperate way of a highwayman.

The roads and turnpikes of the region offer you hiding places and the steam carriages of merchants offer you riches for the taking, if you are bold enough. Once you have collected enough capital, you may be able to buy your way back into the nobility. The real test is whether you will be welcome at the Cliveden Society Ball. Wealth, regardless of its source, opens many doors nowadays.

You have in your possession a **blunderpistol (ACC 6)**, a **sabre (PAR 6)** and a **deck of marked cards**. Your ability scores are:

RUTHLESSNESS	4
ENGINEERING	3
MOTORING	3
INGENUITY	4
NIMBLENESS	4
GALLANTRY	6

Turn to...   **324**

126

You leap onto the driving platform and draw your weapon. The driver jams the steering column and grabs a **heavy wrench** with which to attack you. The hot firebox door, the steering mechanisms and the coal scuttle all make the footplate a dangerous place to fight.

Driver	Weapon: **heavy wrench (PAR 3)**
Parry:	7
Nimbleness:	4
Toughness:	3

Victory!   **149**
Defeat!   **90**

127

When night falls and the manor is quiet, you creep out of hiding and make your way to the outhouses surrounding the west wing of the house. Your afternoon's observations of movements through the windows have made you confident that you can find Lady Dean's suite. Waterbutts, gutters, brackets and architraves all offer themselves to your unorthodox entry, but if you have any climbing equipment with you you can make your own way through the shadows. You must make a NIMBLENESS roll of difficulty 12, adding 3 to your score if you have a **rope ladder**, 2 for a **grappling iron** and 1 for a **rope**.

Successful NIMBLESSNESS roll!   **967**
Failed NIMBLENESS roll!   **900**

128

After studying the map for some time, you find several locations ideal for ambushing the carriages of the gentry: wherever the main routes pass through thick woods or up steep hills, drivers and wagoneers will be particularly vulnerable to gunfire or threats. At Cutthroat Wood, the road between Oxford and London has to climb out of Loudwater. Nearby woods offer you hiding places and getaway routes. Between Marlow and Maidenhead, the steep road at Inkydown Wood also looks promising, while the stretch of the Bath Road running through Maidenhead Thicket is sure to offer opportunities to an enterprising road-pirate like yourself.

Return to the parlour...   **180**
Leave the Crooked Billet...   **291**

129

The driver calls your bluff: he accelerates towards you, ducking down beneath his windshield. Before you have a chance to aim and fire, the carriage is upon you and you are forced to leap aside to avoid being run down. A tumble in the mud is undignified, but you are unhurt, and when you get back up the carriage is steaming away.

Let the carriage go...	**528**
Pursue them...	**284**

131

You turn off the main road beside a short terrace of houses. Beyond them, the road becomes rutted and uneven - still a pleasure to ride on your shock-absorbent forks and your wide tyres. Little regular road traffic comes this way - most probably just logging vehicles and cattle going to pasture. Roll a dice:

Score 1-4	The middle of the wood...	**190**
Score 5-6	A mysterious picnic...	**455**

132

You are recognised by a guard posted by the roadside and before you know it a pair of Constabulary velosteams swing onto the road in pursuit. Each one carries a driver and an armed constable and they are trained to catch outlaws and road-robbers like yourself. It will be a hard ride to escape them - better if you have a getaway planned.

Try to lose the pursuit at Cookham Weir...
            (*Amphibious*)   **853**
Head for your hideout in Windsor Wood...
            (*Ashen*)   **942**
Turn tail and race away...   **922**

133

You open the regulator and hunch low over the velosteam. The machine picks up your speed and, spying a likely looking spot, you swerve off the tracks and onto a plank pathway used by the navvies. At first all goes well, but you cannot maintain your speed on the steep climb and lose control! You and your velosteam tumble back down into the cutting. Your Velosteam now has **Critical Damage** and it is the Railway Guards who pull you from underneath the twisted metal.

They place you under arrest in one of their prison trucks. Lose all your **money** and **possessions.** You are given no food or water for three days and have to slake your thirst by sucking moisture off the cold bars at night. Exhausted and beaten, you barely notice where the truck is moved, until eventually the door is opened and you are hauled out.

Await your fate...   **255**

134

"You haven't understood what you are doing at all." What is that tone in his voice? Disappointment? Frustration? "If you considered murder wrong enough to repent of it, why would you choose to associate yourself with it a second time?" He gets up and leaves the pew.

Leave the church...   **703**

135

The vicar takes your money. "I will pray for you," he says, but makes no sign of being ready to pray now. "I do not care to know what you have done that makes you so sure that you are guilty, but rest assured that not one of us is perfect. Go in peace, my child."

Leave the church...   **4**

136

The rain drifts across the high fields towards you, then passes on westwards, doing little more than dampening the rutted road. A rainbow appears briefly, grounded in the meadows near Widbrook Common. Perhaps the old story of the leprechaun's gold is worth investigating? Gain the codeword *Aurum*.

Ride on...   **650**

137

Wheeler End is really little more than a common dotted around with several mid-to-large houses. It has become a fashionable place for the wealthy of Wycombe to keep a house, ever since the Hughden brewing family settled here. Their mansion is fronted with an elegant cast iron fence decorated with stylised hop vines.

Take the lane north...	**546**
Ride north-east down Bullocks Farm Lane...	**597**
Head west to Bolter End...	
Highways and Holloways	546
Ride south to Lane End...	**684**

138

You carefully hide your velosteam behind a thicket of brambles and overgrown hazel coppice. Once you have found a place to wait, you will be able to pick off the passing traffic. Roll two dice to see how you fare:

Score 2-4   A constables' patrol...   **890**
Score 5-6   An empty road tonight...   **851**
Score 7-12   A private steam carriage...   **905**

139

There is a short row of six brick cottages here. Toys in the yard around one indicate a young family. Gardens are neat and tidy, the lane swept clear of fallen leaves. As you steam by a young woman washing clothes wistfully watches you pass.

Take the lane to High Wood...   **2**
Head towards Burchett's Green...   **727**
Ride south to the Bath Road...   **551**

140

Choosing your spot to waylay travellers is a matter of reading the road, using your observations of steam-drivers and your preference for the style of your attack. You soon have yourself ready where you can see down the road, but where you are hidden by the thick undergrowth and shadow. Woodland birds give the thicket a most misleading air of sylvan innocence. Roll two dice to see what you encounter, adding 1 to your roll for each **Wanted** status you possess:

Score 2-3   A freight wagon...   **221**
Score 4-7   A private steam carriage...   **663**
Score 8-9   The road is empty tonight...   **77**
Score 10+   The constables...   **694**

141

"Welcome, stranger," says the landlord cautiously as you enter. He looks you up and down, then returns to the dining room and chats with his higher-class customers.

Hung on the walls are the destination boards of retired stagecoaches and public steamers, advertising all the places served by the lines. Horse brasses and leathers indicate that while the era of the horse may be passing, this landlord would prefer it to continue.

Buy a drink...   (**2s**)   **744**
Leave the pub...   **429**

142

The heavy velosteam dislikes its road disappearing beneath it and before long you find yourself in the hedge. Gain 1 **Wound** and 1 point of **Damage** for your Velosteam.

If your Velosteam is **Beyond Repair**...   **250**
If you have five **Wounds**...   **90**
Otherwise...   **650**

143

Your final words move nobody. The noose tightens with a jerk and your ears ring as they fill with blood. Suffocation is slow and painful.

Your execution is the end of your adventure. Turn to the **Epilogue** to calculate your final score and see if your reputation will last beyond the grave.

144

The cows do not want to run any further than they have to and you manage to settle them down. They stand about, huffing, and then begin to browse the hedgrows, stripping hawthorn branches and eating the lush, ditch-watered grass. Two drovers come running up.

"Bleedin' cows!" says one.

"What are you? Some kind of magician?" asks the other. "We almost lost them there. 'Ere, take this as a thankyou." You are given **3s** and a small basket of **bird's eggs**..

Leave the drovers to their business...   **280**

145

The drinks help dissolve the company's distrust for an outsider like yourself and eventually you are able to have some coherent conversation with the few still capable.

"Allus a good price for timber at Henley," says one Bargee. "But if you want the best price, stop at Winston's Wharf. Make you a pretty penny."

"That steam fair won't last long," says another, "Atop that hill at Pinkney's Green. Brothers allus fighting, they are. Fell out over daddy's will. I heard he had a whole host of children up in Wycombe."

Several are discussing a raid made by the Constables on a house in Little Marlow. "They came down in the night in one of them fast airships, grappled the missus right out of the bedroom window."

"What did they want with her?"

"Some sort of radical - worked with the printshop, the said. But I reckon she was just too pretty for that Colonel Snappet and his cronies to leave alone."

"Wethered Brewery's in a bad way," says another. "Beer's not what it used to be."

"Hush, Clem! You only drinks Old Eel anyway."

"Fancy picture-show up in Maidenhead. All flickering lights and suchlike - moving pictures, they say. Our Wilhemina went and saw it. The engineer was a black man."

Return to the parlour...   **795**

146

A quick glance behind shows you that your pursuers are gaining. Shots ring out - but if you can stay ahead for another half-mile, you will escape. You velosteam is throbbing and shuddering, the boiler pressure maxed, the regulator wide open and every gas jet flaring. A dash through an open gate takes you off road and cross-country. A rise in the ground gives you once chance - to leap a thick hedge and race away to your woodland hide-out. Make a MOTORING roll of difficulty 15 to jump the hedge: you can add 2 if you have a **reinforced boiler** and 1 more if you have a **gas pressuriser**.

Successful MOTORING roll!   **220**
Failed MOTORING roll!   **207**

147

You are surprised to hear the sound of plainchant over your engine. You pull to one side of the lane, and around the bend comes a procession of monks in brown habits, carrying a large cross, a curtained box of some sort and several banners. They are singing solemn songs of worship as they walk the dusty road.

One of the monks steps aside from the procession. "Abbot Sneer has work for one such as you. Come to the Abbey and he will reward you with an opening to the world of the nobility."

Ride on...   **37**

148

You step back apologetically. "I've no wish to take from you, sir."

He gives a strange grin. "Good. I have business and I must be on my way." The driver looks down at you in confusion. He is mouthing something but it is hard to understand. Gain the codeword *Anhedonic*.

The steamer accelerates away. Who was the blind official? What purpose does he serve the Coal Board?

Ride on towards Wheeler End...   **137**

149

The passengers of the steam carriage step down from their comfortable compartment. It is unavoidable that they will be able to give a good description of you later, so if you are not already, you will now be **Wanted by the Constables**. Roll a dice to see who you meet.

Score 1	A dowager...	**403**
Score 2	An airship captain and hostess...	**205**
Score 3	An engineer...	**315**
Score 4	A professor...	**101**
Score 5	A French traveller...	**224**
Score 6	A famous entertainer...	**158**

150

You show the judge the cufflink you have found and tell the story of your search. He collapses into a seat. "It must be so, then. He is dead. As I had always feared... I gave him those myself. I..." The judge turns pale and falls from his seat.

After his shock, it takes some days for the judge to recover himself, but he remains weakened. Nonetheless, you stay to care for him and continue to entertain him with stories of your adventures. Even when he is out of bed, you return to make sure he is well.

"What have I done to deserve this friendship?" asks the judge. "I have lost one child, but found another. Let me tell you something. I have no heir and no family. So I have decided to make you my inheritor. Perhaps with what is left of my estates you can do some good. But let us hope it is not for many years yet." Gain the codeword *Adoption*. "Treat this house as your own," says the judge. "Return soon."

Leave the house...   **408**

151

A trader standing by a handcart is calling out their wares. "I lost everything in an unwise investment. I'm just trying to get back on my feet, gather a little capital."

Tools	To buy	To sell
waterproof paint	6s	-
wirecutters	12s	9s
titanium alloy	£3	-

Other items	To buy	To sell
clockwork bird	-	£2
revolutionary poster	1s	-

Continue on your way...   **282**

152

A pair of woodcutters are felling an oak tree beside the road. "It's wanted for a cottage in the village," says the elder. "We'll split the trunk lengthways like, take off the smaller side of the fork, got a nice cruck ready to take a roof on it. Good shape in this tree. Need another one of similar size really. Squire Haworth's business - he does right by his tenants, aye, and his labourers."

After helping the woodcutters finish their day's work, you are invited to spend an evening around their campfire with them. One brings out a mecharmonium and plays a fast folk tune, while the older teaches you the steps of a traditional dance. Your feet are still tapping in the morning: if your NIMBLENESS score is 6 or lower, you may increase it by 1.

Ride on...   **646**

153

You brake hard and turn the bike on the spot, accelerating again straight towards the chain. If your new tyres are are good as the salesman promised, you might have a chance of passing unharmed.

Constables dive aside as you approach, but the men at either side tighten the chain. Mercifully your heavy tyres carry you over without a hitch and you quickly head away out of Maidenhead.

Turn to...   **282**

154

A freight wagon has collided with a farm vehicle and spilt its load across the way. Villagers, labourers and freighters are standing around arguing about the best way to clear the.

Steal something from the strewn cargo...	**799**
Help clear the road...	**495**
Ride past on the verge...	**280**

155

The Wagtail tears across the line, spouting flames from the firebox and a narrow stream of steam from the stack. The audience cheer raucously, wild with excitement and wonder.

Dashwood and Harris run over as you coax the machine to a stop. They fall upon you in glee and carry you up to the podium, where you receive the Spenser Cup itself. Dashwood has tears in his eyes. "You did it! Well done, well done indeed. My machine - but driven so finely. Such judgment. All my success, I owe to you."

You have learnt much in these weeks - not just about the road, but also about how a man can pursue his dreams. Dashwood has been a patron like none other - generous, supportive and committed. He has taken your advice, allowed you to shine and footed the bill at every stage. He has become much more than a friend. Increase your MOTORING score by 2 and you may add **Won the Spenser Cup** to your heroic deeds.

If you have the codeword *Able*, turn to 715. If you have the codeword *Anastasia*, turn to 490. Otherwise, read on.

Lady Quarlington's daughter approaches and looks appreciatively at where her scarf, now wind-torn and covered in smuts, flutters over the Wagtail. "A wonderful job," she says. "I am so proud of you all." She rewards you personally with a **diamond brooch** and gives Lord Dashwood a rather more-than-congratulatory kiss.

When eventually the celebrations finish, days later, Dashwood, Harris and Emily Quarlington are all set to return to West Wycombe, taking the cup and the steamer with them. As for you, you must seek new adventures. Lose the codeword *Ambition*, for after all, you have tasted victory on the racetrack now. How else will you choose to be remembered?

Mount your velosteam and ride away...   **137**

156

A steam-bus full of cheery girls in grey pinafore and straw hats comes bowling along the road towards you. It is being driven erratically and slews to a halt

"Ooh," shrieks a girl. "A real highwayman? Come on, girls, let's get a picture." Before you can get away and despite the teacher's protests, the whole class tumble off the bus and surround you. One extends a flimsy-looking portable cameragraph on a pole and the girls all crowd in to be included in the photograph. Which of your attributes has the higher score: RUTHLESSNESS or INGENUITY?

RUTHLESSNESS is higher...	**43**
INGENUITY is higher...	**233**

157

The freight wagon is approaching slowly and the crew expect nothing. You are able to aim directly for the driver: an ACCURACY roll of 11 will hit him and hopefully bring the steamer to a halt.

Successful ACCURACY roll!	**204**
Failed ACCURACY roll!	**287**

158

You recognise the figure before you as the one and only Marvellous Jaffery, the famous entertainer. A moment later, his inseperable companion, Bowzer, leaps down from the carriage and sniffs at you suspiciously. If you have a deck of marked cards, turn to **331**. Otherwise you can force him to turn out his pockets and relieve him of **£5 11s**, a bottle of **soothing lotion** and a **gold ring**.

Ride away...   737

159

"I see you have a powerful friend," says the fortune-teller. "A man of principles, but a man with a flaw. Beware of his rages and keep him from high stakes. Then he will be the friend you hope him to be. One thing I tell you - Davy's fortune is intertwined with yours and you will find more than you bargain for at the sign of the Fighting Cock."

As fortunes go, it is vague enough to apply to almost anyone and any situation. Have you been given your money's worth?

Return to the fair...   326

160

☐

If the box is empty, put a tick in it and turn to **527** immediately. If the box is ticked and you have the codeword *About*, turn to **123**. Otherwise, turn to **358**.

161

You park your velosteam and climb the rough embankment to see the view. At the top you discover that you are not alone, but that a painter in a top hat is standing here throwing paint onto a canvas in a very daring, modern way. He ignores you to begin with, muttering under his breath as he smudges and corrects his work. It seems to be a picture of a railway locomotive travelling over the bridge in front of you, either in the middle of a rainstorm or in a dream.

"Rain, steam, speed," says the painter.

"I'm sorry?" you reply.

"Rain, steam and speed. Fantastic. Watch out, here comes another one."

You step aside as a train thunders past. The painter could have reached out and touched it, but he stands at his easel nonchalantly.

Leave the embankment...   218

162

It is a fair few miles up to Piddington and your veteran hitch-hiker takes the opportunity to tell you about himself. "Going home to my daughter," he says. "Don't know what she'll make of her one-legged dad, no sir! But that's what heavy artillery will do for you. One moment, happy on two pegs, next moment, your foot's the other side of the Iberian peninsula. Took part in four campaigns in the Pyrenees and never a scratch, then one week in the trenches of Valencia and I'm two stone less of a man."

"Does it hurt?"

"'Course it hurts! Got to look on the bright side, though. Could be dead!"

You drop him off by a row of squat brick houses and ride away. Gain a **Solidarity Point** for this simple, compassionate gesture. Your reputation will certainly be improved amongst the common people.

To Piddington...   546

163

Seizing up a chair, you toss it through the window, smashing it noisily. A moment later and you have leaped through! A stumble on the cobbles and you are up again, looking around, but you see that the Constables have placed guards around your velosteam. Their guns are already drawn.

You dive off down the alleyway beside the inn, racing to get away, but turn the corner to see another constable awaiting you, carbine leveled. There is no escape. You are arrested, hooded, and hauled away.

Turn to...   255

164

Remove the **strongbox** from your possessions. It contained a set of **punchcards (Livingstone M)** and **£38.**

Return to your noted passage...

165

The road here is a dream for a velosteamer like yourself. You fairly fly down the slope on a series of gentle curves, heading down to the crossroads south of Bisham. Kites wheel high above you and your engine thrums with finely-tuned rhythm. It is good to be alive and free and on the road!

Turn to...   662

166

There is a large Royal family tree on the wall. It clearly shows the line of descent from the Hanoverian George I to His Imperial Majesty, King James IV. It is interesting to see that if George IV's marriage to Maria had never been declared legally valid, then his heirs James III and the current King could well have been replaced by his niece, Princess Alexandrina. Whom she would have married and whether they would have managed to rule the British Empire with any success, no-one can tell.

Whereas James III took the title 'His Britannic Majesty', Parliament sycophantically voted to give his son the title 'Imperial Majesty', even though the greatest expansion in the Empire was in the previous decades. Now the Royal family are equally loathed and worshipped amongst the lower classes: they are a race apart, of foreign blood, surrounded by the wealthy and powerful and making laws to suit themselves. Yet they have pomp and glory and the current King visits his Empire in an Imperial airship, drawing crowds of thousands and tribute by the million. It is a golden age - with a filthy underside.

The British Empire itself has swollen despite the loss of the American Colonies. Their catastrophic Civil War ended with a victory for the Confederate States, as everybody predicted it would, and a massive expansion programme into the Caribbean has swallowed up nations once ruled by Spain and other imperial powers. Air travel has made much of it possible, together with the technology of telegraphic communication, allowing larger and larger empires to be managed from a single capital.

Last year the King proclaimed that settlers from the northern counties of England and Scotland would be forcibly resettled in far-flung parts of the Empire like Canada and New Zealand. Ever since, the Geat Northern Revolt has been rumbling on, for although the army has not yet been dispatched, many fear there will be bloodshed. What sort of a ruler would make such a decree over his own people - while all know that the West Country is under the sway of warlords as well? Even if the Empire grows, England is splintering.

Return to the library...   **736**

167

"How much is in that chest?" you ask her.

"I don't rightly know." She starts to see the way you are leading her down. "But probably a great deal more than I could make in a year..."

"Exactly," you reply. "So what sort of livelihood do you need, with money like that in your pocket? Take your engine and head west, or to Wales, where the Haulage Guild are just a ridiculous pomposity. Take your family and the chest. Give me a small share - a fifth, say, for knocking you gently on the head and taking the blame. You go and tell the Guild that you were robbed at the roadside, give them my description. We could even arrange a witness. I leave you eighty percent of the money, which you collect after reporting to the Guild. More than enough to start a new life."

She sits silently, considering your offer, then extends her hand. "Let's do it," she says. "But you'll be hunted from here to Land's End."

Turn to...   **541**

168

The hauliers are towing a mixed cargo of pottery and barrel-staves to the Haulage Guild depot at Two Bridges. They nod warily as they steam past, careful of their Guild's requirements to keep to time. If you have a **Guildsman's medallion**, turn to **834**.

Let them steam on by...   **535**

169

Leaving town, the gas-lamps are lit in the streets, reflecting off the damp tarmacadam. You have to weave your way between traffic heading out towards Maidenhead, Wycombe and Henley. The bell of All Saints Church gives a dull ring in the rising fog.

Head to Marlow Bridge...	**277**
Take the Henley Road west...	**786**
Travel towards Bovingdon Green...	**304**
Drive north towards Lane End...	**247**
Ride out eastwards...	**622**

170

A runaway bull comes charging down the lane towards you, closely followed by a shouting farmer, the farmer's wife, a cowherd and several children from the nearest village. The bull easily shoves your velosteam aside, causing one **Point of Damage**, and carries on up the lane, followed by the procession of frantic rurals.

If your velosteam is **Beyond Repair**...	**250**
Otherwise...	**521**

171

You leave your mate with the boat at the abbey's jetty and walk through the yard to the guest entrance. Note that you are moored at **Bisham Abbey**.

Turn to...   **34**

172

Lord Dashwood's butler welcomes you to the house. "Stay as long as you like," he says, showing you to your room. "Dinner will be served at nine and I have taken the liberty of providing some evening wear. Milord will see you at the table."

Will you ever have such luxury at your disposal again? Truly, the surroundings are extravagant. How does it feel to have servants at your command for a change?

You may leave possessions here.

Bandage your **Wounds**...   **619**
Visit the garage...
   (If you have the codeword *Ambition*)   **298**
Leave...   **492**

173

You run the brigand through and kick her convulsing body from the footplate. Then with another shovel of coal in the firebox and the regulator open, the engine forges ahead, leaving the ambush behind.

Fortunately the crossbow-bolt struck the haulier high in the arm, so although he has lost a lot of blood he will not die. When you arrive in High Wycombe the next morning he claps you on the back with his working arm. "Here's your payment," he says, handing you **£4**, "and by gum you've earnt it. Together with my gratitude, I can tell you. Any time you need something of me, just ask it. I live down in Burchett's Green and you're always welcome there with us." You are now the **Friend of Wellesley Garman**.

Bid Garman farewell...   **337**

174

The road is muddy and wet here and you are amazed to see strange tracks in the slick mud: rigid, regular prints of some kind of walking engine. The gaps between its marks indicates its legs must be at least fifteen feet long. Nothing of the sort is anywhere in sight - a new type of transport? An experimental machine?

Ride on...   **310**

175

You recognise Barsali's wagon parked by the side of the road. However, he is sat on the step with none of his characteristic good humour. He looks up.

"Ah my friend. It is a sore day for us. My boy is taken, arrested, by the Constables."

"What did he do?"

"Why, nothing that a boy should not. Gave a marketeer some exercise down in Maidenhead. But they say they will transport him for thievery."

"Where is he being held?"

Barsali shakes his head. "They have him in their wandering gaol, over in Cookham. There is no appeal with them."

"I shall rescue him..."   **418**
"I am sure a clever young man like him will escape..."
                                                            582

176

As you wander through the fair you see past the professional smiles of the stall-holders and detect something of their frustration and annoyance. From the mutterings and the gossip you pick up, it seems that the entire fair has split into two factions, each side favouring one of the Curtiss brothers, Greg and Davy.

"Davy has spent 'is whole life on the fair," says the bald-headed proprietor of the swingboats. "'e knows the business and 'e knows the people. Gregory 'as all these fine ideas, but what it boils down to is wanting to modernise the fair and get rid of them what don't want to see things 'is way."

He is interrupted by a lady running the candy-floss

stall. "Well, that's because Gregory unnerstan's money, isn't it? We're losing money all the time and Davy's pig-headedness is the cause of it, I say. He won't ever modernise and he don't listen to those of us who want to."

You become aware of a chill. Davy Curtiss himself is standing behind you in shirtsleeves. "Stirring up trouble, eh? You workin' for my bleeding brother?"

"He is your brother, Davy," calls the swingboat man.

"Hist!" Davy turns on him in a moment. "Just you mind your business, William Thorne and you leave my family to me." He turns back to you, looks you up and down and smiles. "You look like a killer. Well maybe I have need of you. Come and see me in my wagon."

Davy walks off into the fair and the stall holders pointedly ignore one another - and you. After finding another group of fairspeople to talk to, you hear more of the story. "Well, he's the younger brother, right? His pop, Albert Curtiss, sends him off to London to get educated. That's why Davy's always had a chip on his shoulder abaht it. Now when the old man died, Gregory comes back, insists it's time to change, but Davy says that he'll run the fair just the way his dad did, whatever Gregory thinks. Gregory says now that his brother has cheated him out of his inheritance. Don't know how it'll end."

Continue to explore the fairground...   **326**

177
After a steep climb up the hill, you reach the foot of Odds Hill Plantation. Rows of identical conifers stand on the slope, planted where ancient woods used to stand between small, irregular pastures. At the crest of the hill looms the skeletal structure of an optical telegraph tower, its battens clacking and switching by day, shutters spinning and winking by night, all powered by a static steam engine whose smoke rises as ceaselessly as the messages fly. Only thick fog can loosen the Telegraph Guild's grip on information and stop their codes flying across the Thames valley. Only thick fog or the direst accident.

Approach the Telegraph Guild tower...   **770**
Ride down towards Wooburn...   **515**
Take the Road to Bourne End...   **599**

178
You flash your **Guildsman's medallion** and make your way straight to the Director's office. He dismisses the businessmen who were with him with a brusque wave of the hand. He obviously recognises you. "Well," he says. "Anything to report? How have you responded to my trust?"

If you have the codeword *Aorta*...   **401**
Otherwise...   **448**

179
The driver, fireman and cargoman all step down from the wagon, their hands in the air. "Don't hurt us, yer honour," says one. "All the stuff is insured anyway. The Guild will cover it."

"Aye," says another. "The Guild'll remember too." The description they will give their employers means that you are now **Wanted by the Haulage Guild**. Roll a dice to see what you gather from the wagon.

Score 1-2	**12s** and an **axe**
Score 3	**12s** and a roll of **telegraph wire**
Score 4	**£1** and a **lantern**
Score 5	**£3** and a tin of **waterproof paint**
Score 6	a set of **welding gear**

Ride away...   **351**

180
The Crooked Billet is a small country inn, hidden well away from the noise and smoke of the steam revolution. No heavy freight wagons pass this way, nor the private steam carriages of the gentry, and the local folk are suspicious of outsiders. It is an ideal hideout. To take a room here, you will need to pay **£2** and tick the box below.

☐ Rest in your room...   (Ticked box)   **53**
Study the map on the parlour wall...   **128**
Leave the inn...   **291**

181
The river turns south where it meets the chalk cliff of Cliveden. The water is deeper, faster and colder here in the shadow of the hill. The steep hill is covered in woods, and somewhere atop is Cliveden House itself, out of view. Here on the river a whole variety of traffic passes slowly by. Roll a dice to see what you encounter:

Score 1	An economic opportunity...	**969**
Score 2	Bobbing along...	**916**
Score 3	Three men in a boat, to say nothing of the dog...	**892**
Score 4-6	Plain sailing...	**637**

182

The fat Beadle looks you over as you make your donation. "Never fear," he says. "One hundred percent of your donation will go towards the running of the workhouse. These poor wretches will all benefit, directly or indirectly, from your generosity." He licks his lips.

As you look around you see many children, both boys and girls, born into a life of servitude and confinement. Their clothes are rough, ragged and plain. Their hair is lank, their skin pale and their eyes dim.

"Sponsors," says the Beadle loudly. "What they need are sponsors. I can find good apprenticeships for these young people, but they must have a sponsor. The apprentice-price varies for each trade, but it is generally in the region of five pound. And then the Workhouse must also be remunerated. But once that is paid, they are free to spread their wings and to earn their way through the world, rather than depending on the charity of their betters."

Offer to sponsor an apprenticeship...	(£5)	225
Leave the Workhouse...		602

183

As you continue to observe, your eye is repeatedly caught by the fantastic jewels that Maria Roberts is wearing. They must be worth a fortune - the equivalent of hundreds of ordinary people's yearly wages. You are not the only person there to be interested: "I heard they cost more than ten thousand pounds," says one impressed party-goer. "Imagine the expense! You could launch a steam battleship for that!"

Stealing the Dervish's Eye would be a deed of legend. But is it possible? Late in the evening, Mrs Roberts and a companion disappear into one of the Duchess's dressing rooms and reappear in a much simpler change of dress and jewels. The weight of the gems must have been exhausting... Of course, you make your way upstairs and seek out where the jewels are being kept. The armed guards outside one of the rooms are a very good indication.

You work out a route into the dressing room that will avoid the guards: all you need to do is to enter a vacant bedroom, leave by the window and edge along the ornamental ledge to the dressing room with the necklace. Inside is a single guard - wide awake, but nonetheless vulnerable. If you have a **bottle of chloroform**, turn to **63** immediately.

Surprise the guard...   **837**

184

There is no escaping the inevitable judgment: guilty. The sentence: to be hanged by the neck until dead.

Next morning you are led out to the Maidenhead public gallows. Amazingly, the Constables have brought your velosteam here to show the crowd how the Steam Highwayman's crimes were committed. Perhaps you have one last chance...

As the noose is lowered over your head, you ask for a moment to address the crowd before your life is forfeited. The officers agree and step back. If you have at least 6 **Solidarity Points**, you can make a GALLANTRY roll of difficulty 14. You can add 1 to your roll for every **Wanted** status and 3 if you are the **People's Champion**.

Successful GALLANTRY roll!	**262**
Failed roll or insufficient **Solidarity Points**...	**143**

185

The Cricketers has a welcoming, bustling air, with log fires always burning and good food on every table. It looks out onto the green and is decorated with the split bats, old leg pads, caps, crests, shields, gloves and shirts of the village's successful cricket team.

"What's your pleasure?" asks the man behind the bar.

Ruby Red...	(2s)	480
Wethered Fine IPA	(2s)	567
Cookham Orchard Cider...	(1s)	592
Leave the pub....		1014

186

The lane skirts Mount Hill with its massive Telegraph Guild compound. From this side you can see the supply wagon park, the subsidiary towers and the barrack blocks. But the road continues between a cherry orchard and a hay barn into the village of Cookham Dean.

Head to the Guild Compound...	1004
Ride into the village...	563

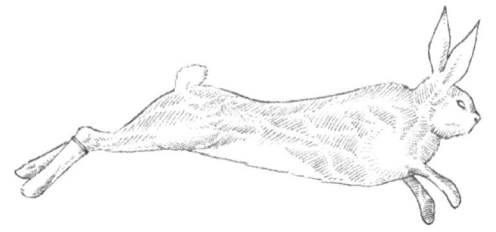

187

You are arrested as a wanted criminal and stripped of your **money**, **weapons** and **possessions**. Your mate is arrested too and taken off somewhere, while several constables board your steam-barge and take it away as 'evidence'. You will not see it again: erase it and any cargo from your adventure sheet.

Under arrest...   **255**

188

Trying to do too much at once is a recipe for disaster! You manage to overbalance and lose control of your velosteam, which pitches you painfully onto the road. Gain a **Damage Point** and a **Wound**. The carriage races off.

If your velosteam is **beyond repair**...   **250**
If you have **five Wounds**...   **90**
Otherwise...   **394**

189

You seek out the dwelling of the lame engineer that Father Bourdain told you about. You find him in the darkened parlour of a narrow house, rocking backwards and forwards with the pain from his stumps. He has no legs.

"Had to have 'em off," he tells you grimly. "A beam fell on me at the works. The master paid for someone to saw me up, then gave me the sack. Took my pins and my livelihood, the miserable son of perdition."

He is a skilled engineer but since his accident has been unable to get work. His wife and children are out, trying to earn what they can to pay the rent. "All I want is a fair chance, mate," he says desperately.

Recommend him to Lord Dashwood...
    (**Friend of Lord Dashwood**)   **447**
Recruit him for the Compact...
    (**Member of the Compact
    for Workers' Equality**)   **215**
Give him a Guildsman's Medallion...
    (**Guildsman's medallion**)   **558**
Offer him money to start a workshop... (**£20**) **636**
Leave him for now...   **574**

190

The trees of Horton Wood block out any sound. Once you quieten your velosteam it is silent beneath the boughs.

Ride south out of the wood...   **602**
Ride north to Winchbottom Lane...   **442**

191

You track the driver with your gun as the wagon comes nearer. A clean shot will almost certainly bring the vehicle to a halt. Make an ACCURACY roll of difficulty 12 to hit the driver.

Successful ACCURACY roll!   **110**
Failed ACCURACY roll!   **252**

192

It is a harsh existence, inside. Many times you are forced to make decisions that you could avoid in the civilization of freedom. One day a thief, imprisoned with their family, steals your meagre portion of gruel.

Hunt them down...   **213**
Let it pass...   **227**

193

You lead the Constables deep into Maidenhead thicket, where the ancient trees hide the evening sun and the thick foliage deadens even engine sounds. The little stream-side track is most likely unknown to these officers - but you must be quiet if you are to avoid them. You turn off your lime lantern and head into the bushes. Make an INGENUITY roll of difficulty 10 to escape, adding 1 if you have a **muffled exhaust**.

Successful INGENUITY roll!   **24**
Failed INGENUITY roll!   **207**

194

The driver sneers at you as he tears past and you are left choking on the dust kicked up by the steamer's wheels. Lower your RUTHLESSNESS score by 1 as a result.

Ride on towards Wheeler End...   **137**

195

You pull your cloak over your head and bend yourself over in mockery of an old beggar-woman and quickly grasp a few wet branches from the hedgerow. Then you hobble out into the roadway towards the tableau.

"Ohh, kind young sir, lend a poor widdy-woman a cup of hot water?"

He turns on the spot. Make an INGENUITY roll of difficulty 9 to take him off his guard.

Successful INGENUITY roll!   **729**
Failed INGENUITY roll!   **58**

196

Mrs Juste smiles. "How too rarely do I hear that. Then accept my thanks." She closes the door. You are now the **Friend of Mrs Juste** and have also gained a **Solidarity Point**.

Return to Maidenhead...   **594**

197

The Honourable Doira Marchpane sneers at you. "How desperately unfunny," she drawls. "How too, too sick-making."

You are grabbed by the hotel porters and thrown in the lock. A sharp blow on the head as you fly through the air means you must gain 1 **Wound**, and in addition any **paper objects** you possess must be discarded, ruined by the water (**tickets, books, letters**).

If you have **5 Wounds**...   **102**
Otherwise...   **94**

198

To set the explosives and successfully destroy the rails here, you will need to make an INGENUITY roll of difficulty 14. You can add 1 to your dice roll for every level of **Explosive Expert** you possess.

Successful INGENUITY roll!   **19**
Failed INGENUITY roll!   **104**

199

Wooburn Mill stands beside filthy ponds in the centre of town. A massive coal depot towers over rows of terraces, their windows smirched with soot and grime.

The steam revolution has gripped Wooburn Green like nowhere else: the ready supply of water from the River Wye has resulted in the mushrooming of factories and depots, terraces and slums. Close to the road to the capital and linked by telegraph to the computational heart of the empire at Maidenhead, Wooburn Green is an industrialist's heaven - and a labourer's hell. Day and night furnaces roar with flame, fed by coal brought down from the north. That coal stands in depots, watched over by the men of the Coal Board in their black and yellow livery. With a finger in every pie, the Board can profit from every engine in the land.

Look into a drinking house...   **68**
Head up into the wood...   **709**
Leave town...   **30**

200

The landslip here still obstructs part of the road and several wagons are waiting to pass up the steep slope. There is no opportunity for you to rob them, however, as a Constable is standing by the heap of soil and rock managing the traffic.

Ride on...   **428**

201

The fields are full of labourers making hay. A massive reaper-binder churns through the meadows, its mechanical scythes clacking rhythmically. Men and women gather the bundles it drops and stook them patiently for the winter. At least nobody has to wield a scythe for fourteen hours a day anymore, but with machinery like this, farmers can produce more - and the labourers have to keep up.

Ride on...   **646**

202

The road here has little steam traffic. You pass an ox-drawn farm cart and several women trudging along with mounds of basket-work high on their backs. After a final, glorious stretch of straight road on which your velosteam feels like it has grown wings, you arrive on the outskirts of the busy market-town of Marlow. If you are **Wanted by the Constables**, turn to **132**.

Head towards the High Street...   **4**

203

You leave the smog and wickedness of High Wycombe behind you. Which way will you turn?

West on the Oxford Road...	**492**
Up the hill to Handy Cross...	**25**
Eastward on the main road...	**574**
Over the hill towards Winchbottom Lane...	**11**

204

The bullet knocks the driver backwards. The fireman and assistant are terrified - they have no idea where you might be hiding. They quickly tend to their friend and shout out their surrender: "Come and take what you want! We give up!"

Roll a dice to see what you can take from them:

Score 1-2	**17s** and an **adjustable wrench (ENG+1)**
Score 3	**12s** and a pair of **goggles (MOT+1)**
Score 4	**£1 4s**
Score 5	**£3**
Score 6	**£2** and a pair of **engineer's gauntlets (ENG+2)**

You are now **Wanted by the Haulage Guild** and also lose **a Solidarity Point** for hurting an unarmed driver.

Ride away...	**662**

205

The airship captain staggers towards you, struggling with a sheathed **sabre** in one hand and a bottle in the other. "You'll never besmirch Judy's honour!" he slurs. "I'd die before you lay a hand..." He collapses in an inebriate heap.

You may take the **sabre (PAR 2)**, **£2 3s**, a **gold ring** and a **bottle of whisky**.

Ride away...	**737**

206

Doris takes you aside. "That lady you brought in here cost us a pretty penny. Dr Smollett had to be called - and you know doctors get paid in guineas, not pence. But she got better after a week or so in bed. Hired herself a steamer to take her off into the West Country, of all places. Now, there's **£4 4s** to pay in all."

Can't or won't pay...	**92**
Give her the money...	**426**

207

Your pursuers manage to overtake and surround you. No options remain - other than surrender.

"Well, chum," says a Captain, as he swings his truncheon. "This'll be the end of your particular adventure, I'm sure." He nods to another officer, who locks your hands in a pair of heavy manacles.

Turn to...	**255**

208

Two steam trucks are top-and-tailing a long trailer up the slope. Aboard are long, curved girders destined for the airship works - perhaps parts of a new hangar? Either way, the slow progress and road-blocking width of the convoy are holding up other travellers. You dismount for a while and take a rest.

A man comes up to you and offers to sell his warm **cloak** for a **shilling**. "I just need a bite to eat."

Turn to...	**247**

209

The fortune teller has a small tent lit by a single, tiny gas jet. As your eyes become accustomed to the gloom she motions you to sit and looks deeply into your eyes.

If your GALLANTRY score is greater than 6...	**393**
If your ENGINEERING score is greater than 7...	**460**
If you are **Friend of Dr Smollett**...	**159**
Otherwise...	**777**

210

The Thames runs sluggishly eastwards here, carrying barges loaded with all the goods of Oxfordshire and the Midlands, each spilling their waste into eddies that churn beside the bank with every turn of a steam-powered propellor or paddle-wheel. If you are wearing a **hat** of any kind, turn to **342** immediately.

Ride on..	**654**

211

If you are **Wanted by the Constables** turn to **132** immediately. You pass a constable's hut just outside Marlow, but the officer inside is either asleep or uninterested in a single velosteamer racing into town. Past several chequered flint-and-brick houses, along a narrow street marked with trailer-gouges, you steam into Marlow.

Ride up the High Street...	**4**

212

Unwilling to risk the dubious shelter of the tree, you ride on through the puddles. It is uncomfortable to be so wet, but unlikely to have any serious effect.

If you are wearing a **cloak**... 650
If you are not wearing a **cloak**... 83

213

You manage to find the thief and exact a dreadful punishment. In their weakened state, your beating is the final straw and the thief dies shortly afterwards. For several weeks the prison buzzes with the story of your wrath - but no-one interferes with you again. Gain the codeword *Arthropod* and also increase your RUTHLESSNESS score by 1.

Turn to... 227

214

You are in the lane by Hedsor House, not far from Bourne End and beneath the steep hill leading up to Cliveden.

Take the Bourne End route... 457
Head uphill to the southeast... 366
Head to Hedsor House... 362
Ride to the Riverside... 230

215

The engineer listens intently as you explain Jensen's philosophy of labour to him. He nods rapidly. "That's it exactly. The old gentry own our houses and the new rich own our labour. What do we have to call our own? So you say this Compact can help me?"

"I'm sure they can," you reply.

After a visit to the Compact headquarters, you convince the leaders of the local cadre to take the engineer and his family under their wing. He becomes a famous example of the cruelty of the rich and the revolutionaries are quick to show how they can care for him and his family, paying his rent, employing him in their (legal) printshop and educating his children. Your reputation as protector of the weak is boosted too: erase the codeword *Assistant* and gain a **Solidarity Point**.

Turn to... 574

216

You are on the long straight road between West Wycombe and High Wycombe. The surface is smooth, firm and well-kept. It is a fine place to open your regulator and let your velosteam fly!

Ride up to West Wycombe... 492
Ride into High Wycombe... 308

217

A few sweet words with the receptionist gets you the room number you are looking for. After a few moments, the door is opened by a pale young man in a dinner jacket, fitting the exact description of the blackguard Ennis. If you wish to scare him and take a ransom for his life, you must make a RUTHLESSNESS roll of difficulty 15. He has proven that he feels little. Otherwise you can attack him directly and he can pay with his blood.

Successful RUTHLESSNESS roll! 431
Attack him directly! 309

218

The Occidental Steam Railway and the main road to London both run from east to west here, at the foot of Taplow hill. Both are busy with traffic, watchmen and sharp eyes.

North towards Taplow... 429
West towards Maidenhead... 282
Onto the railway line... 161
East on the London Road... *The Reeking Metropolis* 450

219

Discard either the **bandages** or **cloak**. You manage to staunch the bleeding and bind up the worst of your cuts. Remove one of your **Wounds** in the normal way. Somehow you manage to start your velosteam and ride away, but in your dazed state you have no sense of direction. Roll a dice to discover where you end up:

Score 1-2   Horton Wood...   190
Score 3-4   Wooburn...   310
Score 5-6   West Wycombe...   492

220

Gain the codeword *Alba* if you don't already have it.

Here between the coppices stands your hideout. Simply built from the material the wood offers, roofed over with a tarpaulin, it offers complete isolation from the troubles of society. If you have brought the makings of a meal with you, it is a good place to spend a night and recuperate by the fire. You can also leave possessions here in safety, hidden near your bivouac.

Bandage your wounds and rest...
(bandages and **pheasant, rabbit,
deer carcass** or **large pike)**   **243**
Fix your damaged velosteam...   **627**
Ride down to Burchett's Green...   **727**
Steam on to Hurley Bottom...   **513**
Take the path to Appletree Cottages...   **139**

221

A slow-moving road engine and trailer come chugging slowly up the hill. The driver and firemen are unlikely to be carrying much money, but the freight might include some valuables, if you dare risk the wrath of their employer.

Let them pass...   **77**
Threaten them...   **524**
Hail the driver...   **504**

222

The master brewer is pleased to welcome you back to the brewery you saved. "What a success it's been!" she crows. "Let me pour you a glass of our newest best-selling brew: The Wanderer's Ale."

What a beer it proves to be: a clean aroma, reminiscent of a floral woodland, with a strong, even carbonation, a toffee-ish foretaste and a strong hoppy end. Your mouth feels as clean as after a trip to the dentist.

It seems that your efforts are well-repaid - if you value a good pint.

Return to the High Street...   **4**

223

You manage to cut a trunk free from its leather straps. It bounces onto the road surface where you can open it at your leisure. Roll a dice to see what you find:

Score 1   a set of **false teeth** and a **bottle of wine**
Score 2   some **fencing gloves (NIM+1)**
Score 3   a **dinner jacket** and a **bow tie (GAL+1)**
Score 4   some **white pills (ING+2)** ☐ ☐ ☐
Score 5   a **gold necklace** and an **artisan's loupe (ING+1)**
Score 6   a **strongbox**

Turn off by the Golden Ball Inn...   **394**

224

A tall man with a flamboyant hat bows. "Good evening," he says in a thick French accent. "'ow delighted I am to meet ze real Steam 'Ighwayman. Would you sign my 'ankerchief?"

He is carrying **£8 5s** and you may also take his **wide-brimmed hat**.

As you remount your velosteam, you see the Frenchman settling himself back into his seat, poring over your blotchy attempt at a signature on the little scrap of linen. He is radiant with joy, despite your robbery, presumably considering his empty purse well repaid with proof of his experience. His return to his homeland will be accompanied by a fond tale, it seems.

Ride away...   **737**

225
☐

If there is a tick in the box, turn to **484** immediately. Otherwise, tick it and read on.

The Beadle's eyes light up with greed at the sight of your gold. "Yes, yes, there is a candidate," he says. "A young man showing promise and diligence in the workshop. I shall summon him here."

A boy of around twelve is brought up to the Beadle's parlour, where you are being served bad sherry.

"Well, Braddins, your lucky day has come. You shall go to work for the butcher in Cookham. He's been looking for an apprentice and mind you serve him well, or he'll cast you out, I'm sure, no pity like your soft old Beadle here at the old Workhouse."

"'m obliged," says the boy meekly. "Much obliged. My sister?"

"Don't be so impertinent. Your sister will find a

place if she mend her ways. No doubt you'll be given a day off this time next year and will have a chance to visit her. Now thank your noble benefactor here and gather your belongings."

"Belongings? What belongings, sir?"

The boy is led out and a passing cart agrees to take him to Cookham. Gain the codeword *Additive*.

Leave the Workhouse...   **602**

226

You are close behind Lord Akroyd's True Patriot again, watching for any opportunity to pass, but the race has less than a lap to go and you have only a little ground coal left to feed into the furnace of your machine. Akroyd seems to lose pressure and you come alongside - but then as he snarls and steers into you, hard, you realise that it was only a feint to get his beaked wheels into play. You have to pull off the main track and onto a service strip to avoid having your expensive tyres shredded and spokes sprung.

You will have to pass Akroyd, or he will destroy you and the Wagtail. Your machine is faster, but you will have to survive his wrath as well as the race.

Wait for the final straight...   **283**
Pass him early and speed ahead...   **771**

227

Eventually your sentence is complete. Who really knows how long you have been cooped up like an animal in a cage? You lost count of the days long ago. Eventually the prison wardens collect you and take you to the front gate.

If you are a **Famed Lawbreaker**...   **545**
Otherwise...   **740**

228

The Three Horseshoes has a brick archway into a yard where most of the drinking and socialising is done. A pretty maid carries trays of beer and bar snacks out to the travellers and resting farmers.

Buy a drink...   **(1s)**   **435**
Leave the pub...   **50**

229

If you are **Wanted by the Constables**, turn to **344** immediately.

There is a fine stone bridge over the Thames at Cookham, guarded by a small group of sharp-eyed consta-bles. They look you over carefully, before raising the barrier and letting you cross.

The river below is clogged with steam-barges towing their butty-boats through the narrow arches, queuing a half-mile or so up and downstream. Talk has been heard of replacing the bridge: the villagers are unenthusiastic..

Travel north towards Bourne End...   **350**
Travel south to Cookham...   **246**

230

A small brick wharf stands here at the riverside. A couple of barges are moored up, their masters chatting as they prettify the rudder posts with intricately wound rope patterns.

"This is the ram's head," says one, thumping the oak. "'cos it be so stubborn. Gets knotted all over with these Turk's head knots, see. Samuel there has a pretty one." He points downstream where a tail of horsehair is woven into the ropework of another rudderpost.

Cross the weir to Cookham lock... (*Amphibious*) **12**
Go aboard your boat (if it is moored here)...   **488**
Return to the road...   **214**

231

In the relative safety and privacy of your room here at the Golden Ball Inn you can rest and treat your **Wounds** if you are hurt. You can also leave your possessions and money here by adding them to the box below.

```
┌─────────────────────────────────────┐
│                                     │
│                                     │
│                                     │
│                                     │
│                                     │
│                                     │
│                                     │
│                                     │
│                                     │
│                                     │
└─────────────────────────────────────┘
```

Rest and treat your **Wounds**...   **390**
Return to the parlour...   **394**

232

You steam up to Cookham lock, carefully negotiating the narrow and crowded channel and avoiding the strong flows over the weir. A sign advertises local charcoal and the ubiquitous coal-dump has a board advertising today's price for a load of coal. There are few other products to load here, but bargees can make a few pounds profit on a load of frozen meat or beer.

	To buy	To sell
Charcoal	£13	£10
Furniture	-	-
Machinery	-	£24
Pottery	-	-
Cotton	-	-
Woollen cloth	-	£10
Coal	£12	£12
Beer	-	£17
Wheat	£3	£3
Malt	-	£7
Frozen Meat	-	£14
Ice	-	£6

Moor here...	613
Continue downstream...	
(**2s** or **Bargee's Badge**)	181
Return to Cookham Reach...	693

233

The flash stuns you for a moment and when you look around, the girls are clambering noisily back onto the bus. Who knows where that photograph will end up! Will fame be kind to you, in your assault on society? Or will your face be recognised all the more easily?

Ride on...	703

234

You are locked in cellar in the Abbey while the Constables are fetched. You make an attempt to widen an old window high in the wall, but have only just begun by the time they arrive. The Constables chain you and take you without trial directly to the prison on Frieth Lane. It seems they are used to dealing with anyone the Abbot' considers a troublemaker in this away.

Turn to...	722

235

Lights on the road ahead warn you of a roadblock. The Constables must have heard that you were in the area: their net is getting ever tighter. Dr Smollett asks why you pause the velosteam - his mission is urgent. You have a simple choice: attempt to break through the roadblock and risk injury or arrest, or leave Dr Smollett here. You are only a short distance from Bullock's Farm.

"I can take you no further, Doctor."	383
"Hold on tight, Doctor. This might get hairy."	108

236

A travelling dentist trundles past in his little steam van. He politely waves, then hails across the road. "Need any teeth pulling? Any lotion for your gums?" He will also offer some minor medical treatment.

Medical items	To buy	To sell
cough medicine	5s	-
soothing lotion	2s	-
false teeth	£1 2s	£1
gold tooth	15s	12s

Medical treatment	To buy	
Treat a **fever**...	6s	
Soothe a **toothache**...	9s	

As you leave, he wishes you well. "Take care to brush twice a day. And floss too!"

Ride away...	534

237

"Well it makes better sense for our donors to give into one pot, you know? Then the trustees and the parish council can decide how best to use these gifts to the church. The poor have their share and so do the servants of the church." The vicar seems entirely free from shame in describing the process. "We could call the collection 'building fund', but we've found that anything labelled 'poorbox' collects more." Gain the codeword *Aggregate*.

Leave the church...	4

238

You creep up on Harris with a sack and a rope to restrain her, but somehow she gets wind of you and leaps up. She swings at you with a heavy steel ruler and manages to knock you out with a single powerful blow to the temple. Gain a **Wound**. While you are unconscious, she ties you up and hands you over to the Constables.

Turn to...	255

239

The road continues by the water's edge and although there are still a few steam carriages carrying socialites to parties in Maidenhead, this area is mostly given over to the world of freight. Barges are unloading into tall warehouses and trains of wagons await their engines and their scheduled times. Roll a dice to see what you find:

Score 1-3   A dejected trader...   151
Score 4-6   The Two Bridges..   282

240

The marketplace at High Wycombe is surrounded by fine buildings and shops. Traders and craftsmen come from far and wide to buy and sell here.

Food and Drink	To buy	To sell
bird's eggs	-	3s
rabbit	2s	1s
pheasant	4s	3s
tin of fruit	3s	2s
wheel of cheese	£1 2s	14s
bottle of wine	10s	6s
bottle of champagne	-	15s
picnic hamper	£3 3s	£2

Clothing	To buy	To sell
cloak	£1	15s
dark cloak (RUTH+1)	-	£2 10s
dungarees (GAL-2)	£1 10s	15s
eyepatch (RUTH+1)	15s	5s
wide-brimmed hat	-	18s
silk scarf	£2	£1
bow tie (GAL+1)	1 10s	£15s
top hat	-	£2
dinner jacket	-	£2
ballgown	£24	£12

Tools	To buy	To sell
rope	4s	2s
rope ladder	9s	7s
lantern	6s	4s
heavy wrench	18s	12s
grappling iron	12s	8s
fishing line	1s	-
snare	2s	1s
tarpaulin	4s	4s

Weapons	To buy	To sell
club (PAR 4)	3s	1s
sabre (PAR 6)	£3	£1 10s

Jewellery	To buy	To sell
locket	6s	4s
pocket watch	-	£1
silver ring	-	5s
silver bracelet	-	6s
silver necklace	-	10s
gold ring	-	£1
gold bracelet	-	£2
gold necklace	-	£3

Other items	To buy	To sell
parasol	£5	£2
chess set	-	£2
box of cigars	-	£1 10s

Leave the market...   337

241

"It's a dirty evening and I've just finished a job," you announce at the bar. "It's best we all stay inside and dry. So order what you will at my expense, ladies, gentlemen."

A chorus of approval rises from the drivers, engineers, firemen and hauliers. Nobody is likely to turn down this opportunity.

☐ If the box is empty, tick it and turn to **303**. If the box is ticked, turn to **130**.

242

A poor woman takes pity on you and brings you under her roof. There you slowly recover your strength, but it takes several weeks before you are fit to ride again. Convert any **Wounds** you have into **Scars**, and check for **Intimidating Scars (RUTH+1)** by rolling 11 or higher on two dice. You don't ask the woman where your **money** has gone, but presumably she took it in payment for your stay. Your velosteam is in the same condition as when you last saw it and your **Wanted** statuses are unchanged. When you leave, you realise that you never asked the poor woman's name, and she never told you.

Turn to...   337

243

The tarpaulin shelter is primitive, but it has kept a stack of wood dry and allows you to build up the fire and stay warm despite the rain. First you prepare the food and fetch water from the spring a short way off in the wood. Then comes the uncomfortable work of removing your blood-encrusted clothing and peeling back the cloth that has dried in the wound. Discard the food and the **ban-

dages. By the time you have cleaned your **Wounds** (remove them and replace them with **Scars** instead) you are tired by the effort and the pain and fall into a deep sleep.

If you have the codewords *Arthropod*, *Astrakhan* or *Apogee*, turn to...   **706**
Otherwise...   **220**

244

It starts to rain heavily and you are surprised by a figure holding an oilskin cloak over their head who dashes across the road in front of you, forcing you to slam on the brakes. The Ferguson skids, but stays upright, and you manage to keep it under control. The man turns to see if you are alright.

"Sorry," he says gruffly. "I didn't see you. I thought someone was after me... I thought I heard..."

With his unkempt uniform, unshaven face and fearful attitude he is plainly a deserter. You wave aside his panicked apologies and shelter with him under the trees of a roadside coppice.

"Where are you coming from?" you ask him.

"Left the barracks at Highmoor Cross three days ago," he says. "They were going to send us back to Spain. I've already done one tour. Lost my best mates and nearly lost my mind too in the trenches. Thump, thump, thump, that's the shells again and again. I can still hear them. I can't go back. I'm making for London, lose myself there."

"You got family?"

"I used to. Don't know now. My wife stopped answering my letters. Bleeding war."

The rain stops eventually and he heads on his way, furtively diving between stands of trees and expecting to be picked up by the constables at every turn in the road.

Ride on...   **646**

245

The wharf is busy here and brisk set of unionised porters ferry cargoes between barges, road wagons and the railway yard. Almost anything can be bought and sold here: the prices for goods change hourly and are displayed on a mechanical board, but many cargoes desired in London sell for a better price here than in Marlow or Henley, while consumables like **Malt** and **Frozen meat** are cheaper to buy here than further up the Thames. If you want to buy a shipment, make sure that you have empty space on your barge first!

	To buy	To sell
Charcoal	£13	£13
Furniture	£27	-
Machinery	£28	£25
Pottery	£24	£21
Cotton	£6	£4
Woollen cloth	£11	£10
Coal	£9	£9
Beer	-	£18
Wheat	£3	£3
Malt	£8	£8
Frozen meat	£12	£12
Ice	£12	£12

To ship Frozen Meat or Ice, your barge must be fitted with a **Perkins Machine**.

Disembark and leave your barge here...   **82**
Sail downriver...   **672**
Steam to Maidenhead riverside...   **333**

246

Welcome to Cookham! This little town has a genteel air, but its wealth is largely of the old-fashioned kind, drawn from agriculture and the land. There is a fine pub, the Swan Uppers but few shops here, as the villagers tend to do their buying and selling at the weekly fair on the green to the west.

Visit the Swan Uppers...   **271**
Head to Cookham Lock...   **12**
Leave town...   **305**

247

You are at the foot of the Telegraph Guild's main trunk tower here at the High Heavens. Except where your view is obscured by the workshops, furnaces and accommodation block of the guild's outpost, you can see all around for miles.

The smog of High Wycombe smothers the town to the north-east, glowing dully with gaslight. Marlow stands at the bottom of the long slope in front of you. Here on the hilltop a racetrack has been cut into the turf, and the woods all around are marred with the signs of industry.

Ride towards Lane End...   **684**
Investigate the nearby racetrack...   **642**
Head down the hill towards Marlow...   **54**
Take the lane between the fields...   **25**

248

You notice a short, smartly-dressed woman in the corner looking at you closely. She has grey hair and a particularly gleaming, hard eye. After a few minutes' discomfort, you walk over and confront her. "What do you want with me?"

She shakes her head and puts down her drink. "It's what they want with you that should worry you," she replies, pointing out of the window. There stand a posse of Constables around their Imperial velosteams, leafing through the all-too familiar Constable's printofit books.

It turns out that Mrs Petty, as she introduces herself, is an important official in the Constabulary with an offer to make you. "How about a clean slate?" she asks. "All forgiven? We forget your crimes and you are free to travel where and how you will."

Obviously there is a cost. "At what price?"

"I need a spy," she says, "Inside the Compact for Workers' Equality. I need to know their plans. They are a reckless and dangerous group of anarchists, seemingly unaware of the great danger of lawlessness they will unleash upon the land. Look what happened to France! And to Greece!"

"And if not?"

She nods towards the door where the Constables have already entered while you are talking. "Then you will rot in gaol," she replies. "I'm a practical woman. Your service is more helpful to me than your death, - and cheaper than your imprisonment. And obviously you'd prefer it, wouldn't you?"

Accept her offer...	**278**
Attempt to get away...	**163**

249

Cliff Wood is full of steep slopes, sharp drops and tiny criss-crossing paths. If you push yourself and your velosteam you may be able to make it over the uneven ground safely, while luring your pursuers over a precipice. Make a MOTORING roll of difficulty 12, adding 2 if you have **off-road tyres**.

Successful MOTORING roll!	**27**
Failed MOTORING roll!	**207**

250

Your trusty velosteam has taken more than it can bear. There is nothing more you can do to patch it up, fix it, or bring it back to life. And without it, what life is there for you, a mere unlucky footpad? It is time to draw your adventuring days to a close.

Turn to the **Epilogue** to discover what sort of tale you leave behind.

251

"I can take you as far as Handy Cross," you offer. "Piddington's a bit out of my way."

"Fair enough," he responds, and clambers onboard. "Lost this leg in the Spanish War. Taken me long enough to get back here. A little longer until I see my Meg isn't too bad."

As you ride away it begins to rain and the soldier settles inside his coat and says no more. The discomfort of the wet and uneven ride on the velosteam elicits no protest from a man as inured to suffering as he. Perhaps taking him to his destination would be the kinder action - if kindness motivates you.

To Handy Cross...	**25**
Travel all the way to Piddington...	**162**

252

Your shot goes wide and the driver ducks down behind the windscreen. Suddenly, shots ring out from the passenger compartment: the occupants are firing back! You dive into the undergrowth to avoid the bullets: roll a dice to see the outcome.

Score 1-2	Shot! Gain a **Wound**...
Score 3-4	Your velosteam gains a **Damage Point**
Score 5-6	Escape unharmed...

If your velosteam is **beyond repair**...	**250**
If you have **five Wounds**...	**90**
Otherwise...	**528**

253

The Wagtail purrs as you take it down the drive and out onto the open road. You save the steam pressure until you reach Booker Racetrack, where an official meets you.

"Pretty thing. Let's see your best time around the course," he says. Make a MOTORING roll of difficulty 14.

Successful MOTORING roll	**367**
Failed MOTORING roll!	**509**

254

You return to the Curtiss wagon, holding the will out in front of you like a talisman. Your knock is answered by an angry Davy, who recognises you instantly.

"What do you want?"

"I know that you and your brother are fighting over ownership of the fair," you say. "But I think you'd better take a look at this first."

Davy takes the envelope (remove the **will** from your possessions) and reads it slowly. He steps back into the wagon, stunned. "'Ere, Greg. You're a reading man. Look at this. I never knew dad left a will."

You tell the brothers how you came to find their father's will in the inventor's study. They share a significant look, before Gregory speaks. "Look here. What we should do is, open it in the sight of all the fair. Every stall-holder, every share-holder. Then, whatever he says, we'll abide by it, fair enough?"

"Fair enough," replies Davy.

The news races around the fair. Rides stop, customers are turned away, furnaces are left untended, and within an hour the people of the Curtiss steam fair are gathered in the night around a great fire. The chatter dies down eventually and Gregory begins to read.

"I, Albert Horatio Curtiss of Curtiss Steam Fair, being of sound mind but unfortunately of less than sound constitution, do solemnly declare this to be my final will and testament concerning the guvnership of said fair, also of all my effects and worldly wealth.

"My wagon, I do leave to my son, Davy Curtiss." A roar goes up from Davy's faction, but Gregory carries on reading. "All my possessions and wealth I do hereby leave in equal share to both Davy and Gregory. Authority over the fair I do pass into both of their hands with the following proviso: it was always my intention for Gregory to become educated in business matters so that the business of the fair could be carried on in the best and most profitable manner. However, Davy who has been my constant support and companion, is better at understanding the daily needs of the fair people, who are a family to us. Therefore I bid them put aside their differences, which have caused myself and their mother such pain, and to share in the family business together."

The fair is quiet. Only crackle of logs breaks the silence of the night, while the people wait to see how the brothers will react.

Davy steps forward first. "Brother Gregory... Forgive me my foolishness. I have been a selfish man. Will you share the guvnership with me?"

Gregory does not hesitate. "Of course, brother. All is forgiven."

A great cheer rises and before you know it, the fair people are celebrating as only fair people can. Drinks and food appear out of nowhere, fiddlers and accordion players start up and the entire community breathes a collective sigh of relief. The brothers turn to you.

"Thank-you," says Davy, offering you his hand.

"Without your help, I would of killed 'im." You are now the **Friend of the Curtiss brothers**. "You'll be welcome with us any time. In fact, we'll fix up Missy Elma's old wagon for you, so you can have your own place right here with us. You're the sort we want to keep close, it seems to me." Now one question remains: do you want to hand over the money as well? No-one is asking for it.

"There was also this money in the box."
(**thirty guineas in banknotes**)	**1007**
"I'm glad that no-one ended up dead."	**700**

255

Since your appearance matches the description of a wanted criminal, you are handed over to the officers of the Town Gaol in Maidenhead. The Chief Constable rubs her hands with glee. "We have you now, my little flying bird. You'll be tried and hanged for your crimes, I'll see that you are."

You are locked up while the trial is prepared.

The night before you appear in court, a doctor comes to look you over. She treats any **Wounds** you may have (convert these into **Scars** without checking for **Intimidating Scars**) and checks your pulse.

"A little anxious," she says. "As to be expected. But I make it a point of honour not to lose a single man for King James' gallows." It is time to call in any favours you may have.

If you have the password *Adoption*... **648**
If you have at least **100 guineas** in Coulter's Bank... **537**
Otherwise... **317**

256

When you announce that you are buying drinks the barman looks at you in disbelief, then whistles loudly. More faces look in from the door. "Drinks are on the stranger," he announces. "Come and get them!"

If the behaviour of the drinkers was coarse before, then it is nothing compared to what you experience now. A scrum quickly develops around the bottles, cups and beakers are broken, more and more drinkers pile in from the streets outside. A brawl starts over who has the right to enter and who doesn't. Nobody gives you any attention at all - until the gin runs out.

"You owe me eight pound six shillings," says the barman. "That'll cover the drinks and the breakages."

Pay up... (**£8 6s**) **577**
Can't or won't pay... **374**

257

The drinks you buy push the crowd onto even more brazen brawling and fighting. The drinking goes on, well into the night, complete with shows of strength, attempted proofs of sobriety and more than one drinking competition. You are holding your own with the steady drinkers until the challenge of the Yard of Beer gets the better of you. Dazed and drunk, you are thrown out with the others at closing time and wander through town, eventually finding a nice warm crate to hide in and wait out the headache.

You awake with a shudder of nausea and a horrible feeling of churning guts. Then you realise that the crate you slept in last night was on the deck of a Thames Barge, and you have awoken somewhere along the river. Miraculously, someone has loaded your velosteam on board as well. Roll two dice to discover where you are.

Score 2-4	Hurley...	**569**
Score 5-8	Cookham Lock...	**12**
Score 9-12	Bourne End...	**703**

258

The councillor surrenders before you are forced to run him through. He is carrying a large wallet containing **£13 2s**. "Why are you preying on the likes of me?" he splutters. "What have I done? Eaten while others starved? Is that a crime in your eyes?"

Ride away...   **535**

259

The landlord ushers the young gentleman into an inner room and the inn servants are sent rushing for hot water, hot food, warmed wine and every luxury that nobility demands.

"You know something about it, I reckon," says a man, recognisable as the local miller from his flour-dust covering.

"What is it to you?" you ask belligerently.

"Starving crows, I don't mind if you thieve off a nob or two. Maybe I would, if I dared. I just want to know, what makes you do it?"

"The rich deserve punishment..."   **474**
"The poor need help..."   **302**

260

A building crew are constructing an iron frame over the roadway here in Cookham, as part of a mechanical unloading system that will make carts quicker to unload. The wonders of the empire never cease! Roll two dice to see what else you find:

Score 2-5	A poacher...	**565**
Score 6-8	Everyday traffic...	**351**
Score 9-12	A building accident...	**792**

261

The young man quivers and grasps at his driver for support. "Good God! Would you kill a man in cold blood for a few coins? I've no wish to die." He tosses you his purse: it contains **£3 10s**.

Ride away...   **23**

262

You appeal to the angry and disenfranchised masses. "I stole, yes, but not from you. From the rich and the powerful. I took from them because they took from you. Now they seek to murder me - just as they will murder you through overwork and the choking smog!"

The officers come to quieten you, but the crowd are incensed. In a wave they pour forwards, clambering onto the platform, wrestling aside the guards and knocking the gallows post down. Chaos ensues - shots ring out from the constables posted around the square, first in warning, then in anger. You manage to leap from the platform as the post falls and use a dropped penknife to free your hands. With the cut noose around your neck you fight your way to your velosteam and start her up. She roars into life, faithful as ever, and you steam through the maelstrom as cavalry bugles are sounded behind you. You have made your escape!

Ride away...   **707**

263

You will have to be light on your feet to spring from your moving velosteam to the driver's platform of a racing steam carriage. Make a NIMBLENESS roll of difficulty 9 (adding 1 if you have a **grappling iron**).

Successful NIMBLENESS roll!   **126**
Failed NIMBLENESS roll!   **22**

264

Widbrook Common is flat and grassy. Your velosteam ploughs through the meadow leaving a swathe of flattened stalks behind it like the trail of some heavy, selfish beast. You surprise several ground-nesting birds and send them up into the summer sky, singing in alarm.

At a small rise you find a boundary stone marking the edge of someone's land. If you have the codeword *Aurum*, turn to page **20**.

Head west towards the railway embankment... **618**
Ride across the common to the Maidenhead road... **107**
Cross the common towards Cookham...   **246**

265

Down towards the river you find the Two Brewers. Its homely, brick facade has a young wisteria vine beginning to creep over it. Inside there is a warm fire and an inviting stool at the bar.

Several locals look up as you enter, but choose not to see you or meet your eye. They can tell they are better off able to claim they have never seen or met you. The barman gives you a wary nod, neither rude nor welcoming. He is waiting to see exactly who has entered his establishment.

Buy a drink...	**(1s)**	**384**
Ask to see Mrs Petty...	(*Ascorbic*)	**301**
Leave the pub...		**4**

266
☐

If the box is empty, put a tick in it and turn to **741**. Otherwise, turn to **407**.

267

After several hours of watching the road nothing has approached other than a few impoverished pedestrians and a couple of farm wagons. Finally the noise of a heavy engine and a pillar of smoke announces the arrival of a steam vehicle, but it turns out to be a freight wagon in Haulage Guild livery.

Head to your woodside hideout...(*Alba*)	**220**
Ride to the Golden Ball Inn and rest there...	**394**
Hail the driver of the freight wagon...	**807**
Threaten the driver...	**41**
Shoot at the driver...	**157**

268
☐

If the box is empty, tick it and read on. If it is already ticked, turn to **548** immediately. It takes a flash of Director Short's medallion before the Guild Hauliers trust you enough to let you join them around their brazier. Business is good for them, "Though we have to crack on proper to make our wage. Paid by the mile and the minute, you see. If the delivery ain't made on time - or better - we pay the Guild back!"

Several proudly show you their haulage engines, customised for hill-climbing or long-distance routes, painted gaily and hung about with coal-oil lamps. They are just as interested in your velosteam. "What sort of speed does it make?" asks one.

"She can top thirty-eight miles an hour," you explain.

The hauliers whistle appreciatively. "Well I never! And a little boiler like that too!"

"You should get a paint job," advises one driver. "Henners'll do it! He's the best hand.

Henners, one of the older firemen, tells you about when he worked at the Curtiss Steam Fair down at Pinkney's Green. "That's where I learnt to paint and letter. Was in the old days, when the boys' pop was the big man. They've fallen out, I heard, Davy and Greg. But when I worked there, it was a happy place. He was always working on those rides, Mr Curtiss, painting 'em up, inventing something fabulous and new. Before he died, he was negotiating with some inventor in Bovingdon Green, to get the designs for a new ride that was going to top the lot. But nothing came of it in the end. But that's where I learnt to paint." Gain the codeword *Ambidextrous*.

You spend several more hours talking with the Guildsmen, hearing of their journeys on the road, with their engines, learning much of the lore of the tarmacadam empire. Roll a dice and add 3: if the result is greater than your MOTORING score you can improve your score by 1.

Return to Wycombe...   **337**

269

"I brought you something," you say. Erase the **bottle of whisky** from your possessions. Dr Smollett takes it carefully and his eyes light up. "My, my! Now this is a malt indeed. I won't ask where you got it - no, I've long since realised not to ask you questions. How you come by your wounds, how you come by your money, that's your business." He takes down two glasses and chips some ice off a block in a lead box beneath his desk. "I'll admit I've thought the worst of you. But you proved you were ready to help - that somewhere inside your there remains at least an ounce of selflessness."

The whisky helps thaw him out at last. After the first glass he is a lot more ready to talk. "I wasn't always so bitter," he says. "But I didn't always treat cut-up hauliers and criminals in a little village in the Chilterns. I served in the Imperial Navy, the Carribbean, the Med. I saw my share of splinter wounds and shrapnel-ridden boys. But I took my retirement after the shelling of Ibiza. God, that was just a slaughter. They brought the bleeding townspeople to the fleet after the surrender for treatment. What man does to man! So I took my discharge. I didn't come to Lane End to find more slaughter."

He tells you more of his stories. Sad ones of the sea, burials far from England's green fields, awful wounds. Then the ridiculous ones. Foolish captains, unbelievable coincidences, life at sea. Late in the night, when the bottle is long finished and the embers of his office stove are cold, he claps you on the shoulder. "Come back again," he says. "You're a better listener than you look." You are now the **Friend of Dr Smollett** if you were not already.

Leave the Doctor...   **684**

270

You take up position in a tree, downwind of a clearing that looks promising. After several hours uncomfortable waiting, you see a deer and fawn trot out into the grasses. Your view is hampered by the grass and by the branches of the tree, but it looks like this is your best shot. Make an ACCURACY roll of difficulty 14.

Successful ACCURACY roll!   **810**
Failed ACCURACY roll!   **29**

271

Inside the Swan Uppers the walls and ceiling are decorated with a plethora of strange river paraphernalia, marked with all manner of heraldry. "'Tis all from the swan uppers," explains a toothy woman with a pot of beer. "They come up from the city and count the swans or some such foolery. Well, such swans as are left from our ' pots and feather pillows. Haw haw haw!"

Order a drink...   (**1s**)   **841**
Leave the pub...   **246**

272

In the dark and the danger of the midnight ambush, the controls of the unfamiliar engine are beyond you. Although you keep the engine on the road, rising pressure threatens to blow the boiler, so you let out the steam and come to a halt. The brigands appear on horseback, their crossbows levelled. There is little you can do. You are knocked out, thrown from the engine and robbed. Gain

two **Wounds** from the rough treatment and if you have **five Wounds**, turn to **74** immediately. Otherwise, lose all your **money** and roll a dice for each of your **possessions** and items of **clothing**: a roll of 4 or lower means you must cross it off.

When the brigands have gone, the haulier's partner brings you round with a splash of water from the engine's saddle tanks. He is less than pleased, but allows you to accompany the convoy as it limps into High Wycombe. There you are dismissed without payment.

Slink away...   **337**

273

As you cut through his fine clothes once more and tear into his upper arm with the tip of your blade, the Honourable Gerald Gilling throws down his rapier in disgust. "Alright, alright. I've no wish to die on a trip to Slough. Take the money - you probably need it for your gin habit or something anyway."

His purse contains **£3 10s** and you can also take his **rapier (PAR 7)** if you wish.

Ride away...   **23**

274

The prison guards usher you into the courtyard and officially take custody from the Constables who have brought you. However, rather than being released into the prison general or being chained in a cell, you find yourself escorted to the Governor's apartment. He gets up from his work and greets you warmly.

"Welcome to our little prison! We are honoured to have such a terror of the road here, such a person of renown. You will bring us quite the air of gentility, I can say." He asks after your financial situation. "If you are in possession of any moderate amount of finance, we will be able to make your stay quite comfortable here. I believe the West suite is free, Mr Smithers?" He takes a look at some paperwork in front of him. "And if you find yourself embarrassed, then I can arrange for some assistance in that quarter - good credit, sufficient for your stay. Which, although lengthy, should by no means be forever. I hope you will dine with me tonight?"

The governor arranges for you to be quartered in private rooms which, though relatively bare and still locked every night, are at least dry and wholesome. However, you may find yourself paying for such favour upon your release!

Turn to...   **638**

275

Comrade Feaver studies you. "You are not yet ready to join us as a full member," she says. "But if you prove your value, you may in time become able to participate in the revolution. I want you to plant some material I have here in a certain lady's dressing table. It will not only ruin her, but her husband too, an enemy to the cause. You will only have this one chance to please me, so proceed quickly to Harleyford and get these notes into Lady Dean's room." You are handed a **sealed packet**, blindfolded and led away. If you have the codeword *Antipodes*, gain the codeword *Ascorbic* as well.

Turn to...   199

276

You step into the road and ready your weapons. "Stop that wagon or I'll blast a whole through every one of you!" Make a RUTHLESSNESS roll of Difficulty 13 to scare the driver into stopping. You can add 2 to your roll if you have a **double headlamp**.

Successful RUTHLESSNESS roll!   149
Failed RUTHLESSNESS roll!   129

277

If you are **Wanted by the Constables**, turn to **419** immediately. Otherwise turn to **389**.

278

"Good," replies Mrs Petty. "You have chosen wisely. Now listen carefully. I want someone who can get close to Feaver and her assistants. Work with her, then bring me news of her plans. I'll arrange a certain tidying up of the file on your citizen number."

"How can I be sure?"

"You'll have to trust me," replies Mrs Petty.

Following her suggestion, you wait until she dismisses the Constables. It is only later at a checkpoint that you realise she has worked her magic after all: you are no longer **Wanted by the Constables**. Gain the codeword *Antipodes*.

Turn to...   4

279

The velosteam glides down the road from Handy Cross. The gentle curves and rises make more beautiful riding as you bank, accelerate and whizz past the uphill traffic. At the foot of the hill you meet the road running between Marlow and Bourne End.

Head west to Marlow...   18
Take the road east towards Little Marlow
        and Bourne End...   602

280

The road continues south towards Maidenhead, but a mile or so out of town you come to Boulter's Lock. This has always been a busy place, full of pleasure-punts, steamers, private cruisers and Thames lighters. The main road continues north towards Cookham, but several haulage and delivery vehicles pull aside here around the green. Then there is the queue of carriages for hire, the Maidenhead locobus carrying day-trippers out to the water and several private steam-carriages of nobility who like to be seen here.

Stop for a while at the lock...   94
Continue south to Maidenhead...   282
Take the road north again...   246

281

The driver laughs and shouts back. "Who are you, then? Robin the 'Ood? We ain't scared of you!"

Fire at them...   157
Let them pass...   725

282

Two bridges cross the Thames here; the lower road-bridge and Mr Brunel's brick masterpiece carrying the Imperial Western Railway. The houses and workshops of Maidenhead crowd together beneath the smog and at the waterside stands the high warehouse of the Haulage Guild. A smog hangs in the air, compounded of sooty smuts, river mist and dust from the shaken-up roads. Several wagons have their lamps lit, despite the hour.

Enter the Haulage compound...   71
Take the road signed Boulter's Lock...   94
Head into Maidenhead...   594
Cross the roadbridge east...   218
Board your barge if it is moored here...   245

283

The Patriot powers on, its twin flues spitting sparks amongst the smoke and steam, keeping ahead of you. Forced to slow when Akroyd slows, you find yourself being slowly caught by the other engines. You know that you only need one opportunity to pass, but without the safety of the finish line you are not ready to risk the Wagtail's destruction.

Then finally, after hurtling around the bends at ever increasing speeds, Akroyd pulls out onto the final straight. He too opens his regulator, increases pressure and stokes the furnace hard. Dropping the intake cover, you open your own furnace and the rushing wind fans the flames until they leap twelve feet behind you! The pressure in the boiler builds, the pistons churn further and faster, spitting grease and lubricant and scabs of corrosion, but you pass the *Patriot* at last and steam ahead, leaving Akroyd in your wake.

The crowd cheer triumphantly and you see Lord Dashwood's hat waved in the air ahead of you. You are nearly there - gain six Race Points!

If you have 13 or more Race Points...	**155**
If you have fewer than 13 Race Points...	**517**

284

You ride up to the racing steam carriage, matching speed with it despite the ruts and the twists in the road. The driver looks up fearfully, then begins to try to weave around to drive you off the tarmac.

Try to cut some of the luggage free...	**345**
Attempt a leap aboard...	**263**

285

Gain the codeword *Augury*. Drawing your gun, you march directly over to the safe-keeper at the grill and point the loaded muzzle of the gun through the bars.

"Open the vault, or by thunder I'll blow this man's brains across the floor!" You must make a RUTHLESSNESS roll of difficulty 17.

Successful RUTHLESSNESS roll!	**514**
Failed RUTHLESSNESS roll!	**630**

286

In your dream that night you come across a collapsed building. Bricks, tiles and rafters are lying about in strange patterns, as if not subject to gravity. Nonetheless, somebody is trapped beneath the rubble - you see their hand and part of their hair, whitened by the dust - and you cannot shake the certainty that you have caused the house to collapse on them. Bending to uncover the body, you find your own face, still and breathless in the dust.

You awake in a fit of coughing, choking on the dream. It has not been a restful night. Gain the codeword *Apprehend* if you do not already have it.

Turn to...	**172**

287

Your bullet whines overhead and alerts the crew of the steamer, who quickly unfold several armoured partitions, closing themselves in. Before you know it, they are impregnably defended. Your bullets are nothing more than wasted ammunition. They steam past, unperturbed.

Ride away...	**662**

288

A tall stone building stands amongst trees and barbed wire fences just to the north of here. You are outside the Royal Buckinghamshire Prison. Frieth Road runs on to the west, higher into the Chilterns towards the villages of Frieth, Fingest, Turville and Stonor. The secrets and intricacies of that region would take an entirely new adventure to discover...

Head west...	*Highways and Holloways 88*
Cut through the fields towards Lane End...	**684**
Head towards Marlow...	**304**
Investigate the prison...	**734**

289

You have come to Bockmer End, a tiny hamlet of no more than five dwellings spread around the crossing of two lanes. Immediately to the north of here is the expanse of Heath Wood.

Enter the wood...	**118**
Follow the lane east...	**304**
Ride south to the Henley Road...	**534**

290

Your money buys ale for a motley crew of roisterers, most of whom are already drunk. One hoary-haired old farmhand takes you aside, though, and offers to share something he's heard that might interest a motorised brigand like yourself.

"I hear the Bishop of Barnsbury is coming over to inspect his holdings down at Hambleden," he says. "A nasty piece of work, but a wealthy one, that Prince of the Church. Ha! Prince in title, though not in nature. He turned three families out in the cold last winter and used the roofs of their cottages to fuel his computing engines there at Hambleden."

You ask the old man, "What was he computing?"

"I don't know, the date of Easter or some nonsense. But he rides in a russet-and-gold steamer and don't keep to no speed limits neither."

Gain the codeword *Alacrity*.

Return to the High Street...   **4**

291

You are midway along the dusty little thoroughfare known as Sheepridge Lane. This tiny road bypasses Bourne End entirely and runs between Flackwell Heath on the high ground and the Marlow road beside the river. High hedgerows fringe the roadway and nestled between the trees stands the Crooked Billet Inn.

Enter the Crooked Billet...	**180**
Ride towards Marlow...	**602**
Head into Bourne End...	**654**
Drive towards Flackwell Heath...	**50**

292

You run him through and leave him slumped on the floor. An open drawer reveals **thirty guineas in notes**, which you take, and then you make sure the curtains and bookcases are alight before you make your escape. The staff do not deserve to burn, but to awaken them you will risk your capture, so you smash several windows to alert them before driving off.

Comrade Feaver will be very glad to hear of the assassination: you should return to tell her of your success. Gain the codeword *Andronicus*.

Turn to...   **727**

293

The town councillor is outraged. "You can't rob me! I'm on the side of the poor! I'm travelling to an important debate to establish social housing for my constituents!" He draws a sword to defend himself.

Councillor	Weapon: **sabre (PAR 6)**
Parry:	11
Nimbleness:	5
Toughness:	2

Victory!	**258**
Defeat!	**90**

294

The woman takes your head in her hands and parts your hair. "Not many can read the future in a scalp," she says. "But I have some skill. Yes, as I thought. You tend towards wild decisions. Be careful! Not everyone you support will support you! Gun-running is a dangerous business, but a profitable one. Where the unicorns dance, take the riskier way. And beware of the turn of the tide! You are not a river-creature, I can see that." The gypsy dismisses you. "Go and ride the road, stranger."

Turn to...   **113**

295

The mausoleum stands high on the hill commanding a clear view of Wycombe down the long straight road. Beyond an iron fence, a polygonal, flint and concrete structure circles the tombs of the Dashwood family, open to the sky. It is a place fraught with memory, sorrow and mystery.

Between the tombs, your foot kicks against a metal hoop in the grass. A complex padlock holds a trapdoor fast into the ground. To open it, you will require a **rope**, some **wirecutters** and an ENGINEERING score higher than 6 - or simply a **skeleton key**.

Open the trapdoor... (**rope**, **wirecutters** and ENG >6 OR **skeleton key**)	**554**
Leave the mausoleum...	**492**

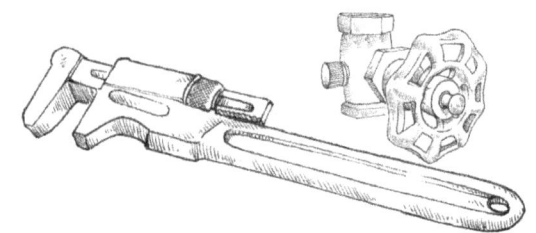

296

Your merciless captor strips you of all your **possessions** and **money** and dumps you by the roadside along with your velosteam, which they disdain to take with them. Roll a dice to see where you have been left:

Score 1	South of Bourne End...	350
Score 2	Handy Cross...	25
Score 3	Piddington...	546
Score 4	Flackwell Heath...	50
Score 5	Loudwater...	574
Score 6	Henley Road...	445

297

To pass the footmen's eyes you must look the part. Total your GALLANTRY score with any modifiers from clothing, accoutrements or other bonuses. If your score is not high enough, they will simply turn you away.

Score 10 or higher...	**738**
Score lower than 10...	**612**

298
☐

If the box is empty, tick it and turn to **406** immediately. If it is already ticked, read on.

Lord Dashwood and his team are preparing the Wagtail for the Spenser Cup. The garage is full of noise, jets of steam and the smell of shaved wood.

☐ A **lady's colours**
☐ **pneumatic tyres**
☐ A **time trial certificate**

If you have any of the three items above, tick the box beside them and cross the item off your inventory. When you have collected all three, turn to **387**. To gain the **lady's colours** you will need to accompany Lord Dashwood to the Cliveden Ball, whereas the **time trial certificate** can be obtained by testing the car in the presence of an official. You will have to source the tyres for yourself.

Attempt the time trial...	**253**
Leave the garage...	**172**

299

Despite your injuries you manage to clamber back aboard your velosteam. You head north, but angry railway workers uncouple a steam engine and chase you along the track. The sides of the cutting are steep and slick with mud. To negotiate your way up at high speed you will need to make a MOTORING roll of difficulty 10, adding 1 if you have **off-road tyres**.

Successful roll!	**15**
Failed roll!	**133**

300

Rainclouds gather overhead. Roll two dice to see the outcome:

Score 2-3	A brief shower...	**136**
Score 4-5	Downpour!	**1012**
Score 6-9	Just a few drops...	**650**
Score 10-12	Road washed out!	**364**

301
☐ ☐ ☐

If any of the boxes are empty, tick one. If all three are ticked, turn to **323** immediately.

Mrs Petty is sat in the corner by the fire, shuffling through papers and enjoying a good meal. She looks up as you approach. "So you have something to tell me? You've done the right thing in coming here." You give her all the details you have discovered about the Compact for Workers' Equality and she is very pleased.

"Excellent work. Bring me more like this and I will make sure you feel appreciated." Erase the codeword *Ascorbic* and roll a dice to see how she rewards you:

Score 1-2	**£15**
Score 3-4	A **pocket watch** and a **letter of introduction**
Score 5-6	A set of **punchcards (Aramanth A)** and **£5**

Return to the parlour...	**265**
Return to Marlow...	**4**
Leave town...	**169**

302

"You're right the poor need help!" replies the man. "A mate of mine makes ten shillings a week on the freight wagons, if he's lucky. He's got a wife and six children to support out of that - rent two shillings a week and bread rising all the time. And you know who keeps the price of freight down? The Haulage Guild! If he makes more than ten shillings, they lay him off for the week and employ some other poor beggar. No, they need help, it's true. Why, Father Bourdain at the church was a-preaching on it just the other day. He's no friend to the rich - gave up a fat living to come and help the poor folk of Bourne End."

"Where can I meet this Father Bourdain?"	573
"Everyone has to help themselves."	180

303

You are soon sat in a circle of roadsmen discussing the journey one of them is making. She is hauling a mixed freight load over to Wallingford, but amongst the cargo is a paychest destined for the town guard. "I don't feel quite right about carrying it," she says. "Suppose some road-thief hears about it and attacks me on the way. The guard aren't popular. And I could be in the middle. But haulage rates are lower than ever and I need the commission." The other hauliers murmur in agreement.

"That dratted Haulage Guild keep the rates low a-purpose," says one driver. "It's the honest drivers like us that suffer."

Try to arrange a robbery with the freighter...	756
Plan an ambush on the road...	470

304

You have reached Bovingdon Green. Here stand several cottages, a workshop, and a small telegraph station. The village is as small, sleepy and unremarkable as any other Chiltern hamlet. If you have the codeword *Ambidextrous*, turn to **719** immediately.

Visit the widow...	(*Aspidistra*)	452
Ride downhill towards Marlow...		4
Ride up Frieth Lane towards the prison...		325
Head south through the plantation...		786

305

You mount your velosteam and leave sleepy Cookham behind you.

Head to Cookham Bridge...	229
Ride south towards Maidenhead...	107
Travel west towards Cookham Rise...	122

306

Director Short has little time for visitors without appointments. You will need to convince his secretary by making a GALLANTRY roll of difficulty 10, or make her a gift of an **ivory fan** or a **parasol**.

Give her a gift or successful GALLANTRY roll!	369
Failed GALLANTRY roll!	71

307

The strongbox has to be smashed before it can be opened. Between the pieces of bent iron, you find a bag containing **£42 13s** and a **Coalboard accountbook**.

Continue...	Return to your noted passage

308

The wide road brings you up to a row of tall factories, smoke and smog billowing from their stacks. A constables' barrier has been placed across the street here. The officers look at you keenly through binoculars, and you can see one at his station shuffling through papers.

If you are **Wanted by the Constables**...	132
Otherwise...	337

309

Ennis draws his blade and takes up a fencer's posture - ready to defend himself.

Desmond Ennis Esq.		Weapon: **swordstick (PAR 5 GALL+1)**
Parry:	12	
Nimbleness:	7	
Toughness:	3	

Victory!	431
Defeat!	255

310

The road passes through the poverty-stricken hamlet of Wooburn. Women and children, cripples and old men tend meagre gardens and scour the hedgerows. Every able-bodied inhabitant has left for the cities.

Take the road to Bourne End...	703
Head on to Odd's Hill...	177
Ride north to Wooburn Green...	199

311

At first everything seems to be going well. Your velosteam's massive, chunky tyres grip the stone and concrete as long as you stick to the parts freest of streaming weed. A sheet of water rises behind you as you accelerate along the precipice. Suddenly, you feel the Ferguson slip beneath you and the river knocks you into the lower stream. It is all you can do to stay clear of the heavy machine as it is pounded into the chain-linked posts, snapping one entirely in two and coming to a rest on a shallow bank.

You are wet, but unharmed. However, even after a helpful bargee soaks himself to help push your machine to the north bank, your velosteam is badly damaged. Any **food** or **paper objects** such as books or letters you were carrying are also ruined and must be discarded.

To get your velosteam working again, you will need help.

If you are the **Friend of Madame Juste**...   483
If you are the **Friend of the Curtis Brothers**... 581
Otherwise...   496

312

The innkeeper thinks for a moment, then agrees. "Alright. When you come through here next, I'll tell you what you owe. There's not a lot of people would make that offer - or would take her in." Gain the codeword *Aspirin*.

Head back to the main road...   534

313

You ride into the outskirts of High Wycombe. Originally the town straddled the river down in the valley, but as the factories and workshops have grown, sprawling terraces have sprouted on the steep hills either side. Perpetual smog and smoke lingers in the air, the noxious result of a thousand charcoal fires smelting, forging, working. A Constables' checkpoint blocks the road, causing a queue to slow the already crawling traffic. If you are **Wanted by the Constables**, turn to **207**.

Ride into town...   337

314
☐ ☐ ☐

If any of the boxes are empty, put a tick in one. If all three are ticked, turn to **674**.

You find Macready in a low office to the rear of a warehouse. He wears a micro-pneumatist's loupe in one eye and has a shock of grey hair. He looks you up and down. "What do you want?" he asks brusquely. "I'm busy."

Macready can help you lose any **Wanted** statuses - but for a cost. He will need to get you a new CIN - a citizen's identification number - and match your appearance to that. Only someone with a very specific set of skills and connections can manage this - hence Macready's high price. Because he will need to telegraph into the main Maidenhead exchange while concealing the source of his message, he will be encoding his transmission us-

ing the small computation engine behind him. If you have a set of **Livingstone M punchcards** he will take them and charge you **£22** for the new CIN. Otherwise the price **is £50**.

If you can afford his price, you may remove any **Wanted** statuses from your Adventure Sheet.

Leave Macready's den...   594

315

Out of the tiny travelling compartment comes a massive, hirsute mountain of a man chewing on a cigar the thickness of your thumb. "'oo the 'ell are you?" he asks. "You want to take my gear? I'll show yer."

Engineer		Weapon: **club (PAR 4)**
Parry:	8	
Nimbleness:	4	
Toughness:	4	

Victory!	85
Defeat!	90

316

Turning a bend you are forced to slam on your brakes by a figure standing in the middle of the road. It is all you can do to keep control of your velosteam, but the pedestrian is oblivious, her eyes fixed to a pair of heavy binoculars directed at the skies.

"Look at that!" she says in tones of wonder. "It's an Italian Marcozzi 29! The fastest airship in the sky!"

Carry on your way...   575

317

The day of your trial arrives. You are led out of your cell into a courtroom under the sharp stare of Judge Morgan's single, baleful eye. The jury is a complement of rich merchants, military men, women of the Telegraph Guild and others, all people threatened by your way of life. After the prosecution make their case - a strong one, considering your past - you are given one chance to defend yourself.

You will need to make a GALLANTRY roll of difficulty 12, adding 1 to your roll for every level of **legal knowledge** you possess but subtracting 1 for each **Wanted** status that you have.

Successful roll!	365
Failed roll!	184

318

Hurley lock is hidden amongst several narrow, wooded islands, each busy with workshops, warehouses and slip-ways. The main trading zone is on the upstream side of the lock, but you still approach from one of the lower channels. However, you will only be able to unload cargo if you have a **cargo crane** fitted to your boat. If you have spare space, you can buy without restriction: gravity is on your side.

	To buy	To sell
Charcoal	£14	-
Furniture	-	-
Machinery	-	£26
Pottery	£27	£23
Cotton	-	£5
Woollen cloth	£12	£12
Coal	£10	£10
Beer	£17	£16
Wheat	-	£5
Malt	£6	£6
Frozen Meat	-	£12
Ice	-	£6

Head downstream again... 443
Moor up here... 47
Pass through the lock...(**2s** or **Bargee's Badge**) 360

320

After a few discreet questions you knock on a cottage door in a Bourne End backstreet. It is opened by a lank-haired, wicked-looking woman with a glint in her eye. "Come to see what Old Meg can do for you, eh?" she cackles. "Got some lovely things inside. Maybe you've some lovely things for me..." Old Meg deals exclusively in jewellery and stolen goods. To find items to buy you will have to venture elsewhere.

Jewellery	To buy	To sell
locket	-	4s
pocket watch	-	£2
silver ring	-	7s
silver bracelet	-	10s
silver necklace	-	18s
gold ring	-	15s
gold bracelet	-	£1 15s
gold necklace	-	£4
ruby ring	-	£5

Return to Bourne End... 703

321

The workhouse stands on the outskirts of Little Marlow behind a tall brick wall. It is a bleak place where poor people in plain clothes sit around, the children picking oakum apart into shreds, the women, segregated into their own part of the yard, toiling at vats of laundry, the men, all unqualified for work in some way, knocking stones into gravel for the roads. Visitors are not welcome - unless they bring a donation.

Make a donation to the workhouse coffers... (**2s**) 182
Leave the workhouse... 602

322

You make a stop for a short while to dry your clothes from the showers of rain and to give your saddle-sores some respite. However, when you awake, you find that your pockets have been picked. Remove the first two items on your list of **possessions**!

Ride on... 288

323

Mrs Petty is not staying here any longer. The barman informs you that she has left for London. "But she left you this note." He gives you a doubtful look as he passes it over.

Mrs Petty's note reads: "I am taking the information you have given me to my superiors in London. We almost have enough to arrest the ring-leaders of the Compact. Ask for me at the Leopard Inn on the Strand."

Lose the codeword *Ascorbic*.

Return to the parlour... 265

324

And now you sit astride a fast machine, armed, ruthless and shrouded in the dark like a bird of prey in its folded wings. Several wagons and engines pass on the road, but none presents you with a suitable target, until a private steam-carriage with fashionable oriental styling makes its way up the slope. It stops a small distance down the road and you can hear the plummy voice of the passenger berating his enginemen.

"Get that pressure up, Jackson. We should be in Slough by now! Slowly, I say, at the foot and then full steam ahead at the crest!"

The fireman and driver dismount to check the drive chain. The rich young man who must be their employer gets out to look as well. "Get out of the way, Harris.

Look, you're running her on too little pressure. No wonder the drive is slack."

The driver tugs at his forelock. "Begging your pardon, milord, but the pressure's right where it should be for this 'un. She's new and..."

The sound of an angry blow to the face rings through the wood. "How dare you, Jackson," says milord, his voice rising to a fervent pitch. "She's my engine and I'll tell you how to drive her."

It seems this son of privilege has not yet completed his education: you are perfectly placed to teach him a thing or two. All that remains is to choose the manner in which you will deal with him: you can use your natural INGENUITY to try to fool him, your RUTHLESSNESS to terrify him or you can attack him without warning and knock him down.

Trick him...	**195**
Frighten him...	**838**
Launch yourself into him...	**555**

325

The velosteam hums contentedly beneath you up Frieth Road. The thicket of Marlow Common rises on your left, then several reservoirs with their smoking pumps on the right. Roll a dice:

Score 1-2	A wandering minstrel...	**119**
Score 3-4	Barsali's caravan...	**701**
Score 5-6	An empty road...	**288**

326
☐

If the box is empty, tick it now and turn to **176** immediately. If it is ticked and you are the **Friend of the Curtiss Brothers**, turn to **808**. Otherwise, read on.

In the centre of the fairground you are surrounded by the mingled smells of coalsmoke, lubricating oil, frying food and sugary sweets. Shouts of pleasure and delight ring from the swinging Steam Yachts, the Rifle Range, the Big Wheel and the freakshow. As dusk falls the lanterns are lit and the polished engines glow and sparkle.

Pick a pocket...		**391**
Ride the Dive Bomber...	(1s)	**464**
Head to the Rifle Range...	(1s)	**398**
Have your fortune told...	(2s)	**209**
Head to the Curtiss wagon...		**775**
Leave the fair...		**535**

327

The railway is still unrepaired here where you wrought such havoc. However, a team of navvies are at work just a short distance along the track, so perhaps it isn't the best place to hang around.

Ride away east...	**67**
Ride away west...	**646**

328

If your boat is moored at **Cookham (downstream)**, turn to **848**. If **Cookham (upstream)**, turn to **232**.

329

The water rushes over the uneven crest of the weir like molten glass - bright with sunlight, streaked with colour from the water weed and full of power. You manage to maintain your balance and make it across. This route may prove useful when trying to make a getaway: gain the codeword *Amphibious*.

Turn to...	**48**

330

Slam! The Wagtail's bumper smashes into the rear right-hand wheel of Da Silva's heavy steamer, knocking her into Anderson's side. As you brake to control your vehicle's shimmy, then reapply steam pressure, you watch the other two drivers fighting to keep themselves on the road. Anderson skids, then one of his tyres catches in a rut and he spins off the track, swiping Da Silva's vehicle into the hoarding beside him. A moment after you whizz past there is an almighty explosion as one of their boilers bursts, but you cannot look back! Gain three Race Points!

Forge ahead!	**103**

331

"What do you want?" asks the Marvellous Jaffrey. "Are you a highwayperson?"

"Jaffrey! The Marvellous Jaffrey!" You cannot contain yourself. "I worshipped you as a child! Show me that trick you used to do," you say.

"Cards? Is that all you want? Funny thing is, I learnt all my tricks from a chap in prison." You spend a short while sat on the grassy roadside practicing card tricks together and by the time you allow him to leave, you have improved your INGENUITY score by 1.

Ride away...	**394**

332

You manage to make it to Pinkney's Green. Night has fallen and the lights of the Curtiss Steam Fair are shining red and gold over the grass of the common. You steam past the fairground and splash through a puddle, intent on leaving a false trail before doubling back to hide amongst the wagons and engines.

To succeed, you will need to make an INGENUITY roll of difficulty 15, to which you can add 1 for every **possession** you discard on the road. It may prove an expensive way to escape, but lightening your load and distracting your pursuers may buy your freedom.

Successful INGENUITY roll!	**808**
Failed INGENUITY roll!	**207**

333

The river is almost choked with traffic here below Maidenhead. Steam cranes are unloading from long river-lighters heaped high with coal. The black gold is worth a fortune to the engineers, freighters, computation magnates and furnace-men of Maidenhead - small wonder most of the inhabitants burn wood or charcoal in their tiny, back-to-back houses.

Across the river at the export dock, regional products like beer and fashionable furniture are piled into immense pyramids, awaiting transport to London. You may buy a cargo here, as long as you have the capital and the cargo space. If you have the codeword *Actinium* and any Beer as cargo, turn to **938**.

	To buy	To sell
Charcoal	-	£10
Furniture	£24	-
Machinery	£28	£26
Pottery	-	£24
Cotton	-	£5
Woollen cloth	-	£12
Coal	£12	£9
Beer	£19	£18
Wheat	-	£4
Malt	-	£8
Frozen meat	-	£14
Ice	-	£9

Visit the River Union building...	962
Disembark...	507
Unmoor and head downstream...	425
Unmoor and head upstream...	355

334

You carefully creep forward and cut a section of the fence open. It is only a short distance to reach where the chain gang are working.

Turn to...											346

335

If you have the **punchcards (Aramanth A)**, turn to **929** immediately. Otherwise, read on.

The fortunes of the Wethered Brewery are visibly failing. Sheds that were stacked with tuns now stand empty and echoing. Large numbers of workers have been laid off and the smokestacks are cold. If something is not done soon, the local brewery will close for good while the Haulage Guild get rich from carrying machine-brewed ale.

Return to the High Street...					4

336

As you approach your hideout something seems wrong. Snapped branches and the rutted ground imply that other, less careful steam vehicles have come this way. You shift your sword in its scabbard and press on.

Suddenly shots ring out and the noise of an accelerating velosteam approaches. An ambush has been prepared by the Constables, who have tracked you to your lair. Figures in blue serge appear from behind the trees, waving and shouting. You will need to ride well to escape them now!

Make a MOTORING roll of difficulty 10 to escape!

Successful MOTORING roll!						707
Failed MOTORING roll!						255

337

The market town of High Wycombe is flourishing in this age of steam and telegraphy. The local woods are full of furniture makers, woodworkers, charcoal burners and craftsmen whose work is in demand up in London. Investors from the city come here and buy up the land, sending prices rocketing in the region and making many rich. The Oxford Road along the Wye valley is a crucial supply network and the tolls charged by the town council are paying for new roads, new houses and lining many a pocket. It is rumoured that if the freight guilds' stranglehold over parliament can be broken that the railway will reach here within a year. Factories using the water and wood are springing up, together with their rows of hovels and tenements. Warehouses extend along the roads towards Loudwater and West Wycombe, spreading over the cheaper land.

Visit Coulter's bank...							368
Head into the market...						240
Enter the Red Lion Inn...						677
Visit the Freight Yard...						616
Leave town...								203

338

The wagon steams past without hesitating. You have impressed nobody. In fact, once the crew tell of your timidity your reputation will certainly suffer. Lower your RUTHLESSNESS score by 1.

Ride away...								535

339

Mr Penfold's eyes light up as you hand the rock over. "The real thing?" he squeaks. "Marvellous!" Tears come to his eyes. "Here, let me give you something in return." He rummages around and lays a few items out on the counter. You may take one of the following: **deck of marked cards**, **pocket watch**, **bottle of wine**.

Return to the village...						492

340

The driver slams on his brakes in terror. You fling open the door, crying "Your money or your life!"

Inside is a pale, bald figure with his limp hands resting on mounds of paperwork. "Who are you?" he says, turning his blind eyes towards the doorway. "A road thief? What do you want from me?"

Let the blind man go...						148
Rob him...								381

341

Madame Juste sends two of the girls in to help you tend your wounds. They carefully peel back your blood-crusted clothes and wipe clean the cuts and bruises. Once bandaged up again they even anoint you with perfume before leaving you to sleep on the couch. For every **Wound** that you remove, increase your number of **Scars** by 1 and check for **intimidating scars.**

If you have the codeword *Astrakhan*, *Arthropod* or
		Apogee, turn to...						466
Otherwise...								91

342

As you are speeding along the road to Bourne End, your **hat** suddenly flies off! Pulling on the brakes, you see it dangling on the end of a long line, hooked by a small boy high in the hedge. He scampers away and is out of sight before you have a chance to catch him. It seems your hat is gone for good!

Ride on to Bourne End...   703

343

In the midst of the mass of vehicles, herds and hand-wagons is a long train of mixed freight towed by a splendid red and yellow striped engine. A brass wheel mounted proudly on the front of the boiler indicates that the owner is a member of the Co-Operative of Freight Hauliers and Road Transportation.

Ride straight past...   337
Sabotage the engine...
    (guildsman's medallion)   754

344

Constables posted at the bridge are checking Identity Cards. When your turn comes, your number is near the top of their wanted list. The Constable at the roadside goes for his holstered repeating pistol.

The velosteam leaps forward and you charge off the roadside and crash through a fence into a boatyard. An overturned barge hull bridges a deep pit, so you steer the velosteam over the slick wood and into the meadow on the other side. Shots ring out as the Constables open fire. You must ride between the riverside willows to confuse their aim. Make a NIMBLENESS roll of difficulty 9 to dodge beneath the branches as you speed along.

Successful NIMBLENESS roll!   386
Failed NIMBLENESS roll!   255

345

To cut a piece of luggage free, you must make a NIMBLNEESS roll of difficulty 9. You can add 1 to your roll if you possess a **grappling iron**, and 1 more if you have a **net**.

Successful NIMBLESNESS roll!   223
Failed NIMBLENESS roll!   188

346

As you approach the chain gang, a loud explosion rocks the camp. Barsali has succeeded in causing a boiler to burst. The resulting smoke and steam cover your final approach to the gang. "Come this way," you shout, "If you value your freedom!"

The men and women pick up their chains and begin to jog heavily towards the fence. Constables are running in the opposite direction, towards where you can hear Barsali hallooing. You help the prisoners through the fence and into the wood, mounting your velosteam to draw off the pursuers and to allow Barsali to find his son.

It is several hours later, after you have lost and confused your pursuers, that you make your way back to Barsali's caravan. He has his arm around his boy and laughs to see you approach.

"Glorious exploit, my friend!" he crows. "My son is free - thanks to you. We fired up our little forge here and split the chains off every prisoner of those vile Constables. What an exploit!" Gain **two Solidarity Points** and you are now the **Friend of Barsali**.

"We cannot stay around here long," he says. "We'll go travelling a while. But when we return, look for us in Maidenhead thicket."

Ride away...   377

347

You leap aboard, weapons ready. The fireman hangs back, but the driver is ready to fight. She snatches up a heavy coal shovel and lays about you!

Driver		Weapon: **shovel (PAR 5)**
Parry:	7	
Nimbleness:	2	
Toughness:	4	

Victory!	416
Defeat!	74

348

The vicar approaches you. "Your gift is appreciated," he says smoothly. "Very appreciated. Do you have any idea how much it costs, daily, to keep this place running? Coal for the heating furnace, water, gas, then the wages of the masons and the carpenters who are still toiling over our heads? The parish really don't appreciate the cost of a place like this, even before you factor in my salary, my staff, the cost of entertaining and maintaining good relationships with the nobles on behalf of the town. And the monthly gift of food to the parish poor as well."

"So the gift doesn't go directly to the needy?"   **237**
"I've been dreaming of my sins." (*Apprehend*)   **98**

349

Your gold wins you an unexpected acquittal. Despite your enemies' rage, you are released, reunited with your confiscated velosteam and dismissed. It seems prudent to put distance between yourself and the officers of the court, so you do not stop until you are far away. At least you are no longer **Wanted by the Constables**. However, if you have other **Wanted** statuses, they are unaffected.

Ride away...   **513**

350

You are on the road a little way south of Bourne End. The River Thames dominates the valley here, its meadows and locks, the cool river breeze and the smoke of the distant steam barges.

Ride towards Bourne End...   **703**
Skirt the town and head west...   **408**
Head south towards Cookham Bridge...   **229**

351

The road winds up from Cookham Dean to Winter Hill, between cottages, smoking workshop chimneys, and old ponies out to grass. Passing traction engines pulling trailers of hay and firewood, you speed up the slope and are struck by the sudden view of the countryside around.

Travel down the hill to Bisham...   **737**
Head to Marlow Bridge...   **277**

352

☐

If the box is empty, tick it and read on. If it is already ticked, turn to **944** immediately.

Abbot Sneer sends a monk to fetch you to his study. "I know who you are," he says, peering over the rim of his half-moon glasses. "You are that ruthless and godless highwayman, are you not? I have a job which I would not sully my brethren with, lest it disturb them."

"What do you mean?"

"The Abbey has tenants, yes? Some of them are proving stubborn. We need to move a family on, so that we can develop the land. Will you assist me by making it plain that they must move or risk harm? They have somewhere to go - it is not as though you will be making them homeless. And you will be paid."

"I will not be your bully."   **742**
"I can help you."   **696**

353

You continue over the high ground, heading south along the edges of fields. Roll a dice to see what you discover:

Score 1-2   A wanderer...   **1006**
Score 3-6   Nothing of interest...   **139**

354

Life in prison is a strange mixture of the mundane and the ridiculous, coloured by the severity of your restriction. Every day the gates open to let pie-sellers and washerwomen in to serve those prisoners with any cash - or credit. And one of these washerwomen seems quite taken by your story.

"You don't deserve to be here," she croons. "The high road is the place for one such as you!"

The opportunity to swap clothes with her and escape with her massive basket of dirty laundry is too good to pass. However, although she is impressionable she will face a severe punishment when your escape is discovered. Add your **Solidarity Points** to your GALLANTRY score to convince her: if the total is 16 or greater, you succeed.

Success!   **385**
Failure!   **227**

355

Beyond Maidenhead the character of the traffic changes: fewer working boats and more and more pleasure-seekers. The reach below Cliveden and around Boulter's Lock is a fashionable place for the upper classes to holiday from their labours in London - such labours as they have!

Steam on to Boulter's Lock...   **363**

356

A fast steam tricycle tears around the bend, its bell jangling, armed Constables hanging on the outside rails. It seems that someone has tipped them off! Mount up and make a quick decision - how will you attempt to escape them?

Lose them over Harleyford Bridge...(*Alluring*) **52**
Hide amongst the Steam Fair...

    (Friend of the Curtiss Brothers)   **332**
Take the Boyn Hill track...   (*Abstruse*)   **193**
Head for Cookham Weir...   (*Amphibious*) **16**
Ride into Cliff Wood...   **249**
Steam west and outrun them...   **388**

357

Your adventures on the road have weakened you. When you awake from a swoon, you discover that **all your money** and **possessions** have been taken from you, and your trusty velosteam is nowhere to be seen... Whether you like it or not, your time as a Steam Highwayman is finished. Turn to the **Epilogue** to discover whether you left any legend behind you.

358

"Welcome back," says the Doctor. "More scratches into your living flesh? More miracles for me to perform with your perforated body? I think I'll have drink now."

For each wound that you want healed, the doctor will charge you **15s**. However, his treatment does not result in your **Wounds** becoming **Scars** - you can simply erase them from your sheet. If you have a **bottle of whisky**, turn to **269**.

Leave the surgery...	**684**

359

You ask around discreetly for Comrade Robin and eventually find a haulier who knows someone by that name. "The wheelman? Yes, he's up here sometimes, but he took a job down to Maidenhead. Have to ask for him round there."

Return to the Freight Yard...	**616**

360

The roaring of the long weir infills the heavy breathing of your boat's steam engine, the whistles of the lock-keepers and the occasionally croak of the riverside crows. Along the banks, riverkeepers lop the osiers, alders and water-loving willows that have seeded along the bank or sprung from a lodged piece of driftwood. All life seeks to continue, it seems, but the particular tenacity of a stick of green willow to regenerate into a river-slowing tree, blocking traffic and creating its own shady shallows, despite being snapped, chewed and stripped and thrown into the stream - that tops all the determination of men.

The riverkeepers have their barge and their steam-axes, but they also have a job for life keeping the banks free, with opponents so vigorous.

Head to Freebody's Yard...	**611**
Sail to Hurley Lock...	**988**
Sail to Medmenham...	**846**
Head upstream...	**964**

361

The drinkers are toasting the success of the rascal airship pirate Captain Coke. "What a man! He tears down in his swift Marcozzi and threatens to blast those rich beggars out of the sky!"

"He was flying north of Henley last season," says one drinker. "I wouldn't go up in one of those gasbags with him at large."

Return to the High Street...	**4**

362

Do you have any of the following codewords:

Adoption? Turn to...	**376**
Astrakhan? Turn to...	**805**
Abapical? Turn to...	**392**
The **griffin cufflink**? Turn to...	**150**
None of the above...	**675**

363

You are forced to keep to a narrow goods channel most of the way, while the main part of the river is reserved for pleasure craft. As a result you chug along within easy earshot of several bargees and pick up a few tips about cargo on the river: the monks at Bisham Abbey have their own ice-house, making it a profitable cargo for anyone with a refrigeration machine on board.

The lock-master has reserved most of the lockspace for the pleasure-boats, whose skippers will tip and spend money at the pleasure gardens. Consequently there is quite a jam here beneath the island while you wait your turn. Above the lock stands a fine hotel with a long veranda, flooded with sounds of music, dancing and eating. You can also see a gaudy parade of shops selling expensive goods.

Moor here...	**497**
Pass through the lock...	
(**2s** or **Bargee's Badge**)	**463**
Return back downriver...	**437**

364

The heavy rain sluices off the high fields and fills the ditches. Before you realise it, you are in the middle of a torrent. It will take careful riding to come through this! You must make a MOTORING roll of difficulty 9 to pass, adding 1 if you have **off-road tyres**.

Successful MOTORING roll!	**650**
Failed MOTORING roll!	**142**

365

Your eloquence manages to win you some sympathy from the jury and clemency from the judge. You are sentenced to a year's imprisonment in the nearby Royal Penitentiary, but the sight of your stoic, implacable face under sentencing impresses the public in the galleries. Newspaper cameras flash: you are now a **Famed Lawbreaker** and may add 1 to your GALLANTRY and RUTHLESSNESS scores. You must discard any **weapons**, **guns** or **tools**, but you may keep your purse.

Clapped in irons...   274

366

You pull over by a signpost in the road. A straight, well-made road runs due west, marked Bourne End. A tall brick wall runs beside the road, enclosing Cliveden house, and a little way along is the rear gate.

Ride to Cliveden rear gate...	21
Take the road towards Bourne End...	408
Steam on south through the wood...	612
Leave this region...	*The Reeking Metropolis* 87

367

"Really quite impressive," says the official. "You stand a fair chance with that machine. Maybe I'll be making a wager." He hands you the **time trial certificate** you need.

Lord Dashwood is very pleased. "Well driven. I knew I had chosen well. Meet me back at the garage when you're ready." He drives off in the Wagtail in a cloud of steam.

Turn to...   642

368

Coulter's Bank is entered down several dingy steps on a narrow side-street at an awkward angle to the marketplace. The low door is guarded by a pair of ill-matched guards in antiquated uniforms and what little light filters through the slits of barred windows is quickly absorbed by the troglodytic atmosphere. Nonetheless, Coulter's is the region's richest and longest-established bank.

If you have the codeword *Forceful*...	644
If you have the codeword *Augury*...	32
Make a deposit or withdrawal...	596
Plan to rob the bank...	724
Return to the High Street...	337

369

Director Short lives up to his name: he is a small, round man, but he has fierce eyes and a hard waxed moustache shaped like a buffalo's horns. He is looking at an extensive wall-map as you enter.

"Got to find a way," he mutters. "Takings are down for another quarter. That wretched Freight Co-operative, they're to blame." He notices you. "Hmmm. What would you do, in my place? Why you'd go to war, wouldn't you? Yes, you would. I thought as much." He explains that the rivalry between his own guild and the Co-operative of Freight Hauliers and Road Transportation has escalated to outright hostility. "And all the time they're cutting into our business. What we need is to convince the public that the Freight Co-operative are not the safe option. Certainly not as safe as our wagons. If several of their road-trains were to have accidents, maybe get stopped by highwaymen, then I'd be very grateful to anybody who could help that happen. Am I being blunt enough? Burn those blighters and rob their passengers and I'll see you're made very rich. If you dare. God knows I would, if I weren't the ruddy director."

As you are bustled out to make way for the next visitor, Director Short flings something after you. It is a **Guildsman's medallion**. "If you show them this you won't have to deal with my fool of a secretary next time!"

Leave the compound...   282

370

The road passes through a tiny hamlet on the edge of the Thicket. Before long, you leave the silent cottages behind you and roar around the side of the steep hill to join the Henley road.

Ride on...   662

371
□

If the box is empty, tick it now and read on. If it is already ticked, turn to **646** immediately.

You pull over by a man in military clothes resting on a tree-stump. A crutch leans beside him and his left trouser leg is pinned up. "Nice wheels," he says cheerily. "Got room for a little one? To Piddington?"

Give the man a lift...	162
Take him part-way...	251
Offer him a couple of shillings for the bus...	(2s) 485
Ride on...	646

372

The cows do not slow down and charge straight into you. You are knocked off the velosteam and trampled by their remarkably sharp hooves. Gain 1 **Damage Point** and 2 **Wounds**. When they are gone you drag yourself up and check yourself over.

If you have five **Wounds**...	**90**
If your velosteam is **beyond repair**...	**250**
Otherwise...	**280**

373

The port parlour is quiet and stuffy. You get talking to a merchant who tells you that if you are looking for work, freight wagons travelling from the Golden Ball Inn are always looking for protection from highwaymen. Outside, rain spatters the glass. It looks like it will be a dirty night.

If you have the codeword *Afterthought*, turn to **820** immediately.

Return to the High Street...   **4**

374

The barman is not pleased. "We'll take what you owe, one way or another." He whistles once more and pair of workmen with shovel handles appear at the door. "Help me beat the loose change out of this blighter's pockets," he says.

Barman and friends	Weapon: **clubs (PAR 4)**
Parry:	9
Nimbleness:	5
Toughness:	9

Victory!	**199**
Defeat!	**427**

375

The crying mother refuses to take any comfort. She savagely spits out her vengeful cries. "The master of Hedsor. I worked there for seven year. And he turned me out, with the babe only a month old. I had nowhere to go. He killed my baby! He killed my child."

Can the nobles of the land do as they wish? Will no-one right these wrongs?

If you have the codeword *Adoption*, turn to **608**.

Swear vengeance on the master of Hedsor...	**69**
Leave her...	**703**

376

You are welcomed by Judge Hector's servants. They park your velosteam in the engine sheds, clean it up, and re-fuel it. You may repair it yourself here if you have sufficient skill.

ENGINEERING score		Materials
Critical damage...	10	**welding tools**
Serious damage...	8	**high pressure valve**
Minor damage...	6	**heavy wrench**

Inside the house you are warmly greeted by your adoptive father. He is becoming increasingly frail with every visit, but his sternness is by no means diminished. You are shown to your room, where you may leave possessions and cash if you wish, and then later called down for dinner.

You rest here for a while, enjoying the sumptuous food and soft sheets, but it is not a place you can stay for ever. The road calls. Your **Wounds** all have time to heal, but each will become a **scar** telling its own dumb story. For each new **scar**, roll two dice and on a roll of 11 or 12 you have gained an **intimidating scar (RUTH+1)**. If you have the codeword *Arthropod, Astrakhan* or *Apogee*, turn to **711**.

Leave Hedsor house...   **366**

377

Coming out from between the trees, you suddenly arrive at the top of the top of a steep drop looking down over the Thames. The view over the valley shows you Marlow, Little Marlow and Bourne End, the high ground opposite of Handy Cross. Far to the East you can make out the hills around Cliveden house. Plumes of smoke rise from every village and town, every road junction and every roadway where steam vehicles pass. If you have the codeword *Anniversary*, turn to **175**.

| Head to nearby Cookham Dean... | **563** |
| Head further on to Cookham Rise... | **575** |

378

The gyspy studies your palm, then looks into your eyes. "Hmmm. You are untouched by your past, so it is hard to read your future. Beware! If you do not dare to build friendships with those who offer friendship to you, then you will certainly die alone on the road. I can see your velosteam in the ditch on the Marlow road, its wheels spinning."

Turn to...   113

379

The Honourable Doira Marchpane sneers at you. "How desperately unfunny," she drawls. "How too, too sick-making."

You are grabbed by the hotel porters and thrown in the lock. A sharp blow on the head as you fly through the air means you must gain 1 **Wound**, and in addition any **paper objects** you possess must be discarded, ruined by the water (**tickets, books, letters**).

| If you have five **Wounds**... | 102 |
| Otherwise... | 94 |

380

Colonel Snappet accepts you as an under-artificer in his laboratory. You are put straight to work fixing steam machinery and creating some complex copper moulds. "What are these for?" you ask another artificer.

He looks at you through narrowed eyes. "Don't ask me no questions and I won't tell you no lies," he says. "The Colonel's got his own plans for bringing the world on, so he has. But it's more that you or I should know."

The work is hard and long, but you persevere and over several weeks you befriend a telegraph clerk. He confides in you: "Some time ago he went out with the airship in the night, came back with an old man, an inventor. Had him down in the cellar for weeks, drawing this, making that, but tortured him so badly that he wasn't able to do much any more. Then he disappeared ."

The clerk is disgusted at what he has been drawn into. He tells you about other secrets he knows. "The Colonel is paranoid about his communications - and with reason! He's been accepting bribes and had the last Mayor of High Wycombe murdered. Then there was Alice de Lacey who he threw out of his airship - her family are still looking for her." He gives you a **telegraph transcript**. "This proves everything. You need to get it out of here and bring him down."

That night the clerk disappears. It seems clear that the Colonel has discovered his treachery - and you will be next. The house is as hard to leave as it was to enter, but late that afternoon you manage to get away, find your hidden velosteam and put the house behind you.

Confronting Colonel Snappet will be difficult. He is always surrounded by armed men and prefers to be out by night. You will have to find him alone somewhere and at your mercy, to untangle this tale.

| Ride east... | **786** |
| Ride west... | **534** |

381

"You'd take from a blind man, would you? May God strike you down!" spits the pale man.

You can take his purse of **£6 4s** as well as a **gold ring** and a **Coal Board accountbook**. You are now **Wanted by the Coal Board** as a result of your robbery.

Ride on towards Wheeler End...   137

382

You heat a canteen of water over the little fire and use it to wash the dried blood off your limbs. Strips of clean bedsheet make satisfactory **bandages** - and if you want to take some with you, add them to your possessions. For every **Wound** that you remove, increase your number of **Scars** by 1. In addition, for every **Scar** roll two dice: a roll of 10 or above indicates that you have gained an **intimidating scar (RUTH+1)** which can be added into your other notes.

Return to your room...   53

383

Dr Smollett looks at you as he climbs off the velosteam. "I won't ask what the Constables want with you. You promise much but you don't deliver on your word. It's all too common nowadays." He marches away up the hill into the dark night. Erase the codeword *Afterthought*.

Return to West Wycombe...   **492**

384

"Here we drink our own Marlow beer," says the landlord as he pulls you a pint. "Brewed just behind the High Street. Wethered's Thames Bitter. You'll enjoy this."

The beer has a hoppy aroma, but a sweet, rounded taste. There is a nutty richness given by the toasting of the malt but the colour is pale. What magic of brewery has achieved that?

The locals tell you about the woman who has taken on the ferry by the Bounty, west of Bourne End. Apparently it is the only river crossing that the Constables overlook.

If you are **Wanted by the Constables**, turn to **248**.

Return to the parlour...   **265**

385

After swapping clothes with the red-faced washerwoman and leaving her in your accustomed cell, you haul the massive basket of dirty laundry towards the gate. Choosing your time to leave carefully, you manage to mumble and gurn your way through, keeping your mop cap low and mimicking the woman's country drawl.

To your amazement, the Constables who confiscated your velosteam have delivered it to the prison, and it stands in the yard beside the entrance. The laundry is tumbled into the moat and, hitching up the skirts of your new pinafore, you climb aboard your beloved machine and speed away! You may now add **Escaped from gaol** to your heroic deeds!

Make your getaway!   **304**

386

After a fast ride over fields, through woods and along the lanes you successfully lose your pursuers. Roll a dice to see where you reach:

Score 1	Horton Wood	190
Score 2	Wooburn	310
Score 3-4	Flackridge Heath	50
Score 5-6	Cliveden Corner	366

387

The Wagtail is ready. Its aluminium glows, its wood gleams, the pistons of its high-pressure motor are synchronised to a fraction of a second, the titanium alloy hidden within the engine, forged into piping, rods and wheels. On the front of the bonnet stands a raked figurehead of a swooping bird, a silken scarf swathed about the stand. Dashwood addresses his mechanics and helpers, Harris and yourself.

"We have created a marvellous thing. The Wagtail is going to be faster than any steam carriage ever built - and the machinery bearing the imprint of your own hands will be flying down the racetrack, showing your own abilities, the manifestation of your minds. I am honoured to be your sponsor, but this is your machine as much as it is mine. How does mere money express ownership, anyway?"

After toasts, bonuses for the mechanics and the foreman, the team roll the Wagtail onto the bed of a long trailer and swathe it in canvas. A picked team of mechanics, Harris, Dashwood and yourself will travel to the racetrack at a place near Whittlebury, a day's journey to the North. There you will compete in the Spenser Cup, the internationally renowned competition for the fastest steam vehicles on four wheels.

Turn to...   **5**

388

You tear down the slope, banking hard at the bends, your rear tyre kicking up gravel and dirt, cut across a meadow and make for the Henley road. Your pursuers however, are just as fast. Unless you have another trick up your sleeve they will surround and capture you. If you have the codeword *Alba*, turn to **146**. Otherwise, it looks like the game is up: turn to **207**.

389

Marlow Bridge is a fine suspension bridge crossing the Thames between two tall, iron towers. It sees many a road-train lumber over the river from the Maidenhead road, many a steam-carriage speed recklessly across, and barges, barges, barges chug their way beneath, bringing grain or coal or wood down to the capital.

Ride into Marlow...	**4**
Head towards Bisham village...	**737**
Take the lane through Cliff Wood...	**377**

390

The servants bring you hot water and clean bandages with which to treat your cuts and bruises. For every **Wound** that you remove, increase your number of **Scars** by 1. In addition, for every **Scar** roll two dice: a roll of 10 or above indicates that you have gained an intimidating scar (**RUTH+1**) which can be added into your other notes.

If you have the codeword *Arthropod*, *Astrakhan* or *Apogee*, turn to...   **440**
Otherwise...   **394**

391

The crowds are a good place to dip into the pockets and purses of the passers-by - if any place is good to do such a thing. Make an INGENUITY roll to see what you find.

Score <6   Caught!   773
Score 7-8   Steal **9s**
Score 9-10   Steal **13s** and a **silver bracelet**
Score 11-12   Steal **6s** and a **locket**
Score 13-14   Steal a **pocket watch**
Score 15+   Caught!   773

If you manage to escape capture, you must leave the fair before people become suspicious: turn to **535**.

392

The judge is disappointed that you have found no news of his son. "Will he never be found?" he wails. "Try again, I beg you. Scour the land - and the skies. The airfield at Rotherfield Greys—surely they will know something of him? He cannot simply have disappeared!"

Leave him to his misery...   **408**

393

Madame Pastelengro closes her eyes and shudders. "I see a ballroom, filled with lords and ladies. I see smoke and flames and a great conflagration. I see you standing amidst the rubble and in your hand is a clockwork bird... The bird flaps its wings and casts shadows on the walls as you hold it up to the flames. In the shadows there is writing—but indistinct and unclear."

She opens her eyes and gives you a wink. "That's all for a florin, darling."

Return to the fair...   **326**

394

The Golden Ball Inn sits back from the busy road. Steamers, freight wagons and even light dirigibles are parked outside. A row of enginesheds is topped by rooms to let and the parlour is always full of good cheer and even better food. If you wish to take a room here, pay **£3** and tick the box below.

Chat to the barman...   **794**
Buy drinks for the drivers and steamsmen...(**8s**) **523**
☐ Go to your room here...   **231**
Leave the pub...   **725**

395

Inside the World's End it seems to be even smokier than the smog-ridden streets of the city outside. Cigar smoke and the fumes of gas lights mingle above your head in the garishly-lit hall. Posters advertise upcoming performances and projections and attendants offer you snacks, drinks and all manner of treats - all at fantastic prices.

Head to the bar...   **978**
Take a ticket for the show...   (**1s**)   **641**
Leave the music hall...   **594**

396
☐

If the box is empty, put a tick in it and turn to **81** immediately. If it is already ticked, read on.

Here at the freight yard you mingle with the engineers and hauliers and keep your ears alert for news of departures and arrivals. Soon you have information about a variety of journeys being made in the locality.

There are a few tools and pieces of machinery for sale here, in an unofficial, unlicensed kind of way. If you would like to purchase any or sell your own, make the adjustment to your possessions and purse before leaving. An engineer here is also willing to fix your damaged velosteam - for a price.

Tools	To buy	To sell
heavy wrench	**18s**	-
welding tools	**£1 10s**	-
copper pipe	**6s**	-
high pressure valve	**18s**	-

Velosteam Customisations	To buy	
muffled exhaust	**£3 15s**	

Repairs	To buy	
Per **damage point**	**£2**	

Leave the freight yard...   **703**

397

You explain why you've come, but Harris shakes her head. "Dashwood's already made me an offer. I've got too much work here to waste my time on playthings." She shows you the design she is currently working on. "I need to redesign these valves for our main haulage engine. That's my priority right now."

Offer to help complete her work...   620
Resolve to kidnap her...   702

398

The little compressed air-rifle you are given looks unlikely to do anything more than puff air, but if you hit one of the targets you are promised a prize from behind the bench. Make an ACCURACY roll to see what you win - using the **air rifle (ACC 6)**.

Score 10 or less   Win nothing
Score 11-13   Win a **tin of fruit**
Score 14-15   Win a **silver bracelet**
Score 15 or more   Win a **chess set**

Return to the fair...   326

399

Standing beneath the broad boughs of the oak, you are spared the worst of the downpour. Then there is a giant flash and an ear-splitting crash. You have been struck by lightning! Gain a **Wound** and reduce your NIMBLENESS by 1.

If you have five Wounds...   90
Ride away when the rain stops...   650

400

The Southern Sour is the drink of choice here: a strong rum and lime concoction straight out of the Confederate Caribbean. It is not inaccurately named - the reduced lime essence pulls your face out of shape even as you try to sip it. You overhear several young men boasting of their intention to head down to the Red Lantern later, to complete their debauch with an opium pipe.

The crowd swells as punters arrive for the evening's floorshow. They have come to watch the flying skirts of the girls, to drink, to enjoy the music and the freedom from their engine-driven lives.

Return to the bar...   978
Leave the World's End...   395

401

You tell the director all about your recent exploits at the expense of his rivals. "Excellent, excellent," he says gleefully. "I am so very glad to hear of it. Well, you won't find me ungrateful." Lose the codeword *Aorta* and roll a dice to see how he rewards you:

Score 1-2   **£10** in cash
Score 3   a **shotgun (ACC6)**
Score 4   improve your ENGINEERING score by 1
Score 5   a waterproof **cloak** and **a skeleton key**
Score 6   a **Letter of introduction**

Turn to...   282

402

The tenements of Maidenhead along Blackamoor Lane and Ray Moor Road are desperate places. Filth and ordure lie in the narrow streets between dilapidated shop fronts and dirty doss-house doors.

Visit the Red Lantern...   477
Enter Bird Court...   926
Return to Maidenhead...   594

403

A tall lady in a grey dress stands before you. "Audrey," she says to her maid. "Give this person whatever they ask to make them go away."

"I'm afraid I won't be bought off, ma'am," you say.

"Heavens! I am addressed directly!"

In the end you manage to take a **silver neck-lace**, an **ivory fan** and **£5 2s** without having to search her yourself.

Ride away...   737

404

A rest is in order after all your travels and travail. Sometime in the night, however, a familiar face appears in your dreams. The figure has a hold on you, somehow, as they are dead and you know that you are responsible for them. They repeatedly ask you for mercy...

Waking in a cold sweat, there has been little benefit to the rest. Gain the codeword *Apprehend* if you do not already have it.

Return to your room...   645

405

A dense stand of holly provides a good place to wait. Dusk comes early beneath the shadow of the boughs and you check your velosteam is up to pressure and ready to head out onto the road, should you need to make a quick getaway. Roll two dice to see what you encounter.

Score 2-4	Constables approach!	**73**
Score 5-8	Steam carriage spotted!	**115**
Score 9-12	A long wait...	**267**

406

Lord Dashwood greets you warmly. "We need three more things to have our best chance of victory in the race. **Pneumatic tyres** to improve the handling, a **time trial certificate** issued by the race organisers and a small matter of sponsorship. Nobody races without a lady's colours, so I will invite you to come with me to the Cliveden Ball." He hands you a **Formal Invitation**. "You will need this to be granted entry - as well as your very best outfit."

Start your preparations...   **298**

407

You hear many tales while you are in prison, but none to match the story of Toothy Braddock's Cornish gold, buried beneath the altar of a ruined clifftop chapel.

Turn to...   **227**

408

You steam down the slope between rows of dark trees and find yourself at a large barn and a signpost just beneath Hedsor House.

Take a look at Hedsor House...	**362**
Head on to Bourne End...	**457**
Try the road south-west...	**366**

409

Inside the Bounty there are several parties of drinkers, families eating the famed picnic fare and all manner of travellers. There is even a posh parlour where city folk eat crustless sandwiches. If you have a **large pike**, turn to **935**.

Buy a drink...	(**1s**)	**589**
Leave the Bounty...		**444**

410

You open the regulator fully and accelerate into the tight bend. The Wagtail hasn't been tried like this before and the driver of the Coal Board steamer flashes you a look of confused anger through his driving goggles as you appear to bear directly down on him. At the last moment you haul on the steering lever and apply the brake, skidding just within the larger steamer's turning circle and pointing uphill again. The rear wheels bite into the mud of the racetrack and you are off again! Gain a Race Point!

Accelerate down the straight...   **424**

411

Temple Lock is not a Union Lock: it is privately owned by the monks of Bisham Abbey, who charge some of the highest tolls on the river for the use of their water and machinery. They also have a small trading post here, but most of their needs are met from their own estates. However, their beer is rightly famous and some of the most profitable cargo on the river: the further you can carry it, the more it will be worth. They also trade in furniture made in their workshops in Temple and the farms nearby.

	To buy	To sell
Charcoal	£14	-
Furniture	£29	-
Machinery	-	-
Pottery	-	£23
Cotton	£5	£5
Woollen cloth	-	£12
Coal	£12	£10
Beer	£16	£16
Wheat	£5	£5
Malt	-	£6
Frozen meat	-	£12
Ice	-	£6

Pass through the lock... (**4s** or **Abbey Ribbon**)	745
Return upstream...	487

412

If you have the **titanium alloy**, turn to **831**. Otherwise, the Butler sends you on your way. "Milord is occupied. Come back another time."

Return to West Wycombe...   **492**

413

You plummet towards the night-time river and plunge into the depths. Mercifully you have hit one of the deeper spots and the water absorbs your momentum with a massive splash. On the surface again, you are just in time to see the *Nevaeh* strike the hillside to the south, first crumpling like an eggshell, then rippling with flame as the gas lights. A resounding explosion echoes across the valley.

Then all is dark again. You swim ashore and lay out your possessions to dry. The **pocket book** is safe within a watertight gut wallet and is completely unharmed. It contains notes to many of Snappet's nefarious schemes, including the notes of Professor Benner's torture and interrogation.

The Professor has been imprisoned in Stonor, north of Henley, within easy reach of the Colonel's airships. Whether you will find him alive or dead there, only time will tell.

Your adventure has exhausted you. A kindly farmer takes you in and you rest with him and his wife for several days while you recover. Remove any **Wounds** and convert them into **Scars**. Then, one bright morning, you hear a familiar sound and look out onto the road to see a Cliveden footman riding your velosteam.

"Milord heard that you were staying here," explains the footman. "And he could not countenance keeping your machine. Also, he sends you his thanks for ridding him of Colonel Snappet at last."

The footman soon hitches a lift back to Cliveden and the generous farmers refuse to take anything for their care. So once again you head out on the road, ready to see what adventures await.

Turn to...   **289**

414

A woman does an impression of a solemn priest, much to the amusement of the company. "Exactly how Abbot Sneer walks!" chortles one. When you ask who he means, you are told about the rich Abbot of Bisham Abbey. "Practically rules around here. They own half the farmland. Does anyone see the benefit of their munificence? No! Might as well have the Coal Board or some other grasping corporation as landlords. You'd never know Sneer was meant to be a Christian."

Return to the High Street...   **4**

415

"Halt that engine and surrender yourselves!" Your cry rings through the woodland and, whether it is something about the way you look or the weapons you brandish, the steam wagon in front of you grinds to a halt.

"Don't harm us!" cries the fireman.

"Don't be a ninny," replies the driver, cuffing her mate. "What will harming us serve? It's the money this'uns after."

Roll a dice to see what you can take from them:

Score 1-2   **£1 8s** and a **gold ring**
Score 3-4   **£2 6s** and a **cloak**
Score 5-6   **£1 3s** and a **pocket watch**

Leave them...   **535**

416

You manage to overcome the driver. Her fireman flees into the woods, leaving you with the loot. You gather a few coins (**3s**) from the driver and the **strongbox** from the cab of the locomotive. This is not the place to open it: you may either do that at a camp or a workshop. However, you will now be **Wanted by the Constables** unless you have a **cloak** or **mask** of some kind to disguise yourself.

Ride away...   **546**

417

Your calculations lead you to a ditch with an old pollard willow that has fallen for the last time. Its rotten trunk is collapsing and in the soil beneath its roots is a strange, hollow flint shaped like an egg. Inside the stone is a handful of ancient gold coins marked with a stylised horse. Who says there is no truth to rainbow gold? The coins are worth **£12**. If you choose to keep them apart from your money pouch, mark them on your inventory as **treasure trove**. It may be that a museum or collector will pay you even more highly for them.

Continue on your way...   **67**

418

Barsali perks up. "You will? I knew I could trust you." He tells you where he last saw the Constables and their wagon and you set off immediately, with the gypsy perched on the back of the velosteam. "What a fine way to travel," he grins.

The Constables have set up a temporary compound on the outskirts of Cookham. Barsali's son, Sandy, can be seen chained together with several others, breaking rocks for the road.

"I can provide a distraction," says Barsali. "A nice little fire in their wood store, maybe? Can you get through the fence and lead him away?"

Sneak forward and cut the fence...

(**wirecutters**)	**334**
Climb the fence and rush the guards...	**625**

419

As you ride onto the bridge, the constables posted at the northern end let out a shout. You have been recognised! You accelerate off the bridge and down the road to the south, but sirens and the whirring hiss of velosteams can be heard in hot pursuit. You must attempt to lose the constables and make off into the countryside.

Lose them over Harleyford Bridge...

(*Alluring*)	**52**
Hide amongst the Steam Fair...	
(**Friend of the Curtiss Brothers**)	**332**
Take the Boyn Hill track... (*Abstruse*)	**193**
Head for Cookham Weir... (*Amphibious*)	**16**
Ride into Cliff Wood...	**249**
Steam west and outrun them...	**388**

420

How many years was it that you toiled for the Haulage Guild? To answer that, you would need to know your age, and even that is hidden from you. Told that you were born to indentured labourers, all you have known is the loading and unloading, the fueling and mending, the road-ruts and the turnpike camps of the freight-wagoneers. Yes, you know the roads and their ways - you understand the manners of the hauliers, their customs, their engines, their deals. You can fix, drive and tune any steam engine on the road. But what else do you know of the world? And what else were you ever to learn, in such a condition? Nothing.

So you ran away. Somewhere, there is an engine-driver still cursing you and a velosteam-rider still puzzling over the theft of their machine. But there is opportunity for one such as you: you have heard tell of the Spenser Cup - the prize for the fastest steam car in the land - and it must be yours. What a deed that will be!

You have in your possession a **blunderpistol (ACC 6)**, a **sabre (PAR 6)** and a **grappling iron**. Your ability scores are:

RUTHLESSNESS	4
ENGINEERING	5
MOTORING	6
INGENUITY	3
NIMBLENESS	3
GALLANTRY	3

Turn to... **324**

421

"Excuse me," you say, "I can't help but overhear. The Haulage Guild are pressurising you?"

The manager laughs bitterly. "We might look like a successful brewery," she says, "But we're on the ropes. The Haulage Guild are trying to strangle us - to make brewing entirely unprofitable. Ever since our shareholders rejected their buyout the other month. We desperately need new deliveries of hops and malt up the river - but what we really need is a chance to strike back. We have a recipe for a new beer ready, but with the time pressure of our debts and the supply of hops running out, we don't really have a chance to brew and test. That can take months - and we don't have months."

"Is there another way?" you ask.

"Well, we could model the brew on the computation engine. But we don't have a program powerful enough to run the calculations. I've heard of someone running a test like that, but they used a rare set of punchcards indeed - **Aramanth A**, I think they called it. If we had those, I reckon we could run a theoretical test right here."

"I have those punchcards."

(**punchcards (Aramanth A)**)	**929**
"Maybe I can find them for you."	**657**

422

The Prince of Ruritania shrugs. "What a strange coincidence. I had thought that my ministers had conspired to remove me during my tour. But I find you are a simple road thief. No matter." You are able to rob his servant of **£14 2s** in and a **ducal star** pinned to his Highness' breast.

Ride away with your loot... **535**

423

Early next morning the convoy sets out. Several heavy traction engines, each pulling three trailers of assorted freight, steam out of the inn yard and onto the road. Shortly after setting out it begins to rain, soaking you through. Roll two dice:

Score 2-5	Scouting ahead...	**690**
Score 6-8	Clear road to Wycombe...	**556**
Score 9-12	Crossbows in the night...	**640**

424

Ahead, two more steam carriages are duelling for position on the bumpy straight. Senorita Da Silva's long motoring scarf flutters out from the cockpit of her machine like the scrap of a storm-torn sail, but her silver and iron steam vehicle is set on its course. She shunts into the side of Anderson's Wonder-Steamer, her momentary opponent, and pulls ahead as he is forced to steady his course.

Accelerate to pass the duelling racers...	**764**
Wait for an opportunity to pass at a bend...	**97**
Shunt Da Silva into Anderson and try to pass them both at once...	**330**

425

Maidenhead is behind you now and the river is perceptibly wider. The southern bank is still green and rural - kept that way by powerful landowners no doubt, while the other side is lined with factories, each with their own wharf and waste pipe flooding the river. Perhaps the contrast between the industrialised and the traditional ways of life has never been starker than here, staring at each other across the Thames.

Head to the Two Bridges Wharf...	**245**
Continue downstream...	**672**

426

With the money in her pocket, Doris shakes her head again. "I don't know what she did to deserve that." Lose the codeword *Aspirin* and gain the codeword *Attribution*.

Return to the parlour...	**795**

427

Once you are knocked down the drinkers clumsily strip you, take your **money** and all of your **possessions** and go on a further drinking spree in the other gin shops of Wooburn Green. You are left on the cold flagstone floor and when you come round and gingerly feel your broken bones, you realise that your only hope is to get out of Wooburn Green as quickly as you can.

If you are the **Friend of Mr Hibbert**, turn to... **639**
If you are the **Friend of Lord Dashwood**, turn to...
 797
If you have the codeword *Adoption*, turn to... **755**
If you have the codeword *Ashen*, turn to... **518**
Otherwise, turn to... **9**

428

You are at the top of Danesfield hill. The gatehouse to Danesfield stands proudly between two rows of roadside trees. The road passes through a steep ravine just west of here, and the proximity of armed guards and airships means it would be folly to attempt any ambush here.

Approach the gatehouse...	**1002**
Ride east...	**786**
Ride west...	**739**

429

The village of Taplow is on the edge of the quickly urbanising corridor west of Maidenhead. Parts of the village still feel like a rural leftover, but it is also home to a paper-mill and a canning factory. There is a prominent pub, the Fighting Cocks, a tall church and a large house by the riverside.

Visit the Fighting Cocks...	**141**
Head south to the main road...	**218**
Take the road north towards Cliveden...	**612**

430

Make a RUTHLESSNESS roll of difficulty 13 to terrify the driver into stopping. You can add 2 to the score if you are **Wanted by the Coal Board** and 1 if you are **Wanted by the Constables**.

Successful RUTHLESSNESS roll!	**340**
Failed RUTHLESSNESS roll!	**194**

431

"Who are you?" demands Ennis, backing towards his dressing table.

"I am your vengeful spirit, Ennis. Your wicked deeds have caught up with you."

He quivers. "I'm no worse than many others, no worse."

"Pay for the lives of the women and girls you have ruined. Pay now and I will let you go."

He plainly never expected to be hunted down - your very appearance has broken what resolve he had. He takes out a wallet and empties it. You take a sheaf of **a hundred guineas in banknotes** and scatter the rest scornfully. "This I will take. But as for you, flee this land. Go and see if you can build a better life somewhere in the distant empire - but be sure you change your ways... Or I will find you!"

Lose the codeword *Charged* and gain the codeword *Avatar*. You will also gain a **Solidarity Point** for punishing Ennis.

Leave the hotel...   **94**

432
The woman sighs and folds her type-writing machine closed. "Really? Well if you kill me then the world will be without the end of the Alice Darling saga. Or this new piece I've just finished." You relieve her of **£3 2s** and a **gold necklace**, but surely you would not be so heartless as to take her **novel manuscript**?

Ride away...   **535**

433
You open the regulator and forge towards the carriage. The driver, completely surprised by your sudden appearance, yanks the steering column and skids the carriage across the rutted tarmac. You leap onto the footplate and engage the fireman with your weapon!

Fireman   Weapon: **shovel (PAR 5)**
Parry: 8
Nimbleness: 3
Toughness: 3

Victory!   **986**
Defeated!   **90**

434
You brush the butler aside, handing him your motoring gloves. "Get someone to water the vel, will you?" Your tone of natural arrogance is exactly the disguise you need to convince him. He introduces you to Lord and Lady Dean in your assumed name and you regale them with the story of your cross-country ride to visit 'Aunt Lucy' in London - the Duchess of Norfolk. You are able to lard your conversation with just enough detail gleaned from newspapers and gossip to convince the upwardly-mobile Deans that you really are a Norfolk, however distantly related, and they invite you to stay for a sumptuous supper and a good night's rest.

However, you have no intention of staying asleep but creep out to plant the papers in the **sealed packet** among the clutter of Lady Dean's dressing table. Remove the **sealed packet** from your possessions immediately.

In the morning you make an early start - and ride directly back to Wooburn Green to inform Comrade Feaver. She is delighted.

"We will inform the authorities immediately - through our intermediaries, of course. They will be very interested to find that the Deans are involved in treasonous plots."

Your reward is **£5** in cash drawn from the Compact's coffers and a **dark cloak (RUTH+1)**. Then Comrade Feaver turns to you once more.

Turn to...   **996**

435
The maid brings you a foam-topped mug of bubbly summer ale. It is cool and refreshing, with a sweet, malty foretaste and a rather floral finish, reminiscent of sunny days relaxing on grassy banks. She tells you that it is called Cottage Garden. While supping your drink you make conversation with several of the locals. One tells you of his difficulty getting a licence to transport his prize bull up to London for showing, another rails against Colonel Snappet of the Constables, who commandeered his traction engine and returned it damaged. Another long-faced man tells you about his bed-ridden mother, over-worked in service her whole life long and now unable to enjoy playing with her grandchildren. "Who is she to anyone but an anonymous old bird," he asks rhetorically, "Though she was the beauty of the village once and had her own dreams."

Go to visit the old lady...   **784**
Leave the Three Horseshoes...   **50**

436
A woman stands beside the road, wailing with grief. She clutches a bundle to her chest - a tiny baby, its face pale, still and unbreathing.

"Nothing!" she cries. "His life meant nothing!

Born to die on a cold night. Born to suffer and pass away. My son. My son..." If you have the codeword *Astrakhan*, turn to **703** immediately.

Leave her to her grief...	**703**
Try to comfort the mother...	**375**

437
You leave the lock and its gaudy, parasol-waving flotilla behind you. However, some of the boats continue to venture this far, and amongst the little wooded islands you have the opportunity to rob them unseen. Afloat or astride your velosteam, you have a reputation to maintain!

Ambush a likely-looking target...	**1019**
Head to Maidenhead Wharf...	**333**
Continue downstream...	**425**
Return upriver...	**463**

438
The net lands right over the driver and fireman, pulling them down. You leap down from the tree and stand over them with your gun at the ready. They surrender immediately, giving you the chance of taking the **strongbox** that is beside them in the cab.

You do not have the chance to open it here, but at your camp or at a workshop you may be able to crack it open.

Ride away...	**546**

439
☐

If the box is blank, put a tick in it. If there is already a tick in the box, turn to **516**.

You work through your repertoire and note to yourself that the instrument is in tune, the audience attentive and your playing exceptionally emotive. Choosing to make the most of your opportunity, you choose to play an old, bitter-sweet ballad guaranteed to tug at the diners' heartstrings, pursestrings and tearducts. A round of applause follows your playing and you gather **£1 17s** before a man with a velvet bow tie takes you aside.

"That playing was beautiful. Not what my wife and I expected when you took to the stage. But that old tune reminded me... reminded me of my younger days." He shakes you by the hand. "Come and play for me in the city. I'll see you're well recompensed for your time. I'm a wealthy man."

When he returns to his dessert you find yourself holding **Sir Reginald Tort's calling card**: he is the owner of a salvage and waste empire in the capital with a house in Mayfair.

Return to the hotel lobby...	**3**

440
Exhausted and in pain after binding your wounds, the soft bed invites you to slumber.

However, no sooner have you closed your eyes than you see dreadful figures: a body of a woman slumped in a ditch, bleeding from a wound to her back; a burning house and the cries of people trapped inside; a plummeting airship and the faces of the doomed passengers, wailing and beyond hope. Children weep as their mothers spend another night hoping for a father to return... A father whose body now lies discarded by the road. Husbands sit, stoking the fire and brewing the deep sorrow of loneliness. How many of these are your doing?

It is not a good night's sleep. But perhaps you simply have a touch of fever. Gain the codeword *Apprehend*.

Return to your room...	**394**

441
It takes several hours of labour to get the trailers ready. A girl is tasked with keeping a small furnace up to temperature while you help the haulier forge new parts. The orange glow of the coals lights the yard into the evening and you quickly forget the choking smoke and grime.

When the job is done, the haulier thanks you and offers you **6s** and a **pork pie** for your trouble. Also you have improved your knowledge of working with metal: roll a dice and add 2. If the total is higher than your unimproved ENGINEERING score, you can increase it by 1.

Return to the high street...	**4**

442
The lane weaves between trees, along a meadow and back beneath the beeches. It is quiet here. Roll a dice:

Score 1-3	Gypsies...	**735**
Score 4-6	Winchbottom Lane...	**465**

443

You continue downstream between wooded banks. A jetty where fuel is sold stands out into the water on one side and you pass a barge sinking piles for a new private wharf. A long string of Coal Board Barges show that the corporation's influence is never far away. Your mate spits into the water. "Filthy Coal Board. Did you hear what happened in Wales? They dug right underneath a village and let it collapse into the ground, just so they could strip-mine the hill. Whole village made homeless, 'accidental'-like."

Steam on...   **411**

444

Cock Marsh is an expanse of flat meadows and scrubland beside the wide river Thames. It is often flooded in winter and used by farmers for pasture and haymaking. A team of navvies are hard at work extending the railway line from Cookham Rise, throwing up an embankment in a curving line. Right where they plan to build a bridge stands the Bounty Inn, and beside that the post and chain of a flat-bottomed river ferry.

Park at the Bounty...   **409**
Take the ferry...   (**2s**)   **703**
Ride to Cookham...   **246**
Take the lane to Cookham Rise...   **575**

445

The broad road leads you onto a hillside overlooking the river. To the West stands a gatehouse of an estate, and beyond that the road sinks slowly down towards Henley.

Head down to the riverbank...   **1000**
Take the road east...   **588**
Continue westwards... *Highways and Holloways 313*

446

"Your lust for speed precedes you like the stink of a stag in heat," says the woman. "You are seeking the Spenser Cup. There is a woman north of Maidenhead on the road to Boulter's Lock who has what you need. But be quick! If you delay, you will never finish the Wagtail." How has the old woman gained such detailed knowledge of Dashwood's project? It is quite a mystery. She tells you no more, but bids you leave the encampment.

Turn to...   **113**

447

You to speak to him about Lord Dashwood. The engineer's face darkens initially, but you reassure him that Dashwood is both humane and honourable. "He will find work for you," you tell him. "He can use engineers."

You are not wrong to trust Dashwood. All it takes is a coded telegraph to West Wycombe, and soon you hear how the engineer and his family have settled on the estate. The engineer never thanks you directly, but he tells everyone who will listen that the Steam Highwayman cares about everyday people. Erase the codeword *Assistant* and gain a **Solidarity Point**.

Turn to...   **574**

448

"How dare you come back in here and waste my time!" Director Short is furious. "You've done nothing? Nothing? Not even one little murder? Not a single robbery? Useless!" He snatches the **Guildsman's medallion** back off you. "Get out of my sight!"

Leave the office...   **71**

449

"Why, it is very good of you to say so. You have been very polite, listening to me rattle on. Now, let me give you something as an emolument - a thankyou - an appreciation - for returning that which was lost. Hmm, let me see. Will you accept a double guinea and these rather fine cigars?"

Add **£2 2s** and a **box of cigars** to your possessions.

Ride away...   **11**

450

It only takes a split second to make your decision: running along the outstretched gantry arm you throw yourself into space and catch the mooring line still trailing behind the Nevaeh. The airship shudders as you swing, but Snappet has ordered full steam ahead and is dropping ballast around you. Despite the pain in your arms you must haul yourself up to the gondola and find a better hold.

Snappet has gone inside and his crew on deck are focused on managing the big craft as the wind is rising and the earlier drops of rain are now turning into a downpour. In fact you can see an awful bank of dark clouds ahead: this airship should be grounded in such weather. The risk is enormous.

A crack of lightning illuminates the countryside around. From your wet and exposed vantage point, the hillsides dotted with furnace glow look like an embroidered pattern. The airship turns west - towards Medmenham, no doubt - but the wind is driving you further and faster than the crew can handle. They wrestle with the big machine and Snappet reappears on deck, berating and beating them in a vain attempt to get what he wants. It is simply a matter of time: can the craft reach Snappet's home mooring before the wind becomes too strong?

A terrible creak comes from the envelope. The force of the wind is twisting the aluminium frame. Without doubt, the airship is about to fall. The crew realise it too and begin tugging on venting lines, but it is too late. The nose of the Nevaeh dips towards the ground.

The battle with the wind has blown you far along the Thames. Looking down, you realise that if you jump now, you will land in the river. May it be enough to break your fall without breaking your back!

Jump!   **413**

451
Your ride through the dark to High Wood is hairy, to say the least. Feeling weaker and woozier every minute, you have several near misses with other traffic. Eventually you are climbing the steep hill to your hideout.

If you have any **bandages**, you will use them up trying to staunch the bleeding from your cuts. In the end you manage to treat one of your **Wounds** - replace it with a **Scar** - but you will need to seek medical attention soon. Despite escaping death, you still wake to find yourself clumsy and stiff: lower your NIMBLENESS and MOTORING scores by 2.

Turn to...   **220**

452
The inventor's widow lives in the cottage near here. Do you remember taking the contents of her husband's study from her?

Give the widow the money...	(£31 10s)	**904**
Ride downhill towards Marlow...		**211**
Ride up Frieth Lane towards the prison...		**325**

453
Without any particular skills you have little to offer the hauliers, but when several wagons come in one after the other you pitch in, tossing hay bales, unloading sacks and hauling the goods into the distribution shed. Every consignment has a punchcard tied to it, which must be fed into the yard computation engine, which telegraphs Henley to confirm the arrival. It is hot work, but at the end of the job you are handed **3s** - and expected to be grateful for it. Unfortunately, the work has strained your back somewhat - roll a dice to see how seriously you are hurt.

Score 1-2   Minor strains, soon past...
Score 3-4   A nasty cut - gain a **wound**
Score 5-6   A **stiff back** - note this on your Adventure Sheet. You must subtract 2 from your NIMBLENESS until you treat your back with some **soothing lotion**.

Return to the high street...   **4**

454
A branch line from Maidenhead has been built through the farmland here. As you approach, a sluggish construction train heads north towards where the navvies are working.

Investigate the railway...	**750**
Cross over and head east...	**264**

455
You come across a clearing in the wood with a fine picnic laid out in a pool of sunshine. Glasses of champagne are poured, ham is freshly sliced, but nobody can be seen anywhere. You may take the full **picnic hamper** if you wish, but there are no signs of who it might belong to or where they might have gone...

Ride on...   **190**

456
It is only a short while after bedding in the rank straw issued to prisoners that your wounds becomes badly infected. Fighting the fever, spending days and nights on end wracked by pain and nausea, doing your best to scrape together a few pennies for medicine by running what favours will be given to a diseased wretch like yourself, you find you are on the very lowest rung. You have no opportunity to escape, improve yourself or make the most of your proximity to so many experi-

enced lawbreakers. Rather, your months in prison are spent in an exhausted battle with poverty and death. When the time eventually comes for your release, you are emaciated and weakened by your time in gaol. You must lower your MOTORING, NIMBLENESS and GALLANTRY skills by 2 points each. However, your **wounds** are healed and converted to **scars**: for each, roll two dice and a score of 11 or 12 means you have gained an **intimidating scar (RUTH+1)**.

On the day of your release you are simply thrust out of the door in your rags, with neither money nor possessions. Somehow your velosteam has escaped confiscation or wanton destruction and, reunited with your trusty machine, you are at least able to ride away and leave the foul stench of the penitentiary behind you. At least you are no longer **Wanted by the Constables**.

Turn to...   **288**

457
The road brings you down the hill towards Bourne End and the river. The land here is being developed. Crowds of builders are using steam cranes to erect a series of low, prefabricated houses in tight rows. Roll a dice to see what you encounter:

Score 1-2   A desperate mother...   **438**
Score 3-4   The road onward...   **703**
Score 5-6   A school bus...   **156**

458
The Wagtail's lightness and quickness to respond to your controls means that you can approach the vehicles ahead at nearly full speed, then brake sharply. Two drivers move aside as you rush forwards, but you find your way blocked by the True Patriot's massive rear boiler. Lord Akroyd looks over his shoulder, sneers, and stabs at his brakes, smacking into the Wagtail's front left wheelguard.

The Wagtail shudders, its steering responding strangely. Has Akroyd's shunt twisted your axle? You are forced to drop back and the pack close in ahead of you as you nurse the car around the next curve. Then, unexpectedly, part of the fairing on the front wheelguard tears off, freeing the front wheel to run in alignment again. You will need to drive carefully indeed now.

Back towards the race leaders!   **226**

459
If you are the **Friend of Arthur Smeaton**, turn to **804** immediately.

The blacksmith's name is Smeaton. He is kept busy here with repairing all the engines that travel over the hill between Marlow and Wycombe, but he dreams of more. "One day, a flying machine. Can you imagine it? Built by my own hands and flown with my own wits. Not simply a gasbag, but a real flying machine." He is looking for several hard-to-find parts that he cannot manufacture himself. If you can supply him with any of them, tick the box and remove them from your possessions.

☐ **high pressure valve**
☐ **roll of oiled silk**
☐ **telegraph wire**

When you have ticked all three boxes...   **550**
Return to the forge...   **60**

460
The lady takes your creased and soot-stained hand and peers into the lines. "Yes, yes, I thought so," she says. "Did you dream of a river last night?" Without waiting for an answer she launches straight into her prophecy. "You will go far, in the ships of the air. I see sabres flashing and lightning, lightning falling from the sky." She hesitates. "When you find the mountain of gold, choose to take only what you can hold."

Further questions are in vain. She shuts her mouth tight and refuses to tell you any more.

Return to the fair...   **326**

461
The pathway you have chosen becomes narrower and narrower until the hedges either side are brushing against you as you ride. The Thames glints silver and blue-brown to your left and several tall, dark trees loom across the water. They are black poplars - uncommon trees that are usually only found on riverbanks and watersides.

One is particularly impressive - its leaning trunk slanted over, repeated pollardings giving its lower trunk a massive, barrel-like appearance. Who knows how old it is? Gain the codeword *Anthill*.

Straight on...   **37**

462

Slipping through the gate, you find yourself between greenhouses and potting sheds. There is no-one around for now, but if you stay here long you will surely be spotted - and you are neither a gardener nor an employee.

Steal some exotic fruit...		**758**
Head on to the ball...	(*Almost*)	**531**
Leave through the gardener's gate...		**366**

463

The river is full of men and women in launches and skiffs playing at boating, picnicking, drinking and romancing. Picking your way upstream, it is clear that the main channel will be busy for some time. The evening is coming on and waterborne, candle-lit parties will continue late into the night. Perhaps it would be best to moor somewhere nearby and wait for the early morning, when all of these pleasure-seekers will be in bed rueing last night's excesses. If your GALLANTRY score is 9 or higher, turn to **857** immediately.

Take the channel towards Hedsor...	**488**
Travel on now...	**539**
Wait until early morning...	**647**

464

The Dive Bomber is a long, vertically swinging arm with a stylised attack-glider gondola at either end. Painted in the patriotic colours of His Imperial Majesty's Aeronautic Corps, they plummet down towards the ground in repeated arcs, spinning on their axes while they do. Boys and young men line up staunchly at one side, jeering at those who stagger off, sure they will perform more courageously. It is not a ride for the fainthearted.

First you find yourself moving slowly forwards and up in an arc as the operator positions the lower gondola for its own passengers. As you find yourself on your back, staring up into the night sky, the gondola swings sharply and loosely left. Before you know it, you are upside down, and then the counterweights pull you back upright.

For a moment you can see far beyond the fair's lights. The gas-lamps of nearby villages glow, the headlamps of passing road trains on the hill shudder and flash through the lines of trees. Distant furnaces light the night and the moon shines in the mirror of the river.

Then the gondola moves and, with a sickening lurch, you find yourself spinning towards the ground. The Gallopers' organ is playing a fast waltz and the lights of countless coalgas lanterns, the rushing blackness of the night and the chipped paint of the iron bar under your grip each take on a wondrous significance. The grass of the meadow, trampled by countless hopeful feet, approaches, before the black undercarriage of the ride's trailer threatens to blind you, then, with a twist like the shuffle of a bat handle in the hand of a giant, you can see the stars again as you climb upwards, almost unstoppably, except for the force that holds you back on the hard wooden bench, constantly at risk that something will fail and your gondola will dive to the ground for real...

Return to the fair...	**326**

465

You are riding along Winchbottom Lane, out of sight of the busy freightways hidden behind the hills and the thick boughs of Horton Wood to the South.

Up the hill to Handy Cross...	**25**
Uphill and east to Wycombe...	**313**
Into Horton Wood...	**106**

466

After the ministrations and gentle cleaning of Madame Juste's girls, you fall into a deep sleep on the couch. However, your dreams show you images of suffering and horror. You recognise the faces of people you know you somehow hurt, or killed, or punished unfairly. Flames, shadows, strange transformations when you turn your head, all combine to leave you feeling less rested when you awake than when you lay down to sleep. Gain the codeword *Apprehend*.

Turn to...	**91**

467

If you have the codeword *Amphibious*, turn straight to **48**. The river splits into four channels and the weir crosses the broadest and shallowest. To make it across you will have to perform quite a feat of riding your velosteam, making a MOTORING roll at a difficulty of 10, adding 1 if you have **off-road tyres**.

Successful MOTORING roll!	**329**
Failed MOTORING roll!	**311**

468

Father Bourdain smiles as he sees you approaching. "I won't hear your confession again, my child. Either you don't need it or you don't value it." If you have the codeword *Apprehend*, turn to **976**.

Leave the church...   **703**
Continue talking...   **717**

469

Even after a long night's work, you cannot solve Lalage Harris' problem. She is not beaten yet. "I cannot help Lord Dashwood," she says. "I have my own problems." Lose the codeword *Agile*.

Return to Littlewick Green...   **707**

470

That night you prepare your ambush on the route to Wallingford. You know that the roadswoman will be steaming this way, so now it is a simple matter of waiting. If you have a **net**, turn to **511**. Otherwise, turn to **600**.

471

Your attempt leaves you scratched by wire and bruised by a fall from the moss-covered sandstone walls. You must gain a **Wound**, and are also forced to abandon your attempt for now. You catch a final glimpse of Myfanwy's resigned face through the dirty glass.

If you have **five Wounds**...   **74**
Otherwise...   **288**

472

The journalist is delighted. "What a wonderful machine," she burbles. "Perhaps we can get a photograph at the office and do a feature. I expect you'd like that, hmm?" If you are **Wanted by the Constables**, turn to **731**. Otherwise, you tear across Cookham bridge and up the long road across Widbrook Common, reaching Maidenhead shortly ahead of the afternoon rush.

"Now that was fast," says the journalist. "I really ought to get one of those machines. Just think! A little customisation - I could report from just about anywhere. I will put it to my editor. Now, would you like an emolument?" She offers you **10s** as an appreciation for the ride.

Turn to...   **594**

473

A woman is disentangling a pheasant from a snare in a hedge. As you watch, she breaks the bird's neck and puts it under her coat. She is a poacher.

If you have more than 8 **Solidarity Points**... **782**
Otherwise...   **1020**

474

"You're right! Wealth gives them power, but they use the power to enrich themselves, fix the land on their pathetic offspring. We've got to show them! You want to talk to Comrade Feaver, if you think like that. She's got a way of putting things - shows you how things really are. And you know what? The revolution is coming, comrade! It's coming!" The man gives you a small brass disc, engraved with a number. Add **pass-disc 101** to your possessions.

Ask to meet Comrade Feaver...   **708**
Bid the man farewell for now...   **180**

475

The minstrel is a cheery fellow with a gift for fitting words to a melody. He strums on a mandolin as you swap tales of your adventures on the road. "I spent a night in the gardens at Cliveden," he says. "Pinched this key to the gardener's gate. Watch out for dogs, though! And if the constables aren't keen to let you over Cookham bridge, try the weir instead. You'll get wet, yes, but you can probably even get your nice machine over it."

He explains that he is heading west, "Maybe to Cornwall or Wales. Folk ask me if I'm worried about the rebellion, and I say no! Only more material for my songs - and in the west they should appreciate good music. Here, if it isn't steam-powered, people simply aren't interested." Add the **gardener's key** to your possessions and if you have **15 Solidarity Points** or more, turn to **826**.

Leave the minstrel and ride on...   **288**

476

Barsali marches over with an extended hand. "Welcome, welcome, my friend!" He invites you to park your velosteam beside his wagon and insists you sit while he fetches tea and cake. "My wife is working on the pipeline, so I am here with the family. But to be honest, I couldn't stay away from my princess." He snatches up his youngest daughter and gives her a noisy kiss. "Family, my friend, is worth any price. But you are with family now."

After relaxing with Barsali, hearing the tales of his most recent run-ins with the law over a firey glass of his home-brewed spirit, he asks whether you have any jewellery to sell. "Don't take it elsewhere. I'll get you the best price, always. I can always get down to town and sell it on." He tells you about a path that reaches Maidenhead without having to pass the Constables' checkpoints: it leads through the thicket, along a stream, across the Occidental Railway and into a suburb of Maidenhead called Boyn Hill. Crucially, it is just wide and firm enough for you to travel on your velosteam - gain the codeword *Abstruse*.

Clothing	To buy	To sell
cloak	**£1**	**15s**
dark cloak (RUTH+1)	**£4**	**£2 10s**
jewelled eyepatch (RUTH+1 GAL+1)		
	£8s	**£2 2s**
wide-brimmed hat	**£1 10s**	**18s**
silk scarf	**£2**	**£1**

Tools	To buy	To sell
rope ladder	**9s**	**7s**
lantern	**6s**	**4s**
fishing line	**1s**	**-**
snare	**2s**	**1s**
net	**8s**	**4s**
tarpaulin	**4s**	**4s**
brass flange joint	**8s**	**5s**
copper pipe	**6s**	**4s**
roll of oiled silk	**£5 7s**	**-**

Jewellery	To buy	To sell
locket	**-**	**6s**
pocket watch	**-**	**£2**
silver ring	**-**	**10s**
silver bracelet	**-**	**15s**
silver necklace	**-**	**£1 15s**
gold ring	**-**	**£1 5**
gold bracelet	**-**	**£2 6s**
gold necklace	**-**	**£5 5s**
ruby ring	**-**	**£7 5s**
Ducal Star	**-**	**£12**
diamond brooch	**-**	**£20**
emerald jewellery	**-**	**£35**

Barsali has more advice for you. "You can't be-

lieve everything that woman tells you," he says, pointing over to the wise woman's caravan. "I should know! She is my mother."

Visit the wise woman...	**578**
Leave the camp...	**113**

477

The interior of the Red Lantern is filled with a drifting, languid smoke. Oriental hangings drape the brick walls. A low doorway leads to the smoking room, where bunks of the opium smokers lie alternately dozing and imbibing the dreamy breath of the dragon of ease. At a table in the corner of the front room sits a tough-looking woman with a stack of ivory and gutta-percha tokens. "What do you want?" she asks. "Hiding from someone? Well, we all deserve a second chance. I can take you to Macready. He can wipe your slate clean. The Constables, the Guilds, they'll have never heard of you. Or p'raps you need to get your hands on something not quite publically acceptable?"

The fixer can sell and will buy contraband goods, but maybe not at the best prices.

Food and Drink	To buy	To sell
bottle of wine	**10s**	**6s**
bottle of champagne	**£1 5s**	**15s**

Weapons	To buy	To sell
club (PAR 4)	**3s**	**1s**
razor (PAR 2 NIM+2)	**£1 15s**	**18s**
sabre (PAR 6)	**£3**	**£1 10s**

Medical items	To buy	To sell
bottle of chloroform	**£2**	**15s**
pink pills (NIM+2) ☐ ☐ ☐	**£2 5s**	**-**
white pills (ING+2) ☐ ☐ ☐	**£2 5s**	**-**

Other items	To buy	To sell
punchcards (Aramanth A)	**£10**	**£7 4s**
punchcards (Habbukuk K)	**£15**	**£11 15s**
punchcards (Selladore V)	**-**	**£18 2s**
punchcards (Livingstone M)	**-**	**£18 4s**
ten guineas in banknotes	**-**	**£6**

Ask to see Macready...	**(4s)**	**314**
Leave the den...		**594**

478

Discard the **strongbox**. Inside you found a bundle of **thirty guineas in banknotes**, a **silk scarf** and a **clockwork bird**.

Return to your noted page...

479

There are plenty of ladies waiting to be asked to dance and after whirling several around the floor in succession you find yourself with one you can talk to. She is introduced to you as Emily Quarlington, and after an up-tempo waltz of swirling dancers and engineers, nobility and socialites, sponsors and inventors like interlocking cogs in a machine, she inquires whether you yet have colours to race under. There are plenty of people here with two left feet, the minimum of social graces, but plenty of socialites wanting to be associated with a racing driver. By the end of the evening you have distinguished yourself as an able dancer, a courteous partner and an enigmatic racer. Emily Quarlington, the daughter of Lady Quarlington, has favoured you with her colours - a silk scarf in a lemon hue - which will be flown from the Wagtail's slender chimney. Add the **lady's colours** to your possessions.

Leave the ball...   612

480

The Ruby Red lives up to its name. The barman pulls it straight from a shelf-mounted barrel behind him, giving you a good look at the reddish brew as he turns the glass. It keeps an impressive, creamy head more reminiscent of a midland bitter, but he skims that off to make sure you get your full pint.

"Do you brew this?" you ask as he places it on the bar.

He shakes his head. "We buy this in from a place near Aylesbury. Relative of the owner here. Very popular at his place, the Racing Gig. See what you think."

The beer has a mild initial flavour on its first taste but a strong blend of medium-dark hop scents builds up in the mouth. It is very drinkable and you can see what makes it popular, probably as a session ale, here in the Cricketers. An old-timer sees you drinking it and raises his similarly-coloured pint. "He-hee. Good to see you making the most of it, youngster. Don't go telling the world though, or there'll be none left for the likes of us up in Cookham." He leans over. "See a lot of rum folks in here now, from who knows where. Girls with the Telegraph Guild, all sorts of people. Why, even some Frenchies wearing that green last week. Some sort of specialists, folk was saying. Ha! They didn't know good honest beer when they were drinking it! Sent out for wine instead!"

Return to the bar...   185

481

Discard the **bandages** or **cloak**. You create a tourniquet to help stem the bleeding for now. Remove one of your Wounds in the normal way. Although you manage to remount your velosteam and ride away, losing all that blood has made you dizzy and you lose track of where you are. Roll a dice to see where the road has taken you:

Score 1	Hurley...	569
Score 2	The Bath Road...	551
Score 3	Cannon Lane...	646
Score 4	Winter Hill...	377
Score 5	Taplow...	429
Score 6	Widbrook Common...	67

482

The rain drives hard, but you ride harder. The warmth of the boiler turns the flying water into a mist and you roar through the dark, lime-lantern blazing. The doctor clings onto you tightly, his medical bag sandwiched uncomfortably between you.

If you are **Wanted by the Constables**, turn to...
                                                       235
Otherwise...   726

483

Your velosteam, entirely unwilling to start and almost completely ruined by the water, is useless for now. You manage to wheel it to the roadside and after several attempts to rouse helpers, you manage to get it loaded onto a steam-lorry headed to Maidenhead. The haulier watches you unload outside the World's End and laughs. "Don't know what a load of dancing girls are going to do with that!" he says scornfully, before steaming off.

You know that Madame Juste will help you: she is the sort of woman who, once they have attached themselves, never let go. And indeed she works wonders. She asks around amongst the staff and clientele of the World's End and very soon several mechanics are helping you put the velosteam back together. It is a long job and one that consumes all the **money** you have with you.

After several days work the velosteam is once again ready for the road. It will never be quite the same and you were unable to remove all the dints and bumps from the metalwork, but it is usable. Note that it has **Minor Damage**.

Turn to...   91

484

The Beadle takes your money and puts it away in a drawer. "Unfortunately there is no-one amongst the youngsters currently showing the promise deserving of the opportunity. But I shall hold your money in trust until someone is found. Then, rest assured, they will be apprenticed to an honest, hardworking trade, under your generous sponsorship.

Leave the Workhouse...   202

485

You toss the man a florin. He grins and doffs his cap. "Now I just got to hobble to some bus stop. After all, I dragged meself across the Valencia wastelands, didn't I?"

Ride on up the lane...   646

486

The surveyor is enraged. "I told my manager I needed protection expenses! Now look what a fine mess we're in." You can rob him of **£5 2s** and a **Coal Board accounts book**.

Ride away...   535

487

You steam westwards along the Thames and are forced to tie up for a while, as the traffic is forming a queue up towards Hurley lock. You chat with other bargees, including one who is proudly showing his new Malt License. "It didn't cost me much," he says. "There's a lady up at Mount Hill who can forge you anything!"

Continue upstream to Hurley Lock...   318

488

The northern-most stream of the Thames used to be the main navigation channel, but shortly after the completion of Cookham lock the burghers of Bourne End and Cookham constructed the impressive weir. Now this part of the river is a quiet backwater and Hedsor wharf is quiet and overlooked.

Sail downriver to the main channel...   637
Moor here...   802

489

The engine is an agricultural steam-tractor towing a long timber-trailer. The driver blows her steam-whistle cheerily. "Mind my near-side," she yells.

Ride away..   535

490

As you are celebrating, a woman in a fine blue dress approaches, surrounded by an entourage of glittering friends and hangers-on. You have only seen her once before - the Princess Anastasia, whose silken scarf hangs from the Wagtail's smokestack.

"The better engine was proven and the better driver too," she says. "Impressive work, milord Dashwood. This young driver of yours promises much. I hope you will allow me to show some appreciation - after all, my colours were first across the line and I have just won some very large wagers." She takes a **diamond brooch** from her own shoulder and pins it onto your driving scarf. "Take this testimonial too. I had my assistant draw it up - it should help you find further employment." A clerk hands you a **Letter of Introduction**.

You and all of Dashwood's team are invited to a victory feast at the hotel where the Princess is staying. Eventually you know you must leave - the company of lords and ladies suits you less well than the wind and rain of the open road. New adventures hang in the air wherever you turn... Erase the codeword *Ambition*, for from now on you must choose to pursue whatever satisfies you most - if anything will satisfy like racing the Wagtail did.

Mount your velosteam and ride away...   137

491

The boy nimbly leaps aside your velosteam and you swing back onto the road, scattering gravel behind you. He urges you onward and soon you have left Bourne End behind.

"Where will you go now?" you ask him. After all, an apprentice who breaks their contract will have his number marked for good. He seems entirely undismayed. "Just drop me off here. I'll make my way over to the Red Lantern in Maidenhead. Mac there can get me a new number altogether."

Leave the boy beside the road...   602

492

For a very small town, there is a lot to West Wycombe. The houses, shops and workshops at the bottom of the valley stand either side of a busy road, complete with its water tanks, coal bunkers and all the normal paraphenalia of steam freight. Atop the steep hill stands the Dashwood Mausoleum - a resting place for the local gentry, built on an ancient pagan site. Caves dug into the chalk are famous as places of depravity and intrigue, used by the Hellfire Club, and atop St Lawrence's Church hangs a strange golden globe.

Investigate the mausoleum...   295
Ride up to West Wycombe House...   494
Visit the sweetshop...   526
West on the Oxford Road...   521
East towards High Wycombe...   308

493

The young man sneers and draws a sword from his side. "You wouldn't dare kill me! I'm the only son of Sir Ryan Gilling!" He has called your bluff and now you must make good your threat.

Charge at him...   555

494

West Wycombe House has been the home of the Dashwood family for generations. The current Lord Dashwood is known as an adventure-seeker and a steam afficionado.

If you are the Friend of Lord Dashwood...   172
If you have a **letter of introduction...**   62
If you have the codeword *Agile*...   412
Otherwise, you are unable to gain entry to the estate...

495

"What about the winch on your freight engine," you suggest. "If you've still got steam up, you could right it with a chain around that ash tree."

The freighter looks unsure. "She's not a petty machine, my engine. Near on four tonne."

Nonetheless, a heavy chain is found and after an hour or so's work, both wagons are upright and rolling and the road is clear. The freighter presses a couple of shillings into your hand (**2s**). "I thought we were going to have to call out the Haulage Guild's recovery wagons," she says. "And then be forced into joining up. Bless you - I can keep freighting a little longer." If you have fewer than 4 **Solidarity Points**, gain one now.

Ride on...   280

496

It takes you all your resources of sweet-talking, begging and downright obsequious grovelling to convince a passing steam-haulier to help transport your wreck to an engineer's shop in Maidenhead, together with a fat sum of money. There you spend even more and are forced to barter away all your remaining possessions to get the finely tuned engine working again. Even then, the velosteam retains some dents that can't be beaten out and a problem with the timing that may come back to haunt you. Cross off **all your money** and **possessions**, mark your Velosteam's Condition as **Serious Damage** and turn to page **594**. Try to be more careful next time you attempt such a crossing!

497

The lockmaster waves you away from the smart pleasure boats, the slipper-sterned launches and the elegant skiffs. "Get over to the working wharf," she yells, "Where you belong!"

You and the mate find a mooring between a coal barge and a Freight Co-operative lighter. Apparently the co-operative do not restrict their ambition to dominating the road traffic alone - but they have serious competition in the Riverman's Guild. You wheel your velosteam off the foredeck and warm up the engine. Mark **Boulter's Lock (downstream)** as your mooring on your barge adventure sheet.

Turn to...   **94**

498

You continue downriver until you reach the wharf at Marlow riverside. Besides the loading and unloading of malt barges, the noise of the steam engines winching and washerwomen shouting, it is a wonder anyone can hear themselves think.

	To buy	To sell
Charcoal	-	£14
Furniture	£28	-
Machinery	£28	£23
Pottery	£24	£21
Cotton	-	-
Woollen cloth	-	£10
Coal	£12	£11
Beer	£15	£14
Wheat	£5	£5
Malt	-	£10
Frozen meat	-	£14
Ice	-	£6

Pass through the lock... (**2s** or **Bargee's Badge**) **705**
Return to Bisham Reach...   **745**
Moor and leave your boat here...   **679**

499

Your escape attempt goes horribly wrong: you manage to upset a flower stall, but it collapses onto your velosteam, pinning you to the cobbles. The constables arrive momentarily and haul you away.

Turn to...   **255**

500

Hibbert is amazed. "You really find it interesting?" he asks. "Come into the library. Let me pour you another sherry and show you the plans. I need to find people who believe in the work."

Hibbert's explanation becomes more and more detailed, but he is too polite to detain you forever. "I am so glad to have met you," he says. "A chance discovery of my lost purse has brought me a new friend. Do come and visit again." You are now the **Friend of Mr Hibbert**. Who knows what influence this man may have over your future? A man of learning and refinement may make way for you in the Imperial capital or further afield. Eventually you remount your velosteam and ride away.

Leave Hard-to-Find Farm...   **11**

501

Snappet stands over you with his rapier point at your throat. "I should run you through," he sneers. "But why should I dignify your end?" He calls for his Constables, who strip you of all your **possessions** and **money** and lock you up under guard. Then, without trial, you are taken directly to the prison, with no indication of your sentence or how long you will serve.

If you are a **Famed Lawbreaker**, turn to...   **274**
If you are the **People's Champion**, turn to... **1005**
Otherwise, turn to...   **722**

502

Your route takes you along paths more used to foot traffic, up a steep wooded hill. As you peer beneath the boughs, you smell charcoal burners at work.

Ride on...   **11**

503

It takes some time to plan your entry to Hall Place: Lynch, perhaps due to his guilty conscience, keeps a large number of guards and 'gamekeepers' patrolling his estate. Nonetheless, you manage to find your way through and hide yourself in the engine sheds, ready to find and murder him by night.

So after slipping through a service door and up past the laundries, the footmen's rooms and the kitchens, you make your way to the top of the house. You find the Squire instead in a study beneath looking over his accounts by the light of an oil lamp.

He turns at your approach and grabs his sword. "A cowardly assassin," he spits. "Not nearly quiet enough. Many want me dead - do your worst!"

Squire Lynch		Weapon: **rapier (PAR 7)**
Parry:	12	
Nimbleness:	5	
Toughness:	3	

Victory!   **817**
Defeat!   **255**

504

You shout out a greeting to the hauliers. They look over at you suspiciously. Roll a dice to discover their reaction.

Score 1-3 **168**

Score 4-6 **489**

505

Hearing a woman's scream you dash around a corner to see a heavy-set man grappling with a girl. On seeing you he drops her and waves his razor.

Ruffian   Weapon: **razor (NIM+2 PAR 2)**

Parry: 7

Nimbleness: 5

Toughness: 4

Victory!   **512**

Defeat!   **90**

506

If you are carrying one or more shipments of Frozen meat or Ice, turn to **927**.

Approaching Temple Lock you quickly notice that the gates are not painted in Union red: this lock is owned and run by the monks of Bisham Abbey. They can arrange a temporary place alongside their wharf to offload cargo, but you cannot moor here: either continue up the Thames or return the way you came.

	To buy	To sell
Charcoal	£14	-
Furniture	£29	-
Machinery	-	-
Pottery	-	£23
Cotton	£5	£5
Woollen cloth	-	£12
Coal	£12	£10
Beer	£16	£16
Wheat	£5	£5
Malt	-	£6
Frozen meat	-	£12
Ice	-	£6

Pass through the lock... (**4s** or **Abbey Ribbon**) **487**

Return to Bisham Reach... **745**

507

If you are **Wanted by the Constables**, turn to **653** immediately. You nose in between two other barges busy loading pottery. "I won't leave the reach," says the mate. "But you won't mind if we does a little light carrying, just for tea money, will you?"

Mark Maidenhead as your **mooring** on your barge adventure sheet - you will find your barge here whenever you need it again.

Head into town... **594**

508

Making a final desperate effort, you crawl to your velosteam and start the engine. You somehow manage to make your way back to Maidenhead and creep through the back streets towards the World's End, where you can be sure Madame Juste will await you.

Turn to... **91**

509

The Wagtail does not make good time and Lord Dashwood is disappointed. The official shakes his head. "Not on form today. You can't enter if that's your best speed. You'll be the laughing stock."

Dashwood takes charge of the car and sends you away. "Meet me back at the garage when you think you can do better," he says, before accelerating away in a cloud of steam.

Turn to... **642**

510

The master reluctantly hands over his purse. Then he spits at the ground. "I don't care to know who you are," he says grimly. "Just another vulture preying on the hard-working man. The Compact for Worker's Equality are right." Lose **2 solidarity points**.

Ride on... **202**

511

You await the steamer high on an overhanging branch, your pistol ready and your blade in your teeth. At last it appears. You must throw down your **net** to try to entangle the driver and fireman: success will help you overcome them significantly quicker.

Make a NIMBLENESS roll of difficulty 10 to cast the net properly.

Successful NIMBLENESS roll!   **438**

Failed NIMBLENESS roll!   **347**

512

□

If the box is empty, put a tick in it and read on. Otherwise, turn to **38** immediately.

Once your opponent is floored you help the girl up from the doorway where she collapsed. You manage to calm her and find that she is Florence, a dancer, staying with Madame Juste at the World's End Music Hall. "I've always been a tidy girl," she says, "No funny business, no men. What gave him the right...?" She bursts into angry, shamed tears. "What gave him the right to think he could have me?"

You guide her back to the music hall and put her into the hands of Mrs Juste, who tenderly takes Florence under her wing. "'Tis alright, pet," she coos. "You're back with me now." Mrs Juste sets her face into a much more business-like manner and addresses you. "Well, you've done a good job there. Can I offer you a small reward in thanks for your gallantry? Perhaps a weapon to arm you against the bullies of the world."

"Thankyou - your offer will help me continue to fight injustice."	**787**
"I require no reward."	**196**

513

The main road runs along the bottom of the valley here, bounded on one side by the gardens, orchards, coppices and cottages of the straggling Hurley village, and on the other by the steep sided hill topped by High Wood. The road is well-used, both by hauliers taking cargo over to Henley and by the local farmers.

Ride east...	**165**
Ride west...	**588**
Take the lane into Hurley...	**569**
Head up the track to High Wood...	**2**

514

With complete access to the vault but limited ability to carry much away, you must make a fast decision. What will you take? Choose one of the following:

A **strongbox...**
Two hundred guineas in banknotes...
A set of **emerald jewellery...**
£35 18s in mixed coins...

Flee on your velosteam...	**574**

515

On the lane called Windsor Hill you are met by a signpost, helpfully indicating the way. North is the route to Wooburn Green over the hill, and west you will find Wooburn and the River Wye. To your east stands the semaphore and telegraph towers of Odds Hill.

East to the towers...	**177**
West downhill...	**57**
North to Wooburn Green...	**10**

516

This time your playing does not move anyone to tears. The hotel is playing host to the monthly dinner of the Society of Deaf Clerks and nobody has heard you, for all your finesse.

Return to the hotel lobby...	**3**

517

The line approaches, but you have ridden the Wagtail too hard. With no reserves of coal left you are unable to stop the nimble Lucardo Kettle from accelerating past you. He noses across the line just ahead of you, taking first place fair and square.

The ceremony of awards is raucous and noisy, and Dashwood is far from disappointed with you. "You did me proud," he says, slapping you on the back. "You did us all proud! That last moment, well, you'd done everything you could. Next year, perhaps!"

You have learnt a lot these last few weeks of racing and practice. Increase your MOTORING score by 2, and although the Spenser Cup itself escaped you, you have proven your ability to drive with the best. You have tasted speeds that you only used to dream of! Eventually, Dashwood's team pack up and prepare to take the Wagtail back to West Wycombe. "What will you do now?" asks Harris.

"Ride the open road," you have to reply. There are adventures a-plenty still to be found across this land of steam-machines and reckless racers. Lose the codeword *Ambition*.

Mount your velosteam and ride away...	**137**

518

The midnight ride to your hideout in Windsor Wood is exhausting. The loss of blood means that you keep losing consciousness and only just avoid another accident. However, your inability to focus means that by the time you arrive at your hideout, you have dropped many of your possessions.

For each possession roll a dice: a score of 5 or 6 means that you can keep it. Otherwise, erase it from your adventure sheet. Eventually the familiar approach to your hideout is beneath your wheels. You bump up to your bivouac and mechanically go through your depressurizing routine.

Turn to...   **676**

519

The band strike up a waltz - the 'Aether Prince' - and guests clatter and swarm onto the dancefloor. From an internal balcony you survey the gathering: the young Lord Fairfax dominates the centre of the room, showing the new-style dance steps. The Princess Anastasia, the greatest machine enthusiast, stands aside, bored by the chatter. However, even an Imperial Princess is out-glamourised by the presence of Maria Roberts, the King's Mistress. She is laughing at a sycophant's story with a coterie of ladies, and around her neck flashes a weighty diamond necklace set with a central black stone. Who would have thought you would ever find yourself in such company?

If you have the **telegraph transcript**, turn to **598** immediately. If you have the codeword *Ambition*, turn to **31**. Otherwise, turn to **183**.

520

Jackson's green Chariaeoli lumbers around the bends of the track: it is a massively powerful engine mounted on an all-too fragile chassis in an attempt to save weight. Jackson himself is strapped into a wicker seat hanging on the left side of the boiler, struggling with steering levers and a vertically mounted regulator wheel. He doesn't notice the Wagtail's approach until you are almost beneath him, then glances down, pedals in a load more ground coal and surges forward.

You can almost see his boiler distending. You can certainly see the chassis twisting under the weight, heat and stress. Pushing forward again to pressurise Jackson, you force him to lose concentration for a moment and, as the pressure mounts, high-pressure steam suddenly erupts from a boiler seam.

The shriek of vaporised water fills you ears and you and the other drivers veer off to dodge the scalding cloud. Unable to see and probably badly burnt, Jackson ploughs into a stand at full speed, knocking down rows of seats and scattering urchins, clerks and ladies across the track. A scream goes up, but you have not opportunity to find its source. You must keep yout eyes firmly on the road!

It is the perfect moment for you to accelerate quickly away and tear up into second place behind Lord Akroyd. Gain four Race Points!

Accelerate...   **226**

521

You are on the wide Oxford road a short distance from West Wycombe. A signpost marks the lane to the south. Labourers toil cutting silage for a steam-baler.

Take the road west...   **546**
Head up the lane to the south...   **137**
Ride on to West Wycombe...   **492**

522

You stalk around the ballroom, watching the dancers, and find yourself alongside a young woman with flowing brown hair. She recognises you as the racer, and says that she admires you for your disdain for "All this hypocrisy. As if this sort of thing matters to speed! And the engines are better judges of an engineer, aren't they?" She offers you sponsorship and you find yourself with a royal blue silk scarf in your hand: add the **lady's colours** to your possessions.

Lord Dashwood finds you at the end of the party. He has plainly had a riotous time. "Aha! Looks like you have found high favour indeed! Princess Anastasia wears that blue. She loves a race." He claps you on the back. "Well done!" Gain the codeword *Anastasia*.

Leave the ball...   **612**

523

☐ ☐ ☐ ☐

If any of the boxes above are empty, tick one. If all four are ticked, turn to **394**.

An independent haulier wants protection for his freight convoy up to High Wycombe. "You look threatening enough," he says. "I want someone to scare off the bandits - and fight them off, if it comes to that. Aye, and to protect my goods from the dratted haulage guilds. They think they own the roads." After some haggling, he offers you four pounds to accompany them. "Paid when we're safely there , of course."

Accept the job...   **423**
Turn him down...   **394**

524

To threaten the driver into stopping the freight wagon you will need to make a RUTHLESSNESS roll of 13. If you are the **People's Champion,** add 3 to your roll and if you are a **Famed Lawbreaker** you can add 2.

Successful RUTHLESSNESS roll!	**415**
Failed RUTHLESSNESS roll!	**338**

525

The river wends its way past Cock Marsh and turns west. The valley is full of industry here - the gravelling pits on the north bank near Little Marlow, marshy aits used to produce osiers for basket-making and wattling. Roll a dice to see what you encounter:

Score 1-2	Workers in the osier beds...	**858**
Score 3-4	Little to interest you...	**776**
Score 5-6	A string of barges...	**845**

526

The sweetshop is a little, cramped room, walled on three sides by shelves filled with glass jars, each one holding a different sugary delicacy. The proprietor, Mr Penfold, stands proudly at his till. "I have the finest selection of sweets outside London," he says. "Although there are some that I have not sourced. Real seaside rock is very hard to get hold of. Imitation stuff just doesn't have that seaside tang." If you have a stick of **seaside rock**, turn to **339.**

Food and drink	To buy	To sell
mixed bag	1s	-

Leave the shop...	**492**

527

"You can't go in yet," says the nurse. You show him the blood still trickling from your wound and he shrugs. "Suit yourself."

In the operating room you are confronted by a shocking scene. A man lies on an table in the centre of the room, biting on a gag and fully conscious. The doctor is bent over him and the grating noise you can hear is the sound of a surgical saw cutting through bone.

The doctor looks up for a moment, takes in your appearance and gives a grim smile. Then he jerks his head towards the waiting room.

Some time later he comes to find you, wiping his freshly-cleaned hands. "That was a difficult operation," he says, without any pleasantries. "The poor man was shot on the road. A highwayman robbed his steam wagon, left him for dead. Mercifully, a haulier found him still alive and brought him to me. But the man's too poor to pay for anaesthetic and will have to spend the rest of his life without an arm." He looks at you with hard, steel-grey eyes. "I believe I know who you are," he says. "What the hell do you want?"

Dr Smollett is bound by his strict observance of the Hippocratic oath: he will not refuse anybody treatment or help. However, that doesn't mean he has to be friendly and he is known for his cold demeanour when dealing with those he distrusts. For each wound that you want healed, the doctor will charge you **£2.** However, his treatment does not result in your **wounds** becoming **scars** - you can simply erase them from your sheet.

When the treatment is complete he heads over to a glass fronted cabinet and selects one of several bottles of fine whisky. He pours himself a glass and then, in a moment of magnanimity, pours you one too.

"Might have been better before I started probing your wounds," he said. "But we both needed to stay steady." Gain the codeword *Afterthought.*

Turn to...	**823**

528

The road here switchbacks and climbs steeply up the escarpment from the flat-bottomed valley below. Together with a thick shroud of trees, it makes Inkydown Wood an ideal place for an ambush.

Wait for a private carriage to rob...	**405**
Ride south towards the Golden Ball Inn...	**725**
Ride north to Bisham village...	**737**

529

The engine shop here is run by Lalage Harris, a woman known for her improvements to the road engines that travel this way. She and her assistants mend and maintain traction engines and steam wagons here. A weighty box-crane can lift a boiler off its bogie and a roaring forge is busy even now, heating stock to welding temperature. If you have any damage to your velosteam, these are the people to fix it for you.

Velosteam Customisations	To buy
muffled exhaust	**£3 15s**
gas pressuriser	**£10 4s**

Repairs	To buy
Per **damage point**	**£1 18s**

If you have the codeword *Agile*....   **397**
Return to the village...   **707**

530
You are riding down Glory Lane between Wooburn Green and the London Road. Buzzards wheel overhead here, watching the verges and the roadside.

Enter Cutthroat Wood...   **561**
Enter Windsor Wood to the south-east...   **709**
Head south to Wooburn Green...   **199**

531
The servant you met is waiting for you at the servant's entrance to the house. "I can get you in to the ball," he says. "I'm sure you can do much for the poor amongst the company of the rich. Come this way."

He leads you through corridors and passageways and you are led to the front yard where footmen are welcoming the guests from their steam carriages. "Good luck!" whispers the servant. Erase the codeword *Almost*.

Turn to...   **297**

532
The sound of money jangling on the cobbles is enough to bring a crowd of impoverished city-dwellers dashing over. By the time the constables erupt from the alleyway, they are confronted by a full-on-brawl as housewives and urchins struggle over sovereigns and shillings. You are well on your way, laughing as you make good your escape.

Ride away...   **282**

533
Tonight's ball is nowhere near as grand or as well-attended as the last - particularly considering the drama that unfolded on that occasion! Nonetheless, the nobility are out in force, drinking, dancing, carefully weaving the web of status and alliance. The conversation is vapid and shallow, even if the food is tasty, and there is nary an ale to quaff. Yet continuing to mingle amongst the upper class is having an effect on you.

Roll a dice and add 6: if the total is higher than your current GALLANTRY score you may increase it by 1.

Leave the ball...   **612**

534
You arrive at the Henley road just west of Danesfield Hill, with four miles to Henley and three to Marlow. The tower of Medmenham church pokes up over the trees. Another lane leads northwards away from the river plain, soon hidden by overgrown hedgerows.

Visit Medmenham...   **774**
Ride west to Henley... *Highways and Holloways 801*
Take the lane north...   **289**
Travel east towards Marlow...   **816**

535
The dusty, crushed rock road sends up clouds of white dust behind you, steaming past the common at Pinkney's Green. Red wagons stand in glimmering oil-light beneath the Big Wheel and the towering frame of the Dive Bomber. This is the home of the Curtiss Steam Fair. A steady stream of fairgoers approaches from the east, come to find distraction and excitement at the premier steam fair in the land.

Ride on towards Maidenhead Thicket...   **113**
Enter the Steam Fair...   **326**
Ride towards Maidenhead...   **650**
Head up towards the Golden Ball Inn...   **725**

536

You steam up the sloping Henley road. Ahead of you is Danesfield hill with its airship mooring posts. Of course, they are not the public gantries of the Atmospheric Union, but the private moorings of the constables and the dastardly Colonel Snappet in particular. Roll a dice:

Score 1-2	Airship engineers...	**607**
Score 3-4	Nothing of interest...	**428**
Score 5-6	Travelling entertainers...	**649**

537

It will take a great deal of money to swing a judge and jury, so the money you have in Coulter's Bank may just be enough. You will need to commit at least **100 guineas** from your account, but for every additional **10 guineas** you use for bribes you may add 1 to a roll of two dice. Decide how much you will spend and cross that money off your bank account.

Score 2-9	You waste your money...	**184**
Score 10+	Your bribes succeed...	**349**

538

A foreman hails you as you approach. "Have you got our cotton delivery? Production has slowed right down without our cotton."

	To buy	To sell
Charcoal	-	-
Furniture	-	-
Machinery	-	£24
Pottery	-	-
Cotton	-	£6
Woollen cloth	-	-
Coal	£12	£11
Beer	-	£16
Wheat	-	-
Malt	-	-
Frozen meat	-	-
Ice	-	-

Return to Cookham Reach...   **693**

539

The steam engine chugs away and you plough slowly along the darkening river. The ground on the eastern bank rises sharply, lit here and there by the last rays of the sun. You see a short chimney smoking, a couple of workshops, and lower down an ornate boathouse. All part of the Cliveden estate. The grand house itself is high atop its cliff, out of sight.

Continue to Cookham Lock...   **848**

540

You drink with a servant from Cliveden house, who gives you a grin of recognition. He is rather awestruck to be drinking with the real Steam Highwayman and has a proposition for you. "Have you heard? There's a great ball planned up at the house," he says. "I can sneak you in, if you like. But you've got to dress the part. Come in the back gate by the gardens and I'll meet you there." Gain the codeword *Almost*.

Return to the Walnut Tree...   **634**

541

So that is how it happens. Late that night, you find yourself staging a robbery in full view of a locobus of amazed passengers. The freighter succumbs to a single blow to the head and her fireman (with whom she has agreed to split her share) flees into the woods. You have time to take the paychest while flashing a gallant smile to the terrified travellers, making sure that they all see you.

The paychest contains **£50** in small coins. Your share is, of course, **£10**.

Take the entire sum...   **89**
Take your share and bury the rest for the freighter...
                    761

542

Comrade Feaver is deeply impressed. "Few of the Comrades here take the initiative as you have done, Comrade 8236," she says. "I am sending a report about your zeal for the overthrow of the capitalist hegemony to our headquarters in London. Should you find yourself in that accursed city, you will be sure of more work to do in the name of the people."

Remove the codeword *Ammonium* and gain the codeword *Anteater*.

Return to the hideout...   **985**

543

You heat a canteen of water over the little fire and use it to wash the dried blood off your limbs. Strips of clean bedsheet make satisfactory **bandages** - and if you want to take some with you, add them to your

possessions. For every **wound** that you remove, convert to **scars** and check for **intimidating scars (R+1)** as normal. If you have the codeword *Arthropod*, *Astrakhan* or *Apogee*, turn to **404**.

Return to your room...   **645**

544

"Is that a fair question, my child?" Father Bourdain shakes his head. "You're talking about hundreds of thousands of people all in breath. Christians may be complicit, I'll agree. There are people who follow Jesus, or try to, or once decided to, but who have tried to do it without changing their life or having it changed. And they get all wrapped up in the dog-eat-dog world. But the Church, no. The Church is more than people. Until you can see people as individuals, whether they have power or not, how can you apportion blame - or responsibility?"

If you have the codeword *Aggregate*, turn to **822**.

Leave the church...   **703**
Continue talking...   **717**

545

As you leave, the Governor comes to bid you farewell. "We will miss you, your honour," he says. "The small matter of your debts arises, I find." Roll a dice to see how much you owe:

Score 1   **£2 10s**
Score 2-3   **£3 15s**
Score 4-5   **£4 18s**
Score 6   **£6**

Pay your debts...   **740**
Unable to pay...   **668**

546

There is little to the village of Piddington: only a yard by the side of the road where freight wagons are repaired, a row of cottages, a couple of small workshops and a dilapidated pub. Chained bollards flank the roadway, indicating the influence of the Haulage Guild. The steep hill to the south casts a looming shadow over the place.

Take the Oxford Road...   *Highways and Holloways 8*
Ride towards West Wycombe...   **521**
Take the steep lane up to Wheeler End...   **6**

547

You would have to be mad to return to Danesfield after your exploits. Snappet is on the look-out for you in particular, and he has also tightened his security. The end of the clerk who helped you is common talk around here - as a warning. The rumour is that Snappet first tortured him, then chained him onto the rooftop to die of exposure.

Return to the road...   **428**

548
☐

If the box is empty, tick it and read on. If it is already ticked, turn to **337** immediately.

The Guildsmen are busy unloading a big convoy that has just come in from the Midlands. "Lend us a hand, mate?" asks a burly foreman and soon you find yourself in the thick of a carefully choreographed operation. Several hours later, you are rewarded with a pot of beer - a cooling draught of Guild Special, the favoured mild - for your trouble.

You have also improved your co-ordination: if your NIMBLENESS score is 6 or less, increase it by 1.

Return to Wycombe...   **337**

549

Your ability to mend your velosteam yourself depends upon your ENGINEERING skill and your access to materials. To repair each level of damage you must have a minimum ENGINEERING score as noted below as well as one of the items listed. Thankfully there is an ample supply of gas, piping and ironwork at your disposal: the engineers of the steam fair are always tinkering.

	ENGINEERING score	Materials
Critical damage...	10	**high pressure valve**
Serious damage...	8	**heavy wrench**
Minor damage...	6	**engineer's gloves (ENG+1)**

Return to your wagon...   **743**

550

Smeaton is overjoyed. "Thankyou! Now I'll leave the shopwork to my apprentices and I can focus on my dream. But I'll take a look at your velosteam first."

Smeaton will repair any **damage** free of charge

and also fits a **muffled exhaust** to your machine. You help him where you can and his assistance improves your understanding of mechanics: improve your ENGINEERING skill by 1.

Return to the forge...   **60**

551
You are on the Bath Road. It runs right across the land, bringing all the freight and wealth of the West Country up to the Home Counties. Telegraph lines run alongside and the Freight Wardens and the guilds keep a close eye on the traffic, charging high tolls and chasing off brigands. Nonetheless, it offers you rich pickings - if you consider the risk worth taking!

Head up towards Appletree Cottages...   **139**
Steam east towards Maidenhead Thicket...   **707**
Follow the Bath Road...   *Princes of the West 63*

552
Your attempts to coax soothing tunes from your instrument first amuse, then aggravate your audience. A nice popular waltz? It is harder than the sheet music suggests. Something dramatic and Russian? It comes out noisy and crashing. Eventually the diners cease being polite and a woman in a green gown marches up and knocks down your music stand. "Get out of here," she spits. "We are paying to eat."

Demand satisfaction for the insult...   **379**
Leave immediately...   **3**

553
Your front wheel is swallowed by the ditch and you are thrown over the handlebars. Gain a **Wound** and a **Point of Damage** to your velosteam.

If you have **Five Wounds**...   **74**
If your velosteam is **Beyond Repair**...   **250**
Otherwise...   **763**

554
☐
If the box is empty, put a tick in it and read on. If it is already ticked, turn to **492** immediately.

The trapdoor leads down to a low chamber beneath the mausoleum. Taking the lantern from your velosteam, you tread slippery brick steps and come to a tunnel hacked out from the chalk. It winds downwards and suddenly opens out into a chamber, containing a wooden table strewn with cards. Several pieces of iron machinery protrude from the walls and an iron door without a handle seems to lead further into the hill. Beside it stands a **strongbox** and a wine-rack, containing eight **bottles of wine** and a single **bottle of whisky**. You can take as much as you can carry. On the table lies a list, reading: Dashwood, Hibbert, Maloney, Foss.

This, no doubt, is one of the famous hell-fire caves. Apart from the cool, chalky air, there is no atmosphere of the occult or weirdness that you can detect—for now. You must return to the surface.

Leave the cave...   **492**

555
You launch yourself directly at him and knock him to the ground. By the time you are both on your feet, his sword is in his hand and he is ready to fight!

The Hon. Gerald Gilling   Weapon: **rapier (PAR 7)**
Parry: 11
Nimbleness: 4
Toughness: 2

Victory!   **273**
Defeat!   **610**

556
Two days later you steam into High Wycombe. The convoy is intact and your job is done. "Maybe I didn't need you after all," says the haulier.

"Maybe just the sight of you was enough to scare them off," you retort.

He laughs and hands over **£4**. "I'd consider hiring you again, friend. I've got to make the same run again soon."

Go your own way...   **337**

557
A man comes out of the farmhouse to call off the dogs. He is dressed like a gentleman at leisure, with reading glasses pushed up over his head. He introduces himself as Thomas Hibbert, an investor and polemicist. "I spend much of my time in the city," he says, "But when I can I come down here to the countryside. There is so much suffering in London and although I do my best to play my part, I feel hopeless at times. So I return here, walk on the hills or in the wood where the air is fresh and remember why I want to

improve the lot of the poor."

You dig out the **initialled purse** and show him. "Is this yours?"

"Why yes! A thousand thankyous! I really thought I had lost that for good."

You tell Mr Hibbert how you found his purse in the wood. "Very good of you," he says. "Most people would have opened it up without a second thought. Please, stay for dinner." Erase the **initialled purse** from your possessions.

Over dinner you talk more and you find that Hibbert is a sensitive, rather shy soul with a love of learning. He is very proud of his library, his dogs and his scheme to renew the sewerage of the capital of the greatest empire in the world. "Sewers might seem dull, but I've devoted a fair part of my life to them now. Sanitary conditions are key to improving the lives of the people of the cities."

"I hope your vision comes to pass..."   **449**
"Tell me more about the sewers..."   **500**

558

You give the engineer your **medallion**. "This is practically a passport," you say. "Show this to any of the Haulage Guild and they'll consider you one of their own."

"I can't eat it," he says. "Nor do they know me."

"Trust me. You'll find that all sorts of things fall off the back of a trailer as they pass your house. Whatever you think about the Guild, they want to be known to be good to their members."

Sure enough, before the week is out, the Hauliers hear that one of their guild is languishing in poverty. Motivated by guild solidarity, they deliver coal, baskets of vegetables and two mismatching artifical legs. The engineer and his family are able to support themselves once more - thanks to you. Erase the codeword *Assistant* and gain a **Solidarity Point**.

Turn to...   **574**

559

You mention that you are hoping to make contact with the Compact for Workers' Equality. The landlord looks you over and shakes his head. "No idea who you could be referring to," he says. "No idea at all."

Pay him...   (**10s**)   **40**
Back off...   **68**

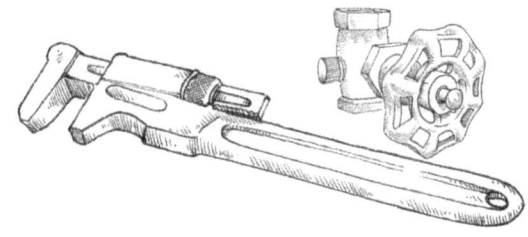

560

The River Wye has been dredged and widened to allow heavy barges to progress a little closer to High Wycombe. The wharves and factories lining the banks all deal in heavy goods and machinery and queues of slow-moving lighters await their cargoes being transhipped onto freight wagons and pulled along the turnpike to Loudwater, Wooburn and Wycombe itself.

One wharf seems empty, its piles beginning to lean and the decking holed and rotten. An air of decay lingers.

Return to the Thames...   **693**
Moor at the Caswell Mill below Bourne End...   **538**
Moor at the empty wharf...   **51**

561

The road to London climbs a steep hill here through the wood and countless years of hooves and wheels have dug a cutting or holloway into the ground. Narrow, dark and shaded, this place is known to all as Cutthroat Wood.

Prepare an ambush here...   **138**
Ride south...   **530**
Ride west...   **574**
Ride east...   *The Reeking Metropolis* 42

562
☐

If the box is empty, put a tick in it and read on. If it is already ticked, turn to **190** immediately.

A mound of leaves beside the path looks like an inviting spot to rest. You take a moment to lie back and enjoy the songs of the woodland birds, the freshness of the country air.

Something digs into your back as you relax into the leaves. It is an **initialled purse**, marked T.H. You can either keep it and hope to find its owner, or open it and take the **£6 5s** inside.

Ride further into the wood...   **190**

563

Cookham Dean is a village of orchards, paddocks and hay-meadows sprawling up the side of the slope. A rambling inn stands opposite the little church and several workshops make a row by the road. Beyond the village stands the semaphore tower on Mount Hill.

Visit the Cricketers Inn...	**185**
Ride North to Winter Hill...	**260**
Head to Cookham Rise...	**575**
Take the lane towards Maidenhead...	**730**

564

The lane takes you over a narrow railway bridge, up a steep hill with a heavy beechwood on your right, and up out of the valley towards Flackwell Heath. Roll a dice:

Score 1-2	Someone in the wood...	**1018**
Score 3-4	Quiet riding...	**50**
Score 5-6	Trouble at the bridge...	**809**

565

A furtive looking man with a moustache, heavy coat and a bowler hat is walking through the village lanes. He is a poacher. "Good hunting in these woods. Plenty of birds. If you want venison, try Horton Wood, or up near Frieth."

Food and Drink	To buy	To sell
bird's eggs	-	**3s**
rabbit	**2s**	-
pheasant	**4s**	-

Tools	To buy	To sell
lantern	-	**4s**
fishing line	**1s**	-
snare	**2s**	**1s**
net	**10s**	**6s**

Ride on...   **351**

566

The Telegraph Guild formed late in the previous century as a group of investors who backed the inventions of Murray and Edelcrantz. Their rapid expansion of the network helped the Imperial Army make its conquests in Asia and southern Africa, and the monopoly they were granted explains why now the Guild has become so secretive and even ritualistic. Almost anybody can read the signalling positions, but the codes used to compress and protect the information are fiendishly complex, using the best Babbage engines to calculate. That has led to the Guild having a massive lead in all forms of mechanical computation: their analytical engines do most of the calculations for the Empire.

Return to the library...   **736**

567

You are served your pint of Wethered's Fine India Pale Ale in a tall, chilled glass. "We get our ice from the Abbey," confides the barman. "Even pay for some of it."

The beer has a pale golden colour and the strong hoppy aroma typical of an IPA. The hop oils are already vaporising as the gentle carbonisation releases the dissolved gases, giving you scents of lemon, pine and leather. On the tongue you first taste the sourness, quickly replaced by the bitterness of the hop blend, finishing with a complex sweetness of honey, treacle, baked bread and sunshine. The flavours continue as you put the glass back on the bar... A grassy note from the hops, a warmer note that you associate with the Fuggles hop. Sure there's Fuggles in there. The beer has been skilfully blended, finely conditioned and served at the perfect temperature. The whole of the brewing industry deserves a round of applause for creating such a beautiful thing.

A beer like this deserves taking your time over, so you carry the precious golden nectar to a chair in the corner and savour it...

Return to the bar...   **185**

568

Your shot ricochets off the cab just below the driver's position, terrifying him into stopping the carriage. You quickly steam over and leap off, brandishing your weapons.

Turn to...   **986**

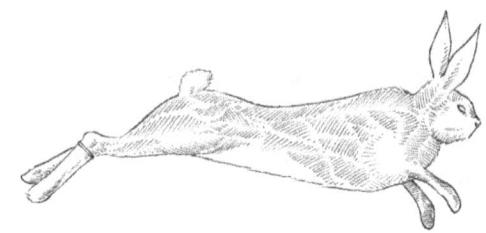

569

Hurley is a small village huddled at the riverside. A busy boat-building yard owned by the Freebody family employs many of the locals and eel-gatherers work the long weir every night of the running season.

Take a look at Freebody's Yard...	**611**
Take the lane to Temple...	**584**
Ride south to the Henley Road...	**513**
Steam onto Lock Island... (*Alluring*)	**1015**
Head to your boat (if it is moored here)...	**860**

570

You throw the mooring lines over a couple of bollards and tie them off firmly, checking the knots yourself. "I'll be back before long," you tell the mate. "You stay here and mind the boat."

"Whatever you say, boss," says the mate, eyeing the Bounty hungrily. Or perhaps thirstily. Mark your Boat Mooring as **The Bounty Inn** on your adventure sheet.

Turn to...	**444**

571

After asking around at the lockside, you find boatmen willing to take you and your velosteam up or down-river. Where will you go?

London... (**£2 10s**)	*The Reeking Metropolis 234*
Henley... (**£1 15s**)	*Highways and Holloways 702*
Return to the lock...	**109**

572

Remove the **pineapple** from your possessions. "Now what is that dreadful thing?" asks the old woman. You cut the pineapple into pieces and give her a mouth-puckeringly sweet morsel. "Delicious," she says, licking her lips. "A pine-happle, you sez? Can't come from near here. Some sort of foreign fruit. Are you a foreigner? You look like a foreigner. What do you want here, anyway? Is it me jewels?" She laughs. "Ain't never had no jewels. Just a poor old woman. But I knows a thing or two, I do. I used to slip down the path through the Thicket to carry my secrets into Maidenhead, right under the gypsies' noses. Pop out in Boyn Hill. Sell your jewels in Maidenhead, young-ster." She unexepectedly falls into a deep sleep. Gain the codeword *Abstruse*.

Leave the cottage...	**50**

573

"St Mark's Church, Bourne End. It's not far from here - down by the river. I mean, there's plenty of other churchmen up and down the Thames, but whether they practices what they preaches, well, you'll find out for yourself I guess."

The miller leaves you with your drink, your meal and your thoughts. What will really improve the lives of the poor? Charity? Or justice? What can a church-man have to teach you? The fire burns down and you settle into your chair for the night.

Turn to...	**180**

574

Riding into Loudwater you can't help but notice the dirt and poverty. Children play in the street, risking death as the heavy freight wagons and speeding car-riages pass by. Squalid terraces are squeezed between the mills and factories. Costermongers sell from bar-rows half-empty, offering vegetables or rich families' leftovers to the inhabitants.

Visit the lame engineer...	(*Assistant*)	**189**
Leave town towards Wycombe...		**308**
Take the road to Cutthroat Wood...		**561**
Take the lane to Wooburn Green...		**199**
Head towards Flackwell Heath...		**564**

575

Here at Cookham Rise the sparse cottages cluster to-gether around a low railway station on the branch line from Maidenhead. Beside the water tanks and coal yard stands a butcher's shop, where you can buy all manner of fine meats.

Food and Drink	To buy	To sell
rabbit	2s	1s
pheasant	4s	3s
large pike	-	8s
deer carcass	-	£1 5s
picnic hamper	£3 3s	£2

Tools	To buy	To sell
snare	2s	1s

Ask after the butcher's apprentice... (*Additive*)	**751**
Take the road to Cookham Dean...	**563**
Ride east to Cookham...	**246**
Go north onto Cock Marsh...	**444**

576

You accelerate and steer your velosteam towards a promising alleyway. You scrape sparks from the walls as you turn in, mounting a cart's loading ramp and jumping a stack of turnips. Emerging onto a busy street, a crowd of people are shopping at flowerstalls and vegetable barrows. They might be the obstruction you need.

Drop a handful of coins... (£3 12s)	**532**
Knock over a stall...	**499**

577

You hand over the money without a word. The publican does his best to hide his own gin-soaked avarice, but seems to come to a decision.

"This one's got plenty of cash," says the publican. "Come on. Let's scrag the stranger."

The gin-sodden mass of drinkers turn their hungry eyes on you. Yes, they are alcohol-befuddled and clumsy, but there are a lot of them and they are blocking your way. You must fight them to get out.

Gin drinkers	Weapons: **fists (PAR 0)**
Parry:	7
Nimbleness:	7
Toughness:	8

Victory!	**199**
Defeat!	**427**

578

You enter the wise woman's caravan. Hanging from the perforated iron beams are bunches of woodland herbs. The gypsy herself is sitting in her chair, puffing on a pipe and tinkering with a small mechanism. If you have a **clockwork bird**, turn to **1009**.

Medical treatment	To buy
Treat a **fever**...	**6s**
Soothe a **toothache...**	**9s**
Treat a **burn**...	**12s**
Heal a **wound**...	**15s**

If you ask her to treat your wounds, convert each **wound** into a **scar** without testing for **intimidating scars**.

Ask her to tell your future...	(5s)	**891**
Leave the encampment...		**113**

579

"I see a dark future for you. There comes a time of blood - your hand reaches out to the branch of a tree and comes away bloody. The tree's branches hold nests - nests of crows, with rats and mice in their beaks. The vision splits - I see you cutting down the tree and letting light into the wood, and the future brightens. Or I see you feeding the crows. You will have a choice to make..."

The old woman's words conjure uncomfortable visions in your mind. You mount your velosteam and ride away.

Turn to...	**113**

580

You tumble the constable into the water and call for your mate to come alongside: other constables are heading your way, blowing their whistles. There is no way you will be able to make your way into Maidenhead in this furore. Instead, you skip nimbly along the topboards of the barges, slide over heaped coal, scare river cats and children and leap into your own moving steam barge, clearing a full six feet.

Head off onto the river...	**437**

581

Your velosteam, entirely unwilling to start and almost completely ruined by the water, is useless for now. You manage to wheel it to the roadside and after several attempts to rouse helpers, you manage to get it loaded onto a steam-lorry headed to Pinkney's Green. The fair people help you unload it, distraught at the damage to the once-admired machinery.

The Curtis brothers look over it together. "It's fixable," says Davy. "But this is going to be hard work."

It is hard work and a long job and one that consumes all the **money** you have with you. However, after several days work the velosteam is once again ready for the road. It will never be quite the same and you were unable to remove all the dints and bumps from the metalwork, but it is usable. Note that it has **Minor Damage**.

Turn to...	**604**

582

"You think he will escape? I hope so," replies Barsali. "But I fear for him..." Lose the codeword *Anniversary*.

Turn to...   **377**

583

"I hear you have joined up with the anarchists." Father Bourdain looks deep into your eyes. "But you have returned here to talk with me."

"Are you such an enemy to them?"

"No. I am no one's enemy. But let me ask you - what do you put your trust in? A revolution in the nation? Or a revolution in the heart? They will justify almost any violence in the name of helping people and they are achieving a great deal. But the cost..."

"You do not like the cost, father."

"Exactly."

Leave the church...   **703**
Continue talking...   **717**

584

You turn between some narrow iron gates and head down the narrow path to Temple, the hedges either side close enough to touch with an outstretched hand. After a short distance the bumpy path begins to sink into the ground: a local landowner has had the path buried in a tunnel so as not to spoil his view with locals crossing in front of his house! You emerge on the other side in the village of Temple.

Turn to...   **37**

585

The road from Professor Benner's wokshop has been long, lonely and dark. The constant beam of the velosteam's lantern has led you away from the screams of your adoptive family, away from the leaping flames that clothed the machine sheds, away from the dark figures who snatched your mentor into the night. You are not going back.

The suddenness of the Constable's raid took you all by surprise. He had spoken of the risks many times, but who expected airships, firebombs and kidnap? His inventions were too provocative, his politics too principled for the Constables to allow him to continue working. You knew he had angered powerful rivals, but he was wrong when believed the law would

protect him: it was the forces of the law who took him. And now you are cast loose on the road, with only your wits, a vengeful hunger and the fine Ferguson velosteam you had been repairing in the shop.

Who knows whether rescue or revenge will be possible. You have heard that none other than Colonel Snappet of Danesfield house, the commander of the local Constables, was responsible. A powerful man to have as an enemy.

You have in your possession a **blunderpistol (ACC 6)**, a **sabre (PAR 6)** and a set of **punchcards (Selladore E)**. Your ability scores are:

RUTHLESSNESS   4
ENGINEERING   6
MOTORING   4
INGENUITY   5
NIMBLENESS   3
GALLANTRY   2

Turn to...   **324**

586

Here a jetty stands out into the river, a heavy chain running under the water to the Bourne End bank opposite. Moored by the other side is a flat-bottomed ferry, captained by a woman with a clockwork arm. If you wish to hail her, she can take you across for a florin.

Cross the river...   **(2s)**   **703**
Enter the Bounty...   **409**
Return to Cookham...   **246**

587

The Head Girl pouts. "What a square," she says. "You're not so wild after all." You must lower your RUTHLESSNESS score by 1.

Ride away...   **703**

588

The broad Henley road leads through farmland here, slowly climbing westwards. Between the fields of wheat and the pastures of grass, this ribbon of compacted stone and tar stretches off beneath your wheels.

Ride towards Henley...   **445**
Ride east...   **513**

589

The company of drinkers at the Bounty are a raucous mix of rivermen, freighters, country folk and engineers. You overhear tales from the city, of the adventurous plans for a great underground railway, of the wounded soldiers seen coming back from the Spanish war, of the price of malt and the rebels in the West. You are served a pint of a hoppy, fresh ale with a strong alcohol content: the barman calls it Traveller's Rest. "Best enjoyed before a short nap in the sunshine," he says. "Take care on that machine of yourn."

Return to the parlour...   **409**

590

"Indeed, we could be mistaken for each other," he replies. "And what confusion that would cause. Tell me of your ancestry."

When you reply that your parentage is disputed and has always been something of a mystery he nods. "The Regal Prince my father did travel to England himself in his youth... Strange are the ways of fate. Cousin, let me give you something in token of our meeting." He hands you a **ruby ring**. "Remember me."

Ride away...   **535**

591

"Thankyou, stranger," says the girl with a curtsey. "What a kushty bauble. I'll show me mam."

The father comes over. "I am Barsali," he says, "And with manners like that you are always welcome to dance and eat with us." Improve your GALLANTRY by 1. "There is work near Winter Hill for us in the woodlands, so we are steaming down. But not too quickly - there is always time for a fire and a dance. Come and find us again!" Gain the codeword *Anniversary*.

Leave the family dancing...   **288**

592

You are handed a glass jar of cloudy apple cider with a perceptible alcohol haze drifting over it. "How strong is this?" you ask.

"Strong enough." You wait for a more exact answer, but it seems that no-one has ever troubled to measure the cider's ABV. Or perhaps the batches are so inconsistent that it would be a waste of time.

The first pull is surprisingly crisp, but then a strong sour taste arrives with a big tanniny aftertaste. Smacking your lips to aerate your suffering tastebuds, it seems that keeping the stuff flowing is the best way to escape the raw parts of the flavour. The pint disappears quickly and you grimace as the alcohol announces itself to your reflexes, eyes and forebrain all at once.

"Another?" asks the barman.

Return to the bar...   **185**

593

You press on up the river, despite the darkness. An otter splashes off the river-bank with something in its teeth. The river must be cleaner than it looks here. If you possess a **fishing line**, turn to **949** immediately.

Tie up at Maidenhead Wharf...   **333**
Steam on upriver...   **355**

594

Maidenhead! The pearl of the Thames - the computational processor of the British Empire - the shame of the mighty. Thousands work in the block-like computer engine sheds, calculating the needs of Imperial projects all over the world. Thousands more man the countless telegraph stations, trunk lines, coding sheds. Row upon row of tenement and terrace built to house all the workforce line the hillside. A perpetual smog hangs over the city, a result of the constant need for power as coal furnaces drive whirring machines. Coal, coal, coal, on every street corner, in guarded bunkers, in gutters, in the trucks of the railway engines, in the wagons of freight steamers, all to feed the voracious steam computers. The city is like a dark maze of brick and coalsmoke.

Explore the streets on foot...   **943**
Head to the market...   **936**
Head to the Freight Yard...   **888**
Stop at the World's End Music Hall...   **14**
Enter the slums...   **402**
Ride to Boyn Hill... (*Abstruse*)   **113**
Leave the city and take the road east...   **282**
Leave the city and head north...   **650**

595

You are shown to Comrade Feaver who uncharacteristically approaches you directly and shakes your hand. "Well done," she says. "Now I know that I am addressing a true comrade in the revolutionary fight. I have heard the news of Squire Lynch's death - and the burning of his manor. We seek to intimidate his evil peers in the region and his refusal to take our warnings seriously have made him quite an example. We mean to do more: to destroy the railway being built on Squire Haworth's land near Cookham and to see Colonel Snappet of Medmenham strung up. And now I can include you in such plans, Comrade 8236." You are now a **Member of the Compact for Worker's Equality** and you will be allowed to come and go as you please - as long as you are discreet. "No more blindfolds for you," says Comrade Feaver.

Turn to...   **985**

596

The clerks of Coulter's Bank are old men in dusty waistcoats. If they don't wear half-moon spectacles, they have little round ones like glass bottle-bottoms, and if their noses aren't dripping with rheum they are bulbous and red. The one you speak to is ready to accept your hard cash regardless of its provenance and will fill out a docket for your accounts - if you care to keep such a thing.

Coulter's Bank accepts deposits in multiples of 10 guineas (**£10 10s**). Write your savings into the **Bank Account** box on your **Adventure Sheet**. You will be able to withdraw your investment from any other branch of Coulter's Bank or from one of their licensed agents. You can only access these savings at these locations, and only in multiples of 10 guineas.

Leave the bank...   **337**

597

The lane runs down the hill obliquely, keeping a relatively even gradient which suits your velosteam fine. Partway down you come to a driveway marked Bullocks Farm. Roll a dice:

Score 1-2   Runaway bull!   **170**
Score 3-6s The lane is quiet...   **521**

598

You spot Colonel Snappet several times during the evening's entertainment, but he does not expect to see you at a society ball, so even if he glimpses your face, you are not recognised. He is far too busy charming Lady Northfield and her daughters, playing alpha-male and throwing his weight around. While the company find him witty, you notice that few feel comfortable in his presence. After all, he is a torturer and a murderer and has arrested people on a whim.

You don't let him get too far. You know that if you can get him alone and blackmail him with the transcripts you found, then maybe you have a chance of seeing Professor Benner's face in the sunlight once more. So when the Colonel heads out into the garden for a cigar late in the evening, you shadow him closely. He seems to be making for a summerhouse for shelter from the first drops of rain, but as soon as you are out of sight of the house you call his name.

"Snappet!"

He turns sharply, his hand flying to the hilt of his sword. Despite the champagne and the rich food, his reflexes are as quick as ever. "What do you want? Who are you?" He peers through the gloom.

"I want the Professor. I want to know where you have hidden him. I want him alive and free - or you will know the disgrace, aye, and the punishment deserved by a traitor." You hold up the transcript. "I have undeniable proof of your embezzlements, of your murders of Mayor Gordon and Alice de Lacey. And they will very soon be on the desks of your superiors, if you do not do as I say."

Snappet wastes not a moment. He draws his sword with a snarl and launches himself at you!

Colonel Snappet		Weapon: **rapier (PAR 7)**
Parry:	12	
Nimbleness:	5	
Toughness:	3	

Victory!   **710**
Defeat!   **501**

599

The lane down from Odds Hill winds between cottages and workshops, commons and coppices. Men and women work outside their dwellings, making parts for road wheels or scraping half-tanned skins in baths of reeking oak bark. Everyone looks up to see you fly past on your velosteam. Roll a dice to see what you encounter.

Score 1-3   Uninterrupted journey...   **703**
Score 4-6   A stranded journalist...   **605**

600

Your best plan of attack on the empty road is to steam alongside and leap aboard from your velosteam. At the sight of the approaching engine, you open the regulator and roar up to it. The driver looks your way and her eyes flash with recognition. You must now jump onto the footplate of the moving engine!

Jump the gap!	**347**

601

The monks lay down their baskets of food. "Abbot Sneer's getting old," says one. "It's the Dean who'll be in charge next, mark my words. And then there'll be some changes. Less vegetable carrying, more steam." They will sell you some of their surplus produce and will even pay a fair price for any game you have.

Food and Drink	To buy	To sell
bird's eggs	-	3s
rabbit	-	1s
pheasant	-	3s
large pike	-	8s
deer carcass	-	£1 5s
wheel of cheese	£1 2s	14s
bottle of Beehive Stout	2s	1s
bottle of Quinta de Vesan	-	£10

Clothing	To buy	To sell
cloak	£1	15s

Other items	To buy	To sell
Abbey Ribbon	12s	6s

Return to the parlour...	**801**

602

Halfway between Bourne End and Marlow stands the village of Little Marlow. The low thatched roofs of the cottages are in poor condition, green with moss and damp, and the squat church looks unloved, its graveyard overgrown and overcrowded. Lowering over them stands the grey mass of the Marlow Workhouse.

Head to the Workhouse...	**321**
Take the road down towards Marlow...	**18**
Travel on towards Bourne End...	**210**
Ride up to Handy Cross...	**25**
Turn up the lane into Horton Wood...	**131**

603

If you are **Wanted by the Telegraph Guild**, turn to **692** immediately.

Here at the Telegraph Guild compound, all manner of people are sending messages or awaiting replies. In fact, there are three waiting rooms of increasing degrees of comfort for the different classes: the most opulent is hidden behind a glass and walnut screen, with leather armchairs, newspapers, refreshments and a good fire. The second class room is somewhat simpler, but the public office is bare and unadorned.

Ask for help with some 'official paperwork'...	(5s)	**655**
Leave the compound...		**186**

604

"I don't think you can outsmart the guild," she says. "I'll still be liable and that'll be my reputation ruined. The Haulage Guild can get a citizen's license to handle a steam engine revoked, you know? And my loco isn't fully paid off, neither. So take your scheming and stuff it where the sun doesn't shine. You don't impress me."

Return to the parlour...	**180**

605

A woman with a portable telegraph tower and a mechanical notebook slung round her neck is sitting on a milestone as you ride by.

"Can you get me to Maidenhead?" she asks. "I need to talk to my editor as soon as I can and I've got stuck out here waiting for a bus or a lift or something."

Take her to Maidenhead...	**472**
Leave her waiting...	**703**

606

To treat your **wounds** you will need some **bandages** or a **cloak** and some food while you rest and get your strength back (for example a **pork pie**, **deer carcass** or even a **wheel of cheese**). For each **wound** you remove from your adventure sheet you will gain a **Scar** and you should check by rolling two dice to see if you have a new **intimidating scar (RUTH+1)**, indicated by a roll of 12. If you have the codeword *Arthropod*, *Astrakhan* or *Apogee* turn to **631**.

Return to...	**676**

607

The Constable backs off, leaving you to untie your mooring lines and steam away. You have managed to escape the Constables one more time.

Turn to... **745**

608

You have always known that your adoptive father could be ruthless when it suited him. Now you see how he considers his tenants and servants - little more than cattle. You have a hard decision to make: you can renounce your relationship to Judge Hector or you can choose to harden your heart towards this woman. After all, she may not be telling you the whole story.

If you choose to renounce Judge Hector, remove the codeword *Adoption* immediately. You then have the option to avenge the woman in front of you, or to ride on by.

Swear vengeance on Judge Hector... **69**
Leave the woman by the road... **703**

609

You fall into conversation with several of the locals. They are discussing the business of the Deans of Harleyford, just across the Thames from Hurley.

"Lord Dean don't give a fig for his wife," says one. "That's why he had that little bridge built - to pay a visit to the girls in Hurley."

Another shakes their head in disgust. "Droit de seigneur, eh? What a century we live in! It's meant to be the modern day."

"Bridge?" you ask.

"That's right. A little iron bridge over to the lock island. Only big enough for walking on, like. Not a big engine."

Gain the codeword *Alluring* if you don't already have it.

Return to Burchett's Green... **727**

610

As you receive your fifth wound and stagger backwards, you see the driver fetch the Honourable Gerald Gilling a sharp blow across the back of the head with a heavy wrench.

"Jumped up little blighter," says the driver. "Look, share the money with the two of us and we'll tell him that there was four of you, alright? And take this for your arm."

The lordling's purse contains his travelling money for his trip to Slough, no more. Your share comes to **£2 5s**. You may also take his **rapier (PAR 7)** if you wish. Your third wound proves to be no more than a scratch - erase it without further consequences.

Ride away... **23**

611

Freebody's Yard is a bustling hive of activity. A steam winch is hauling a barge out of the water as you approach. Old Freebody waves as you approach.

Have improvements made to your boat... **930**
Sell your boat... **972**
Buy a boat... (if you do not possess one) **883**
Moor here... **915**
Sail off... (if your boat is **moored** here) **360**

612

You pause at Cliveden Gatehouse. The long brick wall is broken by a two-story entrance-way with its own miniature telegraph system for signalling to the main house. Nobody can be seen, but you know you are being watched.

If you have a **Formal Invitation**... **297**
Ride north... **366**
Ride south... **429**

613

You and the mate hammer several stakes into the soft riverbank with a mallet and make the boat fast. "This should hold her," says the mate, "But I'll stay aboard to make sure." Mark your boat mooring as **Cookham (Upstream)**.

Turn to... **12**

614

The road rises steadily from Lane End. Ahead of you are the airship sheds of the Atmospheric Union. Beyond that stands a tall telegraph tower, smoke streaming from a chimney near its base. Roll two dice:

Score 2-4   Telegraph Guild Enforcers... **100**
Score 5-9   The way is clear... **247**
Score 9-12   An abnormal load... **208**

615

Inside the toppled steam carriage is a woman in good-quality travelling clothes. Her driver has plainly fled - unless they are buried beneath the landslip. The traveller, though, is still breathing, but bleeding from a gash to her forehead. You gently carry her out, wash her head with water from the carriage's dripping tank and fashion a bandage from a shred of her cloak lining.

The water awakens her. "Don't take me back," she raves. "I'll not go back."

You cannot take her with you. A nearby inn will probably be the best idea.

Take her to the Drowned Badger... **747**

616

The Freight Yard at Wycombe is a long, thin strip of ground beside the filthy river, walled with a tall brick enclosure designed to prevent pilfering. The various groups of hauliers and freighters unload and refuel in their different corners of the yard, maintaining an uneasy peace under the overseer's watchful eye. The Haulage Guild maintain their own watering station and canteen along one wall.

One driver is complaining about the Constable checkpoints that are springing up on the outskirts of the major towns. "I ain't got nothing to hide, no sirree, but every time they stops us to check our cargo it's another 40 minutes added on the run. Have to get pressure up again, and the pipes swelling while we stand."

You overhear another driver advise him. "Well, there's no need to pass the Marlow checkpoints at all. You simply has to take Honeysuckle Lane from Handy Cross over to Bovingdon Green," she says. "If your engine'll take the slope, that is."

Look for Comrade Robin... (**heavy parcel**) **359**
Talk with the Guildsmen...
      (**Guildsman's medallion**) **268**
Leave the yard... **337**

617

Your attempt succeeds and before long the Welsh adventuress is abseiling down the wall beside you. She rewards you with a grateful kiss and a word of advice. "Don't let anyone know that I am free. Not yet. But if you visit the Oaken Vale, I will show my gratitude more tangibly." She slips off into the night. Gain the codeword *Aspect* and lose the codeword *Evergreen*.

Ride off... **288**

618

You eventually reach the railway line that is being forged across the farmland north from Maidenhead. Branch railways like these are unpopular with road-freighters and even more unpopular with the land-owners who are compelled to sell their land.

Investigate the railway... **750**
Cross over and head west... **646**

619

Dashwood's servants bring you hot water, lotions and cloths and very soon you have been able to clean, treat and bandage all your wounds. For each **wound** on your adventure sheet, roll two dice. A roll of 2-10 indicates that it should be erased and becomes a **scar**; a roll of 11-12 indicates that it becomes an **intimidating scar (RUTH+1)**. After your treatment, you lie down to take some rest.

If you have the codeword *Arthropod*, *Astrakhan* or *Apogee*, turn to... **286**
Otherwise... **172**

620

Harris looks at you in surprise, but it only takes a short while to convince her that you understand her blueprints and machinery. You stay up late into the night with her, working by candle-light. Make an ENGINEERING roll of difficulty 12.

Successful ENGINEERING roll! **667**
Failed ENGINEERING roll! **469**

621

You awaken in the tight grip of rope, bound to a chair, still in the dressing room. The Duke of Beverley stands over you, his face puce with rage. "Where is it? And where is your accomplice?" he bellows.

The Dervish's Eye is gone. So is whoever knocked you out and beat you to the prize. For the next few hours Beverley and several others try to beat a confession out of you, but of course you are unable to tell them anything. "What about this?" shouts the Duke, flinging something against your helpless face.

You look down to where it lies on the carpet. A burnt rose.

The Duke and his friends eventually convince themselves that you are innocent of the crime, although most likely guilty of the intention to steal, so they bundle you up and arrange for punishment. "Where am I going?" you ask. "I took nothing!"

"To prison," sneers a guard. "The Duke don't bother with courts and such-like." You are marched out of the room, but before you go, you pretend to stumble, pick up the **burnt rose** and hide it about yourself.

If you are a **Famed Lawbreaker**, turn to... **274**
If you are the **People's Champion**, turn to... **1005**
Otherwise, turn to... **722**

622

At a slight rise in the road stands a lonely signpost, its concrete based reinforced against the heavy wheels of turning semaphore-wagons. Apart from the lights of Marlow behind you, it is quiet and dark.

Ride North towards Wycombe... **25**
Ride East towards Little Marlow... **602**

623

To stop the freighters you must summon your most threatening aspect. Make a RUTHLESSNESS roll of difficulty 10, adding 1 if you are **Wanted by the Constables**.

Successful RUTHLESSNESS roll! **664**
Failed RUTHLESSNESS roll! **202**

624

"Thankyou, oh thankyou," pants Squire Lynch. You haul him to his feet and drag him downstairs, noting that the spilt oil lamp will quickly set the paper-stuffed study alight.

You tie the Squire up in the copse and then raise the alarm, waking the staff of the house lest they suffer for the Squire's evil. Then you take the wretched man and ride, fast, to the nearest airship field, not resting until he is safely on a flight to Casablanca, the captain paid with the Squire's own gold, leaving you with **£13 10s** you took from him. The question is whether Comrade Feaver be convinced. Gain the codeword *Ahasuerus*.

Turn to... **551**

625

You find a stretch of fence that seems to be obstructed from view and begin to climb. After leaping down, you begin to sidle your way around the huts and temporary shelters towards the chain gang. Suddenly you come face to face with an armed Constable. To knock him down without raising the alarm you must make a NIMBLENESS roll of difficulty 10 - but you can add 2 if you have a **club**. Alternatively, if you have a **razor** you can cut his throat.

Cut his throat or successful NIMBLENESS roll! **346**
Failed NIMBLENESS roll! **798**

626

You place the passdisc into Comrade Feaver's waiting palm. "Ah," she replies. "So Hawthorne will get his poisons. Well done." Remove **passdisc 21** from your Adventure Sheet. Feaver rewards you with **£2** and a **bargee's badge**. "You may find this useful in your work for us," she says.

Turn to... **275**

627

Your ability to mend your velosteam yourself depends upon your ENGINEERING skill and your access to materials. To repair each level of damage you must have a minimum ENGINEERING score as noted below as well as one of the items listed, which you must discard to complete the job.

	ENGINEERING score	Materials
Critical damage...	10	**high pressure valve**
Serious damage...	8	**brass flange joint**
Minor damage...	6	**copper pipe**

Return to your hideout... **220**

628

The Cross Keys is a quiet place: the few drinkers here are content to sit and enjoy their game of backgammon or to rest in the windowseats and look at the world outside. Here the barrels of beer stand in the parlour itself, each with its own wooden jug beneath the tap. The landlord has a striking face - a birthmark over his cheek and forehead and a nose broken many times.

Also drinking here is a pedlar who is ready to show you his wares.

Tools	To buy	To sell
axe	8s	-
wirecutters	12s	-
fishing line	1s	-

Jewellery	To buy	To sell
locket	6s	-
silver ring	10s	-
gold ring	-	£1 1s

Other items	To buy	To sell
constable's whistle	3s	2s
chess set	-	£2
ivory fan	£2	-
Bargee's Badge	£6	-

Buy a pint of local ale... (1s)		682
Leave the inn...		727

629

Your rash attempt to ride through the sloping wheat field is a step too far. Your velosteam spills you onto the ground and in a few moments the guildsmen are on you. They knock you into submission with their carbine butts, angrily venting their rage on your unconscious body in return for your crimes. Gain a **wound** from the beating, but at least now that they have caught and punished you, you are no longer **Wanted by the Haulage Guild**.

If you have **five Wounds**...	74
Otherwise...	296

630

The room falls silent. The clerk in front of you shivers, then sneezes in nervous terror, but no-one moves. You repeat your threat: "This man's life is in your hands. Unlock the vault, now!"

A figure moves to the door and a shadow falls across the already dim room. The guards step in, wielding their cudgels but unsure how to proceed. The manager calls to them from behind his heavy desk. "Guards! Arrest that fiend!"

With no other way to assert yourself, you make good on your threat and fire the gun. The clerk falls backwards and the retort of the shot fills the room, the smoke of the discharge billowing around you.

You have a moment to swing and fire at one of the two guards, knocking him down too, but the second barrels into you and swings his cudgel. You must

fight for a chance to make your escape! Win or lose, you are now **Wanted by the Constables** for your audacious crimes.

Bank Guard		Weapon: **cudgel (PAR 4)**
Parry:	9	
Nimbleness:	5	
Toughness:	4	

Victory!	377
Defeated!	779

631

You lie down to rest in your bivouac, listening to the rain dripping onto the tarpaulin. The noise of the rain increases and you look around to see that it is not just water dropping from the sky, by small coins. Stepping out to look upwards, you are surprised to see a heavy anvil dropping towards you. Pinned to the spot, you cannot even turn your head as the approaching metal slams into your head and cuts out your visions. For a moment all is black, then you shudder awake in your bed. It is still raining, but you do not feel rested. Gain the codeword *Apprehend*.

Return to...	676

632

☐

If the box is empty, put a tick in it. If it is already ticked, turn to **683** immediately.

"Help? Well, I know of a man lamed by a work accident in Loudwater. He needs a new direction, yes, and hope too. He is a skilled engineer. Perhaps you can help him find a new employer. I am not a machinist myself. I have no idea where to start."

Gain the codeword *Assistant*.

Leave the church...	703
Continue talking...	717

633

You leave your velosteam hidden in a glade and set off into the wood after the elusive deer. They will be nervy and it will depend a great deal on luck whether you succeed in finding any, before you have the task of shooting one. Roll a dice:

Score 1-2	Turn to...	55
Score 3-4	Turn to...	270
Score 5-6	Turn to...	691

634

The Walnut Tree is named after the craggy ruin of a tree that stands directly in front of the main entrance, forcing the clientele to slip sideways into the parlour. It is a matter of pride that the owner of the house has never rearranged the entrance to make it more convenient for his customers.

Inside there are a mix of farm labourers enjoying their midday meal and several men plainly in service in one of the large houses nearby. A knot of Telegraphers in their green tunics also sit around a punchbowl.

Buy a drink...	(2s)	903
Leave the inn...		703

635

The blacksmith steps away from his pounding steam-hammer and considers your question. "I don't have any of that stuff myself," he says. "Fearful expensive and very finickity. Your best bet is to head up to the big smoke and buy it there, maybe at the engineer's sheds at King's Cross. But I did know of a lady who had a workshop in Maidenhead that used it. But last I heard she was selling up and moving on. Perhaps finding her will help you out."

Return to the forge...   60

636

You explain that you would like to help. The engineer's face screws up with discomfort. "I don't need charity," he says. "I don't want to be trouble to anyone."

"Well, consider this capital an investment, then. If you use it to buy the tools you need to work from here and to take in piece-work for the factories, you may not miss your legs."

"My legs is my legs. I'm not going to bleeding forget I ain't got 'em."

"Would you value the investment?"

The engineer accepts grumpily. "All right. Though I probably won't be able to get any work."

It doesn't take long before the engineer's situation is turned around. With the money you gave him he is able to set himself up as an independent craftsman, deciding his own hours of work, accepting commissions and contracts, employing his elder children as runners and assistants. He insists on paying you back on your investment with interest - gain **£22** -

and lets everyone know that the Steam Highwayman is more than simply a robber of the rich. Gain two **Solidarity Points** and erase the codeword *Assistant*.

Turn to...   574

637

A rowing boat dashes across the river, ferrying a lover to his mistress. You nearly run them down, as the occupants are paying no attention to the rules of the water whatsoever. This is Boulter's Lock - the riverside playground of the rich and idle. If you want to see what London society looks like at its most foolish and fashionable you have come to the right place.

Moor here...	825
Enter the lock and head downstream...	
(2s or **Bargee's Badge**)	437
Return upstream...	463

638

Time in gaol passess slowly. Your attempt to keep track with a wall tally is hindered by the regular shifts in accommodation that the prison guards enforce. Roll two dice to see what your imprisonment holds for you.

Score 2-4	Turn to...	266
Score 5-6	Turn to...	192
Score 7	Turn to...	93
Score 8-9	Turn to...	35
Score 10-12	Turn to...	354

639

Somehow you manage to make your way to Hard-to-Find Farm. When you arrive it is dusk and clouds are filling the sky. Muggins, Mr Hibbert's butler, finds you at the door. He catches you as you slump forward into the welcoming dark.

You awake in an unusually clean bed beneath a window glowing with sunlight. Justin Hibbert is there in a basketwork chair, reading one of his tomes. He lowers it and looks over his glasses at you. "Ahh, my friend. Awake at last. It has been four days - and at last I have been able to repay you for saving my life. No, do not stir. Your wounds are not yet healed, and I suspect you have a broken rib under there too."

Hibbert and his servants do an admirable job of caring for you. He keeps you company as much as he can, never asks how you came by your hurts, pays for medicines and treatments, cares for you like one of his own family. And in the process you learn much about him. "I have no family of my own, you know. When I pass on, this place will go to a distant cousin, a man I have never met. My library contains my closest friends."

Soon you are nearing a full recovery. Hibbert must leave for London, but he insists you stay until you are completely well and leaves you in Muggins' reliable hands. Before he leaves he confides that he has never enjoyed a house guest's company more than yourself.

For each **wound** you have, roll two dice. A roll of 12 indicates it has become an **intimidating scar (RUTH+1)** which should be noted on your adventure sheet. However, a roll of 4 or less indicates that it has not healed properly, and will remain as a **wound** rather than healing. Otherwise, each **wound** will become a **scar** and should be noted on your adventure sheet.

As you prepare to leave, Muggins brings you a few belongings that Hibbert has set aside for you: a purse of **£1 10s**, a warm **cloak** and an old **blunderpistol**. You are almost set to pick up where you left off. Gain the codeword *Ambulatory*.

Leave the farm...   **11**

640

The first day's journey is slowed by a breakdown on one of the engines. To make up for it, the haulier decides to drive on into the night. "After all, we've got you for company."

You are riding alongside the rear engine when a crossbow bolt whizzes through the night and strikes the haulier in the back. He falls to the footplate, leaving the engine without a driver. You quickly hook your velosteam alongside and leap to the controls. You must make a MOTORING roll of difficulty 10

Successful MOTORING roll!   **105**
Failed MOTORING roll!   **272**

641

You settle into your seat as the lights dim. The massive grid of rotating pixel-cubes remains dark and uncommunicative as cheap cigar smoke and chatter rise in the auditorium, but with a martial blare of automatic trumpets, the show begins.

You are taken on a tour of Walkerville, the capital of the Confederated State of Nicaragua. The broad streets running with modern steam-trams and the fine ballrooms are the envy of everyone in the moth-eaten Maidenhead auditorium. Ladies in vast dresses and gentlemen in sharp-edged jackets and wide sunhats dance across the flickering animated board, the tones of grey clearly showing the mixed races of the revellers, but as the presentation shifts to show the vast hillside plantations you can also see the ranks of indentured labourers and slaves. The Confederacy's growth through Cuba, Belize, Mexico and Panama has made them them raw material producer without peer, massively overshadowing their Union cousins to the North, but the human cost is terrible.

The presentation continues, illustrating the Presidential Palace, showing a flickering portrait of William Walker himself (eliciting many a murmour of admiration), and finishing with illustrations of the San Juan River and the Grand Nicaraguan Canal. The Union states of California, Oregon and Washington still depend on sea freight for their contact with the Eastern cities as a result of the Plains Tribes' southern guns, and so the Confederacy can pursue its policy of slave-industrialisation without check. In fact Imperial factories are filled with slave-grown cotton and the very shirt on your own back may have been plucked by a whip-scarred hand.

After the show you are somewhat surprised to see that the narrator is a black man, although perhaps his resonant voice should have led you to expect it. He proudly wears a 'Walker' fashion hat, although he slumps dejectedly into a loose chair when he comes offstage.

Leave the World's End...   **594**
Head to the bar...   **978**

642

The racetrack is cleared every few days for use by speed enthusiasts. Today there are around a dozen steam cars and their drivers competing against each other, jostling for space on the narrow track, overtaking at the contrived twists and turns, powering down the straights, filling the air with the shriek and hiss of steam and the smell of coal and lubricating oil.

A collection of airmen, engineers and enthusiasts stand watching. "These are fast," says one, "But nothing on what I hear Lord Dashwood is building down in West Wycombe."

"He can get speed," says another, "But can he

stay on the road? Crashed his last one up there at Coker Bend, they had to carry him out."

If you want to bet on the races here, you may stake a wager of between **£1** and **£10**. Roll two dice to see the outcome:

Score 2-7   Lose your bet
Score 8-9   Gain twenty percent on your stake.
              (**4s** in each **£1**)
Score 10-11 Gain forty percent on your stake.
              (**8s** in each **£1**)
Score 12   Double your stake.
              (**£1** for each **£1**)

Leave the racetrack...   **247**

643
Night begins to fall and rather than spend lamp-oil and worry trying to feel your way upriver in the dark, it makes better sense to moor up. The cabin at the rear of your craft is small, hampered partly by the steam engine that powers the boat, but at least it is warm. Mist rises over the water and you watch the traffic quieten until it is only the constables patrol boats that churn past.

The morning is bright and cold and you repressure the steam engine with the coals of the day before. "It doesn't do to let this fire go out fully," you explain to the mate. "The boiler is designed to be warm. When it cools, it shrinks, and becomes brittle."

"Aye-aye, captain," comes the reply.   If you have a **Perkins Machine** fitted to your boat, turn to **907** immediately.

Moor at Maidenhead Wharf...   **333**
Steam on...   **355**

644
The clerks stand about muttering, wringing their hands. After waiting to see if anyone will serve you for several minutes, you are approached by a white-haired, bowed old man with a hacking cough.

"The bank has failed! Withdrawal is, lamentably, out of the question and we are unable to provide you with the services for which Coulter's was heretofore renowned."

If you have an account at Coulter's, remove any savings from the account box on your adventure sheet. It seems that the directors' over-enthusiastic investment in airship travel has brought the bank to collapse after the tragic crash of the Great Sovereign. Erase the codeword *Forceful*.

Return to the High Street...   **337**

645
The room kept for you here at the Freighter's Haven is sparse, with a very small fire that is rarely lit. Nonetheless, it is quiet, private and secure. You can rest and treat your **wounds** if you are hurt, as well as leaving your possessions and money here by adding them to the box below.

Rest and treat your **wounds**...   **543**
Return to the parlour...   **79**

646
You stop for a moment where two narrow lanes create a rutted crossroad. To one side stands Cannon Court Farm. One lane leads north, slowly climbing the hill towards Cookham Dean, another westwards, one south towards Furze Platt and another eastwards towards the railway line.

Ride north...   **186**
Ride east...   **454**
Ride south...   **650**
Ride west...   **725**

647
Your night's rest at the riverside is refreshing. Heal one **wound** if you have one, converting it to a **Scar** by the normal process. When you set off upriver in the early morning, the river is empty. You steam past Cliveden boathouse and approach Cookham lock with its islands and boathouses.

Continue to Cookham Lock...   **848**

648

You arrange for a message to be carried to your adoptive father, Judge Hector, pleading for his intercession. Sure enough, on the day of your trial you see him at the bench, his face stern and drained of any sign of compassion. The proceedings continue quickly, your prosecutors have the support of the jury and your end is nearing. Then, after a unanimous verdict of 'Guilty' from the jury, Judge Hector defies all sense by sentencing you to a year's imprisonment, not death. He places all blame for your crimes on himself. "I myself sponsored the accused," he says, "Giving shelter and succour. I too am guilty. I resign my position henceforth."

As cameras flash and the audience and jury begin to shout, you are quickly hustled away to a cell, never to see Judge Hector again. You have escaped with your life (and are no longer **Wanted by the Constables**), but you have been disowned by your adoptive father and will never see him again. Lose the password *Adoption*.

Turn to...   594

649

A caravan of travelling entertainers are camping by the roadside. They offer to teach you a few acrobatic tricks in exchange for something sparkly. Make a GALLANTRY roll and add 1 to it for every piece of **gold** or **silver** jewellery you give them.

Score <8	Turn to...	660
Score 8+	Turn to...	1008

650

You are on the road on the outskirts of Maidenhead, just where the smog and terraces of the future meet the farmland of the past. On one side stands a hedge and lane running north, for now still undeveloped. To the south stand brick houses, wooden sheds, iron and concrete elevated loading platforms. The main road skirts the city to the west. If you are **Wanted by the Constables**, turn to **731** immediately.

Ride south into Maidenhead...	594
Take the Marlow Road...	725
Head to Pinkney's Green...	535
Drive up Cannon Court Lane...	671

651

Remove the **melon** from your possessions. "Ooh, a melon!" chuckles the old woman. "It's year's since I tasted such a thing. We used to creep over the Cliveden wall and filch them from the hothouses. Now that was a lark. We'd watch all the lords and ladies dancing from the summerhouse and sneak down to swim in the river whiles they was all occupied." She launches into other fond reminiscences and when you leave, you know that she has enjoyed at least an afternoon of gladness in her illness.

Leave the cottage...   50

652

Several beautiful, large shire horses come plodding down the lane and you steam to the side to let them and their groom pass. Docile, personable beasts, they are almost redundant now, replaced by engines like the one you straddle. Who keeps these? Surely for little more than nostalgia?

Ride on when they have passed...   37

653

"'Ere, I know you," says a gruff voice as you step ashore. It is Constable with an all-too familiar face. "There's a price on your head, matey, and I'll have it by hook or by crook!"

He attacks you with his truncheon. You must defeat him or you will be thrown into gaol - and likely lose your barge as well.

Constable	Weapon: **truncheon (PAR 4)**
Parry:	8
Nimbleness:	4
Toughness:	4

Victory!	580
Defeated!	187

654

Steaming down the lane beneath the dashing clouds, you are treated to a view of progress in action. To one side stand the hedges, the ditches and fields of the old world. A boy leads a horse over a freshly-ploughed field. And on the other side is a string of terraces leading up towards Bourne End, each house thrown up by bricklayers and steam cranes, prefabricated frames and wall-portions bolted together in the race to house the multitude. You pass navvies digging approach-roads for the steam-cars of the new middle class and labourers hauling pipes slung between their strained shoulders, while tracked steam engines bulldoze and shovel the ground. Who is to say if the fields across the road won't be swallowed by another such estate when you next ride past?

Steam on... **703**

655

"I know who you want," says the Telegrapher. "Quick Jess can sort out any paper issues that you have." He opens the gate and lets you into the back office, where a woman in thick glasses is hunched over a drawing board. Between her time designing and refining Guild machinery, Quick Jess has a lucrative sideline as an excellent forger.

Papers	To buy	To sell
malt license	3s	-
formal invitation...	£15	-
letter of introduction...	£10 10s	-
Grantly's Membership Card... £50		£5

Return to the Telegraph Station... **603**

656

The hat shop in fact sells a variety of high-class clothing and accoutrements, guaranteed to leave you looking your best when you depart. Prices reflect the difficulty of coming upon high-class tailors here, but moving amongst the rich and noble classes requires proper dress.

Clothing	To buy	To sell
cloak	£1	15s
dark cloak (RUTH+1)	-	£2 10s
eyepatch (RUTH+1)	15s	5s
jewelled eyepatch (RUTH+1 GAL+1)	£5 2s	£2 2s
wide-brimmed hat	£1 10s	18s
silk scarf	£2	£1
bow tie (GAL+1)	£1 10s	£15s
top hat	£3	£2
silk waistcoat (GAL+1)	£4 2s	£3
fencing gloves (NIM+1)	-	£4
dancing shoes (GAL+3)	-	£10
dinner jacket	£5	£2
ballgown	£25 4s	£16

Other items	To buy	To sell
parasol	£6	£2
box of cigars	£2 2s	£1 10s
ivory fan	£2	£1 8s
initialled purse	-	£2 2s
letter of introduction	-	£1 10s
Formal Invitation	-	£4 8s
Grantly's Membership Card	-	£6 6s
locket of King Charles' hair	-	£15
opal cufflinks	-	£6
griffin cufflink	-	£1 3s

Leave the shop... **94**

657

"I hope you can find 'em," says ... "I'll pay you well for them - they're not the sort of thing you come across everyday." Gain the codeword *Advertise*.

Leave the brewery... **4**

658

You tell the quartermaster about the dockers' request for guns and give him **passdisc 33** as proof. He seems to recognise the little brass disc and disappears to talk to Comrade Feaver. He returns some time later.

"Our noble comrade has agreed to release the weaponry. You should take a boat to Medmenham wharf and load the guns by night, then transport them down to the dockers on the Wye. Their readiness to strike will be our opportunity to galvanise the region." He gives **passdisc 67** to show to your contact in Medmenham. If you have the codeword *Antipodes*, gain the codeword *Ascorbic*.

Turn to... **985**

659

You must fight the woman unarmed, unless you have a blunt weapon such as a **blackjack**, **truncheon** or **club**. You must subdue her quickly, or you will have the entire yard ganging up against you!

Female Haulier		Weapon: **club (PAR 4)**
Parry:	7	
Nimbleness:	3	
Toughness:	4	

Victory! **814**
Defeated! **296**

660

The acrobats teach you some vaults and cartwheels - pleasant tricks for entertaining. Gain the codeword *Advent*.

Ride on...   **428**

661

□

If the box is empty, tick it now and read on. If it is already ticked, turn straight to **177**.

Remove the **punchcards (Habbukuk K)** from your possessions. The manager is amazed. "I really did not expect you to give these to me," he says. "They're really very hard to get hold of and can be worth quite a lot. Wait here, will you?"

He bustles off to hand them over to the clerks who will reboot the system. Then he returns with a finely written **letter of introduction**. "This is a reference from the Telegraph Guild, recommending you to the great and good of the land. It may help you with persons of influence."

Leave the tower...   **177**

662

You are at a junction on the Henley road. A tall signpost points five hands in five directions:

Ride north to Temple Village...   37
Ride north-east to Bisham Village...   737
Ride west on the Henley Road...   513
Ride south towards Burchett's Green...   727
Ride south-east towards the Bath Road...   113

663

How will you stop the carriage?

Dig a ditch in the road...
    (**shovel**, **pick** or **explosives**)   769
Ride alongside and jump aboard...   433
Shoot at the driver...   785

664

The freighters, unsure of your intentions, bring the heavy steam wagon to a stop at the side of the road. The elder of the two stands protectively in front of the other, a slight young man in dirty overalls.

"What do you want with us?" asks the master. "We're none of your landed gentry with cash in our pockets. We've less than two pound on us all together and most of that's due for refueling in Marlow, together with a shilling for the boy's dinner." He opens his purse and shows you how little they have.

Take the money...   Gain **£1 17s**   510
Give them a few coins...   (**£2**)   781
Ride on...   202

665

□

If the box is empty, put a tick in it and read on. If it is already ticked, turn to **517** immediately. Sure enough, a freight wagon flying a Co-operative banner appears at the foot of the hill. They are laden down with bales of hay.

Set fire to the hay...   790
Chat to the driver...   718
Ride away...   535

666

The priest nods. "Many people come to such a conclusion. That to see justice we must intervene. I cannot condemn you for such a decision - only warn you. St Bernard teaches that the road to hell is paved with good intentions. Do not let yourself be satisfied with the option that is least bad. Such a perspective will habituate you to compromise and inure you to the suffering of others."

Erase the codewords *Arthropod*, *Astrakhan* or *Apogee* if you have them. If you have the codeword *Apprehend*, turn to **976**.

Leave the church...   703

667

Eventually you crack the problem. Lalage Harris is impressed. "You plainly know your way around an engine," she says. "I can hand this over to my assistants now. I'll come with you."

She collects a bag of tools and climbs aboard your velosteam. Before long, you are back on the open road, heading up to West Wycombe and Lord Dashwood's garage. He is overjoyed to welcome you both and rewards you with a purse containing five guineas (**£5 5s**).

The three of you start work on the steamer, which Dashwood has named the Wagtail. Tuning the engine is a long process, combined with frequent trial runs on the West Wycombe Estate. Harris calls a stop after a week of work.

"We can't do any more with what we have," she says. "We can't mill the cylinders any more closely as long as we use copper. But there is an alloy I've heard of that will withstand even greater pressures. It's hard to get hold of, though."

Lord Dashwood looks at you. "You're a resourceful sort of person. Get me this alloy and you can name your price." You will need to seek high and low for this **titanium alloy** if you are to get the Wagtail finished.

Turn to...   492

668

The Governor shakes his head. "Alas, I did not think that such a famed personage would deceive me in such a way. We will have to detain you a little longer, alas, alas." You are no longer considered a **Famed Lawbreaker** (erase it from your titles) and the Governor delays your release in punishment.

Turn to...   638

669

The Freight Yard in Marlow is full of laden trailers waiting to be hauled away to Henley, Maidenhead, Wycombe, Oxford, London or further abroad. Several road engines are undergoing repairs and the air is thick with the smell of grease and coal dust.

Look for work...   836
Return to the High Street...   4

670

The boat moves gently up against the wharf at Marlow riverside. A stationary steam engine is pumping water out of the river right alongside a family trying to picnic on the grass. If you are **Wanted by the Constables**, turn to **832**. Otherwise, mark your Boat Mooring as **Marlow (downstream)**.

Head into town...   4

671

You turn up the lane running north from Furze Platt, beneath a hovering buzzard and a cloudy sky. Roll two dice:

Score 2-6   A hitch-hiker...   371
Score 7-8   The dusty lane leads on...   646
Score 9-12 Haymaking...   201

672

Your voyages have brought you to Bray Reach. The Thames flows on, broadening with every lock and confluence, past Bray, Windsor, Weybridge, Walton, Hampton, Kingston, Teddington, Twickenham and then into London itself. Downstream from here the great city's influence is felt strongly and the country-folk begin to fall into the minority: larger and larger steam barges have proliferated with the rebuilding of larger locks, carrying the heavy cargo that London demands to keep its pressure up.

Steam upstream...   593
Wait until the morning to travel upstream... 643
Head downstream towards London...
                         The Reeking Metropolis 513
Moor at the wharves at Two Bridges...   245

673

The steam wagon approaching is a long, articulated loader with its boiler slung beneath the freight deck and the driving cabin perched high to one side. The driver has to steam carefully past overhanging branches, keeping to the centre of the road. There are two guards sat near the front, each armed with a high powered carbine. If you are **Wanted by the Haulage Guild**, turn to **42** immediately.

Talk to the wagoneers...
            (Guildsman's medallion)   833
Leave them well alone...   202

674

Macready's den is empty and quiet. His boxes and trays of forgeries, punchcards and tools have been tidied away. It is as though he was never here. You ask one of the warehouse women about him. "Who? Never heard of him," is all the response you get.

Leave the warehouse...   594

675

You ride through the open gates of Hedsor House and up the drive. The place has a sorrowful look - the air of a house once loved and now somewhat decayed. Several statues of griffins stand in prominent places. You head up the drive but see no-one about other than an old, shabbily dressed man pruning roses. He looks up and admires your velosteam.

"Handsome machine. But machinery is a lure to the young."

"Why do you say that?" you ask in reply.

"My son... My son loved machinery. Or perhaps he still does. He would be about your age, but I have not heard from him for over a year. Tell me - have you ever flown in an airship? That was my boy's delight and my mistake. I took him up, travelling by those infernal gasbags, and nothing would satisfy him other than flight, flight, flight." He puts down his secateurs. "But I find I am morose this evening. I am in need of company - varied company. Perhaps you can tell a story? You have the look of an adventurer, and I would have my mind diverted with a story. Come in and dine with me and tell me about your wonderful machine and the places it has taken you."

Accepting his offer and entering the grand house, you discover that the old man is the Master of Hedsor and Judge - Judge Hector. He is a stern man but his table offers you an impressive spread. He drinks up your stories of the heroic and the shameful, ironically passing no judgement at all.

"I too have brought about suffering, even death. That is the lot of people with power, I find. You cannot renounce your power if you are born to it, for then, who would you be?" asks the Judge. He then tells you of his own life, his wife's death, his son and heir's departure from his life, how he became obsessed with joing an airship crew and disappeared.

"Do you think," asks the Judge, "That an adventurer like yourself could find my son? I do not know whether he is alive or dead and when I am gone he will inherit all that you see around you. Perhaps he has travelled to a distant land and has found happiness - God grant it. But I do not know and I spend my time here worrying and distraught. Help me answer my question, stranger. Find my Gregory."

You stay overnight at the Judge's request and are treated with the utmost civility and service by his numerous staff. In the morning, as you prepare to leave, he tells you one more detail. "My son was a healthy young man but had developed an addiction to opium-smoking. Return here if you learn of him - alive or dead. But do not come back if you find nothing." Gain the codeword *Abapical*.

You mount your velosteam and leave Hedsor house.

Head east... **366**
Ride down to Bourne End... **703**

676

Gain the codeword *Ashen* if you don't already have it.

Your shelter in Windsor Wood is rudimentary, but a fireplace and a windproof bivouac will do wonders for your morale and well-being. You can leave possessions here, but it will simply be a matter of hiding them under a fallen tree or in another such place, like a squirrel, and you haven't any guarantee that they will be there when you return here.

To open a **strongbox** you will need either an INGENUITY score of at least 6 and a **skeleton key** or an INGENUITY score of at least 8 and some **welding tools**. If you have these, note this passage and turn to 821.

If you want to repair your velosteam, you will need tools and an ENGINEERING score proportional to the damage.

ENGINEERING score		Materials
Critical damage...	10	**high pressure valve**
Serious damage...	8	**brass flange joint**
Minor damage...	6	**copper pipe**

Rest and treat your **Wounds**... **606**
Head towards Cutthroat Wood... **530**
Head towards Wooburn Green... **199**
Head towards Odds Hill... **177**

677

Above the entrance of the inn prowls the original red lion: a life-size, wooden sculpture painted a throbbing gloss red. It is something of a tradition for the young men of the town to prove their mettle by decorating, adorning or even kidnapping the lion. Several traders are continuing their market business here inside the parlour, but more are gaming and drinking in the gloom.

Buy a drink...	(1s)	956
Leave the inn...		337

678

The bar at the World's End serves fashionable Confederate-style beers and cocktails and is full of working girls, engine clerks, speculators and adventurers. An automatic pianiola plays incessantly in the corner, jangling its ill-tuned strings beneath the hubbub and rausous laughter.

Try a Southern Sour...	(4s)	400
Order a Condor Ale...	(4s)	894
Leave the bar...		395

679

You steer your boat into the bank and prepare to moor up. If you are **Wanted by the Constables**, turn to **832**. Otherwise, write **Marlow (Upstream)** in the Boat Mooring section of your Adventure sheet.

Go ashore...	4

680

You open the door but nobody climbs down from the compartment. "Wait a minute, youngster," says a bird-like voice, "I'm just getting to a good part."

Peering inside you see a dumpy woman sat at a portable desk typing frantically at a large type-writing machine. "Now, after she writes the letter, oh yes, it can be all 'You never supported me in my career and now I'm going to prove to you that I can be the woman you never were' and then we'll have the best friend come in and that's when the news of her father's arrest can be broken. Yes, yes."

"Excuse me," you interrupt.

"Really, now is not a good time," she says, not looking up. "Flow, darling, flow!"

"Your money or your life!"	432
"I guess I'll leave you to it, then."	535

681

All Saints Church has a fine flint and stone facade and an elegant spire rising beside the river. It is a recent building, testifying to the prosperity of the people of Marlow, and inside rich colours dapple the floor where sunlight streams through painted glass. A poorbox stands by the door and the sound of music flows from the direction of the organ.

Linger and listen to the music...		757
Make a donation to the poor box...	(1s or more)	803
Leave the church...		4

682

"What can you serve me here?" you ask the scarred barman. He gives you look, then a leer.

"Try the Highwayman," he suggests. "A well-hopped, amber ale. Maris Otter hops, mainly, but with some fancy business to keep you interested."

He pulls you a pint into an sturdy clay pot. The head settles and you can see into a clear, shining draught. "Looking for your future? The gypsy lady in the thicket can do that for you. Or her sister at the fair."

The beer has a clean and bitter taste with some fruitiness from the late hopping. Delicious.

If you have 3 or more **Solidarity Points**, turn to **609**.

Return to the bar...	628

683

If you are a **Member of the Compact for Workers' Equality**, turn to **583**.

Father Bourdain smiles. "You are so zealous! Well, let me tell you of some more in need. It isn't glamorous work. I know of a bedridden woman in Flackwell Heath who longs for company. And then there are the families who work the steam barges - who long for their children to have schooling. Have you visited the workhouse in Marlow? A dreadful place - but at least it is a shelter. I do wonder what more can be done."

Leave the church...	703
Continue talking...	717

684

You are in Lane End, a small but busy village where the high road from Marlow splits towards the villages of the high Chilterns. A tall water tower stands over the houses directly opposite a striking iron steeple, and the place bustles with refueling and rewatering road engines. Everyone seems to be wearing overalls or smocks, carrying tools or pushing barrows of coal, loading or breaking cargo down.

Look for Dr Smollett's surgery... **823**
Enter the Freighter's Haven Inn... **79**
Ride towards Wheeler End... **137**
Take the Marlow Road... **614**
Steam south-west cross country... **288**
Head up into the Chilterns...
                    Highways and Holloways 546

685

If you have the **telegraph transcript**, turn to **547** immediately. Otherwise, read on.

"Back again?" Colonel Snappet is becoming bored. "You'd better be able to complete my challenge now. This time, I want you to increase the pressure by exactly 2psi across the whole system. You may begin."

Again, you must make an ENGINEERING roll of difficulty 13.

Successful ENGINEERING roll! **380**
Failed ENGINEERING roll! **772**

686

You steer the Wagtail out around the outside of the bend, the pneumatic tyres flying over the smoother, unrutted surface. As you watch, the gap between the Coal Board Steamer and the legs of the raised stand narrows sharply: you would almost certainly have been crushed had you tried to fly through there.

Pedal in more fuel! **424**

687

You are offered a pint of Cliveden Deep Stout, named for the reach of the Thames where the river narrows and darkens beneath the cliff. It has a velvety texture and an oaty, almost woody taste.

"Strange lady passed through here with her dog a few days ago," says the barman. "Headed south. Had a story to tell about an adventuress and a sham marriage up north somewhere. Bit potty. She was asking directions to the Bath Road."

Return to the parlour... **801**

688

The gin you are poured flows thickly and has a slight yellowish colour, but in the cheap stoneware tumbler it quickly loses any suspicious quality.

The raw alcohol bites like a dog, screwing up your face involuntarily and bringing tears to your eyes. The other drinkers laugh. "Not to your taste, stranger? Buy a round and we'll show you how to drink it."

A woman sits up. "And give you something for your trouble too."

Buy a round... **256**
Leave the gin shop... **199**
Ask about the Compact for Workers' Equality... **989**

689

The doctor shakes his head in disgust. "I was right about you. A woman in labour, for God's sake, and her child like not to live." He pulls his broad hat onto his head and marches out into the rain.

Finish your port... **4**

690

The convoy make snail-like progress down to Marlow and up the long haul to Handy Cross, so you steam ahead to scout out. Approaching a line of trees, something seems not quite right. Sure enough, you spot a group of brigands preparing an ambush. To scare them off you will need to make RUTHLESSNESS roll of difficulty 10.

Successful RUTHLESSNESS roll! **556**
Failed RUTHLESSNESS roll! **716**

691

Hours spent trudging through the damp woods leave you with nothing but a closer relationship with bracken. It seems to be in your shoes, your underclothing and your hair. When the time comes to return to your velosteam, you slowly realise that you have lost your way completely. Night falls and you are forced to try and shelter outside without even the warmth of your coal-gas boiler. In the morning, you are just as lost, but following a path think you can find your way back to the glade. Scrambling up a slope, you slip and tear your arm open on the branch of a yew tree. Gain one **wound**. Only then do you find yourself back where you started, the day before. You start your velosteam and ride away in disgust.

Leave the wood...   **289**

692

A guard posted at the entrance to the compound looks up from his papers. "Hang on," he says. "I know who you are!"

You must fight him to escape!

Telegraph Guard	Weapon: **truncheon (PAR 4)**
Parry:	8
Nimbleness:	4
Toughness:	3

Victory!	**186**
Defeat!	**763**

693

You are on the stretch of river between Bourne End and Cookham: this reach is tight with river traffic of all types, mooring, unloading, trading in the very middle of the stream. Cookham Bridge presents a bottleneck to the bargees, who sound their steam-whistles angrily in their attempt to get through. Just east of Bourne End Wharf, the Wye joins the Thames. It is only navigable for a short distance, but connects the heavy industry of Wycombe, Wooburn and Loudwater with the main river route.

Sail downstream to Cookham Lock...	**232**
Dock at the riverside Mill...	**538**
Steam to Bourne End Wharf...	**713**
Negotiate the Wye...	**560**
Head upstream towards Marlow...	**525**

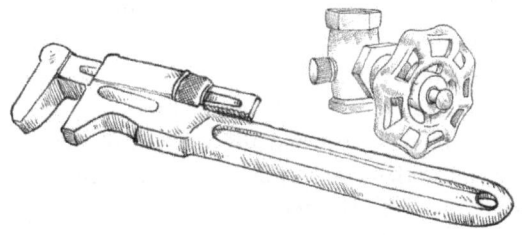

694

A shout rings out from the constables: you have been recognised! Sensing their chance to clap you in irons at last and rid the road of your threats, they accelerate their velosteams towards you. The powerful Imperial steam engines are fast, but less manoeuvrable than your Ferguson. Nonetheless, you will have to ride for your life to escape!

Lose them over Harleyford Bridge...		
	(*Alluring*)	**52**
Hide amongst the Steam Fair...		
	(**Friend of the Curtiss Brothers**)	**332**
Take the Boyn Hill track... (*Abstruse*)		**193**
Head for Cookham Weir... (*Amphibious*)		**16**
Ride into Cliff Wood...		**249**
Steam west and outrun them...		**388**

695

You ride beside the little River Wye as it trickles and burbles towards the Thames. The river is little more than a stream and gives off a chemical stench from all the mill effluent further upstream.

Ride on to Bourne End...   **703**

696

"Good," replies the Abbot. He gives you a few more details and later that night you proceed down to Temple, where the family are living on a riverside smallholding. After placing smouldering bundles of hay beneath the thatch, you watch as the family come running out with the few belongings they can rescue.

Gain a point of RUTHLESSNESS but lose a **Solidarity Point**. The Abbot gives you a **letter of introduction** for your trouble and sends you on your way. "I have recommended you to an employer here," he says. "You need rob and steal no longer. The nobility of the land will respect my reference."

Turn to...   **37**

697

Your shot clips the young driver and he staggers back from the controls and slumps against the coal tender. The master immediately leaps inboard, hauls on the brakes and cradles the boy. By the time you have drawn closer, the master is weeping.

"He's only a boy, by heaven! What can you want of us to be so cruel? Take anything you want - you've already taken his life." He tosses down a purse of **£1 17s** in scorn and anger. You can also take an **adjustable wrench (ENG+1)**, but lose **three Solidarity Points**.

Ride on... 202

698

The instructions you were given lead you up and out of Boyn Hill, towards the area where the countryside again claims an influence. It takes a few attempts to find the right unpaved lane, but when you find the one that leads to the railway crossing it is only a few moments before you slip into the shadow of Maidenhead Thicket. A tiny stream leads you beneath the hornbeam and beech boughs to the Bath road.

Ride on... 113

699

You spy a gold and black steamer with the distinctive Coal Board crest approaching. Seeing as the vast majority of their workforce are carted around in open-sided transports, you expect the passenger to be someone of importance.

Let the steamer pass... 137
Threaten the driver... 430

700

Davy Curtiss laughs one last time. "I would've killed him, for sure. Now, let me tell you about an idea I've had. That velosteam of yours... Very exciting. My dad always wanted a Wall of Death here at the fair. If you ride for us, you could make a pretty penny. And it won't hurt our reputation either. Think it over."

Eventually you leave the celebrations and head off on the open road once more. It won't be a quick process by which the brothers learn to trust one another again, but with proof of their father's love for both of them and with the tangible evidence of his concern, at least they are no longer at each other's throats.

Ride away... 725

701

You come across a fine steam caravan drawn up beside the lane. A brightly dressed family are dancing at a fireside to the music of a violinist.

"Come!" calls a mustachioed dancer. "Come and join the family. It is my daughter's nameday." The man seems to have several daughters, as well young teenage son, a fierce wife and a grandfather. They invite you to eat and dance with them, patiently teaching you the steps to the **gypsy dance** (note your new talent in the **Other Skills** section of your adventure sheet). Perhaps it would be polite to honour the birthday girl with a gift?

Offer her a piece of jewellery...
(eg **gold bracelet**) 591
Bid them farewell... 288

702

As Lalage Harris seems so unwilling to help, her help must be recruited against her will. You make some preparations and wait until nightfall before making your attempt. Her assistants are all long gone, but she remains at her desk by candle-light. Make a NIMBLENESS roll of difficulty 10 to surprise and capture her. You can add 1 if you possess a rope and 2 if you have a net.

Successful NIMBLENESS roll! 749
Failed NIMBLENESS roll! 238

703

A brightly-painted road sign proclaims that you are now entering Bourne End. The town itself is small and struggling, despite a coal depot by the river-side and a freight yard full of wagons.

Visit St Mark's Church... 717
Investigate the freight yard... 396
Visit the Walnut Tree Inn... 634
Do some buying and selling... 320
Take the ferry to the Bounty... (**2s**) 444
Leave town... 732

704

After Ma Curtis' treatments she insists you bed down in your wagon. "There's no need to be out riding the roads tonight, whatever you get up to," she says. "Those wounds won't heal if you don't rest."

The unfamilar cot and the warmth of the little coal fire mean that you stay awake long into the night, unable to drift off. The hoot of an owl, the creaking of the big wheel outside you window, these are all that fill your mind. Then the door of your caravan opens and a shadowy figure enters... A figure in a cloak, with a sabre at its side and a blunderpistol in its hand. An assailant? Here? You try to sit up, but find yourself paralysed. The figure approaches, slowly, slowly, swinging its gun at its side, so that you can see down the flared muzzle of the blunderpistol. Inside you seem to see a tiny head, its lank hair wrapped around its face. You look up and watch the figure drop its hood, revealing your own features looking down at you. The gun is raised and you peer again down the metal barrel, which grows wider and wider...

With a sudden bang, the charge goes off, and you awake on the floor of your wagon, tangled in the bright squares of the patchwork quilt. A dream. The product of a guilty conscience, perhaps, or maybe simply a reaction to one of Ma Curtis' herbs. Gain the codeword *Apprehend*.

Turn to...   **743**

705

Leaving Marlow behind you pass a large paper mill, its wheel churning with water from its own private stream. The evening is starting to close in and as you slowly head downstream you see other Number Ones tying up for the night.

Continue on in the gloom...   **693**

706

The night is cold and you wake shivering. Your fire has gone out and the wood is dark, with only a little starlight filtering through the branches. Someone is approaching your shelter. They are wearing a hooded cloak and dragging something heavy... Something large, lumpen and heavy in a sack. The figure struggles to tug their load over tree-roots and over the leaf-strewn, uneven floor or the wood. They continue dragging their load right past you shelter, not lopking up, keeping their face completely hidden. The sack has the size and weight of a dead body - something you are all too familiar with. As you realise that and look once more at the face of the hooded figure, they look up at last and you find yourself staring into the empty eye-sockets of a polished skull.

You wake up a second time, still cold, but your fire is lit and the wood is empty. That is all the sleep you will get tonight. Gain the codeword *Apprehend*.

Turn to...   **220**

707

Littlewick Green straddles the Bath Road. It is a very small collection of thatched cottages, but to one side stands an engineer's forge and construction sheds. A tall water tank and a chimney overshadow the village.

Head east towards Maidenhead...   **113**
Head west along the road...   **551**
Investigate the engineer's sheds...   **529**

708

He smiles. "I can't take you there, Comrade. She's the Regional Director of the Compact for Workers' Equality. What you want to do is to head to Wooburn Green - that's where we're in force, you see? Show this **pass-disc** in the ginshops down there and you'll quickly get through to Comrade Feaver."

The miller leaves you to finish your meal and settle into the chair for the night. Could these revolutionaries really have an answer to the injustice of the land? You stay awake, long into the night, as the privileged and the poverty-stricken march past your mind's eye.

Turn to...   **180**

709

If you have the codeword *Ashen*, turn to **676** immediately.

The woods here would make a good location for a temporary hideout, meaning you could rest and hide before ambushing traffic on the London Road. If you want to create a hideout, you will need an **axe** and a **tarpaulin**, discarding the **tarpaulin** to create the shelter.

Build a shelter here in Windsor Woods...
          (**axe** and **tarpaulin**)   **676**
Leave the woods towards the London Road... **530**

710

With a final flourish and flick of the wrist, you send Colonel Snappet's blade singing through the air. He is bleeding heavily, but still defiant. He pretends to stumble, but instead grasps a handful of gravel and flings it in your face before making a dash for the mooring tower.

Yet as he does so something falls from his jacket. He hesitates for a moment, then carries on running. You pick up **Colonel Snappet's pocket book** and give chase, but Snappet is simply reckless in the way he throws himself up the gantry. The guests of the ball, hearing the commotion, come to the windows and out onto the balcony, unsure which side to take. "Run the blackguard through!" yells one - but whom does he mean?

Snappet reaches the mooring line of the *Nevaeh* and clambers directly along it, hand-over-hand, without waiting for his crew to approach. "Ready the engines," he roars.

You are not far behind but Snappet aboard by the time you reach the top of the platform. The airship begins to move...

Leap for a line...   **450**

711

The comfortable bed and hot water bath at Hedsor House are luxuries you could never have imagined enjoying, and far from the everyday experience of many of those you ride past or rob. Do you bear any guilt for enjoying such privilege?

Well, at least the water and steam of a good soak can relax you and wash away the troubles of the road. But by night you find nothing has been done to wash away the memories of your murders. Indistinct figuers appear before you and you cut them down with hallucinatory slowness, only to see them multiply and cry for mercy. You awake with the dawn, unrested. One of your old **wounds** has reopened. Gain the codeword *Apprehend*.

You mount up on your velosteam and ride away without taking leave of the Judge.

Ride east...   **366**
Ride into the woods...   **541**
Ride down to Bourne End...   **703**

712

You must clear a wide ditch and then negotiate the low branches of conifers to get away. Make a MOTORING roll of 13 to lose your pursuers.

Successful MOTORING roll!   **288**
Failed MOTORING roll!   **763**

713

Here at Bourne End jetties stretch out into the flowing river, lined with barges, boats and skiffs, loading up charcoal from the nearby woods, furniture from the village workshops and mountains of coal.

	To buy	To sell
Charcoal	£13	-
Furniture	£28	-
Machinery	£27	£24
Pottery	-	£21
Cotton	-	-
Woollen cloth	-	£10
Coal	£12	£11
Beer	-	£15
Wheat	-	£4
Malt	-	£8
Frozen meat	-	£14
Ice	-	£6

Look for the Albright family....   (*Albright*)   **813**
Disembark here...   **835**
Cross the river to the Bounty...   **124**
Head upstream...   **525**
Follow the river downstream...   **693**

714

The track to Hard-To-Find Farm is unmarked and straggles along the crest towards the farm. Dogs bark as you ride up - in recognition, or alarm?

If you have an **initialled purse**...   **557**
If you are the **Friend of Mr Hibbert**...   **17**
Otherwise...   **11**

715

Maria Roberts was not at the races, but your success was telegraphed to her the moment you crossed the line. Her response was short: could she have already transferred her enthusiasm for another project? Nonetheless she extended her congratulations to Dashwood and arranges for a purse of twenty-five guineas (**£26 5s**) to be awarded to you.

"It's the race that really matters," says Dashwood. "Perhaps I'll be able to profit off this, but in all honesty, the feeling of seeing that car fly across the finish line... That's an unbeatable feeling. I owe you a great deal, my young friend. Come and see me soon." He throws a party for the whole team, including the engineers and workers, and joins them at the long tables laden with bread and beer and spit-roast pork, but eventuallt the time has come to part ways. Erase the codeword *Ambition*, and you must seek new adventures on the open road.

Mount your velosteam and ride away...   **137**

716

Your show of strength doesn't seem to impress the brigands at all. One takes a pot-shot at you with his crossbow. Your only option now is to ride straight up to their leader and launch yourself at him. If you can defeat him you should be able to get rid of these rogues.

Brigand Leader		Weapon: **club (PAR 4)**
Parry:	9	
Nimbleness:	5	
Toughness:	4	

Victory!	**28**
Defeated!	**74**

717

St Mark's church is cool and quiet. An old-fashioned box-style confessional stands near the entrance, pools of green and blue light are cast over the flagged floor and a surprisingly simple, unadorned altar table stands beneath a large crucifix.

The vicar approaches. He wears a surprisingly fashionable suit with a frock coat and sash about his waist.

"Will you absolve my sins, father?"	**791**
"I want to make a gift."	**955**
"Why is the church complicit in the sufferings of the poor?"	**544**
"How can I help the needy?"	**632**
Leave the church...	**703**

718

The driver waves to you. "Can't stop to talk. Dratted Guild wagon took all the water at the last tank. We've got to get to Maidenhead on a quarter tank!"

You show her where a steam runs along a side-track just off the main road and she refills with her pump and hose. "Much obliged," she says. "That Guild won't push me off the road yet!"

Ride away...	**535**

719

Asking around the village for an inventor, you are taken to a small cottage with a run-down garden. Inside you meet an old widow, who tells you that her husband used to be a designer of machinery. "I remember Old Curtiss, yes. He was going to buy my William's plans for a Rolling Coaster, he was! He worked long and hard on that. Curtiss used to come up here and plan with 'im. They was negotiating, but he passed away and we never saw no money for it. Then my William passed too."

"Do you still have your husband's papers?"

"Oh yes, in the shed. Those I haven't burnt up for firestarters. They ain't no good to me, not being able to make head nor tail of the drawings, and I can't read anyway, darling."

She shows you the little shed at the end of the garden where the inventor did his work. The room is strewn with designs for mechanisms and machines, but a leaking roof has spoilt many of the plans and papers . "You can have any of this junk," she says. "If I had the space clear I could take in a lodger."

The widow leaves and you seach the studio. You find a **pneumatic manual (ENG+3)** and a wooden box, marked "Curtiss". You lever it open, snapping the simple lock, and inside find **thirty guineas in banknotes**, and an envelope labelled **Albert Curtiss's Last Will and Testament**. Remove the codeword *Ambidextrous*.

Take the items directly to the Curtiss Brothers...	**304**
Take the items to the woman...	**812**

720

□

If the box is empty, tick it and read on. If it is ticked already, turn straight to **200**.

The steep banks of the cutting have been weakened by days of rain and have fallen in a chalky slump, catching a steam carriage on the road ahead of you. The vehicle lies on its side, partly buried, with its fire out and a figure just visible through the windowglass.

Ride by without stopping...	**428**
Take the opportunity to rob the occupant...	**780**
Stop and help...	**615**

721

The insurance broker will not give up his purse without a fight. He draws a sword and attacks!

Insurance Broker		Weapon: **sabre (PAR 6)**
Parry:	10	
Nimbleness:	4	
Toughness:	3	

Victory!	**752**
Defeat!	**90**

722

You are thrown through the gate into the prison court-yard with little ceremony and less concern. The door-keeper does no more than make another tally-mark in his book and you are left to pick yourself out of the filth and try to find a corner in one of the common cells. Survival here in this antiquated, stratified, dog-eat-dog place will depend on your ability to wheedle and connive - as long as you are healthy enough to remain on your feet at all.

If you have one or more **wounds**...　　　　**456**
Otherwise...　　　　　　　　　　　　　　　**638**

723

The horns of the other steamers are in full play as the drivers try to announce their approach and clear the road, but each engine is now in the running for a prize. Stealthy and unannounced, you focus on steering your lighter vehicle around the steamers as they slow round the bends, and manage to pass three in a row through a combination of good timing and control. Gain two Race Points!

Head on to the front of the pack!　　　　**226**

724

You take up a newspaper and sit amongst the customers waiting or resting in the entry parlour, but of course your attention is fixed upon the movement of money through the room. Clerks routinely wheel a small, heavy trolley to a low doorway and hand down small sacks of guineas, parcels of banknotes and other valuables to the safe-keeper, who sits locked behind a grill and in front of the safe door. You might be able to choose your moment and intimidate the clerks into opening the safe, but you will need to be very sure of your RUTHLESSNESS before taking such a risk.

Hold up the bank...　　　　　　　　　　**285**
Leave the bank for now...　　　　　　　　**377**

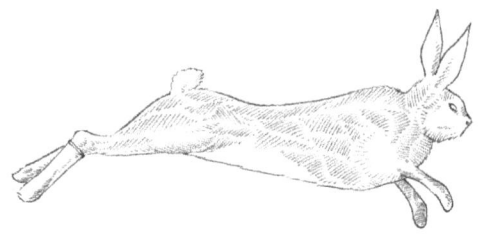

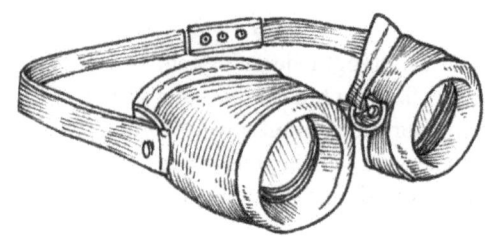

725

The grassy common of Pinkney's Green is full of butterflies by day, moths and owls by night. If it weren't for the drone of airships lumbering west, this scene could seem almost free of man.

Ride north to Inkydown Wood...　　　　　**528**
Visit the Golden Ball Inn...　　　　　　　**394**
Ride south-east towards Maidenhead...　　**300**
Take the road towards the Thicket...　　　**113**
Drive east down Malder's Lane...　　　　　**646**

726

Despite the weather you reach Bullocks Farm quickly. The doctor leaps off without thanks, splashes through the farmyard and pushes open the farmhouse door. After securing the engine and steadying the pressure, you follow him inside.

In the front room of the house a woman lies, howling with pain and surrounded by bloodied sheets. The midwife has not arrived, the baby is suffering and it will depend upon Dr Smollett's skill whether the mother and child survive.

It is a long night. You are kept busy fetching hot water, bracing the mother, cleaning the Doctor's retractors. But by the dawn, somehow, the world has another tiny inhabitant, the farmer has a daughter, and for once you have been responsible, in a small way, for the beginning of a life rather than the end of one.

The Doctor will stay with the farmer and his family. But before you leave he offers you his hand. "Maybe there is humanity in you," he says, looking deep into you with those hard eyes. "When you are in Lane End again, come to the surgery."

You have now gained a level of **Medical Training**. (If this is your first, you can mark **Medical Training Level 1** on your Adventure sheet. If you already have **Medical Training Level 1** or higher, you may increase one level.) Lose the codeword *Afterthought* and gain the codeword *About*.

Leave the farm...　　　　　　　　　　　**521**

727

Burchett's Green is a scattering of small houses and cottages along the hard-packed road. To the North of the village stands Hall Place, a fine house on the high ground. A villager tells you that the house belongs to Squire Lynch, the local landowner. In the centre of the little hamlet stands the Cross Keys Inn.

Visit Wellesley Garman...

(Friend of Wellesley Garman)	**733**
Ride up to High Wood... (*Alba*)	**78**
Break into Hall Place... (*Abound*)	**503**
Ride west to Appletree Cottages...	**139**
Take the road towards Bisham...	**662**
Enter the Cross Keys Inn...	**628**

728

The evening falls and Davy Curtiss takes to the megaphone to announce the highlight of the evening's entertainment. "Ladies and gentlemen, boys and girl, officers and guildsmen! Tonight! The Curtiss brothers are proud to present for you the one and only masked rider, the fearless, the death-defying, the reckless rider of the wooden o! Make your way to the Wall of Death to observe the high drama of a high-powered custom velosteam thundering past on a vertical wall! Swoon, at the daring and bravery of the riders!"

You join two other riders preparing their machines. Once the audience has been gathered into the high stand, surrounding the arena on all sides like a cockpit, you ride out onto the wooden boards, slowly circling Davy Curtiss, who is still armed with his megaphone. Gas light flutters and steam rises from your engines and the whole structure shakes perceptibly with every revolution.

The show begins with a mechanical fanfare from a steam organ. Make a MOTORING roll to see how you fare, adding 1 to your score for each customisation you possess (for example, **reinforced boiler** or **muffled exhaust**).

Score less than 10... Horrific crash! Gain **two Wounds** and **two Damage Points**

Score 11-13	Gather **£5 2s**
Score 14- 17	Gather **£6 8s** and a **bottle of whisky**
Score 18 or higher...	Gather **£12 3s** and a **gold necklace**

Return to your wagon to rest...   **743**

729

The young man is bemused. "Hot water, old woman? At this time of night, shouldn't you be in your cottage or someth - ow!" By the time he finishes his sentence you have him in an armlock with your blade at his throat. He quickly loses his arrogance and his bladder control. You take his purse (which contains **£3 10s**) and leave him to try and regain his composure.

Ride away...   **23**

730

The lane twists beside a cherry orchard and out of Cookham Dean. Roll a dice to see what you encounter on your way through the fields:

Score 1-2	A deserter...	**244**
Score 3-4	Only sparrows...	**646**
Score 5-6	Woodcutters...	**152**

731

Driving up the road into Maidenhead, you are surprised by a constable who steps into the road with a load hailer. "Halt, wanted criminal! Stop your machine!"

A glance over your shoulder shows you that you have ridden into a trap: constables have strung out in a line across the road behind you, trailing a spiked chain to puncture your tyres. They are armed and determined.

Ride into the alleyways...	**576**
Surrender...	**255**
Turn and break through the line...	
(off-road tyres)	**153**

732

Bourne End has nothing more to enthrall you. You must now choose where to head next.

Take the ferry to the Bounty...	**(2s)**	**444**
Along the river towards Hedsor...		**214**
West on the Marlow Road...		**602**
Up the hill to Odds Plantation...		**177**
Take the Wooburn Road...		**310**
Head to Cookham Bridge...		**229**

733

You find the haulier Garman's cottage. It is a pretty place with a garden overflowing with roses, hollyhocks and old-fashioned flowers of every kind. Inside,

Garman is still recovering from the crossbow bolt he took in the shoulder and no longer goes out to deliver the freight himself. "That's a younger man's job," he says as he pours you a cup of tea. "My son-in-law can do that now. Business is well, steam is up, the garden looks just lovely. Have another of these nice biscuits. How they get the jam inside them I don't know."

Garman and his wife are keen to repay you in any way they can. They will bandage any **wounds** that you have and you may leave **possessions** here in their spare room. "We don't need to know how you come by things," says Wellesley Garman. "You saved my life and I'll stand by you for as long as I have breath."

Leave the Garman's cottage...   **727**

734

The prison is a bleak, inhumane place. Barbed wire runs atop dirty sandstone walls and a wide moat separates the little kingdom inside from the world of the free. The few windows are dirty, cracked and lifeless. For a moment you glimpse a young girls' face at one, then it is gone.

How dreadful it would be to be enclosed in such a place yourself. If you have the codeword *Evergreen*, turn to **760**. Otherwise, you must return the way you came.

Leave the prison...   **288**

735

A family of gypsies are burning charcoal here. They are gathering straight hazel rods and building a clamp - an earth-covered mound that surrounds the upright bundles of wood. When it lights they will have to tend it for three days and three nights continuously to produce their charcoal.

"Where do you sell it?" you ask.

"The forges all rush to buy it. We produce very clean charcoal. The blacksmith at Handy Cross is a friend of ours - he needs good clean charcoal for his machinery. But they buy it in London too, although we rarely travel that far. Sometimes we take it down to the wharf at Bourne End and sell it to the bargees. They go to London all the time." Gain the codeword *Albright*.

Ride on into the wood...   **190**

736

The library has a fine collection of books shelved on all four walls. A gallery, giving access to the upper shelves, runs around at a mezzanine level and the whole room is lit by a large pyramid-shaped skylight. Comfortable chairs, a table spread with a map of the world and racks of weekly newspapers complete the haven.

Research the Royal Family...   **166**
Find out about the Telegraph Guild...   **566**
Brush up on your legal skills...   **1013**
Leave the library...   **11**

737

The thatched roofs of Bisham huddle between apple trees and lush meadows, the high escarpment to the south-east and the wide River Thames to the west beyond the Abbey. Even here though, the power of steam is felt. A stubby tower smoking away shows where the cider-makers have thrown in their lot with mechanisation and the rambling roof of the Bull straggles wonkily down the lane.

Investigate the Abbey...   **34**
Visit the Bull...   **801**
Head north to Marlow Bridge...   **277**
Take the steep road into Inkydown Wood...   **528**
Ride down the lane towards Temple...   **762**
Ride down Hurley Lane...   **662**
Take the road up Cliff Wood...   **377**

738
□

If the box is empty, tick it and read on. If it is already ticked, turn to **533** immediately.

Cliveden is wearing glamour tonight. Hundreds of flickering oil lamps line the long driveways, the terrace and the lawns. Searchlights shine into the night, illuminating the private airships mooring up at the two mooring pylons, catching the dresses of disembarking ladies and the braid and satin of the immaculately dressed officers and gentlemen stepping down from the sky. A long line of highly polished steam cars is parked under the watchful eye of liveried servants and firemen: all at the Duke of Beverley's personal expense.

You are welcomed into the house: a grand hall hung with a massive chandelier leads straight into the ballroom, where the air is full with the sounds of musicians playing steam-amplified waltzes, the chatter of the rich greeting one another in mock surprise, admiring dresses and hairdos and presentation sabres, fine moustaches, rare leather holsters, all the time making deals, introductions, alliances, fixing marriages and dalliances, selling and exchanging tracts of land and thousands of man-hours of labour. Lord Cobham stands near the door bargaining a price for Lower Matabeleland with a grey-suited man with a facial scar. Several Confederate Americans are here in a posse of brightly-coloured flounces, flaunting their artificial Caribbean dyes. A lady dances, wearing a bouquet of burnt yellow roses - another has her hairpiece decorated with several tiny clockwork birds.

The noise is fantastic: the colour and movement are dizzying. A footman - perhaps the very same who would have turned you off the estate previously - inquires whether you would like any refreshment and gracefully clears a path for you towards the buffet.

Enjoy the ball...   519

739

The ravine cuts through the chalk here where roadbuilders have smoothed the ascent. Roll a dice to see what you encounter:

Score 1-2   A travelling dentist...   236
Score 3-6   Nothing of interest...   534

740

The prison guards unlock the dreadful front gate and herd you out. On the other side you are issued with a **convict's pass**, which you must show if you ever seek employment, and also led to a shed beside the entrance workshop. There, underneath a tarpaulin, is your beloved velosteam! After all this time it has been kept safe, awaiting your return to freedom. Goodness only knows how it escaped being sold, scrapped or destroyed. You are also no longer **Wanted by the Constables**, having served your sentence and paid for your crimes.

Mount up and ride away...   288

741

During the long weeks in the prison you befriend a ragged old troublemaker called Toothy Braddock. He is a long-term resident here and has been imprisoned before. "It was the silver fraud the first time," he confides. "And then robbery. Well, they caught up with me, but they never found my loot."

Toothy is weakening. He has the prison fever, but your friendship gives him some relief in his final days. On the night before he dies he tells you his secret. "It won't profit me now. But a youngster like you... Maybe you can do something with all that I hid away. There's a ruined chapel overlooking Pendower beach, down in Cornwall. That's where I did most of my killing for the Prince of the West. Well, beneath the old altar. That's where to look." Gain the codeword *Amalgam*.

In the morning the guards take the old man's body away and bury it outside the prison walls in an unmarked grave.

Turn to...   227

742

"I am sorry to find you so unco-operative," replies the Abbot. "Brothers?"

Two strong monks appear from nowhere and grab you before you have a chance to respond. "I am prepared to hand you over to the Constables immediately. What fate you will meet there, I do not know but I am sure you deserve. You have a final chance to assist me."

"Since you threaten me so."   696
"Do what you will with me."   234

743

Your wagon is right how you left it. Ma Curtis has been in to clean and to make sure the fire is ready to light and all the glassware is polished, so you are able to settle down and rest here. It is a good, safe place to leave any possessions or cash, as the Curtis family will make sure that nothing is stolen.

Treat any **Wound**s...	**95**
Fix your velosteam...	**549**
Leave the wagon...	**808**

744

"What's to drink here?" you ask. The woman behind the bar points at the pumps. "The Seaside Mild is out, I'm afraid. Not easy to get hold of and we just finished the keg. But perhaps you'd like to try something special? The Terrier? An independent brewery from up near Newcastle, of all places."

"Pull me a pint of Terrier, then," you reply.

She leans on the handle and out comes a golden stream of aromatic light ale. "Got it in for them at the big house," she says conversationally. "Comes down sometimes, they does, and always likes something original. Big old do in the preparations right now, you know? Some ball or other. I heard there'd be all manner of society there. Ladies from London, Constables, military men. Good business for us: their drivers all need somewhere to stay, you see? In fact I heard that the Marquis of Effingham will be there too."

"Who's that?"

"Well, that's exactly the question. Who is the Marquis of Effingham exactly? Some say 'tis a man, others say 'tis a woman: but 'e's meant to be the one behind all manner of the computations. Sends out a new set of punchcards, they run 'em, the guilds do, and find ways to make another million out of their workers. Perhaps it's just a name, but I tell you, I'd like to know if there's a real flesh-and-blood person behind the reputation. You ask me, it's a lady, taken a nom-de-plume or some such."

You raise the empty glass in salute. "Another, then?" asks the barlady.

A guest that nobody could recognise would provide you with the perfect disguise if you wanted to bluff your way into the ball - as long as the real Marquis were taken out of the way.

Return to the parlour...	**141**

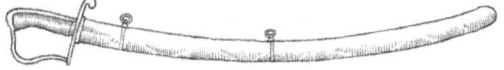

745

You are on the river between Marlow and Temple, floating between the tree-lined banks. The white, squat tower of Bisham church peeks between poplars and yew trees. A little way along the bank stands Bisham Abbey, the home of the Order of St Aloysius.

Moor at the Abbey...	**783**
Head downstream to Marlow Lock...	**498**
Steam upriver to Temple Lock...	**506**

746

The master nods to the boy who lets out steam and slows the road engine beside you. They aren't going to stop the wagons completely - it would waste too much fuel - but they share a few words with you after you ask after their business.

"Still room for a few independent-minded folk on the roads, despite all the dratted Steam Guild and the so-called Co-operative can do. Care to pay their fees? No I don't! Some protection that would get me! I don't choose to feed a guard and I don't choose to insulate fat cats in their offices. I haul."

You ask where he's headed. "Well, freight yard in Marlow for most of this, then the brewery for the barrel-maker. We'll leave the engine there tonight and stay at the Two Brewers - quieter than the Ship. Maybe a chance to hear that gifted organist in the church. They say he's a holy boy. Then some deliveries for Hurley - something heavy with its own trailer for the mill there. It's a never-ending job, freighting."

Wish them a safe journey...	**202**

747

At the Drowned Badger you explain to the lady of the house. She agrees to take care of the stranger. "But what if she needs treatment? I can get Dr Smollett down from Lane End, but he's expensive."

"There's money in her purse."	**815**
"I'll cover it."	**312**

748

The manager looks at you askance when you tell him of your musical ability. "You don't look like a musician," he says doubtfully. Somehow you manage to talk him into allowing you to play for the diners that evening. Make an INGENUITY roll to find the outcome. You may add 1 to your roll for each level of MUSICIANSHIP you possess and if you have no instrument to play, why then, you play the fine hotel piano.

Score 6 or less...		**552**
Score 7-8...	Receive **6s**	
Score 9-10...	Receive **15s**	
Score 11-12...	Receive **£1 8s and a silver bracelet**	
Score 12+...		**439**

Leave the dining room...   **3**

749

You manage to haul the struggling engineer onto the back of your velosteam and ride off towards West Wycombe. She is not at all impressed when you unload her in front of Lord Dashwood, but despite herself she is fascinated by the steam carriage he is building. He has called it the Wagtail and its sleek aluminium lines are quite captivating.

Lord Dashwood takes you aside. "Good work," he says, handing you a purse of guineas (**£5 5s**). "I knew she'd see sense."

The three of you get to work on the engine, but after a week's tinkering and tuning, involving many trial runs, Lalage Harris puts down her tools. "We need a stronger material for the shafts and cylinders. There's a **titanium alloy** that people have been using that is what we need, but it's not easy to get hold of."

Lord Dashwood claps you on the shoulder. "If anyone can get hold of it, you can! I put prodigious faith in you. Bring me that alloy and you can name your price."

Leave West Wycombe House...   **492**

750

If you have the password *Ammonium*, turn to **328**. The railway is a single line of broad-gauge track. Here it is bounded by spindly hedges and a wire fence and the lane is given a simple crossing. The rails themselves are set on heavy sleepers laid in gravel. If you have some **explosives**, you might be able to sabotage the railway here.

Sabotage the tracks (**explosives**)...	**198**
Ride away east...	**67**
Ride away west...	**646**

751

The butcher scowls. "Yes," he says, "The workhouse foisted a scrawny runt of a boy on me. The beadle gave me three pound - barely enough to feed and clothe him for a year, let alone his apprenticeship. But he ran away! Good riddance, say I!"

"Where did he go?"

"How should I know? London, probably."

Leave the butchers...   **575**

752

The insurance broker collapses to the ground, dropping his **sabre (PAR 6)**. He fought bravely for a desk-jockey. His wallet contains **£7 14s** and he also has a set of **punchcards (Terebinth M)** in his pockets.

Ride away...   **535**

753

Wellesley Garman will help you. After all, you saved his life on the footplate of his freight locomotive after the brigand attack. Despite the loss of blood and the sure sensation of a broken bone somewhere in your arm, you manage to get back on your velosteam and make for Burchett's Green. You arrive after dark and tumble off your engine, just as Garman's wife is coming home from church. She doesn't recognise you beneath the dirt and clotted blood, but Wellesley, coming out to find out what the fuss is, sees you for who you are.

You stay with the Garmans for three weeks, slowly recovering your strength and regaining movement in your arm. It will always be stiff now, but you can do little other than carry on: lose 1 from your NIMBLENESS, ENGINEERING and MOTORING scores.

Eventually you insist on leaving. Mrs Garman tries to insist you stay, but the lure of the road is too strong. Starched sheets and breakfast in bed are fine - for a while - but you have things to achieve.

Turn to...   **727**

754

□

If the box is empty, tick it and read on. If it is already ticked, turn to **313** immediately.

With the crowd pushing around the stationary engine, no-one notices you dismount and slip beneath the firebox. You take a loose cobble from the street below and knock a retaining pin out of place, then jam a steam pipe shut for good measure.

A few minutes later, when the Co-operative engine has trudged a few dozen yards further down the road and when you are safely out of the way, the street is rocked by a sudden explosion. Hot metal showers into the streets and shouts of pain rise up into the air. The co-operative's reputation as a safe, reliable transport network will not last much longer. The director of the Haulage Guild will be pleased: gain the codeword *Aorta*.

Ride into Wycombe...   **313**

755

By the time you coax your velosteam into the yard behind Hedsor House, you are faint from loss of blood and exhaustion. However, Judge Hector's staff help you off your engine and upstairs to bed.

For each **wound** you have, roll two dice. A roll of 12 indicates it has become an **intimidating scar (RUTH+1)** which should be noted on your adventure sheet. However, a roll of 3 or less indicates that it has not healed properly, and will remain as a **wound** rather than healing. Otherwise, each **wound** will become a **scar** and should be noted on your adventure sheet.

It takes some time before you are ready to travel again, and when you make your intentions known the Judge comes to warn you. "You cannot continue long like this," he says. "I've come to care for you, after all this time and friendship. The Constables will get hold of you for sure. Be careful."

Leave Hedsor House...   **214**

756

"What if you were to be robbed," you suggest quietly. "But you were sure that you would be paid for it. If you trusted the robber."

She looks at you. "Well, I know the Haulage Guild wouldn't use me again, would they? My livelihood wouldn't be worth much to me."

To convince her, you will need to make an INGENUITY roll of difficulty 9.

Successful INGENUITY roll!   **167**
Failed INGENUITY roll!   **604**

757

If you have the codeword *Burnish*, turn to **61** immediately. Otherwise, read on.

The organist is playing something slow and mournful, beginning with low, quiet phrases that pass like waves in the dark river. The chirping pipes of the upper register only accent the sorrow and the loneliness of the writer. It is a plea in melodic form - a prayer or request, resigned, not desperate, all the sadder for the tinge of hope that looks upwards. And then, as you listen, the organist segues into a livelier piece, the answer to the prayer, the thankfulness of cascading, brassy pipes, punching rhythmically and exuberantly. The same flowing melody is there beneath it all but transformed from sorrow into joy.

At the end of the piece you move to catch the eye of the organist. It is a young man, clumsy in his movements, except as his hands fly over the keys and stops. The vicar has crept up to your side and speaks from your elbow.

"Gregory doesn't understand if you thank him. He understands very little - even of the creed. But he undeniably has a gift for playing the machine. It relieves him and saves us all from his rages. I have had complaints that we should find another organist - one more able to converse with the congregation, to teach the choir - but he is very territorial and won't let anyone near the organ. Not even me. So I let him play." The vicar sighs. "It is a shame. We could be quite a successful church if it weren't for the old ways that cling."

Leave the church...   **4**

758

Looking around the greenhouses you try to find the ripest of the unfamiliar fruit. Roll a dice to see how you succeed:

Score 1-2   Caught and beaten by the gardeners! Gain a **Wound**.
Score 3-4   Steal a **melon**
Score 5-6   Steal a **pineapple**

Whatever the outcome, you don't stay long, but dash back out of the gate to where you parked your velosteam.

Flee the vengeance of the gardeners!   **366**

759

A pair of brothers service the freight wagons and their engines here. You manage to get them to take a look at your velosteam, and they rattle off prices for work they can undertake. "Special rates for members of the Freight Co-Operative," says one.

"I shouldn't think that'll apply to this one..." mutters his brother.

Clothing	To buy	To sell
dungarees (GAL-2)	£1 10s	15s
goggles (MOT+1)	£2 15s	£2 2s

Tools	To buy	To sell
high pressure valve	18s	9s
pneumatic tyres	£3	£1 2s

Velosteam Customisations	To buy
off-road tyres	£5 2s
gas pressuriser	£10 4s

Repairs	To buy
Per **damage point**	£2

Return to the Freighter's Haven...   **79**
Leave the Inn...   **684**

760

The message of your mission has reached Myfanwy Thomas and there you see her signal: a tiny blue handkerchief at a high tower window. You wait for night before signalling with your velosteam's lime-lantern and receive the reply of a candle moving in front of the window.

You must scale the prison walls and help her escape. To do this you will need to make a NIMBLE-NESS roll of difficulty 13, but you may add 1 if you possess a **grappling iron**, 2 more if you possess some **wirecutters** and another 3 if you have a **rope ladder**.

Successful NIMBLENESS roll!   **617**
Failed NIMBLENESS roll!   **471**

761

Add **£10** to your wallet and **a Solidarity Point** to your reputation. You are now **Wanted by the Wallingford Town Guard** and **Wanted by the Haulage Guild** as well. Leaving the majority of the loot buried beneath a clearly marked beech coppice, you head back onto the road, to let the freighter work out her own success.

Ride away...   **546**

762

The lane twists down beside cottages and smallholdings. The burble of water is never far away, as the Thames flows just beyond the trees. Roll a dice:

Score 1-2   A procession of monks...   **147**
Score 3-4   Temple Village...   **37**
Score 5-6   Shire horses...   **652**

763

You have fallen into the merciless hands of the Telegraph Guild! Making enemies of this secretive, power-hungry group might have been unwise, for you find yourself beaten, blindfolded and thrown into a mobile iron cell. After a cold and uncomfortable journey, you are hauled out and chained into a line with others unwise enough to stir the Guild's wrath. They march you, still blindfolded, to a labour camp and for the next several weeks you are forced to build prefabricated towers and mechanisms in their private prison.

The other prisoners are mostly peasants bought from heartless landlords or sold into servitude by desperate family. However, a group of labourers with Cornish accents seem likely to be rebels captured and sold into the Guild's workforce.

The work is laborious, painful and demeaning. After weeks of exhausting work you are handed over to the Maidenhead Constables to stand trial for your crimes. At least the Guild consider you to have paid your debt to them: you are no longer **Wanted by the Telegraph Guild**.

Turn to...   **255**

764

The Wagtail surges forward as you crank the regulator into emergency acceleration and you tear over the bumpy ground. Jolts and jars shake the vehicle's frame and toss you about, despite the leather straps of your quick-release harness. However, despite your speed Da Silva catches sight of you in her reflecting mirror - a very nice piece of design - and swerves to block your path. Rather than hit her at full speed you are forced to steer aside and run onto the grass verge, losing momentum on the slope. Da Silva and then Anderson, on the firmer ground, pull ahead.

Find your place on the track again... **103**

765

As the door of the steam-carriage opens, a well-dressed man with a foreign air appears. His servants bow low and sweep the ground in front of him, but he pays them no attention. He fixes his eyes on your face and steps forward.

"Good God! What is this?" he cries in a Ruritanian accent.

Other than the moustache he sports, your faces bear an uncanny resemblance. Looking up from the ground, the servants are also struck by the likeness and deeply disconcerted.

"I must divest you of some of your heavier accoutrements, your majesty." **422**
"We could almost be siblings." **590**

766

The footman heads through the back rooms of Hedsor house and you follow as silently as possible. He leads you directly to the hallway where the master of Hedsor, Judge Hector, is talking with his butler. They both see you at once.

"Who the devil are you?" cries Judge Hector.

In reply, you snatch down a heavy pike from the grip of a posed suit of armour and strike the Judge down. The footman flees, shouting for help.

Turn to... **87**

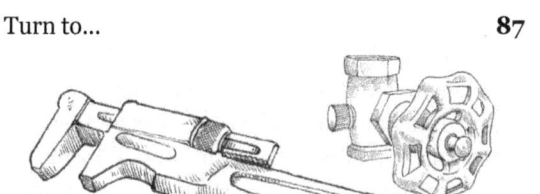

767

Your attempt fails. The trestle resists your charge and you drop the velosteam, spilling Doctor Smollett off the back and coming to an undignified and painful stop yourself. The Constables quickly gather round and cuff your hands, despite your pain, and a hood is thrown over your head.

Discover your fate... **255**

768

You knock the guard down quickly and grab the jewellery box on the dresser. A glimpse inside tells you that you have the Dervish's Eye in your hands.

But as you clamber back onto the windowsill, you feel a massive blow to the back of your head and you collapse to the ground. All is dark.

Turn to... **621**

769

The ditch you have prepared is filled with water running down the hill and looks like nothing more than a broad puddle. However, when the steamer's front wheels splash into the water they lock, tear the axle from the carriage and throw the driver clear. As you approach, you see the passengers climbing out of their compartment. Your RUTHLESSNESS score will decide their reaction:

RUTHLESSNESS 6 or greater... **986**
RUTHLESSNESS 5 or less... **811**

770

If you are **Wanted by the Telegraph Guild**, turn to **763** immediately.

The Telegraph Tower here has a clear line of sight above the smog and smoke and the Guildsmen are constantly busy encoding and transmitting the messages of the Empire across the hills - at least, when it isn't too foggy or cloudy to see the other towers. There is a public waiting room, not as fine as the one at Mount Hill, but the clerks seem agitated and are not taking any messages for now.

"There's some kind of problem with the calculations," says the manager. "We've sent someone out for a fresh set of punchcards to reboot the controls, but they're hard to get hold of."

"What do you need?" you ask.

The manager smiles condescendingly despite his anxiety. "I wouldn't expect a layperson like yourself to understand. Punchcards have a name, indicating the sort of programme they run, and an initial that indicates the complexity of code. We need something like Habbukuk K - but why am I telling you this?"

Offer the manager the punchcards...
   (Habbukuk K)   **661**
Leave the tower...   **177**

771

To build up speed you drop the intake cover and allow more air into the furnace. The last of your ground coal blossoms into a fan of flame and you feel the whole of the Wagtail tense as the temperature rises and the pressure spikes. You shoot past Akroyd, who opens his regulator too and charges forward in his massive machine, pressing hard. The other racers catch up as well and you are hard pressed to stay in front until the last straight. Gain five Race Points!

If you have 13 or more Race Points...   **155**
If you have fewer than 13 Race Points...   **517**

772

You step back from the machinery. Colonel Snappet looks it over and tilts his head. "Not bad," he sniffs, "But not good enough for me. You show promise, though. Come back when you have a little more finesse. Work on your engineering skill. Or perhaps get some glasses."

Leave Danesfield House...   **428**

773

"'Ere, what you doing?" A large man grasps your hand and shakes you, hard. "Some dirty sneak-thief, here!"

The judgement of the fairgoers is swift and merciless. You are kicked, beaten and scratched - and this won't help your reputation either. Gain two **Wounds** and lose **two Solidarity Points**. You manage to get away and reach the edge of the fairground once they have finished their terrible work.

If you have **five Wounds**...   **90**
Otherwise...   **535**

774

Medmenham is a simple enough place. The square-towered church of St Peter and St Paul stands by the main road - with, intriguingly, a small telegraph relay station mounted on top. Cottages run down a single street towards the river, where a small wharf and a waterside inn serve the Thames barges.

Find somewhere to buy and sell...   **793**
Board your boat... (if it is moored here)   **846**
Enter the Drowned Badger...   **795**
Leave the village...   **534**

775

If you have the **Albert Curtiss' Last Will and Testament**, turn to **254**. As you approach the Curtiss wagon, you hear shouting from within. Gregory and Davy are at loggerheads again, and soon to be at blows. Nonetheless, you knock on the door. It is thrown open by Gregory Curtiss, a slimmer but equally firey version of his brother.

"What do you want?" he asks.

"Davy wanted me to talk something through with him. A business proposition."

Gregory barks a short, angry laugh. "Ha. Well, one thing you need to understand is that my brother couldn't spell the word 'business'. He loses money on every deal he makes."

Davy Curtiss appears and knocks his brother down the steps. "Just you wait," he shouts. "This fair'll be mine."

You have no option other than to leave them to their brawling for now.

Return to the fair...   **326**

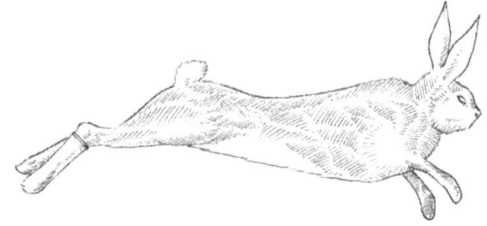

776

Marlow lock takes advantage of islands in the river, like many of the locks, and is bordered on one side by a massive paper mill. The towering steeple of All Saints' Church and the chimneys of the Wethered brewery show over the rooftops as you approach, but fine, drifting rain and coalsmoke soon obscure them.

The main export here is beer, brewed in the massive facility just behind the high street, or in the several pubs. To keep production going the brewers constantly demand shipments of malt, hops and coal. A refrigerated shed sends its chill wafting over the wharves - this is an important market for meat from the colonies, frozen and shipped upriver, sold to the booming population.

	To buy	To sell
Charcoal	-	**£14**
Furniture	**£28**	-
Machinery	**£28**	**£23**
Pottery	**£24**	**£21**
Cotton	-	-
Woollen cloth	-	**£10**
Coal	**£12**	**£11**
Beer	**£15**	**£14**
Wheat	**£5**	**£5**
Malt	-	**£10**
Frozen meat	-	**£14**
Ice	-	**£6**

Take the lock upstream...
    (**2s** or **Bargee's Badge**)   **745**
Go ashore...   **670**
Return downstream...   **705**

777

"Your future is confused," says the lady, running her fingers through a set of jingling chimes. "On the one hand, you have the desire for glory, driving you on to greater and greater exploits. Will it be you to find the Cornish gold? On the other hand, your heart for people advises caution. Pain is all around - will you cause more through your action or your inaction? Do the Haulage Guild deserve your emnity or your service? But the one thing I see for you is a long, long, winding road, over the hills and between dark woods."

Return to the fair...   **326**

778

You were one of the fortunate: poor, like many another Woolwich factory hand, desperate, like everyone looking for a way to put food on your family's table, but more determined, more decisive, more ruthless. That was why when the opportunity came, you did not hesitate to steal the courier's unguarded Ferguson velosteam when it was parked in the factory yard: that was why you did not look back or concern yourself with your dependents. You can serve them better on the road.

Robbery and theft might be able to support you for a while, but even these are means to an end. You've been told that the Compact for Workers' Equality has a strong following in the mills of Loudwater and Wooburn Green. The factory-workers, the indentured labourers, the rural poor dominated by the landowners - revolution cannot come quickly enough for them. And if you can speed it, you will.

You have in your possession a **blunderpistol (ACC 6)**, a **sabre (PAR 6)** and a **revolutionary poster**. Your ability scores are:

RUTHLESSNESS	3
ENGINEERING	5
MOTORING	3
INGENUITY	6
NIMBLENESS	5
GALLANTRY	2

Turn to...   **324**

779

You are handed over to the Wycombe Constables. If you are **Wanted by the Constables**, turn to **255**. If not, they confiscate all your **possessions** and lock you up in the cell beneath the Guildhall. After several days, they have had enough and let you go, but not before relieving you of **£1 10s** (or all your **money**, if you possess less than that) for your bed and board.

Turn to...   **337**

780

The lone occupant is already dead and has no use for her purse of **£3 2s**. She also has an **ivory fan**.

Ride on...   **428**

781
☐

If the box is empty, put a tick in it and read on. If it is already ticked, turn to **7** immediately.

The purse you hand back to the master is two gold sovereigns heavier. The haulier is gobsmacked. "Well I never! We'll be drinking your health tonight, that's all I can say." Gain **a Solidarity Point**.

Ride on...   **202**

782

The poacher gives you a big wink. "Got to find something for the pot," she says. "Tho' Bray the Butcher gives four shillings for a fat bird down in the village. Sells them to Londoners, now the train's come."

Ride on...   575

783

The ancient buildings of Bisham Abbey stand on a laboriously-maintained green bordered by willows. In fact, as you watch you can see several monks on their knees, clipping the grass with shears. Are they making some kind of penance? The monks and their Abbot have a reputation for keeping a very good table, but are also known for their avarice and greed. They will pay good prices for any cargo they are in need of, but they do not sell cheaply if they can help it.

	To buy	To sell
Charcoal	-	-
Furniture	-	-
Machinery	-	£24
Pottery	-	£25
Cotton	-	£6
Woollen cloth	-	£12
Coal	-	£12
Beer	£17	-
Wheat	£3	£3
Malt	-	£8
Frozen meat	-	£14
Ice	£6	-

To ship Frozen Meat or Ice, your barge must be fitted with a **Perkins Machine**.

Tie up and visit the Abbey...   171
Leave the Abbey...   745

784

"I'd like to visit her," you say, startling the long-faced man.

"Who? My gran? Well, she might be glad of a fresh face. But she might be more glad of a wholesome diet."

The drinker doesn't come himself but gives you directions to a cottage in the village where you find an old woman listening to a boy trying to read her the newspaper.

"Who are you, dearie?" she asks. "Another fellow from the officers come to make me tell what I don't know?" She is both suspicious and hostile.

Read her the newspaper...   954
Offer her a **melon**...   (melon)   651
Offer her a **pineapple**... (pineapple)   572
Offer her some **tinned fruit**...(tinned fruit) 819

785

To hit the driver and stop the carriage you will need to make an ACCURACY roll of 13.

Successful ACCURACY roll!   568
Failed ACCURACY roll!   970

786

The white road passes an unassuming gate standing between the trees. There is no gatehouse, but a small sign reads 'Harleyford Manor. Private.' If you have the **sealed packet**, turn to **843**.

Steam between the trees...   (*Alluring*)   1016
Head north through the plantation...   304
Ride towards Henley...   428
Ride towards Marlow...   211

787

Mrs Juste disappears into the back room and returns a few minutes later with a fine sword in a scabbard. "Some gentleman left this," she says. "Not been claimed. But perhaps it'll find a better use with you." Along with the **stossdegen (PAR 5)** you gain a **Solidarity Point** as a result of your deeds.

Return to Maidenhead...   594

788

The landowner quivers at the sight of you. "I know I should have left before lunch," he stammers. "But the mistress's delights were too much to resist. Oh, the weakness of the flesh!" You can rob him of **£7** and a **pocket watch**.

Ride away...   535

789

You throw the tarpaulins off the crates and beckon over your mate with his crowbar. "Come and see what you have been sent, Comrades," you cry.

Forty Blackwater Rifles lie in their greased sacking, ready to arm the proletariat. The dockers surge forward and take their guns. They are soon all hidden away, and by the time you unmoor there is a completely different look on the dockers' face. Gain the Codeword *Arithmetic*.

Turn to...   **560**

790

It is a simple manoeuvre to ride alongside the wagon and toss a smouldering rag into the hay bales piled across the bed. Before long you watch as the drivers are forced to pull over and empty their water tank onto their own cargo. They certainly won't be earning their bonus this month. Thankfully nobody saw you, so your reputation is unaffected - but perhaps your conscience is? Gain the codeword *Aorta*.

Ride away...   **535**

791
☐ ☐ ☐ ☐ ☐

If a box is empty, put a tick in it. If all of them are already ticked, turn to **468** immediately.

You recite the deeds you regret to the vicar in the cool of the church while he nods and listens, never interrupting or even asking. When you are finished, he sighs.

"There is a gentleness in your spirit, my child, despite all these things you regret. I know that within you is the desire to do good. Jesus did not teach that we could make up for our sins with altruistic deeds, but deeds of mercy prove that one's spirit is not entirely depraved. You need to decide - will you listen to that voice advising restraint, pity and forgiveness? If you do not, you will lose the ability to hear it altogether. Let me ask you directly. What about when you leave here? Will you kill again? Steal again?"

"Yes. If confession cleans me from these things, why
    stop?   **134**
"Only if I must."   **666**
"I vow never to do such things again."   **839**

792

A steam-crane drops a heavy girder across the road, toppling a steam-wagon of building supplies and blocking the way entirely. You will have to return the way you came.

To Cookham...   **563**

793

The shops here in Medmenham sell little of interest to a road pirate like yourself, but they do equip hunters and a few local engineers, so some of their products might be to your liking.

Food and Drink	To buy	To sell
rabbit	2s	1s
pheasant	4s	3s
large pike	-	8s
deer carcass	-	£1 5s

Clothing	To buy	To sell
cloak	£1	15s

Tools	To buy	To sell
rope	4s	2s
lantern	6s	4s
shovel	8s	5s
axe	8s	6s
wirecutters	-	9s

Jewellery	To buy	To sell
locket	6s	4s

Return to the village...   774

794

The barman is a mine of information. "See those chaps in green overalls?" he says. "Telegraph Guild. They're all over Mount Hill. Pay their tabs, good customers, but you can't say it's natural, messages whizzing over your head through the air, can you? Now if you were looking for a mechanic, you should head down to Littlewick Green and ask for Lalage Harris' garage. Or I hear there's a chap up at Handy Cross. Maybe you'd like someone who can patch you up after a fracas, not that I'd expect a respectable customer like yourself to necessarily get into any trouble. Look for the gypsy lady in Maidenhead Thicket - or if you have the cash, you could go and visit Doctor Smollett in Lane End. He's known all round for his skill with the retractor. If it's paid work you want, you could do a lot worse than look up the Haulage Guild Director down at Two Bridges."

Return to the parlour... **394**

795

The parlour of the Drowned Badger opens directly onto the wharf through large barn doors, pulled back to let the light in. In fact, one barwoman keeps the boatmen amused and refreshed through a bar hatch directly over the water, so that bargees can order a quart of ale without even leaving their tiller. Most of the drinkers here work on river and with the cases of stuffed river fish covering every wall, the room does have a rather submarine atmosphere.

If you have the codeword *Aspirin*, turn to...		**206**
Order a drink...	(1s)	**830**
Buy a round of drinks...	(12s)	**145**
Leave the pub...		**774**

796

"Good luck!" Lord Dashwood leans into the low cockpit and shakes your hand. "I know you'll do me proud."

To track your progress in the race you will collect Race Points. Mark these in the 'Other Notes' section of your Adventure sheet: you will need a total number to find out whether you have succeeded at the finish line.

The warning horn sounds and you check the engine pressure, the steam reservoir, the response of the steering levers. You pedal a little more powdered coal into the furnace, turn the regulator and, just as the starting horn sounds, release the brake. You are off!

From your starting position you manage to accelerate into the midst of the pack, dodging the other vehicles with regular tugs on your steering levers.

The track heads downhill and takes a sharp turn to the left between a coal dump and a stand of yelling audience. A steamer sponsored by the Coal Board is just ahead of you, heading into the bend. How will you steer?

Take the inside of the bend...	**410**
Steer outside the steamer...	**686**

797

The way to West Wycombe has never felt so long, or so confusing, but then you have never tried to get there in such a condition before. The night falls as you ride and your lime lantern stutters as you shudder over the bumpy road. Eventually you turn into the drive of West Wycombe House and stagger up the steps. The Butler puts his shoulder under your arm, shudders at the bloody footprints you have left on the marble, and brings you to a nook where you can rest.

Turn to... **619**

798

If you have any **Wanted** statuses (for example, **Wanted by the Coal Board**, **Wanted by the Constables**) turn to **255**. Otherwise, the Constables throw you into a holding cell for a couple of days to cool off. They have someone treat all your **wounds** (convert them to **scars** as normal), confiscate your **money** and **possessions**, then send you up to the prison to pay for your crimes.

If you are a **Famed Lawbreaker**, turn to...	**274**
If you are the **People's Champion**, turn to...	**1005**
Otherwise, turn to...	**722**

799

The cargo is mostly ordinary market goods. Roll a dice to see what you take off the road:

Score 1	**wheel of cheese**
Score 2	**silver ring**
Score 3	**locket**
Score 4	**fishing line** and **sack**
Score 5	tin of **waterproof paint**
Score 6	**wirecutters**

Ride away... **280**

800

You moor your boat between a brick-barge and a pleasure skiff under the watchful eye of an old bearded river-man. He chuckles and knocks out his pipe. "Anyone can see you ain't born to the water, chum," he says. Mark **Cookham lock (downstream)** on the mooring section of your Adventure sheet.

Go ashore... **12**

801

Inside the dark parlour of the Bull it is as though the troubles of the world are fenced away behind the diamond-leaded frames of the windows. Several freighters are enjoying a game of backgammon and a couple of monks from the Abbey are making a delivery of produce for the kitchen.

Talk to the monks..		**601**
Order a drink...	**(1s)**	**687**
Leave the parlour...		**737**

802
You tie up alongside a small watermill, in the shelter of a long brick wall. Your mate bustles about and then settles down to touching up the paintwork. Mark your Boat Mooring as **Hedsor**.

Turn to... **230**

803
If you donated more than **5s**, turn to **348**. If not, turn to **681**.

804
Arthur Smeaton is pleased to see you again and shows you his flying machine prototype. "By no means finished, but I am making progress! Have a cup of tea while I show you something else..."

Smeaton offers to melt down any **gold** jewellery you may have to create a gold bar. "It'll take six pieces to make a small bar, but you'll find it easier to store and carry." To go along with his plan, exchange six **gold necklaces**, **gold rings** or **gold bracelets** in any combination for a single **gold bar**.

Return to the forge... **60**

805
With the Master of Hedsor dead, his house is shuttered and quiet. Through the gates you can see the weeds over-running the drive and the rose-bushes choking on fallen leaves. If he has an heir, then they plainly have not returned to claim the estate.

Head uphill towards Cliveden Corner...	**366**
Head downhill towards Bourne End...	**457**

806
Your shot goes wide and before you know it the heavy goods wagon is bearing down on you! You manage to leap off your velosteam but the massive road wheels of the engine smash the delicate machinery aside and knock it off the road. Increase your velosteam's damage by **2 points**.

If your velosteam is **Beyond Repair**...	**250**
Otherwise...	**202**

807
You steam alongside the Haulage Guild wagon. "Going far, friends?" you ask.

"Just down to the depot at Two Bridges," says the fireman, adding another shovel of coal into the furnace. "Got delayed leaving Wycombe - so we'll be steaming through the night. Next time we're up in Lane End we'll get some better lamps fitted, right George?"

"That's right, Freddy," says the driver. "Now free up the road, we've got to make steam!"

Turn off by the Golden Ball Inn... **394**

808
The steam fair is doing better than ever now that Davy and Greg have made peace. As you stroll through the dusk, lanterns are lit all round. Youngsters from Maidenhead, couples in their finery and a whole throng of villagers and townsfolk are feasting on the delights of the fair.

Perform on the Wall of Death...		**728**
Head to your wagon...		**743**
Ride the Dive Bomber...	**(1s)**	**464**
Head to the Rifle Range...	**(1s)**	**398**
Have your fortune told...	**(2s)**	**209**
Leave the fair...		**535**

809
A haulier towing a trailer of furniture is struggling to get his underpowered engine over the crest of the bridge. She stands beside the engine mopping her brow. If you want to help her squeeze some more power from her boiler, make an ENGINEERING roll of difficulty 10.

Successful ENGINEERING roll!	**1021**
Failed ENGINEERING roll or leave her alone...	**50**

810
Your stalk has been successful! The **deer carcass** needs some processing, but once emptied of its innards and with feet tied together it makes an impressive, though unwieldy, addition to your possessions. You may find a high-class butcher or a local cook to

take it off your hands - or prefer to cook it yourself in a woodland hideout somewhere.

Leave the wood...   **289**

811

The occupants quickly reach for their firearms stored in handy compartments to the sides of the carriage. Before you know it, you are under fire! Diving off the road to get out of sight, you are aware of being outgunned for once! Roll a dice to see the effects:

Score 1-2   Gain a **damage point**...
Score 3-4   Gain a **wound**...
Score 5-6   Get away unharmed...

If your velosteam is **beyond repair**...   250
If you have **five Wounds**...   90
Otherwise...   535

812

The widow's eyes widen at the sight of the money and she begins to cry. "All this time that little box sat there. But paper money's no good to me. The Constables will take it off've me. I can't go flashing that around!" Gain the codeword *Aspidistra*.

Offer her the equivalent in coins... (**£31 10s**) 904
"I will take this box to the Curtiss brothers. It belongs
    to them."   **304**

813

You recognise the Albright family from Horton Wood. They are here to sell a load of prime charcoal and offer you the purchase first. You may buy as many loads of charcoal as you can fit aboard: add any cargo to your manifest after subtracting the cost from your purse.

	To buy	To sell
Charcoal	£8	-

Return to the wharf...   713

814

The woman soon lies sprawling in the dust. A watching engineer laughs. "Foolish to injure your own apprentice, anyway. Looks like Marge got what was coming to her this time."

   The apprentice has disappeared from sight, taking the opportunity to escape his mistress and seek his fortune elsewhere. Gain a **Solidarity Point** for standing up for the underdog.

Return to the Freight Yard...   **396**

815

The innkeeper nods. "So there is. I'm surprised you didn't empty it. Maybe your tale about the accident was true, then."

Leave the Drowned Badger...   **774**

816

You steam out of Medmenham and begin to climb the ravine beside Danesfield House. Roll a dice to see what you encounter:

Score 1-2   Landslide!   720
Score 3-6   Nothing of interest...   428

817

Remove the codeword *Abound*. The Squire falls back, grasping at his desk and knocking over the lamp. "Spare me!" he cries. "I may have done ill, but do I deserve death?"

"You do indeed deserve to die."   **292**
"Leave the land and it will be as though you are dead."
                                                      624

818

You tell the professor about the knarled black poplar in the fields by Temple. He wiggles his eyebrows with glee. "Hmm! Not a woodland tree, but by no means a common one. Fascinating. I'll have to take a look at it. Here, for your trouble." He hands you the **pink scarf**. "I shan't need it. The weather is warming up, anyway."

Continue into the wood...   **190**

819

Remove the **tinned fruit** from your possessions. "My favourite," she burbles. "Tinned pears! You got any condensed milk? They go together a treat. When I was at Lord Haversham's place we'd have his leftover custards in the morning, us girls. Course, that was years ago. He was always shooting and riding and flying. Remember one time he brought a black man back with him in his steam coach and we all went to look. Sold half his estate, so he did, and we moved to the town house. But it didn't last. We was all sent home before long. Lord Haversham blew his brains out. Course that was years ago." You talk with the old woman a little longer, amusing her while she munches on the tinned fruit.

Leave the cottage...   **50**

820
Lose the codeword *Afterthought*. The weather outside worsens, rain spattering the glass and you take the opportunity to enjoy the house's hospitality and a good meal by the fire. You recognise the figure of Dr Smollett in his long coat at another table, and before you have a chance to greet him - or avoid his glare - the landlord enters the parlour with a slip of paper and goes over to him.

"Good Doctor Smollett. Just had this telegram come in. The boy picked it out for you."

Smollett reads, puts down his cutlery and looks around the room. He walks directly over to you.

"I have an urgent call up at Bullocks Farm," he says. "A woman there having a child. You can take me quickly on that machine you ride. Will you do it?"

"I am about my business. You go about yours." **689**
"I will take you, Doctor."   **482**

821
Tick the next empty box in the list and turn to that page number.
- ☐ Empty? Tick then turn to...   **307**
- ☐ Empty? Tick then turn to...   **84**
- ☐ Empty? Tick then turn to...   **164**
If all the boxes are ticked, turn to...   **478**

822
You tell Father Bourdain about some of the other priests you have met on your travels. He slips away from your questions. "I can't answer for them and I can't judge them. I'm sure they all make peace with their conscience, in one way or another."

"By ignoring it, you mean?"

"Possibly. If you ignore any voice long enough, it will die away. Even a voice given to help and warn us."

"But you don't spend your poor fund on luxuries?"

"No. And perhaps it is my responsibility to challenge my brothers and sisters. Particularly now you have brought my attention to it."

Leave the church...   **703**
Continue talking...   **717**

823
Dr Smollet's surgery is on the main road, beside a country post office with a telegraph tower. A burly nurse looks up as you answer and puts aside his paperwork. "Dr Smollett is busy. What can I do for you?"

The medical staff will deal with any minor ailments and can sell you basic medical supplies, but if you need your wounds treating you will have to wait for the doctor.

Medical items	To buy	To sell
bandages	3s	-
cough medicine	5s	-
soothing lotion	2s	-

Medical treatment	To buy
Treat a **fever**...	6s
Treat a **burn**...	12s

Request treatment for your **wounds**...   **160**
Return to Lane End...   **684**

824
Bullets now kick up white dust from the road - it is now or never. Make a MOTORING roll of difficulty 11 to escape, adding 1 if you have a **gas pressuriser**.

Successful MOTORING roll!   **521**
Failed MOTORING roll!   **553**

825
Once moored amongst the working boats you find your way over walkways and arched iron bridges to dry land. Your velosteam is ready to go. Mark **Boulter's Lock (upstream)** as your Barge Mooring on your Adventure Sheet.

Turn to...   **94**

826

The minstrel is very impressed by all your tales of derring-do and protecting the weak. "There's good material in there," he says, "For a whole collection of songs - maybe a piece of musical theatre! I should write some of this down."

He collects some of your stories and starts work immediately. Increase your **Solidarity Points** by 1 and add **Legend in Song** to your Great Deeds on your adventure sheet. As you continue to travel through the towns and villages you may indeed find that the tales of your good deeds now proceed you with a catchy tune.

Leave the minstrel...   **288**

827

You find the wholesale manager pacing her office. "This has gone too far!" she shouts to her secretary. "That dratted Haulage Guild! They can't just lock our hauliers up in their private gaol!"

"I'm afraid that's exactly what they've done," replies her secretary. "Roberts, Fluellyn, Masters and Shaw have all been detained for not having the correct transportation licenses. I have the telegraph here."

"First they slap new tolls on malt and hops - on the road and the river - and now they arrest my drivers! We have to do something about it. We'll never be able to finish our next brew. It's a stranglehold!" If you have the **Guildsman's medallion**, turn to **950** immediately.

Offer to help...   **421**
Mind your own business...   **4**

828

After drawing your gun you see the wagon accelerate. You have one chance to make a shot, so you aim for the driver. Make an ACCURACY roll of difficulty 14.

Successful ACCURACY roll!   **697**
Failed ACCURACY roll!   **806**

829

Many of the clientele are enjoing stout-handled mugs of a dark, foamy ale. "'Tis from up-country," the barman tells you. "We get it from the North Road wagons. York City Pride, 5.2 percent and a lovely filling flavour too. It'll put some hair on your chest, I tell you."

"It's all they drink up on the Great North Road,"

one haulier tells you. "From Stamford to Edinburgh. But I heard they was struggling to keep brewing it. York's practically under siege, what with that Earl of Chester. It's a place a desperate man can make a bob or two, running the blockade."

You ask about private steam carriages. The drivers shake their heads. "Precious few come this way. They take the Oxford road, from Piddington, stop in Wycombe, then head on up to London through Cutthroat Wood. Aye, and the Bath road west of Maidenhead."

"And between the two," says another driver. "The Marlow road, through Inkydown wood, across the bridge and then up Handy Cross. You get a lot of private traffic that way. You'll be wanting employment of a sort, I imagine," he finishes with a grin.

Return to the parlour...   **79**

830

Besides the more usual handles on the bar, promising the reliable draughts of machine brewed Oxford King and Wethered's Double Hop, you can see a label advertising Old Eel.

"Quite an acquired taste," advises the barwoman. "Strong, something between a stout and a heavy bitter, quite carbonated. You should be able to taste the bottom of the river in it, they say."

It does indeed have a heavy flavour and pours thickly. The bubbles carry a strange flavour right up into your eyes.

"It's brewed here in the village," she says, watching you drink. "An eel in every barrel."

Return to the parlour...   **795**

831

You enter Lord Dashwood's garage triumphantly bearing the **titanium alloy**. "I knew you could do it! Now we can get this steamer up to speed!"

The next few days see a drastic redesign of the Wagtail. Between you, Harris and Dashwood, the steam car is prepared and tested until you have nothing left to give to the project.

Dashwood has the butler bring out several of the family heirlooms as a reward. You may take any three from the following: **dancing shoes (GALLANTRY+3)**, **bottle of Quinta de Vesan**, **locket of King Charles' hair**, **white pills (ING+2)** ☐ ☐ ☐ and a purse containing **£20**. Lose the codeword *Agile* and gain the codeword *Ambition* as well.

"I was going to drive the Wagtail myself," says Lord Dashwood, "But your help in the trials convinces me that you have a better grasp of the machine than I do myself. Would you be willing to race for me?" He explains that either way, he has owed you all the success of the endeavour so far and invites you to come and stay at West Wycombe House whenever you desire. You are now the **Friend of Lord Dashwood**.

Turn to... 172

832

As you step off onto the quay, you feel a heavy hand land on your shoulder. "'Ello, 'ello, 'ello," says the gruff voice of the local chief Constable. "We've been looking for you." Before you have the chance to draw your weapon or dive into the river, a posse of Constables surround you and have you in irons.

Turn to... 187

833

The freighters wave merrily to you, recognising Director Short's brass commission. One tosses you a **bottle of Beehive Stout**. "Breakages on the road!" he shouts. "Unavoidable really!"

Ride on... 202

834

The driver recognises your medallion and gives you a wave. "Come to check we're alright, have you? Well, listen up. There's a Co-operative wagon down the road behind us, trying to muscle in on our route. Perhaps you should let them know that they ought to seek out the Guild's protection. In your own way."

Wait for the Co-operative wagon... 665
Ride away... 535

835

It is not easy to find a mooring here at Bourne End: every jetty is lined and a queue of boats waits to find a space. A man with mutton-chop whiskers and a bowler hat waves to you from the quay: if you give him **10s** he will find you a mooring. If you choose to do so, subtract the money from your purse and mark your Boat Mooring as **Bourne End**.

Moor up... (**10s**) 703
Steam on... 693

836

You ask around about casual work here at the freight yard. One haulier is looking for an engineer of sufficient skill to help him repair and upgrade some trailers, while another is looking for some hands to unload freight from Henley.

Offer your help on the trailers...
(ENGINEERING score 6 or higher) 441
Unload some freight... 453
Return to the High Street... 4

837

You swing through the window and draw your weapon. The guard staggers as you knock into him, but manages to right himself. You must fight!

Guard   Weapon: **truncheon (PAR 4)**
Parry: 11
Nimbleness: 7
Toughness: 2

Victory! 768
Defeat! 56

838

You draw yourself up to your full height, raise your blunderpistol and your sabre and look him straight in the eye. "You life is forfeit, milord. Your life... or the petty purse at your side!" Make a RUTHLESSNESS roll of difficulty 9 to scare him into giving up.

Successful RUTHLESSNESS roll... 261
Failed RUTHLESSNESS roll... 493

839

"You have set yourself a lofty goal - but it is one you may never reach. Either you must turn from this way of life you have found or find a new way to live it. God go with you on that hard road."

Erase the codewords *Arthropod*, *Astrakhan* or *Apogee* if you have them. If you have the codeword *Apprehend*, turn to **976**.

Leave the church...   **703**

840
Your mate has the helm, so you have him close the gap with the supply barges and spring aboard at the crucial moment. Dashing forward along the very gunwale of the craft, you come to the towing chain and quickly unshackle it. The barge charges on, but veers with the current as the tug and its unobservant crew forge on. You dash back down the barge and leap onto the steering platform of your own boat again. The whole endeavour takes less than a minute.

Slowly but surely, the barge approaches the bank, where the vagrants have realised what is happening. They have left their fire and their dinner and are finding sticks and hooks to help hold the barge while they loot it and make off with everything they can. None of them will have any pity on the Constables. "God bless your honour!" cries a voice in your direction. Gain **a Solidarity Point** for your interventions - but you are now **Wanted by the River Union**.

Continue the way you were going...   **776**

841
After ordering your pint of Hodge's Mild, you join a group of locals gossiping about the goings-on up the hill and across the river.

"This ball's going to be the most extravagant since the old Duke gave his Christmas ball back in forty-eight! Or at least, that's what the new Duke said he wanted."

"And how would you know what the Duke said, Margery?"

"Hush, Malcolm. You know 'er boy's in service up there. Go on, love, tell us."

"Well, they're bringing up forty melons from London hothouses - their own greenhouses can't grow enough. And there'll be sixty guests, so they've laid on extra coal just for the steam wagons. A team 'as been stackin' up an extra mooring pylon too. And the ladies. The Princess Anastasia, Lady Castor, Maria Roberts, the King's you-know-what. And they say she'll be a-wearing the Dervish's Eye."

"What's the Dervish's Eye?"

"Don't you read the papers? 'Tis a black sapphire taken from a Sri Lankan temple, far off in the east. She was given it by Major Coppel, before he was killed in a dreadful duel. And they say it's the power of the stone gives her power over the King."

The mild beer has a creamy texture and a gentle, only-just-hopped flavour. Instead of heady resins you are treated to a sweet, malty, flat brew that promises to be all-too-drinkable.

Leave the pub...   **246**

842
Seeing the grim look on your face and your readiness to resort to violence, the monks back off and you are able to work the lock yourself. Before long you have left them behind.

Steam on...   **487**

843
Recalling Comrade Feaver's instructions to plant the **sealed packet** amongst Lady Dean's possessions, you pull off the road beside the entrance to Harleyford Manor to take a look around. After climbing the fence and making your way through a barrier of trees, you come to the hillside from where you can peer down and the house and consider your options. Firstly you could wait until nightfall, scale the wall and break into the lady's dressing room. You would need to rely on your NIMBLENESS to achieve this and could benefit from using a **rope** or other climbing equipment. On the other hand, you could bluff your way in, impersonating a travelling member of the nobility. GALLANTRY would the best way to succeed such an attempt, possibly augmented by dressing the part.

Attempt a break-in by night...   **127**
Ride up the drive and bluff your way in...   **945**
Return when better prepared...   **786**

844
You dismount your velosteam and prepare to load it on board your riverboat. As long as it is securely bolted to the deck and covered with a tarpaulin it should come to no harm. Are you moored **downstream** or **upstream** of the lock?

Downstream...   **363**
Upstream...   **437**

845

□

If the box is empty, put a tick in it and read on. Otherwise, turn to **776** immediately.

You spy an encampment of wandering poor beside the river, making a meagre dinner over a small fire. Approaching from further upriver, a string of barges packed with food and supplies for the Constables appears, towed by a River Union tug. The chains attaching the rearmost barge have come undone on one side: should you choose to leap aboard and set it loose, you have an opportunity to redress some of the river's inequality right now. Make a NIMBLENESS roll of difficulty 9 if you wish to try to detach the barge, adding 2 if you have an **axe**.

Successful NIMBLENESS roll!	**840**
Failed NIMBLENESS roll or did not attempt the deed...	**776**

846

The little quay at Medmenham can only accomodate a single barge at a time. Once you tie up, you will have an opportunity to unload your cargo and try to strike a deal with the trader, Mr Eli, who has a small warehouse here. If you have **passdisc 67**, turn to **917** immediately.

	To buy	To sell
Charcoal	£11	-
Furniture	-	-
Machinery	-	-
Pottery	-	£23
Cotton	-	£5
Woollen cloth	£13	£12
Coal	-	£9
Beer	£16	£16
Wheat	£5	£5
Malt	-	£8
Frozen meat	-	£12
Ice	-	£12

Steam up to the Drowned Badger...	**920**
Moor here...	**1010**
Sail upriver...	**877**
Sail downriver...	**869**

847

This provokes another argument. "Don't you remember, Harris, last time we took a tow? We were almost swamped because you couldn't keep the tow-rope clear."

"Oh yes, I remember. I remember how you sat with your feet up, telling us to bail."

The third joins in. "If I had my way we should have hired a steam-skiff. What sort of bally idea was it to row the Thames anyway?"

There is plainly little you can offer them. As you steam past, one shouts after you: "Buy the book! We may feature you as a character! We're planning a subscription publication..."

Leave them to their madness...   **637**

848

Cookham lock is busy mainly on account of the through-traffic. It is several miles by water either to Marlow or Maidenhead - the far more significant cargo wharves - but a few traders will buy and sell goods here. The fall of the lock is about four feet from the upper to the lower level, and with the steam pumping engine to assist, the lock gates are opening and closing almost constantly. To one side, workmen are busy digging into the ground and lining it with strong brickwork, in preparation for a second lock to speed traffic through.

	To buy	To sell
Charcoal	£13	£10
Furniture	-	-
Machinery	-	£24
Pottery	-	-
Cotton	-	-
Woollen cloth	-	£10
Coal	£12	£10
Beer	-	£17
Wheat	£3	£3
Malt	-	£7
Frozen meat	-	£14
Ice	-	£6

Pass through the lock... (**2s** or **Bargee's Badge**)	693
Moor here...	**800**
Return downstream...	**181**

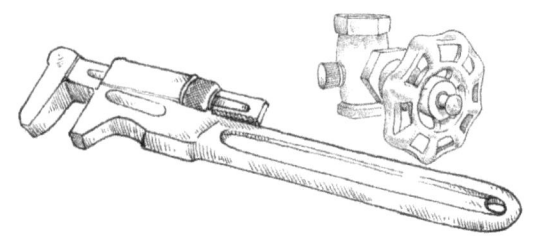

849

The water is cold and deep and you must swim under the surface if you are to escape the constables' shots. You will have to discard any **cloak**, **boots** or **hat** you are wearing and make a NIMBLENESS roll of difficulty 11 to escape.

Successful NIMBLENESS roll!   **855**
Failed NIMBLENESS roll!   **102**

850

The lady accepts your invitation to step aboard and see the cabin, Of course, it is a moment's work to whip a rope around her hands and a scarf over her face, but she does begin to kick and shout rather alarmingly as you steam away up a side-channel. If you have a **bottle of chloroform** you may be able to knock her out and plan how to ransom her. Otherwise you may end up having to put her ashore again.

Knock her out...   (**bottle of chloroform**)   **908**
Otherwise...   **974**

851

After waiting for hours in the increasingly chilly night, you resolve to find somewhere warmer to shelter. Nothing is coming and your vigil has been in vain.

Head to your hideout in Windsor Wood...
    (*Ashen*)   **676**
Ride down to the Walnut Tree at Bourne End... **634**

852

The beer is pale, lighter in colour than you average ale but not straw-bright. "It's called a lager," says the barman. "Drank 'em in Germany. Very nice on a summer's day."

The drink is gassy and sharp. Perhaps in the sunshine it could be as refreshing as the barman says.

"I tried selling it downriver at Boulter's Lock, to the gentry, but no-one took me up on it."

Drinking with the watermen, you hear disturbing rumours about the house on the hill high above Medmenham. "That's Danesfield House," says a woman with a laundry barge. "Colonel Snappet's place. He's a dreadful creature, he is."

"Haven't you heard of the abductions? The torture?" asks another.

"That's right. Last I heard he had arrested that Professor - the inventor - from Wallingford way, who wouldn't give over his inventions. Imprisoned him and tortured him. A cursed place, that old house." The drinkers look with a glare up towards the cliff and the shroud of trees.

Turn to...   **846**

853

The lanes lead you south, over the high ground, until you approach Hedsor and Bourne End. The pursuit velosteams are close behind you - you were forced to slow when moving past several freight wagons and even a short-cut through several fields didn't gain you any ground. The lane leading down to the Thames is nearby - you take a sharp left and steam towards the water. Crossing at speed will be a tricky business - but you are certain that your knowledge of the exact route will take you across and leave the Constables stranded. Make a MOTORING roll of difficulty 10 to get across, adding 1 if you have **off-road tyres**.

Successful MOTORING roll!   **913**
Failed MOTORING roll!   **979**

854

The officer draws his sword as you approach. "I'll be beggared if some low-born road-thief thinks he can order me to empty my pockets!" You must fight him.

Officer		Weapon: **sabre (PAR 6)**
Parry:	11	
Nimbleness:	5	
Toughness:	3	

If he manages to defeat you, turn to **74**. If you are victorious, you can take the officer's **sabre (PAR 6)**, a **pocket watch**, **£2 18s** and his **Veteran's Medal (GAL+1)**, and then turn to **530**.

855

Somehow you manage to swim away from the fight. Your mate has not been so lucky, however. Abandoning him to the constables condemns him to imprisonment or worse as your accomplice - gain the codeword *Aidan*. They will also confiscate (and most probably burn) your boat and its cargo, so you must erase these from your Adventure sheet.

You eventually pull yourself ashore near Taplow, tired and soaking wet. Incredibly, the police launch which stopped you is moored up nearby and your confiscated velosteam is on board. You have another chance! Careless of the danger, you board, mount your vel, fire up the engine, roar down the gangplank and ride off into the night.

Turn to...   **599**

856

The drivers are at the limit of their ability and at the limit of their engines' endurance too. Sooner or later one will slip up. It is Jackson, who has been pushing his engine too hard and loses control as his massive green Chariaeoli bounces over the uneven track. It lands unevenly and the stressed chassis of his vehicle twists, screams, shreds apart and deposits his boiler and him onto a hard bank. Burning coals are scattered across the roadway, the forewheels bounding down the track, still spinning. The other drivers dodge as best they can: one other is tangled in the wreckage, one takes the opportunity to leap ahead and match Lord Akroyd, and then you whizz by, up into third place. Gain three Race Points!

Focus on the final stretches of the race...   **226**

857

☐

If the box is empty, put a tick in it now. If it is already ticked, turn to **879** immediately.

A woman with a parasol waves you over to the bank. "I say," she says, "What an interesting boat. You don't look the type to have to work on the water - is it a game of some sort?"

Rob her...   **859**
Kidnap her...   **850**
Give her a sarcastic answer...   **901**

858

In the osier beds you see an overseer beating the workers. Peering over the reeds and rushes you realise that he is whipping a woman with several children looking on.

Sail on...   **776**
Attack him...   **961**

859

"Come aboard and see," you say sweetly. At first she is a little unsure, but you charm her aboard and pretend to show her the workings of the boat. Then, when she is off her guard, you tear her handbag out of her hands.

"You disgusting rascal," she says as you unceremoniously dump her ashore again. "I shall never trust boat-persons again!"

Her bag contains **thirty pounds in banknotes**, which you may be able to convince a Bank to accept, but you will most likely have to find somebody to exchange them for good hard money.

Steam on upriver...   **539**
Steer towards the Hedsor channel...   **488**

860

Your boat is safely moored where you left it. Your mate pokes his head out of the cabin as he hears the familiar sound of your velosteam approaching over the wooden walkways.

"Lockmaster has been poking around," he says. "We owes **6s** in mooring fees, according to him. Bare cheek, if you ask me! We haven't taken anything from them here - no sirree! I've simply been here enriching the environment."

If you are unable to pay, turn to **569**. Otherwise, subtract the money from your purse. Are you moored above (upstream of) or below (downstream of) the lock?

Upstream...   **988**
Downstream...   **318**

861

The passengers are impressed with your behaviour. "Well, maybe the tales are true," says one portly gentleman. "You must be the Steam Highwayman the papers do keep telling of. Roll a single dice and add 3: if the total is higher than your current unmodified GALLANTRY score you may increase it by 1.

You arrange the wounded passengers as comfortably as you can and leave them under the care of the unwounded, advising them to wait for the next steamer to pass this way.

Ride away...   **530**

862

You tumble off the roof of the carriage and hit the ground hard. A sharp pain tells you that something is broken - increase your **Wounds** by 1. The carriage does not slow and disappears quickly down the road.

If you have **five Wounds**...   **74**
Otherwise...   **530**

863

Your mate is impressed. "I knew you wasn't an ordinary type of bargee, but I didn't expect that! And all that loot - you give it to the needy? That would feed my family for a year."

Steam on downriver...   **425**

864

The driver laughs and accelerates directly towards you. You must make your next decision quickly.

Shoot at the driver...   **918**
Dodge the speeding carriage...   **925**

865

"Ere', I recognise you," says the officer. "I've got a printofit somewhere with your face on it..." He starts to fumble in his jacket, giving you a moment to act.

Jump overboard and swim for it...   **849**
Attack him...   **887**

866
☐

If the box is empty, tick it and read on. If it is already ticked, turn to **693** immediately.

You address the wharvesmen, aiming to motivate them into joining the Compact and rising up in armed revolt. You receive a mixed response to begin with. Make an INGENUITY roll of difficulty 11 to convince them: you can add 2 to your score if you have a **revolutionary poster**.

Successful INGENUITY roll!   **878**
Failed INGENUITY roll!   **560**

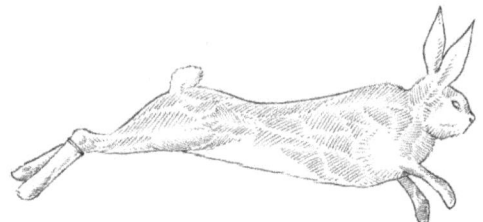

867

The priest shakes his head as you order him to empty his pockets. "Have you no respect for the cloth, my child?" He turns out to be carrying **£4 3s**, a **gold necklace**, a **gold ring** and a **cloak**.

"Whatever happened to your concern for the poor, Father?" you ask.

"Come now," he replies. "A man must have a few travelling comforts."

Ride away...   **530**

868

"I don't want to know how you justify your despicable ways," you spit. "Just give me your purse and you can go on your way."

He shrugs, then tosses you a silken purse, containing **£6**.

Ride away...   **530**

869
☐

If the box is empty, put a tick in it and turn to **953**. If it is already ticked, read on. You are approaching Harleyford and Hurley lock. The string of islands and the long weir cross the river obliquely, making a small change in level into a massive obstacle for river craft. The narrow lock by Hurley village struggles to keep up with all the traffic passing downstream.

Moor at Freebody's yard...   **611**
Approach the lock...   **988**
Steam towards Medmenham...   **846**

870

If you are able to offer the Compact gold bullion, you will make Comrade Treasurer's day. "Just imagine! Gold can become anything! Rifles! Bullets! Assassinations! Bombs! I can't get enough of it, gold."

	To sell
gold bar	£32
gold necklace	£4
gold bracelet	£2
gold ring	£1

Return to the hideout...   **985**

871

You wound the adventuress in her arm and blood seeps into the cloth of her sleeve. She clasps a handkerchief over the scratch and bows. "You prove yourself quite a brawler."

"That is beside the point. Hand over your valuables."

She looks at you coolly. "Valuables? I shan't ask what you mean by that. I presume you mean coinage." She drops a purse and walks into the trees. Something about her poise and the way she bore her wounds convinces you to leave her be... This time.

The purse contains **£5 3s**.

Ride away...   **530**

872

"It's a guild thingummy," says the barman. "Affiliation token of some sort. The Union of Rivermen, Bargees and Canalpersons. Once you join up and pay your dues they see that you get fair treatment at the locks - well, all of the Union ones, anyway. Most of the number ones on the river are members. Most - but not all. The headquarters or council room is down at Maidenhead wharf."

Steam back to the wharf...   **846**

873

Your shot misses and before you know it, the carriage is upon you. The driver, fearing another bullet, accelerates away before you have chance to shoot again.

Ride away...   **530**

874

"I can't swim!" yells the constable as you knock him into the water. He goes overboard with a splash and his friends seem more worried about fishing him out than chasing you. The mate opens the regulator on the steam engine and you quickly head out to lose yourself amongst the working boats and wharves of Maidenhead dock. Unfortunately you are growing notorious and are certainly **Wanted by the Constables** for your assault if you were not already.

Turn to...   **333**

875

It is the body of a man, plainly shot, probably in a duel. He has one bloody wound in his chest that has stained his fine suit, but he has been in the water too long to make his face recognisable. His pockets are empty but you can take his **opal cufflinks** if you wish.

Return him to the river...   **637**

876

After leading the constables on a merry chase you steer straight into a thicket, then pull hard right and silence your engine. Coasting through a curtain of linden branches you gently pull to a stop beneath a sandstone cliff. The pursuit vehicles tear past. After waiting for them to get out of earshot, you re-ignite your burner and carefully steam back the way you came, heading for your woodland base.

Turn to...   **676**

877

The river wends on, between the rising hills, between pastures and rich wheatfields, beneath steep woods and on, on, on. There are few things so stately and slow as the flow of the Thames.

Follow the Thames west...
                    Highways and Holloways 251
Travel east ...   **869**
Travel to Medmenham...   **846**

878

The workers are soon brought to a fever pitch. "We'll do it," one yells! "We just need the guns!"

"Get us some guns!" shouts another. "If the Compact want us to join with them, the least they can do is arm us.

One of the rioters presses himself to the front of the crowd. "Here," he says, pressing **passdisc 33** into your hand, "This'll convince Feaver we're serious. Go and tell her we're ready."

Return to the river...   **560**

879

A party of drunken students in a punt wave to you cheerily. "Enjoy yourself!" says one. "It's a lovely evening!" He hands you a **bottle of champagne**.

Steam on upriver...   **539**
Moor here until the morning...   **647**
Steer towards the Hedsor channel...   **488**

880

"Again, just what Jensen teaches. So now imagine yourself in situation: you have been instructed to carry out the assassination of a member of the nobility. You have the opportunity to plant a bomb in his steam-carriage, although your observations indicate that he may be travelling with his young children and wife. Would you plant the bomb?"

"Of course I would. Orders are orders." **996**
"Since the cause depends on the value of all human
    life, I would not squander it." **275**

881

The travellers brighten up. "So there is goodness still in the world," one says. "This'll help us get to London and there's bound to be work there." You can only hope they find it.

    If you have fewer than 10 **Solidarity Points**, gain one now.

Ride on... **50**

882

The treasurer looks at you for a moment, then bursts out into laughter. "I like the way you think! Yes, if you could take down a bank then we will be able to use as much paper money as you can bring us. Or otherwise if you can lay your hands on bullion - gold bars - that's even better. Bring them to me and I'll give you Comrade's rates. You could try Coulter's Bank in Wycombe - but watch out for the armed guards. Perhaps theres another way to skin that particular cat...."

Return to the hideout... **985**

883

The following boats are for sale here at Freebody's wharf. Some are straight off the chocks and others are reconditioned river boats of considerable age, but each has been fitted out with care and craftsmanship.

Small skiff... **£22** (1 cargo space)
Medium launch... **£30** (2 cargo spaces)
Large barge... **£40** (3 cargo spaces)

And of course you'll have no difficulty finding a mate to crew your barge.

Return to the village... **569**
Board your new craft... **360**

884

You steam out into the middle of the road and flourish your weapons, crying "Stand and deliver!" Make a RUTHLESSNESS roll of difficulty 12. You can add 2 to your roll if you are a **Famed Lawbreaker** and 2 more if you are the **People's Champion** .

Successful RUTHLESSNESS roll! **957**
Failed RUTHLESSNESS roll! **864**

885

The newspaper editor spits as you prod him and threaten him. "I've work to do, you blackguard. What do you know of work? There is news to be told and a paper to fill!" You can take a a box of **white pills (ING+2)** ☐ ☐ ☐, a **silver ring** and **£6**.

Ride away... **530**

886

"Why is it so much?" you ask.

    "We monks of Bisham Abbey hold the monopoly on ice-making by order of Parliament," he replies, slipping the coins into a heavy toll-purse. "The payment makes sure it stays profitable for us, supporting Mother Church. Now, if you wish to moor up, we do keep a small depot here to support the river trade. Otherwise, I'll happily open the lock for you on payment of your toll."

    "You mean that doesn't cover the lock fees?"
    The monk simply smiles and shakes his head.

	To buy	To sell
Charcoal	£14	-
Furniture	£29	-
Machinery	-	-
Pottery	-	£23
Cotton	£5	£5
Woollen cloth	-	£12
Coal	£12	£10
Beer	£16	£16
Wheat	£5	£5
Malt	-	£6
Frozen meat	-	£12
Ice	-	£6

Pass through the lock... (**4s** or **Abbey Ribbon**) **487**
Return to Bisham Reach... **745**

887

The officer parries your first attack and steps backwards. You will have to defeat the man quickly if you are to escape his friends on the launch!

Constable		Weapon: **sabre (PAR 6)**
Parry:	11	
Nimbleness:	5	
Toughness:	2	

Victory!	874
Defeat!	187

888

The Freight Yard at Maidenhead is a tense and dangerous place. Not only are the massive engines and their trailers a constant threat as they rumble between the narrow gates and over the weighbridge, but the rivalry between the Haulage Guild and the Co-operative is only one step away from all-out war here. You overhear several hauliers muttering about Director Short of the Guild and his ruthless policy of intimidation. Nonetheless, you are able to speak to the mechanics and will be able to have your velosteam examined. If you have a **heavy parcel**, turn to **114** immediately.

When you ask about ways to bypass the Constables' checkpoints into town, one freighter shakes her head. "I don't know of any way. But on that little velosteam of yourn, you might be able to find a way through the Thicket. The gypsies'll know. They know them woods better'n anyone else."

Velosteam Customisations	To buy
double headlamp	**£9 9s**
reinforced boiler	**£12**

Repairs	To buy
Per **damage point**	**£3 15s**

Return to Maidenhead...   **594**

889

You spy a small slipper launch making its way erratically down river. Its helmsman is plainly an amateur, unlikely even to drive his own steam carriage on the highway. After all, that is what servants are for, isn't it? Fools with more money than sense are exactly your target.

As they come between the islands, you block their way with your boat and, after bracing yourself for the collision, step confidently onto their foredeck.

"Give me all your valuables," you say. "This is a hold-up!"

The day-trippers panic and wail, utterly unprepared for anything like this. You strip them of their purses, wallets and jewellery and collect **£4 5s**, a **pocket watch**, a **silver necklace** and a **silk scarf**.

"I will be making a report to the constables immediately!" shouts the helmsman after you. "I can give a good description! You will now be **Wanted by the Constables** unless you are wearing a **cloak** or **mask** of some sort to hide your features.

Turn to...   **863**

890

If you are a **Famed Lawbreaker** or you are **Wanted by the Constables**, turn to **952** immediately. Otherwise, read on.

The buzzing of high-powered reciprocal engines approaches: two Constabulary velosteams speed down the London road. On catching sight of you they slow, no doubt comparing your description to their printofit notepads. You are glad to see they find no match, but they still wave you over.

"Out for a little ride, are we?" asks the female officer. "Enjoying the dusk breeze on our customised velosteam, indeed?"

"Is there a law against it?"

"Oh no. Not at all. It's simply that this stretch of road is somewhat notorious for highwaymen and robbers and the like. So we'd advise you to move on through as quickly as possible."

The constables insist on escorting you out of Cutthroat Wood. Which way were you headed?

South...	**530**
West...	**574**
East...	*The Reeking Metropolis 42*

891

Do you have any of the following codewords?

Additive...	**1011**
Arithmetic...	**294**
Ambition...	**446**
Aorta...	**579**
None of these	**378**

892

You come across a boat containing three young men in boater hats and river suits, arguing about whose turn it is to row, whose turn it is to cook, whose turn it is to steer, why one of them has sat on another's hat for the third time, whether they should have brought the ruddy banjo in the first place, when they should stop to cook tea and whether they still count each other as friends. A small terrier is sat on the prow of their skiff looking plaintively at the river bank.

Offer them a tow...	**847**
Sail straight past...	**637**

893

The steam carriage speeds ahead as you turn and coast alongside the fallen luggage. Roll a dice to discover what you find:

Score 1	Only clothes - gain a **dinner jacket**
Score 2	A bag of jewellery - gain a **golden bracelet** and a **golden necklace**
Score 3	An **ivory fan** and a **silk scarf**
Score 4	A **picnic hamper**
Score 5	A gentleman's valet kit - gain a **razor (PAR 2 NIM+2)** and a **bow tie (GAL+1)**
Score 6	A **strongbox**

Ride away with your loot...   **530**

894

The high price of the bottled ale is enthusiastically explained by the bartender, with wiggling eyebrows and a wide grin. "Brewed for Walkerville," he says. "We've only got a single crate ourselves!" You can see another pair of crates tucked behind a curtain.

The beer, poured into a handsome tulip glass, deserves at least some of its accolades. It is somewhat reminiscent of a summer ale or an IPA but with a strong, floral, spicy hop aftertaste - apparently the profile of a hop called citra. Medium sweet and neither flat nor aggressively carbonated, the beer is really characterised by the complicated resiny notes of the dry-hopping, inviting further tastings. It could certainly become a popular style.

As you sit supping your beer, a drunken clerk starts to tell you conspiratorilly of what he hears in the telegraph wires. "Someone is looking for the maker of clockwork birds," he slurs. "Someone with a lot of influence." He slumps onto the bar and the bartender tidily wipes around his balding head.

Return to the bar...   **978**

895

"What?" shrieks the woman. "Henry, you won't let this blackguard take me gems. You gave them to me, after all."

"My dear," says the man, "Our friend is armed and dangerous."

"Why you are less of a man than Dorothea ever said! To think I ever considered giving you my intimicable affections!" She gives him an open-handed slap, scratching his face badly. Her jewels are only a cheap **silver bracelet** and a **silver necklace**, but perhaps you won't tell her that her beloved gems were just paste.

Ride off with your loot...   **530**

896

After letting several pleasure-boats go past, reckoning them either not worth the trouble or too likely to resist, a small steam-launch steams towards you. A small crew manage the boat while rich passengers sip drinks and sit in deckchairs. You can either try to threaten them into submission with your RUTHLESSNESS skill or to board them and overawe them with violence.

Threaten them first...	**912**
Board them and subdue the crew...	**933**

897

The family are aghast. "What have you done? A beating we could have survived, but with this on our heads the master will turn us out - if we aren't punished beyond bearing!"

"We'll have to leave," says the woman decisively. "Come on, father. Gather your children and everything you can. We'll make the best of it we can and go tramping."

Sail on...   **776**

898

The monk makes a massive splash and your mate roars with laughter to see him splutter angrily in the water. Six or seven other monks appear with boathooks and clubs: make a RUTHLESSNESS roll of difficulty 11.

Successful RUTHLESSNESS roll!	**842**
Failed RUTHLESSNESS roll!	**923**

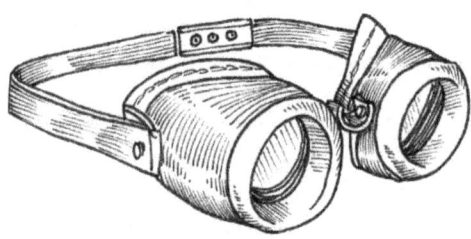

899

An atmosphere of warm, hoppy goodness fills the courtyards of the Wethered Brewery. Even the horses pulling the old-fashioned drays seem to be enjoying the brew mixed in with their oats. The company employs many in Marlow and the townspeople are proud of their part in a drinkable legend. If you have the codeword *Advertise*, turn to **335**. If you are the **Friend of Louise Standler**, turn to **222** immediately.

Talk to the wholesale manager...	**827**
Return to the High Street...	**4**

900

Part-way up the wall you lose your grip and come tumbling to the ground, knocking over a water-butt and bruising your ribs badly: gain a **wound**. The noise also alerts the servants, who come rushing out. You manage to make it away and into the woods before they catch you, but the effort tires you dreadfully.

If you have **five Wounds**...	**74**
Otherwise...	**786**

901

"You are quite correct," you say. "I am actually the heir to a large estate in the North country, but I thought I would like to see how the poor rivermen live. I don't see what they complain about!" You wave to your mate. "This fellow is my butler."

The lady is amazed. "How very romantic! I think that everybody of the better sort ought to at least try to sympathise with the poor - but I would never do such a thing. Do come and visit me in London and tell me more about it!" She passes over **Lady Emmeline's calling card.**

Steam on upriver...	**848**
Steer towards the Hedsor channel...	**488**

902

Despite the driver's desperation, you manage to cling on to the luggage rack and slowly work your way forward until you can put your blade against the driver's neck. "Stop the coach!" you order.

Turn to...	**957**

903

The Walnut Tree serves a variety of fine ales, including the Bishop's Peculiar, brewed for the Bishop of Salisbury and sold in all of the inns under his patronage. It has a distinctly sour flavour, which is balanced by a sweetness that lingers on the tongue. The barman watches you try it. "Quite an acquired taste," he says, "But once you try it, you'll not forget it. If you have **ten or more Solidarity Points**, turn to **540**.

Return to the parlour...	**634**
Leave the inn...	**703**

904

The widow has never seen so much money at once. "My sainted aunt! Who would've thought it! Oh, thankyou, kind stranger. God bless you!" Gain **two Solidarity Points**. Remove the codeword *Aspidistra*.

Ride away...	**304**

905

Your waiting has paid off! A private steam carriage approaches. How will you respond?

Threaten the driver...	**884**
Shoot to kill the driver...	**918**
Swing aboard... (**grappling iron**)	**984**
Ride alongside...	**951**

906

The American draws his sword and quickly takes up a fighting stance: he must be a trained fencer.

Samuel Montauk the third Weapon: **sabre (PAR 6)**

Parry:	12
Nimbleness:	6
Toughness:	3

Victory!	**931**
Defeat!	**74**

907

The gentle juddering of the Perkins engine that refrigerates your cargo comes to an abrupt stop. After handing the helm to the mate, you investigate the problem. Make an ENGINEERING roll of Difficulty 11.

If you succeed, you manage to quickly unblock the intake and get the Perkins going again. However, if you fail the roll you are forced to jettison any Ice or Frozen meat you are shipping before managing to restart the machinery.

Either way, it is a short distance to Maidenhead where spare parts can certainly be had.

Moor at Maidenhead Wharf...	333
Steam on...	355

908

You manage to subdue the lady and leave her in the cabin while you moor in a side-channel north of Cookham lock. The mate is intrigued. "Will you ransom the lady, then? Seems like she must have rich family somewhere, with a get-up like that."

You bring her round and explain that she must write a letter, asking for a ransom of **two hundred guineas**. Until the money is delivered, she will remain your prisoner on board the boat. Make a RUTHLESSNESS roll of difficulty 11 to scare her into following your plan.

Successful RUTHLESSNESS roll!	958
Failed RUTHLESSNESS roll!	937

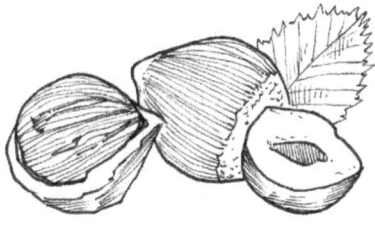

909

Erase the **bottle of chloroform**, which you tip onto a rag and then hold to the woman's face. After few moments breathing in the fumes she falls limp and you are able to lift her from the now-burning carriage.

Turn to...   861

910

The treasurer smacks his lips. "Mmmm. Folding money. Not much use in it to the man in the street. I can understand you'd want to be rid of it. I can exchange it for you - but don't you worry, we'll use the difference for the Cause, we will."

The treasurer will make the following exchanges. Although the rates are low you can be fairly sure that the hard coins in your hand won't bring questions with them.

	To sell
£200 guineas in notes...	**£150**
£100 guineas in notes...	**£60**
£50 guineas in notes...	**£22**
£20 guineas in notes...	**£10**
£10 guineas in notes...	**£4**

Return to the hideout...   985

911

If you are the **Friend of Barsali**, turn to **476** immediately. The gypsies are wary of outsiders in general, but they are willing to show you what they have to sell, including a wide range of mechanical tools and engineering components. After all, they make their livings working wherever they can.

Clothing	To buy	To sell
cloak	**£1**	**15s**
wide-brimmed hat	**£1 10s**	**18s**
silk scarf	**£2**	**£1**

Tools	To buy	To sell
rope ladder	**9s**	**7s**
lantern	**6s**	**4s**
fishing line	**1s**	**-**
snare	**2s**	**1s**
tarpaulin	**4s**	**4s**
brass flange joint	**8s**	**5s**
copper pipe	**6s**	**4s**
roll of oiled silk	**£5 7s**	**-**

Jewellery	To buy	To sell
locket	**-**	**6s**
pocket watch	**-**	**£2**
silver ring	**-**	**10s**

Visit the wise woman...	578
Leave the encampment...	113

912

Make a RUTHLESSNESS roll of difficulty 13 to convince the passengers and crew that you mean business, adding 1 for every **Wanted** status you have and 2 if you have a **double headlamp**.

Successful RUTHLESSNESS roll!   **946**
Failed RUTHLESSNESS roll!   **933**

913

The water splashes up in a curtain either side as you tear over the weir. Carefully judging your speed and balancing even more prudently as you skip over carpets of river weed, you make it to the other side with only water in your boots and sweat on your brow. Looking back, you see one of the velosteamers try to follow, but she misjudges her line and the current throws her into the river. The remaining constables shake their fists at you from the opposite bank. You have escaped!

Ride away...   **12**

915

A grain barge pulls away from its mooring alongside the chain-posts and the mate points with his pipe-stem. "That's the best place for us, skipper. I can put her right alongside there." A few minutes later your boat is moored snugly along the decking and your velosteam is ashore once more. Mark **Hurley Lock (Upstream)** in your Mooring section of your adventure sheet.

Go ashore...   **569**

916

Something is floating in the water just beneath the surface. A body? To hoist it aboard you will need either a **grappling iron** or a **cargo crane** fitted to your boat.

Haul the body in...
    (**grappling iron** or **cargo crane**)   **875**
Sail on by...   **637**

917

You moor up and wait for night to fall, when your contact is due to make herself known. An unlit steam lorry draws up and you wander over nonchalantly and slip **passdisc 67** into the driver's hand. She looks down and smiles grimly. "Right then. Help us unload these crates."

If you do not have room for a unit of "Mineral Samples" then you must jettison some of your cargo now. The guns will only take a single unit of cargo space beneath anything else you are transporting.

Several men you didn't realise were in the back of the steam lorry start carrying long wooden crates across to your boat and cover the deadly cargo with tarpaulins. Before long, the exchange is done and the unnamed Comrade whistles her men back into the lorry. She leans out and shouts as they drive off. "Speed the Revolution!"

Turn to ...   **846**

918

You draw your gun and track the speeding vehicle as it approaches. To hit the driver and stop the carriage you will need to make an ACCURACY roll of 12.

Successful ACCURACY roll!   **948**
Failed ACCURACY roll!   **873**

919

"Why," you ask Father Bourdain, "When I give to those who ask of me, do some go and drink themselves into a stupor or gamble with their chance to get out of their predicament?"

"Don't they have the right to do that? You seem the sort to value choice, my child. Now if they, in their particular situation, choose to value a beaker of gin over a chance of gainful employment, can you change their mind for them? You'd be a hypocrite to insist they lived by *your* morals."

"Isn't that what you do?"

"I try to encourage them to share my morals - or my Lord's morals. But you'll have to learn that giving things away is a risk. When you really give, you don't have any control over your gift. If you give something but still want to remain making the decisions, why, you haven't given at all."

Leave the church...   **703**
Continue talking...   **717**

920

The unique feature of the Drowned Badger that makes it so popular with the river men is its waterside river-hatch: you can steam right up alongside the flint wall of the pub and order a jug directly from the bar if you

so wish.

"I hear this place is famous for its Old Eel," you say to the thin-faced man standing behind the hatch.

He wrinkles his nose. "Landsmen drink it. You want to try the Water Rat."

Order a pint of Water Rat...	(1s)	852
Ask about the **Bargees Badge**...		872
Steam back to the Wharf...		846

921

The woman's leg is not beyond your ability to splint, even though she is wedged into the wreckage. With several broken pieces of rail and some scraps of carriage curtain you manage to steady her wounded limb and you are able to lift her from the now-burning carriage.

Turn to...   861

922

The constables' velosteams are fast, and what is more, each has a sharp-shooter mounted behind the driver. You will have to be both fast and lucky to escape without injury. Roll a dice and add your MOTORING score to find the result:

Score 6 or less	Capture!	979
Score 7-8	Under fire!	993
Score 11 or more	Escape!	965

923

The approaching monks charge forward, intent on defending their brother and teaching you a little Christian humility. You push off and turn the barge around.

Sail back the way you came...   745

924

"The cause needs money. Money is the crystallisation of power - it allows us to prepare the practical necessities for the coming revolution, as well as disseminating the teachings of Jensen and Ambrose. What can you contribute?"

Offer them paper money...	910
Offer to rob a bank...	882
Offer them bullion...	870
Return to the hideout...	985

925

You pull out of the way of the speeding steam carriage. The passengers wave their fists and jeer at you as they tear past: nobody will find behaviour like this initimidating. Reduce your RUTHLESSNESS score by 1.

Ride away...   530

926

Bird Court is a collection of low, unlicensed jewel workshops hidden in the slums of Maidenhead like a bright brooch hidden in a bundle of old rags. The makers, polishers and salespeople are deeply suspicious of outsiders. To deal with them you must either be **Wanted by the Constables**, the **People's Champion** or have a GALLANTRY score lower than 4. If you can't gain their trust you must leave immediately: turn to 594.

Jewellery	To buy	To sell
locket	6s	4s
pocket watch	£3	£1 15s
silver ring	10s	7s
silver bracelet	£1	10s
silver necklace	£2	£1 5s
gold ring	£3	£1 1s
gold bracelet	£3 5s	£2 2s
gold necklace	-	£5
ruby ring	-	£12 6s
Ducal Star	-	£15 4s
diamond brooch	-	£20
emerald jewellery	-	£35

Other items	To buy	To sell
ivory fan	£2	£1 8s
clockwork bird	-	£2
punchcards (Aramanth A)	£10	£7 4s
punchcards (Habbukuk K)	£15	£11 5s
punchcards (Selladore V)	-	£18 2s
punchcards (Livingstone M)	-	£18 4s
Guildsman's medallion	-	6s
ten guineas in banknotes	-	£6
twenty guineas in banknotes	-	£14
thirty guineas in banknotes	-	£22

Return to Maidenhead...   594

927

A heavy-set monk steps aboard as you toss your mooring line over the bollard. "Good day," he begins. "We are permitted to collect a levy on all refrigerated goods passing through the lock. For your cargo a payment of **10s** is due."

Pay the levy...	**(10s)**	**886**
Toss the monk in the water...		**898**
Turn the boat around...		**745**

928

A strange figure steps down from the carriage: a gentleman in a long frock coat and a wide hat, waited upon by a tall black man in a fine waistcoat.

"Where on earth are you from?" you ask.

"My name is Samuel Montauk the third," he replies in a strong American accent. "I'm a traveller in your fair land. I believe I've heard tell of you - you're the Steam Highwayman, am I correct?"

Realisation begins to dawn. "You are from the Confederacy?" He nods. "Then this man is your slave?"

"My body servant, yes. I own him and his whole family."

Cut the man down...	**906**
Demand he free his slave...	**940**
Rob him and let him go...	**868**

929

You hand over the **punchcards** (remove them from your possessions). "Well I never!" breathes Standler. "That changes things. Let me give you something for these - I know their value." She hands you **fifteen guineas in notes**.

You hurry over to the brewery computation room. Standler orders the clerks to halt everything running on the Bardsley - all the order reconciliations, all the monitoring systems - to give the full computational power over to her test. "I had a program ready to load, hoping I'd find some way to run it," she says, opening the little packet of off-white cards and slotting them into the feeder. "Now, let's see what it says."

The program runs for most of the night. While it does, you help Standler prepare everything she will need for a small-batch brew. Hops, sugar, malt, clean well water - all are prepared to make a scientific mash. Some time after midnight, the machine rings its bell and chatters out the final recipe. "This is it," crows Standler. "Wethered won't sink at this rate. Let's brew us a beer!"

The beer itself won't be ready for trial tasting for some time, but something tells you that it is sure to be a success. You leave Standler and her brewers and mount your velosteam once more.

You are now the **Friend of Louise Standler**. Erase the codeword *Advertise* if you had it.

Return to the High Street...	**4**

930

Mr Freebody and his employees offer several modifications, either to your craft or to its engine.

	To buy
Fit a **Perkins engine**...	
(Allows you to carry refrigerated cargoes like Ice and Frozen meat)	**£25**
Build an **enlargened cabin**...	**£20**
Mount a **cargo crane**...	**£20**

If you choose to go ahead with Mr Freebody's modifications, add any improvements that you pay for to your boat's manifest before moving on.

Return to the yard...	**611**

931

You make one final thrust and the man crumples to the ground without a word or cry. His body servant dashes forward to help him.

"You are free now," you tell him.

"Strike you down, what do you know of my life? This here's the best master I've ever had. Treated me right, fed my folks, bought my wife and brought me here to England. What right have you got to go freeing folks?"

The man's righteous anger burns in his eyes. "Don't worry, master. George is here. I'll care for you."

You may take the man's **sabre (PAR 6)** and purse, which contains **£8** and a **fine cigar**.

Ride away...	**530**

932

"I do not think you are at all sympathetic to our cause. Or if you are, then you prove yourself far too weak and indecisive to join us. Do not return here, or we will be less patient next time."

Turn to...	**199**

933

You and your mate leap aboard the launch, armed and dangerous. The mate knocks a sailor into the river, leaving you to deal with the helmsman, who picks up a heavy wrench. If he can disable you he will toss you in the river to drown.

Helmsman	Weapon: **heavy wrench (PAR 3)**
Parry:	10
Nimbleness:	7
Toughness:	1

Victory!	946
Failure!	102

934

The members of the Compact who are unfortunate enough to have been hurt or wounded in the cause of duty have recourse to Comrade Doctor Marbelline, a sharp-faced woman with an even sharper manner. Her equipment is sharp and clean, but she wastes no time on making her patients comfortable. For each **wound** she treats, you should add a **scar** to your Adventure Sheet. For each **wound** converted, roll two dice and a score of 11 or 12 will result in an **intimidating scar (RUTH+1).**

Treatment per **wound**...	15s
Treatment for a **fever**...	6s
Treatment for **burns**...	12s

Return to the hideout...	985

935

You tell the gathered drinkers the tale of your own impressive catch. Anglers to a man, they listen appreciatively as you embellish the story with dives and recaptures. When you produce the pike, several whistle appreciatively. "'Tweren't no tale, then, but truth," says one. The landlord offers you **£2** for the **large pike**, which he will mount behind the bar.

"Bit of a way, but over below the Flowerpot at Aston you'll find some real monsters. Lovely fish up there," says one bargee. He is sailing up from London to buy furniture. "Makes a good profit - prices are high there. I tends to bring frozen meat back upriver. They sends it from Argentina, I hear, and the New Zealand."

Return to the Bounty...	409

936

Maidenhead marketplace is lined with steam engines and their trailers piled with goods. A cattle and sheep fair occupies the lower part of the open ground, with sellers dealing in clothes, food, tools and other items each taking their own place.

Food and Drink	To buy	To sell
mixed bag	1s	-
tin of fruit	3s	2s
wheel of cheese	£1 2s	14s
bottle of Beehive Stout	2s	1s
picnic hamper	£3 3s	£2

Clothing	To buy	To sell
cloak	£1	15s
engineer's gloves (ENG +1)	£4 10s	£2 5s
engineer's gauntlets (ENG+2)	£6	£4
eyepatch (RUTH+1)	15s	5s
wide-brimmed hat	£1 10s	18s
silk scarf	-	£1
bow tie (GAL+1)	-	15s
top hat	-	£2
silk waistcoat (GAL+1)	£4 2s	£3

Tools	To buy	To sell
lantern	6s	4s
fishing line	1s	-
snare	2s	1s
tarpaulin	4s	4s
brass flange joint	8s	5s
copper pipe	6s	4s
high pressure valve	18s	9s

Weapons	To buy	To sell
sabre (PAR 6)	£3	£1 10s
blunderpistol (ACC 6)	£4	£1 10s

Medical items	To buy	To sell
bandages	3s	-
false teeth	£1 2s	-

Other items	To buy	To sell
revolutionary poster	-	3s
pneumatic manual (ENG+3)	-	£6 10s

Leave the market...	594

937

"I don't know who you think you are, speaking to me in such a tone. But I guarantee you that I will never, ever bow to your wicked wishes. A lady will never be intimidated by one such as you."

The lady is quite unafraid of you. So the best thing seems to leave her on an islet in the middle of the river and to steam off. She will order some 'boat-person' to rescue her and find her way back to Boulter's Lock for sure.

Turn to...   **488**

938

You begin to offload the beer barrels you bought from the bargee upstream when your mate wrinkles his nose. "Can you smell that, Captain?" he asks. You broach a cask and a rewarded with a stinking reek. The beer has spoiled and you have been tricked. You must pour the unsaleable beer away and erase it from your manifest. Lose the codeword *Actinium*.

Return to the wharf...   **333**

939

You try to spin a story of how you are a wealthy noble from the West Country, on tour through the home counties and heading towards London to visit your uncle, the Duke of Devonshire.

However, although you manage to convince the wary butler, once he allows you into the house you are unable to sustain the charade. Your hosts, Lord and Lady Dean, become more and more suspicious and when the Lord of the Manor leaves the hall to 'attend to an urgent matter', you glimspe him heading to the house telegraph and decide it is better to make your exit while you can.

As you turn and flee, Lady Dean takes a hunting gun from beside the door and fires it in your direction - surely more to warn you than to maim? Roll a dice to see whether she has managed to hit you.

Score 1   Gain a **Damage Point**
Score 2-4   Miss!
Score 6   Gain a **Wound**

If your velosteam is **Beyond Repair**...   **250**
If you have **five Wounds**....   **74**
Otherwise...   **786**

940

"You are in England now," you say. "Slavery has been abolished here, long ago. And in all civilised lands."

The man coolly draws his sword. "And who are you to enforce the law of the land? George, why don't you tell this road-thief the way of things."

The manservant steps forward. "Don't you touch my master. You don't know what he's done for me and my folks. I'll die first, yes I will."

"You want to be a slave?"

"We're all a slave to something," replies the man-servant. "I'm only glad I belong to a good man. Who do you belong to?"

You can't fight them both, so you have no choice but to back off.

Ride away...   **530**

941

The riverbank is dotted with birds' nests here: you may collect several **birds' eggs** if you choose.

Return to the road...   **445**

942

Your knowledge of the local woods allows you to take turns and routes that the Constables would barely consider. You have planned for a chase such as this. Nonetheless, it will not be easy to get away: make a MOTORING roll of difficulty 9 to escape.

Successful MOTORING roll!   **876**
Failed MOTORING roll!   **979**

943

You wander through the cobbled and narrow streets of the town, past the tall, red-brick walls of the gaol, be-tween the computing sheds and through courts and ginnels. Roll a dice to see what you encounter:

Score 1-2   Tax collectors...   **45**
Score 3-4   Find a **pork pie**...   **594**
Score 5-6   A ruthless assault...   **505**

944

"I am surprised to find you have returned," says the Abbot. "You are becoming quite notorious around here." Without warning, you are grabbed by the monks and a sack is thrust over your head.

Turn to...   **234**

945

You steam proudly down the drive, announcing your arrival with a hoot on your horn and parking directly in front of the grand entry. A butler emerges, but you also have the strong sense that you are being watched from an upper-floor window. Now you must make every effort to charm your way in: make a GALLANTRY roll of difficulty 10.

Successful GALLANTRY roll!	**434**
Failed GALLANTRY roll!	**939**

946

The passengers dare not resist: they pull out their wallets and purses, place their jewellery into your outstretched hand and cower beneath their deckchairs. You collect **£9 3s**, two **silver bracelets** and a **gold ring**. You may also take a **dinner jacket** or **ballgown** from the fancily-attired nobility.

You will be recognised again after this, so unless you have hidden yourself with a **cloak** or a **mask**, you are now **Wanted by the Constables**.

Make your escape...	**863**

947

"'Ere, aren't you that highwayman?" asks a green-jacketed Telegraph officer as you make for the door. "There's a price on your head." You must fight him to escape!

Telegraph Officer	Weapon: **sabre (PAR 6)**
Parry:	10
Nimbleness:	4
Toughness:	4

Victory!	**563**
Defeat!	**763**

948

Your shot finds its target. The driver jerks backwards, then falls from his seat, dead. The carriage careers on and comes off the road.

The RUTHLESSNESS of your action will not go unnoticed: you must lose a **Solidarity Point** for killing the driver. However, you can roll a dice and add 3: if the total is higher than your RUTHLESSNESS score you may increase it by 1.

Turn to...	**999**

949

The gentle progress along the river takes up little of your attention: a fat worm attached to your **fishing line** brings a toothy monster out from his hiding place in the weeds and you gain a **large pike**.

Moor at Maidenhead Wharf...	**333**
Steam on...	**355**

950

It seems that the Haulage Guild's plan of pressurising the Wethered Brewery is having its desired effect. If you are the one to return to Director Short with the information, then you will be sure of a reward. Gain the codeword *Aorta*.

Return to the High Street...	**4**

951

You kick down on the friction igniter, sending a pulse of coalgas to the burner. Your steam-pressure rises almost instantly and you accelerate out from your hiding place. The driver spots you and also accelerates, but the slope is against him. To come alongside you will need to match speed and manoevre over the rutted road. Make a MOTORING roll of difficulty 8, adding 1 if you have **off-road tyres** and 1 more if you have a **gas pressuriser**.

Successful roll!	**997**
Failed roll!	**530**

952

The Constables have caught up with you at last. You recognise the velosteam squad of Captain Lucas, who has been charged with your capture. Notoriety has its drawbacks! To escape the posse you must turn about and flee as fast as steam will allow: do you have an escape route prepared?

Down to Cookham and across the weir...	(*Amphibious*)	**853**
Into Windsor Wood and through the brush...	(*Ashen*)	**942**
Otherwise...		**922**

953

Approaching Hurley lock, your mate points out a light in the dusk. "Do you see that, skipper? Someone on the Harleyford Bridge. There's a wee crossing there from the big house on the North bank, over to one of the islands. The squire owns all of them, but he's got a summerhouse on one. You know, for assignations and rendezvouses and things. But it seems to me rather selfish that he keeps it to himself."

You can just make out the slender bridge. It might just do as a river crossing unguarded by the Constables - if you can get through the Harleyford estate somehow. Gain the codeword *Alluring*.

Turn to...   **869**

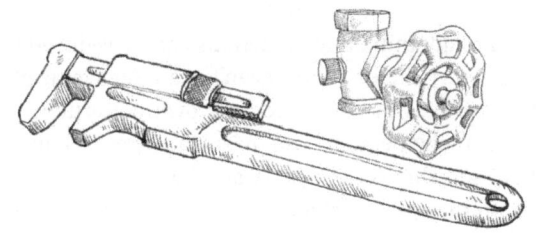

954

You take over from the boy who looks heartily relieved to be able to scamper outside into the sun with his playmates. You can't tell what the woman understands of the stories of royal scandal, the updates from the Galician front, the reports of unrest in Cornwall and airship piracy over the Schwarzwald, but when you read about the Van Diemen's Land Colony she begins to weep.

"My Andrew was transported, you know? For stealing a silver spoon. Stealing a silver spoon from the house of Mistress Marchpane in London. Sent over the sea and I ain't never seen him." She continues down a habitual rehearsal of her sorrows and her loneliness. After an hour or so of keeping her company, you have little left to offer her.

Leave the cottage...   **50**

955
□

If the box is empty, put a tick in it. If it is already ticked, turn to **919** immediately.

"Where do you get all this money?" asks Father Bourdain.

"Does it matter? If it will help the poor?"

"Where are the 'poor'. When I look out there I see only individuals - people with names. And people with names don't simply need money. They need dignity and opportunity and respect."

"Don't be so idealistic. Money will help achieve that."

Father Bourdain chews his lip. "Don't give me any money, my child. If you genuinely want to help people, you need to know them as people. There are people in need in every town and village, but they don't just want a handout. They need friendship and respect. And yet Jesus taught us to give to those who ask from us."

Is he simply too self-righteous?

Leave the church...   **703**
Continue talking...   **717**

956

The barkeep pulls you a pint of dark, nutty stout named for the post-ships that fly the airways overhead: The Traveller. It is fairly strong and has the bold sort of flavour that would suit a nice traditional pie. While you look at the bar menu you fall into conversation with a telegrapher in his green tunic, who tells you that the manager of the Odds Hill Telegraph station is in trouble. "There's something wrong with the algorithm there," he says. "All sorts of errors getting into the transmissions. If he don't fix it soon, he'll be out!"

Leave the Red Lion...   **337**

957

The driver hauls on the brakes and bring the steam carriage to a stop. "Stone the crows, it be the Steam Highwayman!" he says. Roll a dice to discover who was in the carriage:

Score 1	A financier and his lady...	991
Score 2	An adventuress...	977
Score 3	A Confederate traveller...	928
Score 4	A newspaper editor...	885
Score 5	A priest...	867
Score 6	A military officer...	854

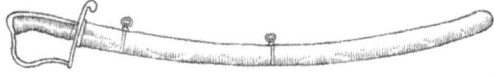

958

The lady does indeed write the letter and you send the mate ashore with it. To make good your threat, that means almost a week spent on board your boat, moored in the narrow channels by the lock.

However, the mate returns with a parcel he has been unable to resist opening. Through the brown paper you see banknotes - **two hundred guineas in**

banknotes. The lady is set ashore and you carry on your way. However, as a result of banditry like this you will certainly be **Wanted by the Constables** if you are not already.

Turn to...   **488**

959

The other passengers are still very wary of you, but when they see that you are genuinely ready to help, they are more sympathetic. Nonetheless you will need to make a GALLANTRY roll of difficulty 9 to get them to help you.

Successful GALLANTRY roll!   **861**
Failed GALLANTRY roll!   **981**

960

"Ah, you've already met our friend the Miller," says the barman. "No doubt he sent you here." He takes **passdisc 101** and tosses it into a box behind the bar. "At least we can be sure that you're no spy." He waves over a man from the corner of the room - a man with an eyepatch.

"Come on, then," says the one-eyed man. "Come and see what we do - the purposes we have for violence."

He leads you through the streets and courts, the alleyways and crooked dens of Wooburn Green, behind the walls of factories to a low doorway. He blindfolds you, then leads you further, further, until the temperature changes as you realise that you must be underground. A dark chuckle escapes your guide. "In the country of the blind, the one-eyed man is king, they say."

Turn to...   **40**

961

You steer the boat into the rushes and leap ashore as it grounds. The overseer turns around, giving the family a chance to retreat from his cruelty, and readies himself to fight you.

Overseer   Weapon: **whip (PAR 4)**
Parry: 9
Nimbleness: 5
Toughness: 3

Victory!   **897**
Defeat!   **187**

962

The Rivermen's Union overlooks the wharf, of course. To become a member takes a payment of **£5**, after which you may wear the **bargee's badge** with pride. This badge will allow you to pass through the local locks with impunity - at least, all the locks that are not privately owned.

Return to the wharf...   **333**

963

"Do you really think that all actions can be reduced to that puny principle? You haven't read Jensen at all. He teaches that the desire for our own betterment is the steam engine that empowers all great change. Without selfishness, we are passive beings, like clouds blown on the wind. I shall give you one more chance. The people despise the Emperor James for his weaknesses, his bending to the whim of the rich. What do you think?"

"This land needs no kings. The people
    are right to hate him."   **982**
"Perhaps if he observes the cry of his people,
    his heart will change."   **932**

964

Beyond the weir the river winds on beneath the shadow of quick-moving clouds and swooping kites. A long airship train, straying from the main corridor, waves desperate signals to an unseen escort craft high up above. On the river, you are passed by a tug shoving a lighter of freshly-sawn timber and a barge carrying machinery bound for the capitol. "Johnson's Hand Tools," shouts the bargee in reply to your hail. "Relocating to Wapping, to be nearer the international trade."

Continue upstream...   **877**

965

You dodge the hail of bullets and steer your velosteam through the woods, along precipices, over narrow deer -tracks, between the trunks of beech coppices and out onto sideroads. It takes many a twist and turn before you shake off your pursuers. Roll a dice to discover where you end up!

Score 1-2   Little Marlow...   **602**
Score 3-4   Flackwell Heath...   **50**
Score 5-6   Glory Lane...   **530**

966

Comrade 109 is in charge of the supplies at the Wooburn Green depot. He is a thin, shabby man with a miserly attitude: he isn't keen to let any of the Compact's hard-won supplies leave his care - even on official business. If you have the **passdisc 33**, turn to **658**.

Clothing	To buy	To sell
cloak	£1	-
dungarees (GAL-2)	£1 10s	-
engineer's gloves (ENG +1)	£3	£2 5s
engineer's gauntlets (ENG+2)	£5	£4
eyepatch (RUTH+1)	15s	-

Tools	To buy	To sell
heavy wrench	18s	12s
explosives	£1 4s	-

Weapons	To buy	To sell
club (PAR 4)	3s	1s
razor (PAR 2 NIM+2)	£1 15s	18s
sabre (PAR 6)	£3	£1 10s

Medical items	To buy	To sell
bandages	3s	-
bottle of chloroform	£2	15s
white pills (ING+2) ☐ ☐ ☐	£2 5s	-

Other items	To buy	To sell
revolutionary poster	1s	-
Coal Board accountbook	-	£4
punchcards (Aramanth A)	£10	-
punchcards (Habbukuk K)	£15	-
Abbey Ribbon	-	6s
Bargee's Badge	-	3s
Guildsman's medallion	-	6s

Return to the hideout... **985**

967

The only sounds in the night are the hoot of distant owls and the muffled roar of Hurley weir. You climb silently up the side of the house and tread along the narrow ledge, gripping any imperfection in the brickwork and heading slowly towards Lady Dean's suite. The shutters are closed so you raise the sash of her smaller, dressing-room window and gently raise the latch.

Lady Dean's boudoir is sumptuously decorated and filled with expensive knick-knacks. However, you are not here to take but to give, and any impression of a break-in will doom the success of the planted letters. You carefully open the **sealed packet** and place the letters within Lady Dean's papers, mingling them so that there is no obvious distinction. Then once again you make your way through the window and out of the house.

Comrade Feaver insisted that you return to the Compact Headquarters immediately after you had planted the documents, so you saddle up and steam through the night, back towards the den in Wooburn Green.

You are met in the street by a contact, who blindfolds you and brings you back inside, where you are made to await Comrade Feaver's reappearance. After several hours, she enters the little room rubbing her hands.

"Well, the Constables have been tipped off and I fully expect to read of Lord and Lady Dean's arrest in the afternoon paper," she says gleefully. "How delightful when our enemies can expend their energies so usefully. As for you, you have done well." She passes you a bag of gold, containing **£12**.

Turn to... **996**

968

A Constabulary steam-launch approaches you, armed men behind their turrets. They bump carelessly into the side of your boat and two step aboard. If you are **Wanted by the Constables** or **the River Union**, turn to **865** immediately. Otherwise, turn to **980**.

969

A bargee travelling in the opposite direction hails you. He has a proposition. "I've a cargo of beer here that I need to off-load. I was heading to sell it at Cookham, but I've had family news and want to turn back straight away. I'll give it to you at a special price - **£30** for the whole cargo or **£12** for a single load."

The bargee has three loads to offer. If you have space, or choose to jettison your cargo to make space, you may buy the beer and add it to your manifest. If you choose to buy some or all of the cargo, gain the codeword *Actinium*.

Continue downstream... **637**

970

Your shot actually hits the driver square in the shoulder, knocking him off his driving position and into the road with a dreadful scream. The carriage careers onwards, off the road, through the undergrowth and over a hidden precipice, crashing to the ground with an almighty pressurised explosion. You lose a **Solidarity Point** for killing the innocent driver and have also lost any opportunity to rob the occupants. You had better leave quickly.

Ride away...   **535**

971

The passengers are dazed but still conscious. Now is your opportunity to rob them. Roll a dice to see who was on board:

Score 1	A financier and his lady...	**991**
Score 2	An adventuress...	**977**
Score 3	A Confederate traveller...	**928**
Score 4	A newspaper editor...	**885**
Score 5	A priest...	**867**
Score 6	A military officer...	**854**

972

Old Freebody will give the following for your boat, depending on its size. He is not bothered by any of the customisations you have fitted and bats your hand away as you try to point out the features. "We'll strip most of that out anyway, for the next customer. Are you sure you want to sell?"

	To sell
Small skiff...	**£12**
Medium launch...	**£18**
Large barge...	**£30**

Should you choose to sell your boat, erase it and any cargo from your Adventure Sheet.

Buy a replacement boat...	**883**
Leave by road...	**569**

973

"Your answer is straight from Jensen's *Statement*," replies Comrade Feaver, sitting back and steepling her fingers. "Either you know what we want to hear, or you have truly internalised it. So another question: when will the revolution succeed?"

"When the producers of wealth grasp their
    responsibility."   **64**
"When the rich believe they cannot be toppled." **880**

974

The lady bites and scratches like a tiger. Gain a **Wound**. If you now have **five Wounds**, turn to **998**. If not, you can either knock her down viciously or let her escape.

Knock her down...	**983**
Release her...	**992**

975

You go over to the door of the carriage, now facing the sky, and wrench it open. The passengers are unsure whether to accept your help as they clamber out. One woman with what looks like a broken leg remains inside, screaming with pain at every attempt to move her.

Send the woman to sleep...
     (bottle of chloroform)   **909**
Check the woman's leg...
     (**Medical Training 1** or higher)   **921**
Get the other passengers to help...   **959**

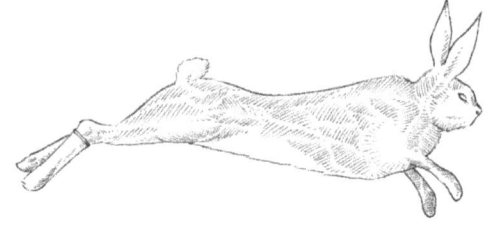

976

You tell Father Bourdain about your dreams. He shakes his head - in pity, or disapproval? He is a hard man to read.

    "It sounds like guilt to me," he says. "Even if you were forgiven for these things, you need to grasp that and believe it to be delivered. So if I pray for you, it will be for you to actually have a change of heart and believe you can be forgiven. And that is an inhuman idea. It is all too human to be subject to guilt and nightmares."

He seems too cool and collected. "What do you know of guilt?" you ask.

"I won't burden you with my confession," he replies. "You are carrying enough." Erase the codeword *Apprehend*.

Leave the church...	703
Continue talking...	717

977

A striking looking woman steps down from the carriage. She has the air of a predator and is utterly unimpressed by your attempt at robbery. "Oh how charming," she says. "A roadside assault. Draw, then, and prove yourself!"

Adventuress		Weapon: **rapier (PAR 7)**
Parry:	13	
Nimbleness:	6	
Toughness:	2	

Victory!	871
Defeat!	74

978

The bar at the World's End serves fashionable Confederate-style beers and cocktails and is full of working girls, engine clerks, speculators and adventurers. An automatic pianiola plays incessantly in the corner, jangling its ill-tuned strings beneath the hubbub and raucous laughter.

Try a Southern Sour...	(4s)	400
Order a Condor Ale...	(4s)	894
Leave the bar...		395

979

A bullet smacks into your shoulder, throwing you off balance and sending you crashing into the ditch. Gain **two wounds** and **two damage points**.

If your velosteam is **beyond repair**...	250
If you have **five Wounds**...	74
Otherwise...	255

980

The officer aboard inspects everything closely, lifting the covers of the cargo hold, poking his cane into your coal store, inspecting your ticket drawer. "Aha," he says. "Your water license is expired. I am authorised to collect a fine of **£1** on the spot."

He is simply resorting to extortion - but with a launch at his back, he is sure to find something to make you pay for.

Pay the fine...	(£1)	995
Resist him...		887

981

The passengers want nothing to do with you. "Get away!" says one. "This was all your doing, you monster! If you daren't rob us now, we certainly want none of your help."

You have little choice other than to leave them here until another carriage passes. Gain the codeword *Arthropod* and if you are not already, you are now **Wanted by the Constables**.

Ride away...	530

982

Comrade Feaver fails to hide her disappointment. "There is no way we can admit you into the Compact as you are. But if you prove your loyalty through serving our cause, you may in time be able to participate in our plans. We need a delivery of some technical equipment making to one of our operatives - but as he is continually on the move, you will suit us as a courier." She waves to another comrade, who brings you a **heavy parcel**. "Find Comrade Robin in one of the Freight Yards in this region and give him this - unopened. He will give you a passdisc in return."

Leave the headquarters...	199

983

You throw the lady to the deck, but she hits her head on the corner of the cabin and you hear a definite crack. Her neck is broken. The mate is shocked. "Oh dear," he says. "What will we do with her?"

You have only one option. You strip the body of valuables (you can take her **parasol**, **wide-brimmed hat** and **silver necklace**) and tie her to some heavy scrap machinery. Then, with a splash, she goes down to the bottom of the river. Gain the codeword *Apogee*.

Turn to...	488

984

You check that the grapple is firmly fixed and swing out into the air, landing atop the steam carriage with a thump. The driver begins to swerve to knock you off: to hang on you must make a NIMBLENESS roll of difficulty 10.

Successful NIMBLENESS roll...	902
Failed NIMBLENESS roll...	862

985

You are brought to the hideout of the Compact for Worker's Equality, deep inside the brick vaults of the embankments. Anarchists and revolutionaries bustle about seriously. Speeches are practiced, posters printed, crates of weapons packed and readied. If you have the codeword *Ammonium*, turn to **542**.

Speak to the Compact treasurer...	924
Speak to the quartermaster...	966
Find medical treatment...	934
Leave the hideout...	199

986

Roll a dice to see who you have stopped:

Score 1	A best-selling novelist...	680
Score 2	A town councillor...	293
Score 3	An insurance broker...	722
Score 4	A Coal Board surveyor...	486
Score 5	A wealthy landowner...	788
Score 6	A Ruritanian Royal...	765

987

The driver becomes more and more reckless in his attempt to escape! He throws the heavy steam carriage from side to side of the uneven road. Roll a dice to see the result!

Score 1-3	A crash!	999
Score 4-6	The terrified driver surrenders...	957

988

The long weir stretches upstream from the islands by the lock, and against the chain-posts lie almost a dozen freight barges, their number ones arguing fiercely about the prices of the cargoes they exchange. This is not an officially sanctioned place to buy and sell, but there seem to be goods of an excellent quality available.

	To buy	To sell
Charcoal	£14	-
Furniture	-	-
Machinery	-	£26
Pottery	£27	£23
Cotton	-	£5
Woollen cloth	£12	£12
Coal	£10	£10
Beer	£17	£16
Wheat	-	£5
Malt	£6	£6
Frozen meat	-	£12
Ice	-	£6

Take the lock downstream...	
(**2s** or **Bargee's Badge**)	443
Return upstream...	360
Moor here...	915

989

If you are a **Member of the Compact for Workers' Equality**, turn to **985** immediately.

If you have **passdisc 21**, turn to...	626
If you have **passdisc 101**, turn to...	960
If you have the codeword *Ahasuerus* or	
Andronicus...	595
Otherwise...	559

990

As you awake, you are aware of a new and crippling stiffness in your limbs. Your dangerous lifestyle is at last catching up with you and you know it is time to retire from your life on the road. Your scarred body has been pushed to its limit and your spirit tires of the restless search for purpose. Turn to the Epilogue to see how you fare in retirement.

991

The occupants of the carriage are a thin, dissolute-looking fellow and a trollop plastered with make-up. The man attempts to distance himself from his travelling companion immediately. "What do you want? Money, I suppose? Or did Gustore send you? Tell me, do you work for Gustore? He'd like to ruin my reputation, I know."

The man's guilty conscience is your opportunity. "What can you give me to tell Gustore I never saw you?"

The man stutters. "Take my wallet... These ledgers will mean nothing to you. But my **pocket watch**, my **silk waistcoat (GAL+1)**, my **top hat**." Together with the **£5** in his wallet it is a fair haul.

"And the lady's jewellery." **895**
Leave them by the road... **530**

992
The lady gets ashore and runs off towards the lock. You cannot pursue her without hurting her now and she will certainly ensure that you are **Wanted by the Constables** if you are not already.

Turn to... **488**

993
Bullets whine past you as you steam for your life through the woods. You prove less than lucky this time: roll a dice to see how badly you are hit!

Score 1   Gain a **Wound** and a **Damage Point**...
Score 2-3   Gain a **Damage Point**...
Score 4-5   Gain a **Wound**...
Score 6   Gain **two Wounds**...

If your velosteam is **beyond repair**... 250
If you have **five wounds**... 74
Otherwise... 561

994
"That is true. We must teach the uneducated poor to value themselves and then teach them to fight for their rights. Respect is earnt, not given. Now what do you think: is it better for a true comrade to pursue making a living in their workplace and hope to radicalise their peers or to leave the workplace to produce propaganda material?"

"Each individual must come to an understanding of their need to act in their own time." **982**
"This comrade should commit themselves to producing the most gripping posters." **880**
"Submitting for a while allows a response of greater strength." **64**

995
The Constable pockets the gold sovereign and grins. "That's right, cully. Pay up quick and proper and you won't have no problem with us Constables. We're all nice fellers once you get to know us."
    The mate spits as the launch steams away.

Turn to... **425**

996
"Ruthlessness is a desirable quality for those who will serve the cause. Without it we would be distracted many times from our service to an ideal. So I have a test for you that will suit your character. Near Burchett's Green stands the house of Squire Lynch, a wicked and oppressive landlord. Kill him and bring me proof. His death will be an example to all the rich who terrorise their workforce. Then I will know that you are worthy of joining the Compact."
    Comrade Feaver waves her hand: you are blindfolded and led away. Gain the codeword *Abound*. If you have the codeword *Antipodes*, also gain the codeword *Ascorbic*.

Turn to... **199**

997
You steam ahead and quickly catch the passenger carriage, despite the driver's desperate attempts to block you. In fact, his efforts only manage to dislodge some of the baggage piled on top of the wagon roof, which comes loose and falls into the road.

Let the carriage escape and rifle the baggage... **893**
Pursue the steam carriage further... **987**

998
You are badly hurt and need to recover from your wounds. Ordinarily, your boat's cabin would be a good place to do this, but your mate sees this as his opportunity to make his way in the world. As you lie bleeding, he rolls you into the water with an unrepentant smile...

Turn to... **102**

999
With a final skidding turn, the steam carriage tilts over too far at last and crashes off the road, breaking through the low branches of the trees and coming to a heavy stop at the foot of an oak. Hissing steam bursts

out of broken piping, water pools beneath the mangled wheels and cries come from inside the passenger compartment. The driver has been thrown clear and lies in a pile of leaves.

Rescue the occupants... **975**
Rob the occupants... **991**

1000

If you have the codeword *Appropriate* or already possess a boat of any kind, turn to **941** immediately. Otherwise, read on.

Approaching the river you come to a wide bank of rushes between the dry land and the river. A heron cries and alights from something hidden by the reed-stems. It is an abandoned steam-skiff, partly sunken, but certainly not beyond repair. If you want to fix it up and try to get it steaming again, you will need an ENGINEERING skill of at least 9 and the following: **copper pipe**, **waterproof paint**, and a **high-pressure valve**.

Fix the skiff...
    (if you have all the requirements) **13**
Return to the road... **445**

1001

The dockers laugh. "You again? All talk, mate. If this revolution is coming, then it's deeds what are wanted, not words."

Return to the dock... **538**

1002
☐

If the box is empty, tick it. If it is already ticked, turn to **685** immediately.

Danesfield house is the base of operations for Colonel Snappet, the wicked commander of the Constables. Rumour tells of imprisonments and torture here in this dark place. To find out the truth, you need access to the house, but the place is guarded like a fortress: dogs, armed guards and tall fences.

However, you know that Snappet will need able engineers for his laboratory work, so you manage to convince a doorman to carry in a brief letter, begging the nobleman's consideration. You give a false Identity Number and write some lies about the various high-profile engineering workshops you have worked in and sure enough, you are given the opportunity to prove your abilities. Colonel Snappet himself appears

- a small man with a monumental moustache and bright, beady, black eyes. He shows you into a long, low room, filled with steam machinery. "This should be synchronised with the clock there in the corner," he drawls. "I want exactly three hundred and sixty strokes of the piston a minute. Can you do it?"

You will need to make an ENGINEERING roll of difficulty 13.

Successful ENGINEERING roll! **380**
Failed ENGINEERING roll! **772**

1003

The lane is narrow and fairly overgrown, yet there are signs that freight wagons have passed this way. It dips down the slope into a hollow and then begins to climb again towards the hilltop at the High Heavens.

Return to Handy Cross... **25**
Continue to the Lane End road... **247**

1004

Approaching the compound you are stopped by a green-coated guard. "No access to the public," she says, hefting her crossbow. "You can use the station at Odds Hill to send messages if you need."

Ride on to Cookham Dean... **563**
Head south... **394**

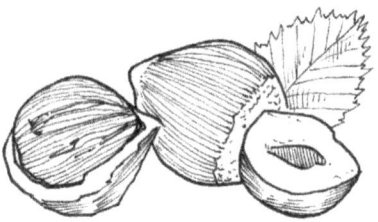

1005

Once the Constables transfer you into the custody of the prison guards you are released into the prison courtyard. You are not long alone, however, as a small crowd of inmates quickly appear. They are quite aware of who you are. A lady in an oversize dress weeps and kisses your hand.

"After all you've done for the common folk of the realm, they lock you up! If there was any justice, you'd be given a knighthood, I say."

An old man with the shreds of a dignified bearing butts in. "Now Mistress Clark, do hold your tears in.

Every new arrival needs a little orientation, however worthy." He bows low. "My name is Gregory Smake, Esquire, of Havering House. Currently serving for debt and fraud, but don't worry about that at all. Let me show you around."

The prison inmates make sure you have a warm nook in one of the common cells and point out which guards to avoid, which food sellers and money lenders you can trust. All in all, they make your imprisonment seem like it could be almost bearable.

Turn to... **638**

1006

A woman with a mongrel dog in tow comes whistling over the field towards you. She gives a jaunty nod of the head and stops to share a mouthful of food and a swig from her bottle of beer.

"I've been walking for a week or so, down from the north country. Spent several weeks working on Lord Bradingfield's estate near Newark. But they ran me out, you see, as a troublemaker. Ha! All I said was that his new bride was an imposter. I knew her in London, see. Jenny Bull, her name is. And there she is, pretending to be some American heiress. Don't know how she pulled that one." The woman laughs. "Good for her!" Gain the codeword *Apparently*.

Ride on... **139**

1007

Gregory Curtiss takes the banknotes, then hands them straight back to you. "You've earnt this, and much more," he says. "After all, if I had paid someone to murder my brother, it would have cost me more than this."

Davy smiles grimly. "I would have killed you first, Gregory boy. Now, let me tell you about an idea I've had. That velosteam of yours... Very exciting. My dad always wanted a Wall of Death here at the fair. If you ride for us, you could make a pretty penny. And it won't hurt our reputation either. Think it over."

Eventually you leave the celebrations and head off on the open road once more. It won't be a quick process by which the brothers learn to trust one another again, but with proof of their father's love for both of them and with the tangible evidence of his concern, at least they are no longer at each other's throats.

Ride away... **725**

1008

The entertainers are acrobats. Their eyes widen as you show them your treasures and tell them of your deeds. "Come, let us show you what we can do!" They teach you several vaults, cartwheels, tumbles and other tricks. Improve your NIMBLENESS score by 1 and gain the codeword *Advent*.

Leave them... **428**

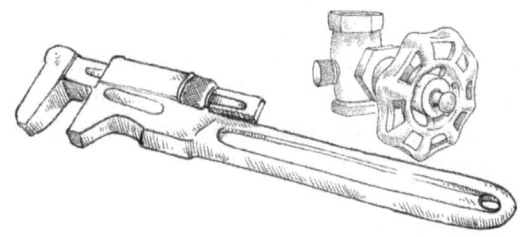

1009

"Oooh, where did you get that, dearie?" The old gyspy lady is fascinated by the clockwork bird you show her. "Not one of the old ones, no. Look there, under the beak. That stamp is a recent one. And does it..?" She twists it sharply. The wings and tail unfold and it reveals a pattern of perforations.

"What are they?" you ask.

"A coded message from the bird-maker," says the gypsy. "He has a lot of influence, if you know where to look." She holds the wings up to the fluttering oil lamp and peers at them intently.

"Who is that? Are they with Compact?"

She laughs scornfully. "That bunch of clowns? No! Look for the bird-maker on the Great North Road. Or follow these little birds." She hands the bird back to you, grinning. "I'll tell you this - the Henley Freight Yard won't be the safest place to visit for a while." Gain the codeword *Artisan*.

Return to the carriage... **578**

1010

You steer towards the bank and throw a loop of mooring line over a bollard, startling a dozing duck into an abrupt take-off. Mark **Medmenham** in the Boat Mooring space of your adventure sheet.

Turn to... **774**

1011

"You have a soft heart," says the old woman. "But hard hands. That is a powerful combination, but beware that your compassion does not make you vulnerable to tricksters. Watch out for charming women and smooth men and their opportunities. Guard your purse - the woman from the sky will take and take and continue to take. Yes, the woman from the sky..." The gypsy drifts off and puffs on her pipe. It is time to leave.

Turn to...   **113**

1012

The clouds break noisily, drenching you and the fields around in sheets of vertical rain. There is little cover other than a single, stag-headed oak tree with leaves around its lower parts.

Head for the oak tree...   **399**
Persist down the road...   **212**

1013

You spend several hours researching the best legal defences for a roadside robber such as yourself. Should you ever face arrest and prosecution, a little reading might well come in useful. Add **Legal Knowledge Level 1** to your Adventure Sheet if you did not already possess it.

Return to the library...   **736**

1014

If you are **Wanted by the Telegraph Guild**, turn to **947**. Otherwise turn to **563**.

1015

Steaming carefully over the ricketty footbridge onto Lock Island is only the first stage of your route, of course. The private bridge from the island into the grounds of Harleyford Manor will lead you to the northern side of the Thames at the only dry crossing west of Marlow. As soon as night falls, you unlock the gate and steam quietly across by the light of the moon. You have to skirt the estate and are soon on the Marlow Road.

Turn to...   **786**

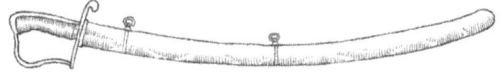

1016

You pass quietly between the trees and wait for night's cloak to swathe you. Then, when the estate is quiet, you make your way to the narrow bridge over to Hurley and cross the Thames, unobserved.

Turn to...   **569**

1017

Retiring from life as a highwayman may be the way to attain a secure and respectable life - if you value that. Many factors will decide your future happiness: the amount of money you have been able to squirrel away in bank accounts; the number of enemies you have made; the sincere affections and friendships of those who trust you; your physical health and the scars you bear; and finally the skills you have managed to tune in this wild way of life. Then there is your reputation: are you known throughout the land? Will tales be told and songs sung of your deeds? Are you loved by the people and feared by the powerful? Is it time to edge away from centre-stage?

Put an end to your career on the road...   **Epilogue**
Return to the Crooked Billet...   **180**

1018

At the edge of the wood two figures sit dejectedly by a spluttering fire. They tell you they were evicted from their cottage in Christmas Common by the Bishop of Barnsbury's land agent. "Said we aden't no right to live there if we wasn't working," says the woman bitterly.
Give them something towards a new start... (£1) **881**
Leave them be...   **50**

1019

Roll a dice. If you are **Wanted by the Constables**, add 1 and if you are **Wanted by the River Union**, add 2.

Score 1-2   **889**
Score 3-5   **896**
Score 6 or higher   **968**

1020

The poacher panics, terrified by your dreadful appearance. "Don't peach on me, your graciousness. I just wanted something for my starving children." She drops the **pheasant**, which you can take if you wish, and leaps through the hedge and across the field.

Ride on...   **575**

1021

You spend some time looking at the haulier's engine and end up rebuilding the crank that connects the flywheel to the pistons: "Whoever fitted this was larking about," you tell the haulier. "This should help you up the hill and save you a lot on your fuel costs into the bargain."

The haulier is deeply grateful. "Not many folks would stop on the road to help someone like me," she says. "Take this warm **cloak** to keep you dry on that machine of yourn."

Ride ahead of her up the hill...   **50**

Epilogue

So your days on the lawless road are over. Before calculating a final score to enter on the Roll of Honour, you can discover what follows your story in this book by using the table below. How did your adventure end?

	Dead	Alive
Money in purse...	0 points / £	1 point / £2
Money in bank account...	0 points / g	1 point / guinea
Scars	-	-3 points / scar
Wounds	-	-10 points / wound
Ruthlessness...		2 points / point
Engineering...		1 point / point
Motoring..		1 point / point
Ingenuity...		1 point / point
Nimbleness...		1 point / point
Gallantry...		2 points / point
Solidarity Points...		5 points each
Wanted status...		10 points each
Friendships...		10 points each
Great Deeds...		20 points each
Famed Lawbreaker....		50 points
People's Champion...		100 points
100 points or fewer...		**Quickly Forgotten**
101-150 points...		**Local Hero**
151-200 points...		**Night Terror**
201-250 points...		**Remembered Fondly**
251-350 points...		**Admired Inspiration**
351 points or more...		**True Legend**

Quickly Forgotten

Even on the roads you used to haunt, your trail is insignificant and your deeds uninspiring. Other roadside robbers quickly outshadow you with their daring and inventiveness. No-one thinks again of the masked stranger who threatened and scared them, only to disappear into the night.

Local Hero

It is only amongst the poor people of the region that you are remembered. For several years, your name and deeds are talked about in the pubs you used to frequent. Freighters, now free from the threat of attack, laugh at your memory. Nobody of any social standing or importance pays any attention to your passing and in a few short years you will pass away into obscurity.

Night Terror

Something of your deeds remains: mothers frighten their children with threats of being carried off by the vicious Steam Highwayman unless they eat their vegetables. Some local people and your few friends mourn you for a time, remembering your occasional kindnesses, but you have failed to make a lasting impression in the hearts and minds of the people.

Remembered Fondly

You are remembered as a loveable rogue - a free spirit and someone who, for a time, made life more bearable for the common folk. However, whether you have had a lasting effect on society is doubtful. The rich are once more free to travel the highways and tollroads with impunity.

Admired Inspiration

Your fame is justly deserved, for you have influenced and inspired many. Tales of your gallantry and self-sacrifice are told up and down the land. Wherever independent hauliers stop to heat up a brew, the legend of the mysterious Steam Highwayman is repeated. A local inn is renamed in your honour and several youngsters vow they will continue your war against injustice and go to live in the woods. Perhaps you have used your power wisely after all.

True Legend

The tales of your deeds will be told through the ages: future novelists will fictionalise your adventures, romanticising your deeds, simplifying your motivation and editing out your struggles. Eventually you will become part of the school curriculum. People will argue whether you truly existed and re-enactment societies and museums will be founded in your name. In your own day, nobles and wicked landowners still fear to travel without heavy escort, fearing that reports of your death are just trickery. It will not be long before their hegemony is destroyed for good.

ROLL OF HONOUR

Date:	Points:	Fate:	Memorable Adventures	Reader's Name
_____	_____	_____	_____	_____
_____	_____	_____	_____	_____
_____	_____	_____	_____	_____
_____	_____	_____	_____	_____
_____	_____	_____	_____	_____
_____	_____	_____	_____	_____
_____	_____	_____	_____	_____
_____	_____	_____	_____	_____
_____	_____	_____	_____	_____

Acknowledgements

L ord! My prayers are more than answered,
My hopes are always heard.
You promise life abundant
And then give it through your Word.

Thanks and appreciation to my wife, best friend and

Cheryl Anne Adamos Noutch

whose constant support and encouragement has enabled the entire project.

Also to:

Ben May; illustrator. What a good day it was that we met in Blackwell's! You've been enthusiastic, hard-working, professional and great to work with at every stage of the project. Long may the partnership continue.

Dave Lowery; teacher. Dave, you have been one of the most influential people in my life. I'm daily grateful to have had you as my teacher back in Lynncroft Upper Juniors. I've taught countless children to create their own CYOA adventures—just they way you taught me.

Jonathan Baker; backer 66 and erstwhile collaborator. Without your partnership, *The Emerald of Wolla-Wolla* would never have been written. Then where would we be?

Jon Ingold; backer 11, author and campaign advice. I've a lot to thank you for, Jon. *Sorcery* and *80 Days* were big inspirations, convincing me that my interest in interactive fiction was worthy of pursuing; *Inklewriter* helped me do that; your *Sorcery IV* launch event was a key networking moment for me and when you generously gave me that Kickstarter video critique at FFF2 I was encouraged and challenged to up my game and aim high.

Jonathan Green; backer 32, community-builder, advisor. Without your hard work in convening Fighting Fantasy Fest and Fighting Fantasy Fest 2, I would never have found the crucial support for Steam Highwayman. Thanks too for blazing the trail in Steampunk Gamebooks and your warm, respectful welcome onto the writer's panel at the Essextraodinaire III.

Ben Henderson; Steampunk community-builder. Ben, your open and sincere invitation to participate in the Surrey Steampunk Convivial catalysed my interaction with the Steampunk community and jolted the project into a whole new phase.

Dave Morris; author and publicity. *Fabled Lands* set me on this gamebook path, more than twenty years ago. When you responded online I was a little in awe, but when you generously blogged about *Steam Highwayman* writing alongside your own writing, dozens of your fans decided to back my work.

Jamie Thomson; author. Thankyou for pushing *Fabled Lands* to be more than any preceding gamebook had been. Great to meet you at FFFest 2.

Steve Jackson and **Ian Livingstone**; authors and gaming godfathers. Thanks for what you started with Games Workshop and Fighting Fantasy. Thanks for sharing your own delight in imaginary worlds with young people (and young at heart) everywhere.

Jamie Stegmeier; Kickstarter guru. I'm indebted to Jamie for the way he generously shares his expertise with any and all who want to learn from him.

Paul Gresty; author and editorial advice. I appreciate the way you've discussed multi-volume open-world planning with me! Thanks for your insight.

Francis Wong; backer 126 and editorial advice. Thanks, Francis, for your interest in all my projects, but particularly for your help in approaching illustrators and in managing this crucial part of the project.

Caleb Simmons; backer 77 and editorial advice. I'm grateful to God for our friendship and to you for your generous advice, time and all the help with finding and working with an illustrator.

Jessica Noutch; editorial advice. Thanks for all the help in writing and shaping my illustration briefs. I couldn't have got far without you, sis!

Noah and **Ruth Noutch**; backers 45 and proof-readers. Thanks for all your interest and encouragement. Ruth, you're one of the most accurate and professional readers I've worked with. This book would look a lot less careful without you!

Kevin Abbotts; backer 2 and proof-reader. Thanks for the level of detail in your responses, including differences between flight of buzzards and kestrels.

Mark Lain; backer 5 and proof-reader. Thanks for your thoughtful corrections and comments, your encouragements online and your friendliness in person.

Martin Randall; backer 21, proof-reader and door-keeper. Thanks for the chance to network at AdventureX - for which you were doubly responsible.

Michael Hartland; backer 57 and proof-reader. Thanks for your speedy turnaround and support!

Simon Day; backer 168 and proof-reader. Thanks for your time and support in correcting the drafts.

James Dickinson; backer and proof-reader 24. Thanks for your help in bug-squashing and making the road smoother for all velosteamers.

Ruth de Leon; backer and proof-reader. Thankyou, dear ading Ruth, for your hard work reading and checking my writing, as well as your enthusiasm, prayers and encouragement from the start.

Jared and Marian Foley; backers 151 and proof-readers. Your welcome into the Steampunk world has introduced me to a whole new group of friends as well as healthy market for my writing. Floreat amicitia!

Hugo de Pelet; backer 0. Few people have the faith and generosity to support a project so prophetically. You can't imagine what it meant to me to have had your interest back at David's Tent.

Gwen, Josh, Jon and Charlotte Winn; backers 1 and hosts. Thankyou for being behind the project from the first moment, for your hospitality and friendship.

Jack Noutch; backer 3 and creative collaborator. I am so thankful to God for a brother with your heart and generosity. Thanks for everything.

Jerica and Rico Castro; backers 4. Thankyou for sharing your lives with me and Cheryl. Everyone should have friends like you.

Philippe Jaillet; backer 6. Thanks for being my first international - and first French - backer.

Planete Ldvelh; backer 7. Thanks for your contribution to the project.

Stevie Smith; backer 8. Stevie, you have the honour of being my first US supporter: YOU are the Steam Highwayman (USA).

Ate Anabelle and Adings Arabelle and Andrew "Ace" Santiago; backers 9. Thanks for your support, your friendship and your prayers.

Michael Phillips; backer 10. Thanks for your online encouragements and getting behind the Highwayman Hype!

Patrick Ewing; backer 12. Thanks for your interest and boosting online, Patrick!

James Spearing; backer 13. Great to have your support and interest - hope you enjoy the adventure.

Colin Oaten; backer 14. Thanks for your support: sorry the copy doesn't stack with your greenspines...!

Martin L. and Anna Noutch; backers 15. Dad, that chat at Christmas 2016 was a powerful challenge to me: what was I doing? Would I finish it? Thanks for all your enthusiasm.

Neil Myler; backer 16 and faithful friend. Thanks for contributing to the project and showing me how much my writing is valued.

Robert Crewe; backer 17. Thanks for your help. I hope you enjoy every adventure.

Javier Fernandez; backer 18. My first backer in Germany - but my first Spanish backer! Gracias!

Joe Tilbrook; backer 19. With your support, the Steam Highwayman rides even unto Canadia - thankyou!

Mark Phelps; backer 20. Thanks for getting involved and helping me get this off the ground!

Zacky Chun-pong Leung; backer22. First backer in Asia and only in Hong-Kong! 谢谢

Nicodemus of NIMH; backer 23. Thanks for taking time out of your rat-leadership duties to contribute.

Michael Reilly; backer and community builder 25. Thanks for your support and your contribution to the gamebook community. Your feature in Gamebook News helped Steam Highwayman reach its target. You're also my first Australian backer!

Paul Senior; backer 26. Thanks for continuing to represent the Australian tradition of choosing freedom!

Rob 2.0.; backer 27. Thanks for your support and interest.

James Schannep; backer 28 and author. It's been great to discuss writing with you and to cheer each other on. Thanks very much for your support.

'Uncle' Ben Tejevo; backer 29 and prayer covering. Dear Ben! Great to have your help and sowing into my project. Your gifts to me have been so much a part of God's redirection of my life. I can't express my gratitude in words.

Lynda and Mike Moran; backers 30 and proof-reader

Stuart Lloyd; backer 31 and gamebook community builder. Thanks for your efforts to support the writers out there!

Christopher Trapp; backer 33. Thanks for getting involved so early on.

Chris Dunnings; backer 34. Great to have you involved in the first hours of the project - a great morale boost!

Jamie Fry; backer 35. Thanks for joining in on day 2!

alx; backer 36. Great to have your support, alx!

Luk Pikey Hekenkamp; backer 37. Thanks for your contribution to the book, Luk.

Y.K. Lee; backer 38. Thanks for climbing aboard the velosteam!

Peppe Fazzolari; backer 39. Thanks for your help getting the book off the ground, but even more for your example in getting out there and making success happen!

Azmi; backer 40. Thanks for participating in the campaign. I hope you find the adventure rewarding!

David Bowman; backer 42. Great to have your support, David. Enjoy the moonlit road.

Mark Buckley; backer 43. Thanks for your support: you've single-handedly brought the project to the Emerald Isle. Happy riding!

Daniel Shaw; backer 44. Dan, great to have your support after all these years! I'm so pleased to be able to have your help in making this happen.

Hans Peter Bak; backer 46. Who is Hans Peter Bak? He is the Danish Steam Highwayman!

Richard Harrison; backer 47. Great to have your help. Exciting to have my book read in exotic Sheffield!

Kristine Dietriche; backer 49. Thanks for your support in publishing the book. I wish you many adventures!

Sherloth; backer 50. Thanks for your support. I'm sure your mysterious manner will make you an excellent roadthief.

Rebecca Scott; backer 51. Rebecca, your pledge and your

support are much appreciated. Thanks for joining in.

Omar Dabasas; backer 52. Thanks, cousin Omar, for your support for my writing. May adventures in a world of steam and intrigue inspire you!

John Berry; backer 53. Thanks for backing my project: I'm honoured you consider me worthy of your pledge alongside works like *Scythe* and *You are the Hero*.

Gaetano Abbondanza; backer 54. Great to have you on board! I hope Kickstarter continues to supply you with many a new and exciting gamebook.

Josh Guerette; backer 55. Thanks so much for your support and encouraging message.

Dafyd Jones; backer 56. My dear friend, thanks for supporting my project! It might have been many years in coming, but you're still there interested in what I might do. That's true friendship.

Shannon Koh; backer 58. Thanks for participating in the campaign. I hope you enjoy the steam-driven world of Steam Highwayman and I hope you manage to convince your daughter of the glory of gamebooks too!

Adrian Briggs; backer 59. Thanks for getting involved and choosing to back my project on Kickstarter. Much appreciated.

Graham Hart; backer 60. I hope that Steam Highwayman makes a proud addition to your collection!

Isobel Bassindale; backer 61. Thanks for your support. I hope you and the unnamed recipient of your second copy have a great time exploring the England that never was (but should have been...)

James Catchpole; backer 62. Thanks for your interest before backing. I hope that your adventure in *this* volume is just the beginning...

Tim and Alison Simcock-Brown; backers 63. Dear Uncle Tim, Auntie Ali! Thankyou for wanting to see my work published and out in the world. I'd love to know what you and the family make of the adventures inside!

Becky Warren; backer 64. Becky, great to have your interest and support on the project. Let me know if your numbers-brain finds reliable in-game ways to break my systems! I know you'll go to any lengths to succeed as a Steam Highwayman.

Wills Allan; backer 67. Wills, I had such a burst of joy seeing your name appear on the list of backers! I don't know how to express my gladness to be sending you this book.

Tonie and Arthur Perkins; backers 68. Thanks for your friendship, your encouragement and blessings. I'm so proud to be sharing the project with you both: I hope you enjoy it!

Fabrice Gatille; backer 69. Thanks for your help in getting the project funded. May every new generation of readers be inspired!

Richie Stevens; backer 70. Thanks for your interest in Steam Highwayman as soon as I began publicising the project online. Your early interest was very encouraging indeed.

Ali, Andrew, Dan and Ellie Kesson; backers 71. Thanks for your friendship, your prayers and your support all the while I was honoured to teach Dan as well as now that I'm working elsewhere.

Charles Revello; backer 72. In the immortal words of Sid

Meier, 'Your service will be remembered', noble supporter. I hope that the pleasure you have in enjoying this adventure is also something of a reward. Happy steaming!

Mervyn Koh; backer 73. Mervyn, thanks for supporting this Highwayman in his bid for glory. I hope you find your share of the loot gives you much satisfaction and hours of absorbed adventure.

Kim Sein; backer 74. To have your help in bringing this project to life has been like seeing old promises kept: thanks for your friendship, Kim.

Visesh Sankaran; backer 75. Thanks for the support, old friend. Let me know how you fare!

Abraham and Nadine Ankers; backers 76. Thanks for contributing to my efforts and believing in your cousin. God bless you!

Daniel Fuerstman; backer 78. Great to have your support: I appreciate you responding to Dave Morris' post and getting on board. I hope you're pleased with the result.

Joseph Snape; backer 79. Thanks for your support—particularly considering your strict Kickstarter backing conditions! I'm glad I seem to have met them.

Scott Ballantyne; backer 80. Scott, I really appreciate your pledge and support. Thanks for messaging during the project and keeping me motivated too!

John Hagan; backer 81. Here we are, John! The book itself should be heavy in your hands, far too large to slip into a phone-case and ready to catch the eye. Grab your favourite dice, pour that delicious glass and settle down for an adventure!

John Ansari; backer 82. Great to have your support, John. Sheffield will quake before the roar of your velosteam!

Antony Quarrell; backer 83, author and motorcycling friend. Thanks, Antony, for the interest you've shown in my project at every stage. I can't wait to be back on two wheels so we can ride the woods together!

Anders Svensson; backer 84. Anders, you have the honour of being the first Swedish Steam Highwayman! Thanks very much.

Jörn Bethune; backer 85. It was great to have your enthusiastic and encouraging messages during the project. I'm glad you're looking forward to further adventures—I hope this one gives you a taste of what's to come.

Jerry and Dot Mendoza; backers 86. Thanks, dear and valued friends, for your prayers, friendship and support in everything Cheryl and I do, not just this book. May God continually grant you favour and blessing - in your projects and in your family.

Ashley Hall; backer 87. Thanks for your support and interest. The best of luck with your own gamebook and **MAJESTIC TRIAL** projects!

Robertson Sondoh Jr; backer 88. Ribuan terimakasih! May all Malaysia resound to the roar of the mighty Ferguson velosteam!

John D Jones; backer 89. Great to have your support, John. May your shelves ever have capacity!

Matthew Lockman; backer 90. Thanks for your encouraging messages during the campaign as well as your support. I hope the rewards of adventure on the midnight road satisfy -

or tantalise you!

David Ibbett; backer 91. My dear friend! I am so grateful to count you among my supporters and my friends. I'm so looking forward to the time we collaborate again. I wish you every success in your **MUSIC of REALITY** projects and in everything else you undertake.

Rebecca Palmer; backer 92. Thankyou, dear Rebecca, for your friendship and your support. I'm so pleased to be sending this copy your way.

Ninong Manoj Shah; backer 93. Thankyou, dear kuya Mick, for much more than your generous pledge: thankyou for your faithfulness to preach, minister and challenge as the Holy Spirit has led you. You've catalysed a lot of change in my life and in Cheryl's and I'm honoured to say that this book is one small fruit of that.

Femi Oluwayale; backer 94 and proof-reader. My friend! Thankyou for your ceaseless encouragement.

Peter Auger and Zen Cho; backers 95. Fellow MRCs and writers - how much I value your friendship and support! Thanks for getting involved.

Toni Mortimer; backer 96. Toni, I was so moved to see you pledge towards the project and I'm grateful for your faithful friendship! Thankyou.

Joshua Abramsky; backer 97. Joshua, thanks for your messages during the campaign and your support for the project. I hope that SH resembles FL enough for us both - but not too much!

Jhoan and Dasha Cordoba; backers 98. My dear friends, thankyou for your constant encouragement and trust. You've always believed in me and honoured my endeavours. God bless you and your family.

Prof. Dr. Oliver M. Traxel; backer 99. Thanks for your support and interest, as well as your reading recommendations. May Norway tremble before the threat of the Steam Highwayman's approach!

Mark Jackman; backer 100. I'm touched and honoured that you would continue to support my projects, dear Mark and Lorraine. Thankyou for your continued friendship.

Dipesh Shah; backer 101. Thankyou Dip for your support and enthusiasm. It means a lot to me to have had your interest throughout the project - God bless you!

Robert Langston; backer 103. Thanks for your support and messaging during the campaign. I hope you find the world of Steam Highwayman enjoyable and satisfying!

Uncle Otis C Parker; backer 104. Thankyou, dear Uncle Otis, for your faithful and generous support! I am looking forward to the day we meet even more keenly.

Jonathan Shaw; backer 105. Thanks for getting involved with the campaign and for your interest in the art too! I hope you enjoy flipping through (and playing through) the book.

Kevin Clifford; backer 106. Great to have your support, Kevin, particularly as you mentioned you were keen to help a new and independent writer. I guess Kickstarter was made for us! Thanks.

Magnus Johansson; backer 107. Magnus, your support is much appreciated. I hope I'm able to do justice, as you hope, to the ambitions of the project. Enjoy the open road!

Ninong Pastor Ojie Ramos and Ninang Pastora

Elena Ramos; backers 108. Thankyou so much for your love and support for Cheryl and me in all we do: your friendship and teaching have been constant blessings to us both, as is your generous support and your interest in my writing.

Moritz Eggert; backer 109. Thanks for your support. I hope that the recommendation you took is proven worth while. Have a great adventure!

Eamonn McCusker; backer 110. Thanks for getting involved with the project and for your encouraging messages during the fundraising period.

Alex and Wylma Papdakis; backers 111 and 122. Dear friends! Thank you so much for being such a wonderful part of our lives. Cheryl and I treasure your friendship and to receive your support on top of all you give us is testimony to how God is blessing our relationship.

Carl Covatto; backer 112. Thanks for deciding to give my adventure a try: I hope the book lives up to your expectations and that you find it replayable!

Vasilis Papaioannou; backer 113. Thanks for getting involved with the project. I'm looking forward to getting Volume II ready, so backers with ambitions like yours can expand your adventures across the lands. Ευχαριστώ!

Anthony Impenna; backer 114. Thanks for your support! I hope you find somewhere with a nice view of the Hudson and warming glass to roll your dice and ride the road.

Demian Katz; backer 115. Demian, thanks for your messages during the project and for your pledge. This book wouldn't have happened without you! I'm honoured to be joining your collection.

Sarinee Achavanuntakul; backer 116. Thanks for backing and for taking the risk on an unknown author! I hope the steampunk flavours tickles your (mental) tastebuds!

Skorpio; backer 117. Grazie mille, Skorpio! May your claws remain snappy and your sting stay sharp.

Joel M Bridge; backer 118. Thanks for your support! I hope that you enjoy defining the Steam Highwayman any way you wish to inside your own adventures.

Ranger Tim; backer 119. Great to have you on board. Thanks for your pledge.

Jack Bodem; backer 120. Thanks for joining the project back in September. I hope the adventure entertains you - and maybe you'll even find a style of steampunk you enjoy!

Ate Erma Paragas; backer 121. Thankyou, dear Ate, for your support for my writing. I'm honoured and blessed to count you among my backers. Thankyou!

Francis Nulud; backer 123. Francis, it means a great deal to me to have your friendship and respect. May God reward you many times over with the riches of his grace as well as his presence in your daily life.

Montie21; backer 124. Great to have your support. Thanks for joining the project.

Neal Culkin; backer 125. Neal, great to have your contribution and your interest. I hope you enjoy the book and your adventure!

Kristopher Latter; backer 127. Thanks for following your hunch, reading the demo and pledging to the campaign. Hope it whets your appetite for more!

Chris Dacaney; backer 128. Thankyou, C-Dac, for getting

on board and believing in my writing. How much I appreciate it!

Aaron Thorne; backer 129. Great to have your support, Aaron. May Missouri be your very own road to glory!

Peter and Jemimah Reid; backers 130. Hooray, dear Reids! Thanks for everything you've contributed. Still can't wait to get on the open road with you (both)!

Matt England; backer 131. Matt, it's been really great to have your support and your help in bringing the book into reality. Thanks for joining in!

Harold and Hannah Mensah; backers 132. Dear friends! I hope that you enjoy the adventure - tell me what the spirit says to you through it!

Josh Spencer; backer 133. Thanks Josh, for taking the plunge and putting up your pledge! It's really appreciated.

Emily Moran; backer 134. Emily, great to be enjoying your friendship again, as well as your generous support for my work. May the Spirit of Jesus continually guide you.

Adrian Jankowiak; backer 136. I'm very pleased to be able to satisfy your curiosity at last and honoured to join your collection. I hope you have a good ride.

Nicola Birch; backer 137. Dear Birchy! I don't know what you'll make of my stories, but I hope they'll prompt many a reverie and many an impassioned discussion. How I value your friendship.

Eva Fritz; backer 138. Thanks for your interest in the project back in September when we met at Crossness. Thanks for your pledge and your support.

Mads Neumann; backer 139. Thanks for your support, Mads, and your friendship too. Let me know how the puzzles and quests feel to you!

Derek Devereaux Smith; backer 140. Great to have your help in getting my book published. I hope the choices engage you and interest you!

Godwin Matthew Teoh; backer 141. Godwin, you're my first backer in Singapore and much, much appreciated!

Pete and Pippa Ankers; backers 142 and dear uncle and aunt. God bless you! Your generous contribution brought such joy to me, seeing how you value this effort of mine to produce something new and fun. I hope you enjoy poring through the book. Lots and lots of love.

Andy Smith; backer 143. Thanks for your pledge, Andy. I hope both you and the recipient of your second copy (fill in name here_____) have a great time on the moonlit road.

Malcolm Tan Qi En; backer 144. Thanks for believing in my project and participating all the way from Singapore!

Adam Doyle; backer 145. Great to meet you at Maldon Museum of Steam: more pressure to your boiler, sir!

Gábor Joe Telekesi; backer 146. The Steam Highwayman ventures even unto Hungary with your help! You are the Hungarian Steam Highwayman!

Jonathan Caines; backer 147. Jonathan, thanks for your support for my book. I hope you enjoy the lifestyle of a Highwayman and an adventurer!

MoiMarcy; backer 148. Great to have your contribution and your help in bringing this to reality. Thankyou"

Mikey Cua; backer 149. Thanks, Mikey, for your pledge and your friendship. May you continue to know and enjoy God's presence day by day.

Cristovão Neto; backer 150. Thanks for your support, meaning that this book will be read in Portugal!

Brendan Mills; backer 152. Brendan, I really appreciate your support and hope you enjoy this book as a result.

Robert Thomson; backer 153. Thanks for getting involved, Robert! Have a great ride!

Adam J Purcell; backer 154. Adam, fantastic to have you joining in and contributing to the project. Much appreciated.

Jane Darnbrough; backer 155. Thanks for the welcome to the Steampunk Community, Jane! Your interest and enthusiasm has been so fantastic.

Mike Jones; backer 156. Mike, thanks for your contribution to the project and your help back when I was sowing seeds through those leaflets back at Crossness. Your permission and welcome encouraged me a great deal.

Niran Vinod; backer 157. Thanks, Niran, for your friendship and your support for my project. I really appreciate you getting involved.

Paul Gaston; backer 158. Paul, thanks for following your nose and finding out more about my project. Great to have your help!

Stuart Whitehouse; backer 159. Thanks for your readiness to investigate my project on Kickstarter and your willingness to pledge and participate! Much appreciated.

Nadine Reuter; backer 160. Thanks for your interest and messages during the project and best of luck for your own Herzensprojekts and the growth of steampunk publishing in Germany.

Philip Christensen; backer 161. Philip, I hope you don't feel you've had to wait too long to get your hands on this! Enjoy every passage and every page!

Bruce McGregor; backer 162. Thanks for making me your first Kickstarter project - I'm honoured.

Dean Soukup; backer 163. Great to have your help in publishing this book, Dean. I really appreciate your help.

Shabazz L. Graham; backer 164. Thanks Shabazz, for your interest, support and friendship in Christ. Let me know when you're ready for a Steam Highwayman screenplay!

Edward England; backer 165. Thanks for your help. I hope you consider this a worthy addition to your steampunk collection!

Malcolm Webb; backer 166. Malcolm, I appreciate your help in getting this book to publication. I hope it reminds you happily of books of old - and brings you something new as well.

Barry Swodeck; backer 169. Thanks for your contribution towards Steam Highwayman. I wish you many happy hours adventuring in the pages!

Dominic Brismail; backer 170. Great to have your help, Dominic, and your encouragement.

Robert Drake; backer 171. Thanks for your contribution towards the project.

Mark Voss; backer 172. Great to have your support. I hope that you feel well rewarded for your pledge!

Ian McFarlin; backer 173. Thanks for pledging and participating, Ian. May Ohio tremble at the sound of the Steam

Highwayman's approach!

Steven Lord; backer 174. Thanks for your help in pushing the project well beyond 200% funding. I hope Steam Highwayman becomes one of the Kickstarters you are most pleased to have backed!

Michael K; backer 175. Thanks for joining with all of these fellow backers and helping me make this book a reality.

Katherine Fisher; backer 176. Thanks for getting involved! May this book inspire you into even more steampunk splendour.

Vécsei Zoli; backer 177. Great to have your help in completing my book and seeing it in readers' hands. I hope you enjoy the adventure.

benjebobs; backer 178. Thanks for your contribution, benjebobs. May the road always be smooth beneath your feet and your tyres resilient and well-pressured.

James Dawson; backer 179. James, thanks so much for your pledge and your support of my project in response to Cheryl's persistence! I hope you have an adventure all of your own in these pages.

Joshua Galinato; backer 180. Thanks for your support and interest, Josh! You inspired me countless times with your go-getting attitude.

Jon Mann; backer 181. Thanks, Jon, for participating and contributing towards my ambition! I wish you many satisfying adventures aboard the velosteam.

T Hayes; backer 182. Great to have your help and support for Steam Highwayman. Enjoy every adventure"

Austin Elwood; backer 183. Austin, with a puzzle-solving mind like yours, I'm expecting to hear you've found all the solutions and intricacies of Steam Highwayman in double-quick time. Enjoy the ride!

David Gunning; backer 184. Thanks for your support, David. Let me know how the Ferguson copes with the dust and head of the outback!

Per Stalby; backer 185. Thanks Per! Warning: if you mean to ride the velosteam in Swedish temperatures, you will need to fit the Buckleby seat-warmer (available at all good artificers).

Allan Jenkins; backer 186. Thanks for joining the project on the final day and helping it become the success it was. I hope the book is as exciting as the Kickstarter was!

Mrs Evangeline Adamos (Mummy); backer 187. Thanks for much more than your contribution to the costs of the project - thanks for including me as an Adamos.

Jodie Sayson; backer 189. Salamat, veggie! Great to have your support. Your ciabbatta appreciates your help for her husband.

Guillaume Trouvilliez; backer190. Thanks for your faithful support and interest, Gim! I hope you enjoy riding the roads astride your very own velosteam.

Hannah Galinato; backer 191. Last but by no means least! Thankyou for your friendship to Cheryl and me over all these years. God bless you in your riding and your adventuring.

BEER NOTES

	Name of beer	Location	Notes
1.			
2.			
3.			
4.			
5.			
6.			
7.			
8.			
9.			
10.			
11.			
12.			
13.			

CODEWORDS

- ☐ Abapical
- ☐ Able
- ☐ Abound
- ☐ About
- ☐ Abstruse
- ☐ Actinium
- ☐ Additive
- ☐ Adoption
- ☐ Advent
- ☐ Advertise
- ☐ Afterthought
- ☐ Aggregate
- ☐ Agile
- ☐ Ahasuerus

- ☐ Aidan
- ☐ Alacrity
- ☐ Alba
- ☐ Albright
- ☐ Alluring
- ☐ Almost
- ☐ Amalgam
- ☐ Ambidextrous
- ☐ Ambition
- ☐ Ambulatory
- ☐ Ammonium
- ☐ Amphibious
- ☐ Anastasia
- ☐ Andronicus

- ☐ Anhedonic
- ☐ Anniversary
- ☐ Anteater
- ☐ Anthill
- ☐ Antipodes
- ☐ Aorta
- ☐ Apogee
- ☐ Apparently
- ☐ Apprehend
- ☐ Appropriate
- ☐ Arithmetic
- ☐ Arthropod
- ☐ Artisan
- ☐ Ascorbic

- ☐ Ashen
- ☐ Aspect
- ☐ Aspidistra
- ☐ Aspirin
- ☐ Assistant
- ☐ Astrakhan
- ☐ Attribution
- ☐ Augury
- ☐ Aurum
- ☐ Avatar
- ☐ Awful

£ and S

NB:
£1 = 20 shillings,
1 Guinea = 21 shillings

COULTER'S BANK
ACCOUNT NO. 345887107
Savings to the amount recorded below are held in trust by the directors and Board of Coulter's Bank, *IN GUINEAS*

ABILITY SCORES

RUTHLESSNESS:

ENGINEERING:

MOTORING:

INGENUITY:

NIMBLENESS:

GALLANTRY:

SOLIDARITY POINTS

AT 50 SOLIDARITY POINTS
GAIN THE TITLE
THE PEOPLE'S CHAMPION

POSSESSIONS

DAMAGE POINTS	MINOR DAMAGE	SERIOUS DAMAGE	CRITICAL DAMAGE	BEYOND REPAIR

0   1   2   3   4

CUSTOMISATIONS

PARRY

(NIM+PAR)

OTHER MODIFIERS

SCARS

WOUNDS
1
2
3
4
5

OTHER NOTES

WANTED BY

FRIEND OF

MEMBER OF

NAME:

SKIFF /
LAUNCH /
BARGE

MOORED:

CARGO:

CUSTOMISATIONS:

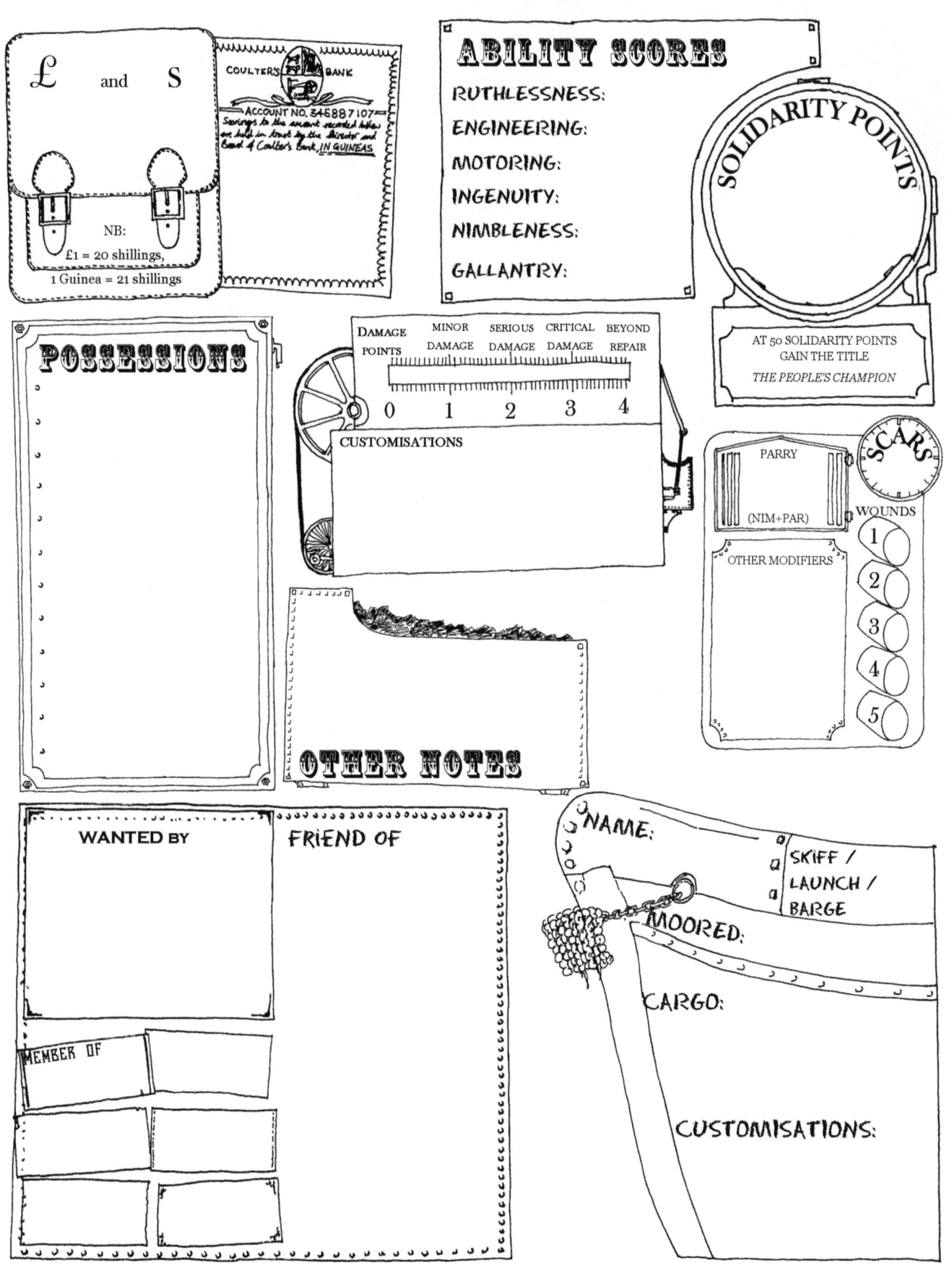

Lightning Source UK Ltd.
Milton Keynes UK
UKHW030751201118
332651UK00003B/338/P